THE INVISIBLE HUSBAND
OF FRICK ISLAND

THE INVISIBLE HUSBAND OF FRICK ISLAND

COLLEEN OAKLEY

THORNDIKE PRESS

A part of Gale, a Cengage Company

LIBRARY OF CONGRESS CIP DATA ON FILE.
CATALOGUING IN PUBLICATION FOR THIS BOOK
IS AVAILABLE FROM THE LIBRARY OF CONGRESS.

ISBN-13: 978-1-4328-8749-0 (softcover alk. paper)

Published in 2021 by arrangement with Berkley, an imprint of Penguin Publishing Group, a division of Penguin Random House, LLC

Printed in the United States of America
2 3 4 5 6   25 24 23 22 21

*For Henry, Sorella, Olivia, and Everett,
the four greatest joys of my life.*

*And for my grandparents
Hugh and Marion,
who showed me the world and
all the stories it contains.*

Life seen without illusion
is a ghastly affair.

— VIRGINIA WOOLF

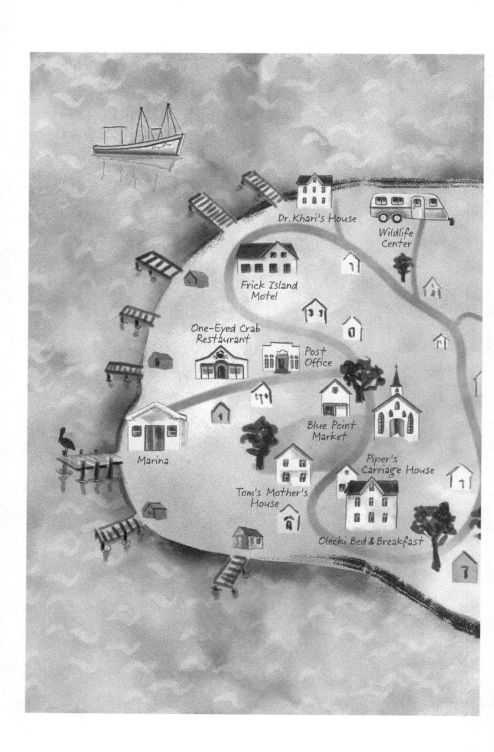

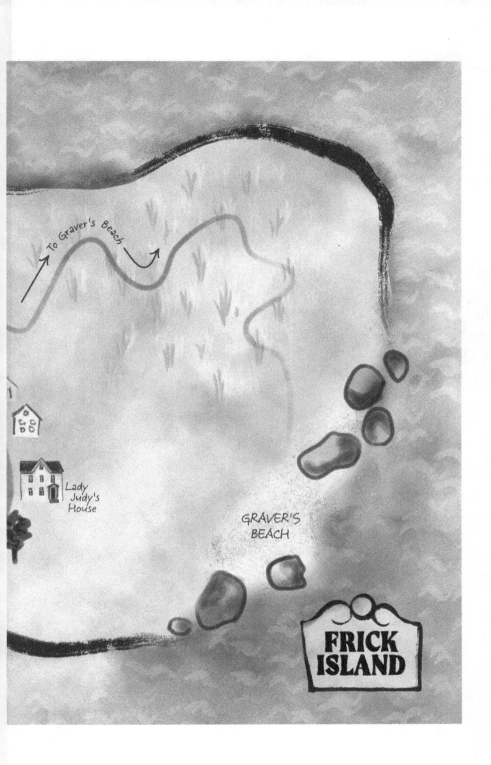

CHAPTER 1

The Storm

At first, when Piper scanned the docks and didn't see the familiar rickety white-pine-and-fir fisherman's trawler, she thought nothing of it. Tom, like most Chesapeake Bay watermen, tried to beat the sun's rays onto the water every morning during crab season, squeezing in every minute of the government-allotted eight hours of crabbing per day. That put him back in the harbor just after lunch most afternoons, with plenty of time for his onshore duties — icing his catch, checking his floats, tending to the boat. But inevitably some mornings there was a delay — a net needing mending, the buy boat running late. On those days, Tom's deadrise would come puffing into the harbor later than the others, when the sun was half-way down the other side of the sky. But whether it was two, three, or four in the afternoon, it didn't much matter. Time on Frick Island had always been more of a theoretical concept measured in *jiffi* or *awhiles* or *later ons.*

Still, even though there was no telling on any given day when Tom would return, every afternoon when the Blue Point market closed at three, Piper flew through her closing responsibilities moving the packaged deli meats, cheeses, and any unsold fresh crab cakes from the display cooler to the back refrigerator, mopping the cracked linoleum floors, hanging up her apron on the hook in the office, and slipping her card in the punch time clock (even though she had never seen Mr. Garrison so much as look at them) — and rushed over to the docks.

Most days Tom was already there, helping tie off boats or diagnosing an outboard engine problem or simply standing around with other watermen, grumbling about the day's haul or the sharp drop in the market price of oysters.

And sometimes, on those days, the breath would catch in Piper's throat. And she'd stop and stare at him for a beat in wide wonder that of all the places in the world, God had found it fitting to put Tom Parrish on the same tiny spit of land that she, too, inhabited. And even more miraculous, that though he could have had his pick of mainland girls at the high school they once ferried over to before the sun woke every weekday, Tom chose her.

Fire. That was what Piper remembered when she thought of those early days on the ferry with Tom. There was a heat to those mornings, even in the dead of winter, when they could see their breath float out into the cold air in great big puffs, as if they were exhaling cigarette smoke. She'd never forget the way the clouds would suddenly blush pink at the first kiss of sunlight and how her face followed suit whenever she caught Tom looking at her. Or the way when Tom, two years her senior, first sat next to her on the boat when there were at least ten other empty spots he could have chosen, and his thigh burned so hot against hers, even through their jeans, that it warmed her entire body from the inside out. And she thought she might die from the sheer pleasure of it.

And she'd been dying a thousand tiny pleasurable deaths every day, ever since. Like the first time he clumsily kissed her, behind his dad's crab shack sophomore year, catching just the corner of her mouth and a few locks of her hair. And the second time, a week later, when he didn't miss at all. Or when he would leave notes for her in the pocket of her jacket, tucked in schoolbooks, or affixed to the outside corner of her bedroom window, and she wouldn't find them until hours later, running her thumb over the tiny block letters

13

of his handwriting, her heart fit to burst. Or when, just a year earlier, they had been lying in the bottom of the very boat she was now scanning the horizon for, and — looking at the moon — he had whispered the words she realized she'd been waiting to hear from him since she was fourteen: *We should get married.*

She agreed immediately, because after seven years, she still felt the same way she did those mornings on the ferry — that when he looked at her, she was alive. And when she was away from him, she counted down the seconds until he would be near again.

But on this breezy April afternoon, Piper would have to count for a little while longer, it seemed. She slunk over to the bench, swiping the beads of water off of it with her bare hand. There had a been a storm that morning when they woke, a spring squall angering the seas, creating choppy waters that slowed even the most experienced boat captains. But watermen didn't stop for weather. As BobDan Gibbons, the official Frick Island ferry boat captain, often explained to the boatloads of tourists visiting from the mainland: *The crabs don't know it's rainin'.*

So Piper sat on the wooden bench, the dampness seeping through the back of her khaki slacks, and pulled a book out of her satchel, cracking the worn spine. Piper and Tom both loved to read, but whereas Piper enjoyed mostly mass-market mysteries, bodice-ripping romances, and even heart-pumping horror, Tom preferred higher-brow literature. For years, Tom tried giving her some of his favorite classics as gifts: *Moby-Dick, A Tale of Two Cities, Frankenstein.* And to please him, she would try to muddle through, even if it meant reading the same paragraph over and over, while her mind drifted to other things. It wasn't that Piper wasn't smart — she was. (Science-minded like her mother, though she was drawn to entomology over ecology. Could tell you the species, genus, family, all the way up to the domain of a number of insects that crawled the earth.) It was just that when it came to reading, she liked what she liked.

And so far, she only liked one of the books Tom had given her, *Their Eyes Were Watching God,* and she was currently rereading it for the ninth time. The first time she read it, it drew her in from the very first paragraph: the idea that for some men, their dreams sail forever on the horizon, resigned that they will never reach them. She thought that perfectly described Tom in a way she might never have put into words. Literally, at times, when she would catch him staring out into the ocean, as if he were looking at another life he could have lived. But Tom was a Parrish. And while some island watermen's families saw the writing on the wall — the marine life in the bay was dying off from pollution and overfishing, and the sea levels were rising, swallowing up their island with it, inch by inch — and encouraged their kids to leave for government jobs on the mainland, join the military, go to college even, Tom's family were stalwarts of the community. Tom's daddy and his granddaddy and his granddaddy before him were watermen. And even though Tom's father was no longer around to see if his son kept up the tradition, or maybe *because* he was no longer around to see it, Tom felt duty bound to take his place at the helm of the trawler when his time came.

It wasn't just that sentiment in the book that reminded her of Tom, though, or really why she loved the book as much as she did. It was, of course, the love story. Maybe she was too young, or didn't have enough life experience, to truly appreciate the deeper themes of independence and feminism, but she wasn't too young to understand the burning desires of love. And she believed with her entire being, the way maybe only young people can, that she was the earth and Tom, her sun, moon, and stars. Tom was her Tea Cake and she loved him in the same way she breathed

— effortlessly and as if it were the only thing that kept her alive.

So that was what Piper was doing — sitting on a bench, lost in the love story of Janie and Tea Cake, when a shadow fell over her pages. She looked up with her well-known smile, ready to greet whomever it was standing over her.

"Hey there, Pipes," BobDan Gibbons said. His face was weathered, in the way boat captains' faces are, as if their skin were competing to match the wood on the decks of their ships.

"BobDan," Piper said, the dimples in both her cheeks still on display.

"I don't know how to tell you this," he said, taking his baseball cap off his head and curving the worn bill in the palm of his hand. "I'm sure everything will be fine, of course, but Tom . . . well, he's gone missing."

Even though the words didn't immediately register with Piper, they did pull the corners of her lips back into a straight line. She cocked her head. "What do you mean, missing?"

He cleared his throat, a sound like a race car engine gunning on the starter block. "Apparently he radioed out for help this morning, during that little rain shower we had. Old Mr. Waverly got the call. Said he was taking on water, but the connection was bad and it went out 'fore Waverly could get the coordinates. Coast Guard's been looking for him since, and we've got some of the guys out there, too. Like I said, I'm sure we'll find him 'fore long and everything'll be fine." He twisted the bill of his cap one more time, and Piper wasn't sure if it was that movement or the grim look in BobDan's eyes that caused her stomach to go hollow.

And then Piper remembered the *Teredo navalis.* Three months earlier, Tom had spotted damaged wood on the hull of his trawler — a few drill-size holes, as if someone had shot a BB gun clear through the wood. Upon further inspection, he discovered he had shipworms, a parasite that fed on docks and boats and had been wreaking havoc at marinas for centuries — there was even a mention of them in *Moby-Dick.* To kill them, Tom had the boat pulled out of the water and sprayed it down with a hose, and after a few days without saltwater, the worms curled up and died, their carcasses like little circles of copper wire. (Piper, of course, took one home to study under her microscope.) The boards needed replacing, but by that time, they had already run through most of their winter savings — and the little bit they had left needed to go to new crab traps for the season. Tom hoped, until he could scrape the money together, that any water that came in through the tiny holes could be handled by the bilge pump.

Piper wasn't sure why she was thinking of the worms, except that Tom was an experienced boater and maybe she was searching for what could have possibly gone wrong. But she quickly dismissed the thought, because speculation wasn't going to get her anywhere, not to mention it ran counter to the only thing BobDan said that she wanted to believe — that everything was going to be fine.

"I believe I might join the search effort, if you want to tag along," he said. "Shirlene is gonna man the marina, in case anyone calls with news."

Piper considered this offer, but decided she wanted to be there, on the dock, when Tom's boat came chugging into the harbor, his mouth bursting to tell the wild story of his day's adventure on the sea. And so she waited, on the bench, not noticing the growl of her stomach when suppertime came and went, and trying not to notice the other watermen that came in to dock one by one, their hats in their hands like BobDan's, their heads bent toward the ground, their eyes avoiding Piper's at all costs.

Four days later, the boat was recovered by a diver at the bottom of the sea.

Tom's body was not.

■ ■ ■ ■

While the rest of the town knew the worst had happened, Piper held out hope. Maybe Tom got disoriented and swam in the wrong direction, washed up on a deserted island, and was currently eating coconuts and writing messages in palm fronds for passing airplanes. Or maybe a ship of Somali pirates picked him up and he was being held against his will, unable to negotiate his release due to the language barrier. Or a whale swallowed him whole and he was contemplating his escape from the depths of its belly. Each of her theories was more outlandish than the next, but to Piper, none were as ridiculous as what the rest of the town believed — that Tom was gone. That she would never lay eyes on him again.

In the days following the Coast Guard's announcement that they were calling off the search for Tom, Piper found herself growing increasingly intolerant. And not just with the rescue teams who were, in her view, prematurely giving up. She couldn't stand the way people started looking at her, their eyes filled with pity. She couldn't abide the way they began referring to Tom in past tense. But the final straw was when the members of the island's Methodist (and only) church — where the Parrish family had been attending for as long as the church had been on the island, and where Tom and Piper had exchanged vows and thin gold bands — started planning a memorial service for Tom. Upon receiving that news, Piper locked herself in her one-bedroom carriage house behind the Oleckis' bed-and-breakfast. She didn't answer the phone, or the door, not even when Lady Judy stopped by with enough smoked ham and beaten biscuits and peach cobbler to feed half the island. She left the food on Piper's stoop and it sat there all afternoon until the sun set. Until Mrs. Olecki retrieved it and set it out in the main house's toile-covered living room for her current boarders to enjoy for supper.

Piper missed the memorial service altogether, where Tom's mother, glassy-eyed and catatonic, stood propped up by her brother Frank on one side and her nephew Steve on the other and the Valium that had been pumping through her veins daily since her husband's aptly named heart attack — the Widow Maker — had made good on its promise. Where Tom's cousin Steve's newborn interrupted the reverend with her insistent squalls, eyes screwed shut tight, giving voice to the pain the watermen were too stoic to show. Everyone asked after Piper, murmuring their condolences to every Parrish in attendance. *Poor girl,* they said, shaking their heads, offering various superlatives: too young, most in love, the worst.

But Piper couldn't hear them. She was in her bedroom, staring at the dent Tom's head had left on his pillow when his alarm clock prompted him to get up at 4:30 a.m. two weeks earlier. Piper didn't dare touch it — not even to try to inhale his scent that surely remained on the floral cover. Nor did she touch Tom's near-empty mug of coffee sitting in the sink, a film of mold growing on the top layer of liquid still left in the cup. Or the book — *Middlesex,* by Jeffrey Eugenides — splayed open, pages facedown, on top of the two wooden crates they stacked in the corner to use as a side table in their tiny den. It was as if all of these things, Tom's things, suddenly sprouted magical properties, transformed into talismans beckoning Tom back to where he belonged — to his bed to sleep, to the kitchen to wash out his coffee mug and hang it on the hook next to the sink, to the threadbare easy chair in the den to find out what happens to the characters of his current novel. They weren't just reminders of Tom, they were promises. He was going to come home. Of that one thing, Piper was sure.

And then one morning, just like that, he did.

CHAPTER 2

Four Months Later

"Caldwell," Greta said, walking toward him from her office, the uneven threadbare-carpeted floor creaking beneath her mules. "Frick Island Cake Walk tomorrow — it's yours."

Anders affixed a smile to his face. "Great," he said, looking up from the three-inch article he was writing about the local sheriff filing for reelection.

"Six inches, couple basic quotes, a photo; you can check the archives for past coverage," she said. The window air-conditioning unit rattled to life across the room. Greta turned on her heel toward it, heading back to one of only two closed-door offices in their space on the second floor of what used to be an old firehouse. (The other belonged to the executive editor, a stooped and liver-spotted gentleman who appeared to be editor in title only, shuffling into the office one day during Anders's first week. "I'm Harry," he introduced himself, and then paused for dramatic effect. "But not all over.")

Anders knew, of course, his first reporting job out of college would be about paying his dues — he'd just rather hoped he'd be paying them at the *Washington Post* or the *New York Times* or the *Boston Globe,* or even the *Dallas Morning News,* covering state senate bill debates or immigration reform or university protests. In the three months he'd been at the *Telegraph,* he'd been dispatched to cover four never-ending school board meetings, a pierogi festival in nearby Rehoboth, and a literal cat burglar — a neighborhood feline who snuck into open windows and doorways to steal ball caps and socks and, in one case, a treasured fountain pen.

But Anders also knew he was lucky to have a newspaper job at all — slashed budgets equaling bare-bones staffs at papers all across the country, if not shuttering the doors altogether — and he reminded himself of this as he turned back to the sentence he was constructing regarding the sheriff's past accomplishments. His plan was to put his head down and do the best job he could do, even on the fluff pieces — especially on the fluff pieces. The faster he proved himself, the quicker he could start working on bigger, more interesting assignments. And the closer he would be to moving up to a bigger, more interesting paper. Maybe he'd be the next Michael Rezendes. Maybe Mark Ruffalo would play *him* in a movie. Maybe he'd even win a Pulitzer.

But probably not for six inches on the Frick Island Cake Walk.

"Oh," Greta called over her shoulder, "and make sure you call to reserve your space on the ferry — I think it leaves at twelve thirty. And you need cash. They don't take credit cards."

"The ferry?"

"Yeah," she said, monotone. "It's an *island.*"

"Right," Anders said, vividly remembering the last time he was on a boat. He had been seven, tagging along on a deep-sea fishing adventure with his dad on vacation in Charleston. He spent the majority of the outing vomiting over the side and the rest of it curled up in the fetal position on the floor of the boat, the putrid scent of decaying fish flesh filling his nostrils. He hadn't stepped foot on a boat — or eaten seafood — since. Then Anders replayed the second part of Greta's sentence. "Wait — call? Can't I book online?"

25

Greta frowned, her crow's-feet deepening. "Frick Islanders don't do the Internet."

Anders heard a snicker and didn't have to look over to know that Jess, the courts and crime reporter (though she seemed to cover everything else, too) who took pride in being a local, was deriving joy from his ignorance. Not meanly — Jess didn't have a cruel bone in her tiny body — but still.

"OK. I'm on it," Anders said, trying his best (but failing) to channel the enthusiasm of Clark Kent.

Clark Kent.

That was the answer Anders Caldwell gave as a child at holiday gatherings to well-meaning relatives who pinched his cheeks (well past the age where cheek pinching was acceptable) and asked him the uninspired but inevitable question of what he wanted to be when he grew up. "Adorable!" Aunt Sylvie would squeal, clapping her hands and cooing as if he were a baby goat wearing a little knitted sweater. "He wants to be a superhero."

It was what everyone thought — that Anders, like most other boys, envisioned himself wearing electric blue tights and a matador's cape, flying through the air to save innocent citizens and hurl clever quips at bad guys. And Anders never corrected them, because he didn't see the point.

But the truth, if he had ever uttered it, was that he didn't want to be Superman.

He wanted to be Clark Kent. The mild-mannered reporter with snappy prose and thick square glasses, yelling, "I'm on it!" when his editor pounded his fist on the desk and blustered: "We're sitting on the story of the century here!"

In other words, Anders Caldwell wasn't like most other little boys.

Jess's head popped over the low cubicle wall that divided their desks. Though she was seven years older than Anders, her makeup-free countenance, small stature, and coarse black hair pulled back tight in a high ponytail made her look all of about fourteen. "Hope you've got your DeLorean," she said. "Because you're about to go back in time."

"What?" Anders raised his eyebrows.

"You know, *Back to the Future*?"

"No, I get the reference." His mom was an eighties movie buff; made sure he'd seen all the classics, including all the original *Supermans*, more than once. "But what do you mean?"

"Frick Island." She grinned. "You'll see."

Anders flipped on the light of his studio

apartment with his elbow, clutching a paper cup of soda and a sack dinner — a Quarter Pounder and five-piece chicken nuggets — in one hand and his laptop in the other. But as had become custom, he didn't enter right away. He stood frozen in the doorway, his eyes scanning his efficiency kitchen for any sign of movement. The day after moving in, Anders spotted three cockroaches scampering along his laminate countertops, and he had been at war ever since. If there was one thing he hated more than being the center of attention, it was bugs.

Assured that all was well, or at least still, Anders set everything on his card table and tried to ignore the thumping rap music that flowed nonstop from his upstairs neighbors, a couple of college kids who attended the local university. As he settled onto the lone folding chair, he almost wished he'd taken Jess up on her offer to grab dinner after work. Though she was an overenthusiastic NFL fan (Ravens) and often told pointless and meandering stories about her two Weimaraners, she was technically the only friend Anders had in town.

Anders powered up his computer, tucked into his cheeseburger, and opened his email, his eyes quickly scanning the new messages — a forward from his mom and a link Jess had sent earlier from the Humane Society. Then he clicked on the URL in his favorites bar: theadventuresofclarkkent.com. He scrolled to the most recent podcast: *Who Gives a Cluck?* and scanned the data: twenty-seven listens, one comment. He sat back and sighed. He'd worked on this one for weeks — an in-depth profile of the founder of Concerned Citizens for Poultry, a woman who traveled the country protesting at fried chicken festivals, and down comforter and pillow factories, and was most recently arrested for driving her Ford Focus into a turkey transport truck off Route 30 ten miles outside of Salisbury.

He scrolled down to the comment, though he already knew who had sent it.

LeonardC404: Wow! Great opener — detailing her inner thoughts as she risked her life and others on the highway to free those birds. I was gripped. Can't wait for your next one. — Dad

Annoyed, Anders rolled his eyes. Leave it to Leonard Caldwell to effuse praise when none was due. Obviously, it wasn't "great," or more people would be listening to it.

Anders had started the podcast in college, after the news editor at his school paper turned down his profile pitch on a notorious student on campus named Mark Harris, a full-bearded, wide-smiled man who had been attending the school for *nine* years — and had no plans for matriculation in the near future. More rumors swirled around him than around JFK's assassination. He was a legend, yet no one knew if the stories about him were true. Had he really been involved in an S&M love triangle with the provost and the women's soccer coach? Was *he* the one who hid a nest of yellow jackets in the visitors' locker room during the school's rival football game? Had he really sung "Papa Was a Rolling Stone" in a duet with Charles Barkley when the basketball star appeared at a karaoke bar in Atlanta?

Anders followed Mark around for weeks, recording interviews, observing his daily life, mostly trying to avoid the contact high from his near-ritualistic vaping sessions — and he edited the material down into a fascinating inside look at Mark Harris's life. That podcast was listened to more than sixteen thousand times, half the student population of his university, and Anders thought he'd stumbled onto something big. Podcasts were the next big thing — the perfect medium to tell stories that newspapers no longer had the time, space, or money for. And what if his took off? He fantasized about those sixteen thousand listeners doubling, tripling, even quadrupling! Forget crawling his way up that very long ladder to *Newsweek,* the *New York Times;* he could sprint to the top. He could be the next Ira Glass on *This American Life* or the next Sarah Koenig and *Serial.* NPR would be banging down his door to hire him.

Except, within a matter of weeks, he soon realized that *Mark Harris* was what the listeners had been interested in, not Anders's own journalistic storytelling prowess, and his audience dropped sharply with each consecutive episode. Still, he had thought this poultry woman story had legs.

He slipped his earbuds in to drown out the rap music and typed "Frick Island" into his search bar. Though he had looked through past issues as Greta suggested and could write the Cake Walk piece in his sleep without ever stepping foot on the island (*It was literally a cake walk,* he had thought to himself, wryly), Anders was committed to treating each article as though it were an A1 feature, carrying on methodically in his research. He clicked on the first result.

Frick Island is a 1.2-mile strip of land in

the Chesapeake Bay, twelve miles off the coast of Winder on the eastern shore of Maryland. With no airstrip or bridges, the island is accessible only by boat. Passenger ferries run twice a day, year-round, to and from the island.

History: Native Americans resided on the island for nearly twelve thousand years until the early 1600s, when it was discovered by Jamestown settlers. The island is one of the oldest English-speaking communities in the region and is known for its unique dialect, which linguists have dubbed Tidewater English.

Present Day: As of the 2020 census, there were 94 people living on the island. Most residents are direct descendants of the first British settlers. The median income for a household was $26,324, and the median income for a family was $29,375. The main profession is fishing. The town boasts one church, one general store/market, and one restaurant. Notably, there are few cars (most people walk or ride bikes for transportation), no street signs, and there is no police force. There is a schoolhouse, although there are no longer enough children to fill it, and therefore children ferry over to the mainland to attend school every day.

Anders's cell vibrated in his back pocket, interrupting his reading. He dug it out, half hoping it would be Celeste.

"Kelsey," Anders said when he answered, swallowing his disappointment.

"I've been texting you all day. Why haven't you responded?"

"Because I don't know what Zoosk is, and I'm not joining it."

"Mom says you're heartbroken."

"I'm not heartbroken." He was. Even though it had been two months since he and Celeste broke up. Theirs was a college romance, a first love, and when Celeste got accepted to Emory's medical school upon graduation and Anders got the job in Maryland, they did what most young lovers do — ignored the facts and held steadfast to the belief that their love could endure anything, including a distance of six hundred and ninety-six miles between them. Turned out, it could not. Celeste met a fellow doctoral student at her orientation in June, and the swoony way she spoke about him that evening to Anders — "he's really smart; an infectious disease major" — should have been his first clue that it was over. The next night it was more facts: "He has this adorable German shepherd, Lola. He showed me a picture." When she finally ended things for good two weeks later, Anders felt a literal pain in his chest. He had loved her. Or admired her, at least. Or just really appreciated the way she laughed at his quips, as though he was the funniest person she'd ever met.

But he knew defending himself further would only cement Kelsey's claim, so he chose to deflect. "Mom says *you're* sleeping in until twelve and have only been on one audition all summer." His sister had somehow convinced their parents to let her defer college for a year and live at home to pursue her dream of acting in Atlanta, which had suddenly become a mecca for filmmaking.

"Well, I already signed you up," she said, ignoring his jab.

"For what?"

"Zoosk."

"I still don't know what that is."

"A dating app. I'm sending you the sign-in now."

His email dinged. He didn't bother looking at it and stuck the straw from his Coke in his mouth.

Anders sighed. "I don't need a dating app."

"Yes, you do. Celeste has moved on and you need to get out of your comfort zone."

"I like my comfort zone." Anders started to wish he hadn't answered the phone.

"Will you just look at it, please?"

"Sure," Anders said, though he had no intention of doing so.

He heard muffled speaking and then: "Mom wants to know if you're coming home for Labor Day. She's ordering the pork butts or something and is trying to get a head count." The Caldwells' Labor Day barbecue had somehow become *the* social event of the year in their suburban neighborhood.

"I've already told her, I'll probably be working," Anders said, though he hadn't even asked Greta yet.

More muffled voices. "You worked on Fourth of July, she says. Surely you get some holidays off."

Anders was about to explain the way a *daily* newspaper worked for the hundredth time, when his sister said: "You what? *Mom.*"

"What?" Anders said, growing impatient with the mediation.

"She says she invited Celeste."

He nearly choked on another sip of soda, the froth sputtering out of his mouth.

"*What?* Why?"

"She's not *practically family,* Mom. They broke up."

Anders cringed. His mind flashed to Celeste in her white sundress last year, her hair swept up in a messy knot. He preferred it that way, her perfect neck on display. There was something vulnerable about it, sexy. He sighed again.

"Look, Kels, I'm working. I've got to go."

"OK — well, just look at the website. Maybe you'll meet someone and can bring her to —"

Anders hung up and slunk down in his chair. He glanced at the Wikipedia page and then clicked off of it, not caring anymore about Frick Island. He navigated to his email and wavered the pointer over Kelsey's newest message before hitting delete. Then, in an effort to forget about his exhausting conversation with his sister and Celeste's perfect neck, he opened Jess's email and clicked on the Humane Society link, which took him to a series of pictures of homeless dogs with names like Chip and Pepe and Stella staring at him with sad, hopeful eyes. Maybe he would get a dog. He could be a dog person like Celeste's new boyfriend, couldn't he? He had no idea what the guy looked like, but he pictured him as one of those Ken doll *Bachelorette* contestants from Kelsey's favorite show — a guy with coiffed hair and skinny jeans and K-Swiss sneakers tossing tennis balls at the park for Lola, showing off a row of perfect toothpaste-commercial teeth when he threw back his head in masculine, effortless laughter.

Movement on the wall drew his attention, and Anders jumped up, letting out a squeak and grabbing the can of Raid he kept out for this purpose. With lightning-quick speed, he popped the top off and directed the nozzle at the offensive target scurrying across the beige wall, leaving a trail of God knows what disgusting diseases in its wake. The cockroach dropped to the ground on its back, its fibrous legs still twitching, as if looking for purchase. Heart thudding, Anders sprayed it again in disgust, waiting for the poison to take effect. He glanced back at the screen of virile dogs and noticed it had gone black, so all he was looking at was the vague reflection of his own freckle-painted pale skin and unmanageable cowlick that refused to be tamed no matter how much he smoothed it. He thought of the coiffed hair, the tennis balls, the teeth.

And he sighed for the third time that evening.

■ ■ ■ ■

Once, in a fit of paternal (and scotch-induced) bonding at his high school graduation party, Anders's father gave him three pieces of advice. Anders couldn't remember the first two, but the third made so much sense, it stuck with him like a piece of gum to a shoe: *Dress for the job you want, not the job you have.*

Which was how Anders found himself sitting on a fiberglass bench in the middle of a passenger boat destined for Frick Island wearing a long-sleeved dress shirt and khaki pants as if he were heading into a budget meeting at the *New York Times.* Unfortunately, the August sun blazed like a furnace in the cloudless sky, raising the temperature of everything it touched to burning, causing his shirt to feel more like a stifling down coat by the second.

At least he had forgone the tie.

The boat rocked heavily as it churned through the water, and the motion roiled the Pop-Tarts still digesting in Anders's stomach. That plus the familiar tang of the sea air conjured vivid and unwelcome recollections of his last deep-water venture on a boat. He closed his eyes.

An old man stood at the helm, speaking into a handheld mouthpiece tethered to the dashboard by a spiraled cord, but Anders couldn't hear him. The latest episode of *This American Life* filled his ears, with the goal of drowning out everything unpleasant around him — the crackling voice distorted by the boat's ancient speakers, the vague lurching in his stomach, and the all-too-top-of-mind realization that Anders was smack in the middle of the ocean, at the mercy of an ancient boat captain on an even older boat, with no control over the destination or his motion sickness or the strength of the sun's rays.

After thirty long minutes, a strip of trees appeared on the horizon, and Anders breathed a small sigh of relief that the end was in sight. That is, until the boat chugged closer and he had a better view. Shacks — about ten of them — sat on the shore, each with its own wooden dock reaching into the water like a crooked finger, the planks like the keyboard of a broken-down piano. Anders knew these were crab shanties he'd read about in his research — the shelters where watermen sorted through their catch and stored supplies — but he did not know they would have all the craftsmanship of a clubhouse nailed together by a child. Each one looked less sturdy and in a greater state of disrepair than the one before. After the last shanty, the ferry pulled up alongside a small dock parallel with the shore, rather than perpendicular. Just beyond the dock sat another small white shack with a hand-painted sign:

Frick Island Marina
Captain BobDan Gibbons
555-6728

Anders blinked. *Marina?* This tiny building with one dock and a couple of benches? It was like stumbling upon a lone apple tree and calling it an orchard. When the boat was secure, Anders stood, Ira Glass's voice still blaring in his ears, and followed the other passengers shuffling forward to disembark. When it was his turn, Anders stepped off the boat, dug a crisp ATM-fresh twenty-dollar bill out of his pocket, and dropped it in the bucket proffered by the captain, but then froze. He had no idea where he was going. He stepped to the side to let the last few passengers walk around him and pulled out his phone.

He knew the day's festivities took place in front of the Methodist church, but when he punched in the address and nothing came up, he realized he had no service. He looked up to ask someone where the church was, but the passengers that had been near him had already dispersed, halfway down the road leading away from the dock. Before he could decide whether to follow, a rumble of a deep voice caught his attention. He removed one of his earbuds and turned his head, coming face-to-face with the captain, still holding the bucket.

"Straight down the road there, take a right at the general store. Sign says *Blue Point.* Can't miss it." The man's voice was as grizzled as his skin and his accent warbled, as if he were talking around a mouthful of marbles. Anders just stared at him.

"You going to the Cake Walk, ain'tcha?"

"I am," Anders managed.

"Well, go on, then. Although, weather like this — prolly get canceled anyway."

Anders looked up at the cloudless sky. *For the heat?* he wondered.

"Storm brewing to the east — see the wind picking up on the water?" The word "water" came out "wudder."

Anders did not, but he nodded anyway so as to placate the senile old man.

On the sunbaked road leading away from the docks, every building Anders passed looked to be larger incarnations of the crab

41

shanties — houses built with wooden slats or shingles, sanded by wind, salt air, and time. A few had their own handpainted, often crooked signs declaring what they were — a restaurant called the One-Eyed Crab, an antiques store, and a post office. A rusted-out Chevy with no windshield and three flat tires sat in front of the antiques shop as if it had died there one day and no one bothered to move it. Although where would they move it to? Surely there was no mechanic on the island, for it was the first car Anders had seen. And it would take a barge to get it off the island — probably the same barge that got it over here in the first place, which couldn't be cheap.

At the end of the road, as promised, Anders came upon a building with a sign that announced: *Blue Point General Store.* Anders stood for a minute in front of it, considering the rickety stairs leading to a cement slab porch, the air-conditioning unit that precariously hung out the front window at an angle and looked like an insurance claim waiting to happen, the way the building sloped slightly to the left as if a strong breeze had one day pushed it sideways and it never recovered. This was, according to Wikipedia, the only market on the island. The only place residents could buy their groceries. And it was a far cry from a Food Lion.

As Anders stood there, slack-jawed and contemplative in the middle of the road, he thought how he had been to a lot of beach towns before. Small towns, even. But he had to admit, he'd never seen a town quite like this.

CHAPTER 3

Two Weeks After the Storm
It was two days after the memorial service
when Piper woke up suddenly, as if startled
by a loud noise, and found herself staring at
her husband's eyes. Eyes she often thought
were the color of the Chesapeake Bay, briny
and gray with a hint of sky. Eyes she hadn't
seen in two full weeks.

"Tom!" she cried, her heart swelling with joy,
relief, and love. Always love.

His face still groggy with sleep, his head lying on his pillow exactly in the dent Piper had
been staring at for days, he blinked at her.

"You're here," she said, sitting up.

"Of course I'm here," he said.

"Why didn't you wake me?"

Tom yawned. "Seriously? I know how much
you like your sleep." He arched an eyebrow.
"Why are you acting so strange?"

Piper stared at him, all the words pooling in
her mouth — that though she knew better,

44

everyone said he wasn't coming home; that she'd started to believe them; that the weight felt so heavy in her chest at times, she thought she might never, ever breathe again — but suddenly none of that seemed to matter. He was here. Tom was home. And then, she remembered her hair. She hadn't bothered pulling it up into a top bun at night or wrapping it in a scarf like she usually did. She couldn't remember the last time she moisturized or combed it. And only now, when she gently patted it with her hand, did she notice the way the corkscrew curls knotted around each other, matted up in patches, like a mangy dog. She could only imagine how terrible it looked. And that was when the sourness wafted up to her nose, and she realized the only thing rivaling her looks was probably the way she smelled. Half of her wanted to immediately jump in the shower, but the other half was terrified Tom would disappear if she did. So she sat still, torn, while Tom just lay there, smiling at her the way he always did — slightly amused, full of adoration.

"I need to get cleaned up," she said, reticently slipping out of bed and padding backward to the bathroom, not wanting to take her eyes off him. And then she froze.

"Don't go anywhere! I'll only be a minute. Don't leave."

"Never," Tom replied simply. "Piper Parrish, I would never leave you."

And true to his word, he didn't. When Piper got out of the shower, Tom was still there.

Seventeen days after Tom's boat went missing in the storm, Pearl Olecki stood in the kitchen of her bed-and-breakfast, turning link sausages over in a hot pan, when the side screen door squeaked open and Piper came walking through it.

"Piper," she breathed, turning her wide hips toward the girl, ready to embrace her or feed her or give her whatever she might need.

But Piper slipped right by her and went to the opposite wall, where she tugged her cat-paw-printed apron off a hook and looped it around her neck, expertly tying the side ribbons behind her back. "Morning, Miz Olecki," she said cheerfully, going straight to the refrigerator to retrieve the carton of eggs, easily falling into their routine as if seventeen days had not passed since they'd last performed it.

Pearl stared at the girl's back, mouth agape, and then promptly closed it when Piper turned around, clutching the eggs in her right hand. She had lived long enough to know the ways people grieved were as varied as the waves that lapped up on Graver's Beach at the far end of the island. And far be it from her to say one way was better than another. If Piper chose to face today with a smile, then so be it. The important thing was she was finally out of that house. Pearl turned back to her pan and busied herself with the browning sausage.

"Sunrise was beautiful this morning," Piper said, as she beat the egg yolks with a fork in the orange ceramic bowl. "Did you see it?"

"I didn't," Mrs. Olecki said. She opened the oven door a crack to peek on the cinnamon rolls, thinking how wonderful it was that Piper could still appreciate the simple things, like a glorious sunrise, in the midst of her pain.

"Pinks and oranges — like the sky was on fire," Piper said.

"Mm," Pearl said, infusing the sound with sympathy and understanding.

For the next ten minutes, the two women strode around each other in silence, performing their well-practiced dance. Mrs. Olecki tonged the links onto a plate lined with paper towels, while Piper cooked the eggs. When the timer dinged, Piper moved the lower half of her body to the side so Mrs. Olecki could retrieve the cinnamon buns.

It wasn't until they were standing side by side at the counter, Piper plating the first course for the three guests currently staying at the bed-and-breakfast, Pearl icing the cinnamon rolls, that Piper finally mentioned Tom.

"You want to hear something funny?" Piper asked.

"What's that, hon?"

Piper paused a beat. And then: "I miss Tom's snoring."

Mrs. Olecki froze, holding the piping bag above the round metal pan of swollen, browned buns. "Oh, Piper."

"I know, it's so silly. I hated it for so long. Nearly drove me crazy with keeping me up. Sometimes, I'd punch him square in the back. Punch him! Trying to get him to stop."

Mrs. Olecki set down the icing, ready to embrace Piper now, to absorb the tears she knew were coming on the lemon apron covering her heavy bosom.

But Piper kept talking. "It's crazy, but last night, he didn't snore. Not once. And I know he's not using those Breathe Right strips I ordered from the mainland, because they're still in the box in the mirror cabinet of the bathroom." Piper spooned another serving of eggs onto a plate. "Isn't that something? Been sleeping next to him for a year now —" It was really longer than that, Mrs. Olecki knew, as she had seen Tom, before he and Piper got married, sneak into the carriage house under the cover of night and sneak out again before the town was awake so as not to scandalize anybody. "And every single night he's snored. I mean, like a freight train running through our bedroom. And last night — silence. I stared at him, his peaceful sleeping face, for the longest time, just waiting for it, but it never came. And the silence was too much. I couldn't sleep!"

Piper giggled then, and Mrs. Olecki, who had been staring at her during the entire soliloquy, trying to make sense of it all, was glad she had set the piping bag down, for she surely would have dropped it. She opened her mouth to say something, but then closed it, not knowing where to begin with her questions.

"Have you ever heard of such a thing?" Piper said, putting the now-empty ceramic bowl in the sink and running water into it. "Snoring being cured just like that?" She snapped her fingers, still grinning.

Yes, death will cure a number of maladies, won't it? Mrs. Olecki thought. But she knew to say it out loud would be cruel, even if true, and she swallowed the words down. Piper, not noticing her restraint, bopped over to the swinging door between the kitchen and the dining room to hold it open, and, having no choice, Pearl balanced the first-course plates in the crooks of her arms and waltzed them out to her waiting guests, where she would serve them and chat with them about their plans for the day, making suggestions for lunch or the best bird-watching or fishing charters, while Piper washed the dishes. But her mind spun while she conversed with a retired couple, Franny and Pat, visiting from San Francisco. By the time she got back in the kitchen, she had convinced herself that surely she had misheard Piper, or misunderstood what she was trying to say. Maybe Piper had been staring at a *picture* of Tom last night, missing him, as she surely did. Yes, that must have been it.

When the door swung back into place behind Mrs. Olecki, she saw that the dishes were clean and stacked in the drying rack beside the sink and Piper already had her apron off. She was holding a plate with two fried eggs, sunny-side up, and two links of leftover sausage. "Taking breakfast to go this morning?"

"Yeah, I hope that's OK," she said.

"Of course," Mrs. Olecki said. "Just bring the dish back when you're done." She eyed the plate again. "I thought you didn't like eggs."

"Oh, they're not for me," Piper said. "For Tom."

Mrs. Olecki's eyes nearly popped out of their sockets. "For Tom?" she sputtered.

Piper's eyes went round, innocent. "Yes,"

she said, and breezed out the screen door, leaving a perplexed Pearl behind her. She thought again how she had lived long enough to see all the different ways people grieved. And how they were as varied as the waves that lapped up on Graver's Beach at the far end of the island.

But if she was being honest, she had to admit — she'd never seen a wave quite like this.

CHAPTER 4

Frick Island was not widely known by anyone who didn't live in the state of Maryland. It wasn't even widely known by those who did. But the people who did know about the tiny island likely had heard of it by way of a dessert. More specifically, a cake: the Frick Island cake, eight to ten thin layers tall, each one carefully spread with frosting, traditionally chocolate. Currently twelve of those cakes filled two folding tables, shaded from the sun's glare by white tents, on the patch of freshly mown lawn in front of the Methodist church. Small groups of people milled around them, pointing, admiring the practice it must have taken to get the layers the same thin width, the skill to keep the cake from toppling over. Anders joined them, snapping photos of the cakes and stopping a few tourists to ask questions, mainly: What are you *doing* here? He tried but failed to keep it from sounding accusatory. But really, the question he wanted to ask was: Why would anyone *live* here?

Around two thirty, a jowly woman with sparse eyelashes and bangs teased up high off her forehead announced that the first walk would start in fifteen minutes and directed people who had not done so to purchase their ten-dollar ticket at the folding table to her right. When she completed her address of the crowd, Anders approached her.

"Anders Caldwell," he said, sticking out his hand for her to shake. "Reporter with the *Daily Telegraph.*" Even after three months, and despite the fact that it wasn't the *Times* or the *Post,* he still got a small thrill from saying it — a sense that his six-year-old self, who stared wide-eyed in admiration at Christopher Reeve announcing, "Clark Kent, the *Daily Planet,*" would be impressed.

"Nice to meet you. I'm Lady Judy."

Anders raised his eyebrows at this. Wikipedia had mentioned that most people on the island were descendants of the British, but the woman looked, and sounded, about as far from royalty as one could get. "Er, is Judy your last name?"

"No, last name's Cullins — that's with an

i-n, not *e-n.*" She nodded toward his notebook and Anders made the notation.

"I see," he said, and scratched his pen on the notepad. He cleared his throat. "How long have you been in charge of the Cake Walk here?"

"Oh, Lordt, honey, I'm not in charge. Or not more so than anyone else anyway. We all just kind of pull it together each year. Used to be a much bigger affair, right after the cake was named Maryland's official dessert — what was that? Ten years ago. Anyway, that's the way of things, iddn't it? Feast or famine." Anders noticed Lady Judy had the same affectation in her pronunciations as the boat captain. *T* words came out with a soft *d* sound. It was similar to the Eastern Shore accent he had slowly been getting used to, but a derivative of it — like the difference between a British accent and Cockney.

Since she'd brought it up, Anders asked the question that had been bothering him since he had noted the dwindling attendance — he estimated about sixty people at the event, which had once drawn nearly five hundred. "Why is the event held on a Thursday? I know it's the summer, but wouldn't it have a greater chance of drawing a bigger crowd if it was a Saturday?"

Lady Judy just stared at him, and then shrugged. "It's always been on a Thursday. That's the way it's done."

"Yeah, but —"

Her eyes flared, effectively cutting him off. "Nobody goes around suggesting we change Thanksgiving, do they?"

"Um, no. I guess not," Anders said. He glanced back at his notebook, eager to change the subject. "The only other thing I'll need is the total funds raised from today's walk. Is that a figure I could get from you when it's over?"

"I reckon I could find that out for you."

"Great," Anders said. "Do you have an email or cell number so I can follow up?"

She cackled. "Wouldn't be any good to you if I did, now, would it? Internet hardly works out here and the only place to get any kind of cell service is clear the other end of the island — Graver's Beach. That's what they say, anyway, though I never had need to test it out. And why it would work all the way out there is anybody's guess." And that was when Anders looked around and wondered how he hadn't noticed before — heads weren't bent toward phones in the crowd the same way they were everywhere else he'd ever been.

The next two hours plodded by, with a

large swath of tourists surprisingly clearing out after the third walk — not even halfway through the event. Anders hadn't noticed the clouds rolling in until suddenly the sun was blotted from the sky and the first fat drop of rain fell on his shoulder. Then the bottom dropped out, rain coming down like bullets, scattering the few people left to shelter beneath tents and open doorways. He stood, stunned for a moment that the old man's prediction had been correct, and then he checked his watch and realized he only had fifteen minutes to get to the dock for the four o'clock ferry departing back to the mainland. And then he ran.

He reached the dock winded but relieved when he saw the yellow boat tied up where he left it. Until he got closer and realized no one was in it. His eyes darted around the docks and landed on the white shack of a building with the Frick Island Marina sign. In small letters above a door was the word *Office.*

The door squeaked on its hinges as Anders entered, grateful to be out of the deluge. And he came face-to-face once again with the boat captain, glasses perched on the end of his nose as he scribbled in a ledger, a stubby pencil gripped in his right hand and a lit cigarette in his other. At least Anders thought it was a cigarette. But the man dispensed with it in such a smooth, quick motion, his hand disappearing beneath the desk, that Anders would have thought he'd imagined it altogether if not for the telltale wisp of smoke rising up in the air. When the captain turned his attention to Anders, his face morphed from alarmed to relieved to annoyed. "Thought you were my wife," he muttered. He opened a squeaky desk drawer and reached for a new cigarette out of the pack stashed there.

Anders nearly apologized for startling the man, but then remembered why he was there. "Has the ferry departure time been postponed?" Anders asked. The captain brought the cigarette to his lips and lit it with the flick of his thumb on a red lighter. He glanced at Anders, then back at his work.

"No," he said, the cigarette impressively staying put between his lips

"Oh. Good." When the man didn't say more, or appear to be finishing up what he was doing, Anders pointed his thumb in the marina's direction. "Should I just go wait on the boat?"

"Suppose you could, if you want," the man said, without looking up.

Confused, Anders hesitated. When he realized the man wasn't going to say anything else, he turned to walk back out the door.

"You'll be waiting awhile, if you're trying to get back to the mainland."

"What? I thought you said it wasn't postponed."

"It's not."

"What do you mean?" Anders asked.

"Boat left at three today. On account of the weather."

"*What?* How was I supposed to know?"

He shrugged, scribbling in the book with his pencil. "I announced it four times on the ride over. And again when we docked."

Shocked, Anders wondered how he had missed it. Then he remembered his earbuds and inwardly groaned. "I had my headphones on . . . I didn't hear."

The man didn't respond and panic started to grip Anders. "How do I get back to the mainland? I need to get back."

The man finally plucked the cigarette from between his lips and tapped the ash into a coffee mug on the desk, while his eyes grazed Anders's face once more. "Walk around the docks long enough, you might could find a waterman'll take you. If the price is right, anyway. Otherwise, you'll need to find a place to hunker down. There's a motel should have room."

"You mean spend the night?" Anders asked, appalled.

"I reckon. 'Less you up for some long-distance swimming."

Back outside, huddled beneath the awning over the office door, Anders glanced around the dock. There wasn't a soul in sight. And he was overcome with a surreal feeling — a familiar one that he had encountered a few times since moving to Maryland, a sense that this wasn't his real life. He was stranded on an island in the middle of the Chesapeake Bay, in the middle of a downpour, with no cell service, and worse, he realized, a story due for tomorrow's paper, with no way to file it. He'd never missed a deadline, and the anxiety of it gnawed his belly. He stood for a minute cursing the rain. Then he reopened the door and stepped back into the marina office.

"Can I use your phone?"

When Anders stepped back out into the storm twenty minutes later, having explained the situation in private (BobDan had generously shut himself in what appeared to be a smaller office room within the office and turned up the radio) and dictated all his quotes and observations to Greta to fill the six inches (they'd have to go without a photo, and Greta would have to call Lady Judy for the final fundraising number), the anxiety had lifted from his belly, but another feeling had taken its place: ravenous hunger. He hadn't eaten since the morning's Pop-Tarts, and saliva pooled in his mouth as he recalled the thick frosting painted on those cakes. He needed to secure lodging, but his first priority would have to be food. Remembering the restaurant he'd passed, Anders retraced his steps out of the marina and entered the One-Eyed Crab wet as a dog.

While the docks and the road leading from it had been bereft of people — nearly a ghost town — the inside of the restaurant was surprisingly bustling with life, people crowded at wooden tables and at the length of a rustic bar lined with Christmas lights, their voices commingling in the din. Anders stood in the doorway, feeling out of place — an unwelcome guest at a party — until a young girl who didn't look a day over twelve greeted him. She stood next to a stack of three overturned wooden crates, which Anders assumed must have been a hostess stand of sorts.

"Just one?" she said.

Anders nodded.

"Do you mind sitting at the bar? When

it's busy, I'm supposed to save the tables for two or more people."

He followed her to the back of the room, where he took a seat on a barstool. Hair matted to his forehead, Anders pulled his camera out from beneath his shirt and set it down on the bar. He picked up the menu the girl had left him, a white piece of paper that had been laminated long ago but was now tattered, the plastic peeling at the edges, leaving openings for grease spots to take hold. There were only five dinner options — crab cakes, fried shrimp, fried flounder, catch of the day, or chicken fingers, all served with coleslaw and chips — and though Anders didn't care for seafood, he had half a mind to order one of everything he was so hungry. He looked up for the bartender and saw a freckle-faced guy in a backward ball cap and T-shirt chatting animatedly with a few men at the far end of the bar. Anders tried to get his attention, to no avail. The group laughed uproariously at something and Anders hoped that signaled the end of the conversation. It didn't.

Finally, ten minutes later, the guy noticed Anders and sauntered down to his end of the bar.

"What kind of beer do you have?" Anders

asked. He didn't drink much, but after the events of the day, he felt a cold pint was in order.

"We don't."

Anders cocked his head. "What do you mean?"

"It's a dry island."

"As in no alcohol?"

"Right."

"Oh."

He ordered a Pepsi and the chicken fingers (he wasn't sure he could eat seafood, after all) and then let his eyes wander around the room. Fishing nets and old buoys hung on the wooden slatted walls, but more haphazardly, it appeared, than as a part of any grand décor scheme. A nineteen-inch box TV sat in the corner of the bar, but it was covered in so much dust, Anders doubted it actually worked. He let his eyes graze over the people seated at the tables. A few he recognized from the Cake Walk, and he found, as he had earlier in the day, he could easily spot the locals from the tourists. Not because of their belongings this time, but by a difference in the way they carried themselves. The locals' posture belied a certain sense of belonging, a comfortable relaxation, as if they had been sitting on these same chairs for years, the wood worn in just the right grooves to fit their bodies perfectly. The tourists were also relaxed — the salt air, Anders noticed, had a way of seeping into your skin no matter who you were, loosening joints and muscles — but they still looked more formal, somehow. As if the chairs knew they were visiting, their worn parts not matching up to the tourists' bodies the same way.

As Anders was contemplating this, the front door opened and his attention was drawn by the jingle of bells. A woman walked into the restaurant, but instead of glancing away as social etiquette directed, Anders found that, for some inexplicable reason, he couldn't stop staring. Maybe it was the wild pencil-thin curls of her hair framing her face like a lion's mane, or her eyes, which reminded him of a cow's, large and round and set a little too far apart, or her lips, perfectly bow shaped and book-ended by two dimples that looked deep enough to swallow a pencil eraser whole. Or maybe it was simply that she stood out in a crowd — specifically, this crowd of burly watermen and retired, linen-clad tourists.

Anders wasn't sure. And so he just stared, until the girl, feeling his eyes on her, met his gaze. Embarrassed, he turned away and noticed that at some point while he was

gawking, his chicken fingers had materialized on the bar in front of him.

And Anders, red-faced and perplexed,
stared down at the glistening breading, just
out of the fryer, a bead of water from his
hair trickling down the side of his face and
dripping from his chin onto the plate.

CHAPTER 5

The first person Piper laid eyes on when she and Tom walked into the One-Eyed Crab Thursday night was Jeffrey Wallace, running plates to a table, a dingy white rag hanging out of his back pocket, swinging to and fro like a horse's tail.

She tried to shrink, avoiding his notice, while knowing it was an impossibility in a restaurant — and island — this small. She loved Jeffrey, of course, in the way you love a distant cousin, even if you don't *like* them that much, because they're family. And they *were* family in a sense, considering she and Tom and Jeffrey grew up together from the time she moved to the island, being the only three kids in the same age range, and she didn't have much of a choice in the matter. But ever since she'd turned him down when he asked her to his senior prom her sophomore year (anybody with two eyes and half a brain knew she'd be going with Tom, who was also a senior), he'd treated her with nothing short of disdain. And she didn't have the energy to deal with him tonight.

Frankly, she was exhausted. She had waited on more people than usual at the market today, thanks to the influx of tourists looking for fresh-picked crab meat and Mr. Garrison's famous crab cakes, which they had been mixing and forming since four o'clock that morning.

Not to mention, she hadn't been sleeping well recently, what with the absence of Tom's snoring — though she recognized the irony in that. Shouldn't she be sleeping better?

She flicked her eyes from Jeffrey to Emily Francis, a girl of fourteen, who could probably get owners Mack and Sue convicted of every child labor law ever written if anyone on the island actually cared about those kinds of things. She was standing at the upturned stack of crates, clutching menus and gazing at Piper as though she had suddenly forgotten the English language.

"Can we please be seated?" Piper asked, flashing her a smile.

"Um . . . well," the girl stammered. "I'm supposed to save the tables for groups of —"

"Three or more," Sue said, swooping in

and shooting Emily a look. "But we can make an exception for you and Tom, Pipes."

"Thank you, Sue," Piper said. She followed Sue to a table, shrugging out of her rain slicker and chatting about the downpour and the influx of tourists (neither one mentioned how it was even smaller than the previous year) thanks to the Cake Walk. Once seated, Piper fluffed her hair, though the rain and wind were no match for her tightly wound and belligerent curls. Sue didn't offer menus; Tom and Piper rarely strayed from their usual — crab cakes for Tom, grilled catch of the day (cobia, this week) for Piper, extra coleslaw. And if they did, like most locals, they knew the options by heart.

"You kids want the usual?" Sue asked.

"Please." Piper nodded.

As Sue left to gather an iced tea for Piper and a Pepsi for Tom, Piper and Tom sat in a long silence, until she remembered the joke Mr. Olecki had shared with her that morning as she helped Mrs. Olecki in the kitchen of the bed-and-breakfast. She opened her mouth just as Sue arrived with the drinks.

"Oh, you'll like this, too, Sue," she said.

"Like what?" Sue asked as she placed the translucent tumblers with worn Pepsi logos on the table.

"This joke," Piper said. Sue waited patiently. "So this man passed a pet store, and the sign in the window said 'Talking Dog for Sale.' Curious, the man went in and said to the dog, 'Tell me about yourself.' The dog said, 'Oh, I've had the most marvelous life. I was born in Great Britain and worked as a service dog in the Royal Guard, helping protect the Queen herself, and then I moved to the Alps, where I spent years rescuing avalanche victims, and now I spend my days with the owner of this store, curled at his feet by the fire at night, reading to him.' Flabbergasted, the man turned to the owner and said, 'What an amazing dog. Why on earth would you want to get rid of him?' And the owner said, 'Because he's a liar! He never did any of that. He can't even read.' "

Sue chuckled and Piper sat back, pleased with herself.

"Food'll be out soon," Sue said, turning away from the table.

As they waited for their meals, Piper curled the length of white straw paper around her index finger and studied the tourists two tables over. "What do you think?" she whispered, cutting her eyes to the prim lady holding her purse in her lap, as if she were afraid it might get snatched at any second. When Tom didn't respond, she said, "I'm gonna go with craft blogger, waiting to be discovered as the next Martha Stewart. She owns entirely too much decoupaged furniture — end tables, coffee tables, even the headboard of her bed. She just couldn't stop. Her friends and family were finally forced to stage an intervention, as they couldn't bear receiving one more Mod-Podge-and-magazine-cutout-covered flowerpot or stool or picture frame for their birthdays or Christmas."

It was a game they'd been playing for years, sizing up the tourists visiting the island and guessing what they did — trying to top each other for the most outlandish careers or hobbies. Piper sometimes felt guilty for the inherent unkindness of the contest, but there was no malice in it, and what was the harm, she reasoned, if the people in question couldn't hear them? She wondered what Tom's assessment of the current woman would be — his were always so much more creative, funny, unexpected. But before she could find out, a man approached the table, standing behind the chair opposite Piper. A tourist, obviously, because Piper knew everyone on the island, and this was a stranger. But even for a tourist, he was peculiarly dressed. Aside from the damp spots at the shoulders of his white button-up, it looked like he was about to attend a business meeting. Or church. But on Frick Island, no one wore long sleeves in the dead heat of August. Not even to church.

Piper stared pleasantly up at the man, curious and patient. Perhaps he wanted to borrow their ketchup or salt. Or maybe he was going to ask if she was an actress. It had happened once before, a few years earlier, and when she said no, the tourist was embarrassed and she never got the chance to ask which actress. On the off chance that this man was going to ask her the same thing, she resolved that this time, she would find out.

Anders cleared his throat, feeling a little out of body and unable to recall the short walk that had propelled him from the bar to this table, where he stood now in front of the curly-headed woman with the perfect bow-shaped mouth. In the fifteen minutes that had passed since he first laid eyes on her when she walked into the restaurant, Anders had spent twelve of them eating his chicken fingers in silence and not giving any more thought to the woman who had caught his eye. But then, his waiter dropped off a rolled

70

napkin — a little late considering he was halfway done with his meal — and Anders unrolled it to find a knife and a *spork*. He stared at the hybrid instrument — part fork, part spoon — and he couldn't help it, he thought of Celeste.

He thought of how she squealed, "A spork!" and held up the utensil that came with her order at KFC one night, on a mashed potato study break. "God — I used to love these when I was a kid." It stuck with Anders, because he never considered that he would be attracted to someone who squealed over plastic cutlery.

And then he remembered — in that shocking, painful way that happens after a breakup, like being blindsided by a sucker punch — that he would most likely not ever be hearing her squeal about sporks again. That honor now belonged to the infectious disease major with coiffed hair and a dog named Lola.

That was when he turned his head slightly and caught sight of the woman, now sitting two tables behind him. She was alone and appeared to be talking to herself, which may have put off some men but only charmed Anders further. His sister's voice echoed in his head — *You need to get out of your comfort zone* — and after some hemming and hawing, that was what actually stood him up on his two feet and made him do something as dumb (in retrospect) and out of character as attempt to — what, *hit on* her? No, no, he certainly wasn't *hitting on* anyone. But walk over and speak to the woman who so piqued his interest.

"Can I help you?" the woman asked now, when seconds had ticked by and Anders had not volunteered any explanation as to why he was standing there.

Anders, who didn't do much of anything without planning out every single detail, cursed himself for not coming up with an opening line, and then cursed Frick Island for being dry, because he couldn't even do something as banal and cliché as offer to buy her a drink. "I just, um . . ." he stammered. His eyes flitted from the girl's expectant gaze to her wild hair and then to the table, where they landed on a pillar of salt and he was buoyed with inspiration. "May I borrow your salt?"

"Of course," she said, nodding toward the shaker on the table. Anders picked it up but didn't immediately turn back to the bar. He closed his eyes and inhaled through his nostrils. He tightened his grip on the salt. Then he opened his eyes and said, "Do you want to join me?"

The woman paused, lifting an eyebrow. "*Join* you?"

Heat rushed into Anders's face. "You know, to eat. At the bar. I don't really know anyone and I just thought . . ."

The woman glanced at the chair next to her and then back at Anders, her eyes round, a pink slowly tingeing her cheeks. "I'm here with my husband." Her voice was still kind, but a tightness belied it, as if she were apologetic but also appalled — as if Anders should have known she was not alone. And that was when Anders noticed the thin gold band on her ring finger. Anders had always prided himself on his keen observation skills — it was one of the things, if not *the* thing, that made him such an excellent journalist. How did he not see the ring before?

"Oh, I'm . . . I didn't . . ." He stumbled backward from the table. "Of course, yes. Enjoy your dinner," he managed, and turned toward the bar, wishing the slats of the floor would open up and swallow him whole, while chiding himself for actually taking his kid sister's advice. When had she ever been right about anything? He slid onto the barstool in front of his half-eaten chicken fingers and looked up for his server, hoping to get the check as fast as humanly possible so he could just leave. Surprisingly, the waiter was standing right in front of him, wearing a large grin.

"Don't worry," he said. "You're not the first to strike out with Piper Parrish."

"Mm," Anders said, not wishing to dwell on the experience any more than necessary. "Could I get my check, please?"

"Sure," the guy said, whipping a dingy terry-cloth rag out from his back pocket and wiping down the space on the bar right beside Anders, even though there wasn't much to wipe as far as Anders could tell. Anders silently urged him to hurry. "She tell you she was married?" the guy asked.

Anders looked up at this. "Yeah," he said, then cocked his head when the man grinned again in a way that suggested this may have been a lie. It suddenly dawned on him that *of course* it was a lie. The girl couldn't have been more than twenty, and really, who on earth gets married that young these days? Anders inwardly groaned at the prospect of being found so lacking that instead of just saying no, the woman felt the need to create a husband out of thin air, but still he found himself saying: "Is she not?"

"Depends on who you ask."

Anders considered this for a minute and wondered then if she *was* really married —

and if this waiter was alluding to some kind of marital strife, maybe a separation or something the couple was trying to work out. Whatever it was, it was definitely none of his business and all the more reason for him to leave, before her husband showed up and she pointed Anders out as the man who had been hitting on her. But though the waiter took the hint and tucked his rag back in his jeans pocket, he still took his sweet time getting the check, and when he did bring it and Anders gave him a twenty-dollar bill, he disappeared once again, making Anders wait on the change.

The minutes ticked by, and Anders picked up his spork — that infernal tool that got him into this embarrassing mess — and poked at one of his chicken fingers, half-eaten and now cold. The tiny prongs didn't pierce the breading, and it occurred to Anders that sporks were one of those inventions that sounded good in theory but in real-life application were positively useless.

Finally, the waiter returned with his change, and Anders left a few bills on the bar top and pocketed the rest. But as he quickly rushed out of the restaurant, head down, he couldn't help but notice that though at least fifteen minutes had passed, the woman — what had the bartender said her name was? Piper? — was still sitting very much alone.

It took two long blinks for Anders to recall exactly where he was Friday morning. He lifted his head off the pillow. Radiant sunlight beamed through the rips in the canvas window shade and directly into his face, causing him to squint as if injured.

"Freakin' Frick Island," he muttered to the water-damaged wallpaper, the Bible on the nightstand, the silent air. He let his head fall back down on the pillow, then eyed the Bible once more. Did the Gideons really come all the way to Frick Island just to deliver them to a five-room motel? That was dedication.

Then he sat straight up, remembering the times of departure BobDan had quoted for the buy boat (5:30 a.m.) and the mail boat (7:00 a.m.). He checked his phone — 6:36 a.m. — and realized he'd missed one but may still have time to catch the other. He stuffed his feet in his loafers and left the room, dropping his key in the rusty metal box beside the glass front door — and not even glancing inside to see if the mirthless woman working the front desk when he checked in was still there. (When he inquired about a room, she had waved her hand to five hooks on the wall behind her head. Four of them had keys hanging from them. "You can take your pick," she said, her eyes never leaving the magazine she was lazily flipping through. "Except the penthouse. It's booked." It took Anders ten seconds longer than it should have to realize this was a joke.)

Carrying his still-damp shirt in one hand, he eyed the road back into the main strip of town and, seeing the cracked, potholed, sunbleached asphalt in the light of day, wondered how on earth he hadn't turned an ankle during his dark walk to the motel the previous night. Quickly, he realized it wasn't the only thing in need of repair. The houses all were in their own state of disrepair — slanting staircases, grimy windows, splintered wood, missing shingles. They weren't abandoned-looking — no broken glass or boarded-up doors — just worn, lived in, loved. The Velveteen Rabbits of real estate.

Air always feels fresher after a storm, and the air on Frick Island was no exception. As it was too early in the morning for the mugginess to have set in, Anders might have enjoyed the stroll, appreciated the cloud-streaked morning sky, the rustle of wind through the blue-green seagrass between the houses, but he was too focused on getting away from it all, and he didn't want to miss the boat. He picked up his pace and was out of breath by the time he got to the marina at 6:51.

The docks were alive with men attending to various duties, tossing metal cages and ropes around as if they were as light as footballs. Anders scanned the various skiffs tied up, searching for a mail boat, but supposed it might be too much to ask that it would actually say that on the side. He spotted BobDan Gibbons wearing the same faded ball cap he'd had on the day before, talking to a man in waders in front of a bench. Anders approached him, and both men fell silent. BobDan looked him up and down.

"Found the hotel, I reckon?"

"I did," Anders said. "Is the mail boat still here? I was hoping to catch a ride back to the mainland . . ."

"No. Left about ten minutes ago." BobDan looked back to the man in waders, picking up where he left off about the rising price of gasoline. "Fifteen cents more than last week and prolly go up again 'fore August is over."

Anders's shoulders fell, and he turned on his heel to leave, before realizing he had nowhere to go. He had half a mind to jump off the dock into the water and attempt to swim the twelve miles in his khakis, or drown trying. Instead, he bent his knees and plopped down on the bench to wait. For four hours.

The two men talked for a few minutes longer and then the one in waders walked off in the direction of the boats while BobDan turned toward the marina. Anders shoved his hands in his pockets, closed his eyes, leaned his head back, and exhaled a long breath. His stomach gurgled, demanding its daily slug of coffee and twosome of raw Pop-Tarts. He wondered, briefly, if the One-Eyed Crab served breakfast, but wasn't eager to return to the restaurant, especially on the off chance that he might run into —

"Hey, Piper! Morning, Tom!" a voice called from the direction of the water, and Anders's head snapped back up, his eyes immediately clamping on the one woman he hoped to never see again. He inwardly groaned. She looked more beautiful in the morning light, fresh like the air itself. She was dressed simply in a purple tank top, the thin straps climbing over her tawny shoulders. Long khaki shorts stopped at her knees, the hems frayed, threads dangling down her legs. Her sturdy calves curved into delicate ankles, ending in gray canvas shoes tied neatly in bows. A wide smile stretched her lips as she waved back to the watermen in their boats — Anders just now noticing that the one greeting called out to her had created a domino effect. A chorus of gruff voices were shouting their hellos to Piper.

And someone named Tom.

Anders squinted, trying to ascertain who Tom was — or rather, *where* he was.

When Piper was within a few feet of the bench and finally took note of Anders, she didn't scowl in disgust or roll her eyes as he had feared; she looked directly in his direction, her dimples deepening in her cheeks, and said, "Mornin'," catching Anders even further off guard. He opened his mouth to say "Hi," but his brain thought it was going to say "Good morning," and he ended up making a strangled nonsense sound, causing his face to turn a brighter shade of crimson.

If Piper noticed, she didn't say anything, and then she was past him, walking down the dock, leaving a sweet scent in her wake, reminding Anders of one of those Strawberry Shortcake dolls Kelsey used to play with as a girl. He inhaled deeply. Apples, he thought. Or peaches. Something fruity and pleasant, and he wondered if it was her shampoo or a fragrance she dabbed on her wrists every morning or a lotion she — He shook his head. And then trained his gaze on where Piper had stopped, in front of a skiff tied up to the dock ten yards down. "Glad you decided to show," the man in the boat was saying. "Like your old man used to say — you always catch more crabs when you're out than when you're not."

Piper laughed, the sound bright as a bell, trilling in the open air. "I'm glad you're still here," she said to the man. "We weren't sure we were going to catch you."

Anders's forehead crinkled in further consternation. Piper had said "we," even though she was alone — and he puzzled over it for a beat until a voice from behind interrupted his thoughts.

"You gonna sit there all morning?"

Anders turned and met BobDan's grizzled face.

"Get up, son. Charlie here runs the buy boat. He'll take you, you don't mind sharing a seat with the crabs."

The buy boat. "I thought that left at five thirty," Anders said.

BobDan narrowed his eyes. "What are you, time management?" He shook his head, mouth turned in half a grin. "You want a ride back or not?"

"Yes," Anders said, chagrined. "I do."

And that was how Anders Caldwell ended up standing on a skiff, the bay wind whipping his cheeks, surrounded by cardboard boxes packed with hundreds of soft-shell crabs wrapped in seaweed, their briny juices leaking on his already-rain-ruined suede loafers. Anders didn't care. The smaller Frick Island — and Piper and BobDan and the One-Eyed Crab — shrunk behind him, the easier he breathed, resting in the knowledge that by this time next year, he would have moved on to a bigger, better paper and would not ever be returning to this godforsaken island for the Cake Walk — or anything else, for that matter.

CHAPTER 6

The musty scent of manure commingling with wet hay hung thick in the air as a 250-pound Andean bear named Baloo swatted a log, trying to dig out a piece of honeycomb from its hiding place — a knot in the wood. A zookeeper narrated, her voice reverberating in a cheap handheld microphone: "We've hidden pieces of the honeycomb around his habitat, creating strategic challenges to encourage the bear's natural problem-solving ability."

The problem, Anders thought, was that this zookeeper had been talking for forty-five minutes, and the crowd (of fifty-seven onlookers; Anders had counted), who most likely had attended more for the free cupcakes and punch than for the unveiling of the zoo's newest addition, was getting restless. The mosquitoes were nearly as thick as the heat and Anders slapped at one on his arm before snapping a few more photos of the bear with the newspaper-issued Nikon. He checked the counter. Certain that sixty-three pictures was more than enough to choose from, he let the camera hang around his neck and dug his phone out of his back pocket.

He scanned Instagram, expecting idle entertainment, but all the photos of feet in sand, perfectly plated quinoa bowls, and groups of smiling friends hugging each other only threw the depressing nature of his current situation into sharp relief.

Instead, he clicked onto his podcast web-site, to check the current status of his latest episode. He had recorded it on a whim, two days after he got home from Frick Island. Whereas most of his episodes were meticu-lously researched, carefully written and edited over weeks of time, this one he recorded in just one night — simply telling the straight story of his experience on the island (well, everything but the unfortunate and embarrassing encounter with the girl at the restaurant). And to his surprise, in the past week and a half that it had been live, it had garnered a whopping 123 listens. Not anywhere near *Serial*'s 250 million down-loads, of course, or even close to his sixteen-thousand-plus record with the Mark Harris episode, but it more than quadrupled his

84

audience for the poultry episode, and at least he was on an upswing for the first time since graduating.

Now, he saw the number had risen again — 152 — and instead of the one comment he expected to see right after he first posted it (**LeonardC404:** Reminds me a little of Daufuskie Island off the coast of South Carolina from Conroy's The Water Is Wide. Great detail; felt like I was there. — Dad), he now had three. Three!

He scrolled down to the second one.

MacLuvsCheese: Is this for real? I've never heard of this place! And I live in Virginia. Crazy.

Anders grinned. A comment! From a stranger! And he had felt the same way, not ever having heard of the island before. He moved on to comment three.

41NM241: Earn $175,000 working from home! Click here to learn how: bitly.sjfl53

Oh. He tried to swallow the disappointment at not having a comment from the one person he hoped to have a comment from, and focused on whether to delete the spam (three comments was still better than two), when the email alert on his phone dinged.

To:

ACaldwell@TheDailyTelegraph.com
From: NoManIsAnIsland@aol.com
SUBJECT: Your Cake Walk story

You came all the way to Frick Island and missed the biggest story out here. For a reporter, you're not very observant.

Anders's forehead crinkled as he scrolled down for the rest of the message — or a signature, at least — but that was it. He read it again and scoffed — there were plenty of things Anders could be accused of, but being unobservant was not one of them. He returned his attention to the stocky zookeeper, who was now droning on about the efforts of the various teams of people it had taken to relocate the bear from Ecuador to the United States. She was thanking each one by name, and if it were the Academy Awards, an orchestra would have long drowned out her words with music.

He looked at the email once more, his thumb hovering over the delete button. Though he'd only been a full-time reporter for a little over three months, he was used to getting weird missives like these. Even at his college paper, reporters got more than their fair share of calls, emails, and even old-fashioned letters from people who always said they had the next big story waiting to be uncovered. Nine out of ten times, they did not. In his experience, they often just wanted attention. Anders read the missive a third time, but instead of deleting it, he let it be. Just in case.

Anders followed his regular routine, head down working, yet always remaining attentive, alert at every assignment he was covering, looking for the more interesting, deeper story that could be his next podcast — something that could be worthy of following up and building on the minor success of his Frick Island episode.

But another week passed by, Anders covering the grand reopening of a renovated Starbucks, a three-day county fair, and the inevitable sale of a local radio station to a national conglomerate, and nothing jumped out at him. He was frustrated. Demoralized, really. He should be patient, he knew. That was another thing his dad always said: *Patience, persistence, and perspiration are the three keys to success.*

But patience was not Anders's strong suit.

He sat at his computer in the office, elbows on the desktop, head down, hands in his hair. One window on his computer screen opened to an email from his sister asking him if he was planning to drive in for Labor Day weekend on the Thursday or Friday before. Another window displayed a press release touting the accolades of the new dean of the school of education at the local university, information for the latest riveting article Anders was writing.

"There are doughnuts in the break room." Anders lifted his head and turned to see Jess standing behind him, clutching a powdered orb in one hand and a coffee mug in the other. "Might help your day get better."

Anders eyed her. "You have jelly on your shirt."

She glanced down at her sleeveless white blouse, dotted with small cutouts of floating Weimaraner heads, which was a bit disconcerting, if Anders was being honest. "Well, shit." She turned to set her coffee mug on the bookcase behind her but was closer than she thought and hip checked the structure, jarring the tan liquid out of her mug and onto her blouse, while simultaneously sending a teetering stack of back-issue newspapers cascading to the floor.

Jess froze, shocked from the commotion.

"You were saying?" Anders deadpanned. "Something about *my* day?"

"Ha ha."

Anders stood up. "I'll get you some paper towels." When he got back with a wad clutched in his fist, half damp, half dry, Jess was on her knees trying to corral the papers currently splayed all over the floor. Anders knelt beside her. "Here," he said.

"Thanks." Jess took the proffered towels and dabbed at the stains, as Anders continued the newsprint cleanup effort.

"Every time," she muttered. "Every. Single. Time. Should have known better than to wear white."

But Anders didn't hear her. He was staring at the front-page headline of a newspaper he had just picked up:

CRAB BOAT SINKS OFF FRICK ISLAND, MISSING WATERMAN PRESUMED DEAD

He rocked back on his haunches, lowering his bottom to the worn carpet, and scanned the article. The name "Tom Parrish" jumped out at him, tickling the recesses of his mind.

"Anders!"

"Huh?" He looked up.

"I was asking could you let Greta know when she gets in? I gotta run home and change before the city council meeting at two. Can't exactly go looking like this."

"Oh, yeah. 'Course."

She stood up, still scrubbing the front of her ruined shirt, though it was clearly beyond saving. Anders glanced back down at the story, the byline catching his eye. "Wait," he called out after Jess, who was already halfway to her cubicle.

She paused. "What?"

He flicked the paper with his middle finger. "You wrote this? About the missing waterman?"

"Oh." Her mouth turned down in a frown. "Yeah, that was sad."

"What happened?"

"A bad storm capsized his boat. He drowned. Least they think that's what happened. Still haven't found the body. Probably eaten by sharks." She shrugged nonchalantly at her gruesome suggestion, in the way only newspaper reporters, doctors, and police officers can. "Anyway, it was like the first waterman death in fifteen, sixteen years?"

"And his name was Tom," Anders said. He stared at the man's picture accompanying the article — young guy, buzzed hair almost like a military cut, friendly eyes. *Tom. Tom. Tom.* What was it about that name?

"Yep," Jess said. She tilted her head. "You know the saddest thing about that island isn't that waterman dying, though."

"What do you mean?"

"Saddest thing is that the island isn't even going to be here in eighty years, and not one of them seems to believe that."

"Why won't it be here?"

"Climate change? Maybe you've heard of it." She grins. "Sea level's rising. Frick Island is disappearing."

Now that *is interesting,* Anders thought.

"Anyway — gotta run."

"Yeah, OK. See ya." He waved her on, then stared at the story a few beats more, searching the recesses of his brain. Nothing materialized, aside from the email he had received: You came all the way to Frick Island and missed the biggest story out here. He folded the paper in half and, standing, tucked it under his arm, then walked back to his desk to flesh out the four inches on the new dean of education due at noon.

After work, Anders went through his routine in a half daze — unlock apartment door, turn on light, scan for cockroaches. He loosened his tie, then pulled it off and started on his shirt — a short-sleeved white button-up that was a gift from his grandmother at his college graduation. Kelsey laughed when he tried it on and said he looked like one of those Latter-Day Saints kids who rode from house to house on their bikes peddling Mormonism to the masses. Anders didn't care. The August heat and humidity was brutal and it was cooler than long sleeves while still being work appropriate. He hung it on the back of the folding chair.

Clad in his white undershirt and Dockers, he microwaved a frozen dinner and ate at the collapsible table while staring at *News-Hour.* He glanced at the folded newspaper he had brought home, where it now sat next to the plastic tray of half-eaten lasagna (that honestly tasted more like the plastic tray than lasagna), his eyes scanning the missing-waterman story again, and he thought about what Jess had said about the island.

His cell buzzed on the table and he experienced a brief hope it was Celeste, and then the immediate, familiar embarrassment. *It's over. Get it through your thick skull, Anders.* He spied Kelsey's name on the screen and turned his phone over, not eager to speak to his sister, who he knew was just calling to find out why he hadn't yet answered her email about Labor Day.

After ditching the rest of his meal in the

trash and scrubbing his fork in the sink —
he hadn't always been so steadfast in his
cleaning, but with the cockroaches, he
couldn't leave anything to chance — he
stretched out on his floor mattress and
pulled up a new web page on his phone,
typing "Frick Island disappearing" in the
search bar.

A string of hyperlinks popped up, and
Anders sat up straighter as he scanned
through them, each headline more alarming
than the next.

THE ISLAND SINKING INTO THE BAY
WASHING AWAY: THE VANISHING ISLAND
FRICK ISLAND: A PLACE IN CRISIS

Crisis? Good Lord, Anders thought, his
eyebrows having risen halfway to his hairline. Except when he visited the island, it
hadn't exactly had the vibe of a *place in
crisis.* Disrepair? Sure. Old-school? Definitely. But *crisis*? Not quite. He clicked on
and skimmed a few of the articles, which all
detailed the same point Jess had mentioned
earlier — global warming was steadily
increasing sea levels, which NASA assessed
could rise up to two full meters in the next
hundred years. And Frick Island — which
lay exactly at sea level in the Chesapeake

Bay — would at the very least be in dire trouble, if not completely underwater.

And while he read through article after article, Anders couldn't help but think the journalists had missed something very vital: What did the people of Frick Island think about all this?

It was egregious, in fact, the oversight. How could you write a story about an island in *crisis* without the perspective of the actual islanders? He knew newspaper budgets were tight — maybe no one thought it was worth it to make the inconvenient trip to that little strip of land smack in the middle of the Chesapeake Bay. And yet, here Anders was. Less than two hours away from that little strip of land. A strip of land that might just contain the perfect story for a long-form podcast.

A story he had missed the first time he was there.

He pulled up his email and clicked on the saved message from NoManIsAnIsland, this time a buzz forming in his belly. The buzz he got whenever he felt maybe he was onto something. Was it climate change? Was that what this anonymous tipster was referring to?

Maybe it was a cry for help. Anders sat up straighter. Maybe he could tell a story that others had missed. Something that could make a difference and save the island, once and for all! That was one of the reasons he'd gotten into journalism — before *Spotlight,* no less — because he knew one reporter following the right trail could make a big difference in the lives of others. One only had to look at *Serial* — the popular true-life podcast about a convicted murderer who may not have committed the crime — to see that podcasts had the same opportunity as newspapers, maybe even more so. OK, so maybe the murder suspect hadn't gotten a new trial in the end, but millions of people had been educated about the pitfalls of the American justice system.

His chest puffed a bit as he briefly allowed himself to imagine the heroic scenario to fruition (because although his intentions were mostly altruistic, he was, of course, still human): the millions of gripped listeners, the grateful faces of the islanders, not to mention the accolades rolling in — maybe he'd win a People's Choice Award, the iHeartRadio Podcast of the Year, a Pulitzer! Though he wasn't technically sure the Pulitzer recognized podcasts.

What he did know was that even though he'd sworn he'd never go back, that buzz in his belly (and resulting hero fantasy) alone was enough to compel him to take one more trip over to that strange little island.

But this time he'd be prepared, he thought, remembering the sweltering heat, the uncomfortable boat ride, the sweat. He eyed the worn shirt hanging on the chair. This time, he'd wear short sleeves.

CHAPTER 7

On Saturday morning, BobDan Gibbons kept one hand on the steering wheel and the other wrapped around the microphone he spoke into as the ferry chugged its way through the thick, salty air of the bay from Winder Cove Marina back to Frick Island. "The crabs don't know it's raining," he said for the eight thousandth time, and waited a beat for the joke to hit. He could give this speech in his sleep — and one time did, if his wife, Shirlene, was to be believed. She said he was always grumbling at night, saying all kinds of weird things, but he wouldn't know. He was asleep.

His mind wandered as he moved on to the bit about Maryland blue crabs being superior to any other crustacean out there. He had plenty to think about this morning — like how he really should quit smoking, and not just when Shirlene was around. Or how it was getting toward the end of tourist season, and he hadn't made nearly half of what he needed in ferry ticket and bird-watching tour revenue to get him and Shirlene through the battened-down cold months of winter. He'd been around long enough to know that money ebbed and flowed like the tide. Some seasons were better than others and that was just the way it was — but he wasn't sure if a tourist season had ever been this light.

And that boat — good Lord, he knew people in town were talking. How long was he gonna leave it there, sitting up on wood blocks in front of the marina, the wormholes still in the hull? An eyesore, is what it was. But what could he do? He'd cleaned it up best he could, scrubbing it down, removing the dried seaweed and ocean debris, but he didn't have the money to fix it up, and it certainly wasn't seaworthy enough to drop in the water and tie up to the dock. It'd sink quick as a lead fishing weight. Though, truth be told, BobDan thought maybe the bottom of the sea was where it should have stayed.

He maneuvered the ferry into the slip — something else he could do in his sleep, or at least blindfolded — at the end of the marina's dock. He tossed the bowline to the Perkins kid, who appeared right on time, which wasn't always the case. Shirlene wanted BobDan to give up more responsibility — at least let someone else drive the ferry a couple times a week. But the only person BobDan trusted at least halfway with something like that was his son, and after he got discharged from the navy, instead of coming back home, he got married to a girl he met at a port in California (California!), and it was like pulling teeth just to get them to come visit for Christmas. When the boat was secured and the Perkins kid dropped the metal walkway plank into the boat, BobDan got out first so he could help any of the passengers — only five today — out of the boat, if need be.

He scanned each of their faces and recognized a mainland couple who had started coming annually for their anniversary about five years ago. He nodded to them, welcomed them back to the island, and then did a double take when he saw the boy bringing up the rear. He must have been lost in his thoughts to have not noticed the boy boarding the boat in Winder, but it was the same kid who got stuck out here after the Cake Walk and asked to use his phone in the marina. BobDan didn't know who he had called — a mother, maybe a girlfriend who had expected him home that night —

it wasn't in his nature to eavesdrop on a private conversation. But he did know that kid did not take to the news that he'd be spending the night on the island well, and he was surprised to see him back.

"Didn't think we'd be seeing you again so soon," he muttered when the boy got close to the steps. "Frick Island growing on you?"

"Something like that," the boy said, stepping off the boat. Then he grinned at BobDan. "I listened today."

"Come again?"

"No headphones." He pointed to his ears. "So I wouldn't miss any announcements. Lot of clouds, but you didn't say anything about the ferry leaving early." He was puffed up and glowing, as if he'd just discovered the Pythagorean theorem all by himself.

BobDan glanced up at the white fluffy clouds blotting out the sun. "Those aren't rain clouds, son." He tried to suppress an eye roll. That's what a mainland education'll get you. Book smart, maybe, but learning nothing about the world around you.

"Oh," the boy said.

"You know, there's no Cake Walk today," BobDan said, wondering why on earth he had come back. Repeat tourists were rare on Frick. There were the regulars, of course, but they were the yearly visitors, the ones who lived on the mainland and used the island as their one vacation each year — like the anniversary couple — wanting a break from their factory jobs or teaching gigs or prison guard work.

BobDan picked up an errant boat line from the deck and made a mental note to remind the Perkins kid what his responsibilities entailed for the six hundredth time. Then he glanced back at the boy, taking in the backpack straps cutting into the sweat-soaked white shirt, and just as the boy said, "I know, I'm actually a —" it dawned on him.

"I know what you are," BobDan said. He should have realized it right off, but it being the Cake Walk day, he just took Anders for a run-of-the-mill tourist. About a year ago, Shirlene had dragged him to the mainland to watch a local theater group put on that musical she'd been dying to see — and it might have been funny, had they not taken the Lord's name in vain so many times. Oh, and the mimicry of bestiality. Call him conservative, but he saw nothing funny about a human having sex with a *frog.* Just disgusting, is what it was. BobDan frowned at the memory.

The boy nodded congenially, as he hooked his thumbs through the backpack straps and readjusted it on his shoulders. Then he started digging in his back pocket. Whatever he was looking for wasn't there, so he slung his bag around and unzipped it. While he was digging, he said, "Could I ask you a couple of questions, then?"

BobDan gave his head a small shake and he grunted, the sound coming from somewhere deep within. He busied himself with the line in his hand, looping it around his elbow, trying to make it clear that he couldn't possibly take a pamphlet. He had no problem with the Mormons — he thought people oughta believe what they wanted to believe — but he didn't want anybody shoving their beliefs on him. "Thank you, son, but I'm already right with Jesus."

The wind was strong on the dock and nearly stole BobDan's words right out of his mouth.

"What? I'm not sure —" the boy started, but BobDan was already halfway down the boardwalk, mind onto his next task, relieved he'd so easily gotten out of what was sure to be a long and unnecessary conversation.

Anders grunted as he sat heavily on a barstool at the One-Eyed Crab, letting his backpack slip off his shoulder and onto the grimy floor, which looked like the last time it had seen a mop — if ever — was decades earlier. But Anders didn't care. It had been a shit day. And not just because it had been so hot as he walked around town he felt like his skin was melting off. Or because he had so many gnat bites his arms reminded him of the way his back looked that one time his mom took him for a battery of allergy tests and he turned out to be allergic to just about every environmental allergen possible. ("Don't ever get a dog," the doctor said with a smile, and then joked, "or go outside.")

No, his day had been terrible because he currently had as much information from the locals regarding their thoughts on climate change and the island sinking as he had when he woke up that morning. Which was to say: none.

After his strange encounter with the boat captain, Anders had methodically stopped into all six storefronts on the main strip of town (if there was a road sign naming it, Anders couldn't find it), starting with the tiny post office, all the way to the Blue Point market, an establishment that had one glass refrigerator case, offering an assortment of fresh seafood and a few packaged deli meats, a deep freezer with a bevy of frozen treats, and two aisles of various boxed, canned, and bagged food.

In each rickety, weatherworn place, he approached the requisite proprietor, and before he could even properly introduce himself, the person quickly busied him- or herself with an activity, as if they couldn't possibly be bothered right then.

This happened time and again, until Anders got the rather paranoid feeling that they knew he was coming somehow, which was impossible. The only place he scored an interview was at an antiques store called Gimby's, where a man with liver-spotted hands and bifocals perched on his nose warmly welcomed him into the store and offered him coffee from a kettle sitting on a hot plate at the counter.

A black-and-white-splotched cat was sitting next to the hot plate and eyed Anders as he accepted and sipped on the bitter brew. "Scram!" the man said, startling both the cat and Anders. The cat slinked away as the man turned to Anders and introduced himself as Ronald Gimby the Third. He readily agreed to Anders recording him, without even questioning it or letting Anders explain why — causing Anders to wonder if perhaps he was the mysterious "you missed the biggest story out here" emailer. He fit the mold — an eccentric older gentleman who rambled on from one subject to the next, starting with his impressive collection of saltshakers, moving on to furniture and the various ways you could tell a true antique from a reproduction (wider dovetail joints, square nails, and rough hand-sanded surfaces are all good indicators, but fraudsters would go to great lengths and you never could be too careful), and somehow finding his way to the conspiracy of the moon landing, though Anders wasn't sure if Mr. Gimby was suggesting that it *was*, in fact, a conspiracy or was not. Most impressively, Anders thought, was the way the old man seamlessly slipped full Bible verses into his soliloquy that seemed to match whatever topic he was on. Anders stood at the wooden counter, shifting his weight from foot to foot as his coffee grew cold, and nodded politely, though Mr. Gimby didn't appear to need encouragement to continue speaking. When the man finally got around to commenting about the weather, Anders saw an opening.

"Speaking of the weather," Anders said, cutting him off in midsentence, as he realized it was the only way he was ever going to get a word in, "what do you think about climate change?"

Mr. Gimby's jaw dropped half an inch,

and he was momentarily silenced — a rare feat, Anders surmised, if the last twenty minutes were any indication.

"Climate change?" the man finally repeated, scrunching his nose as if the two words tasted sour in his mouth. "Tommyrot. Climate change. It's August and it's hot as the dickens out there just like every other August I've been on this island. And in the winter it gets cold enough to chill you to the bone. One year when I was a boy, the bay froze all the way from here to Winder." He waved his gnarled hand in the direction of the marina. "You could ice-skate to the mainland if the spirit moved you, though it did not so move me —"

"But what about the sea level?" Anders interjected. "Surely, if you've been here since you were a kid, you've noticed that it's rising. They say the island might not even be here in as little as twenty-five years."

Mr. Gimby pulled his glasses down to the tip of his nose and peered at Anders over the frames, his eyes narrowing, as if he was just seeing him for the first time. "Where'd you say you were from again?"

"Um, I didn't," Anders said, wilting under the man's stern gaze. He straightened his spine, cleared his throat, and stuck out his hand. "I'm Anders Caldwell. Journalist with

106

the *Daily Telegraph.*"

Mr. Gimby took a not-so-subtle step backward, nearly knocking into a shelf filled with ceramic cherubs. Anders noted the sudden change in the old man — the tightening of his jaw muscles, the hardening of his milky brown eyes — and it became resolutely clear this man was not the anonymous tipster.

"A reporter," Mr. Gimby said with the same distaste with which he had spit out *climate change* a minute earlier. "I don't talk to reporters," he said. And then he muttered, "Climate change. When there's a bona fide drug-trafficking ring on this island and Lord only knows what else, he's in here asking about *climate change.*"

Drug trafficking? Anders waited for more, but the old man just fixed him with a final look from under his furrowed brow and wrenched the half-drunk cup of coffee right from Anders's hand. "Get out of here," Mr. Gimby said. "And take that mangy cat with you." Then he exited through a door to the left of the cherub shelf. Anders hadn't noticed the door until that moment. It could have been a kitchen, bathroom, or broom closet for all he knew. He waited, watching the seconds tick by on an imposing grandfather clock, and then the seconds turned into minutes and Anders realized the man wasn't coming back.

Drug trafficking. Anders added it to his mental checklist to look into, though instinct told him it was more likely the ramblings of a senile old man than a real "bona fide" crime ring on the island.

And now he had an hour to kill before the 4:00 p.m. ferry, and as far as he was concerned, it couldn't pass fast enough. It was a mistake to come back here, he now knew. There wasn't a story, after all — or if there was, he certainly wasn't going to get to the bottom of it — and he'd wasted an entire day and another forty dollars on the ferry with nothing to show for it.

Sitting at the bar, Anders directed his anger at a particularly bothersome bite on his forearm, vigorously scratching it, as the same freckle-faced, backward-ball-cap-wearing waiter from his last visit approached, handing Anders the same oil-stained menu.

The place was dim, the afternoon sun unable to find its way through the filmy windows, and empty, aside from one table of three men, who all had the same weathered look as the captain at the marina — bronzed necks carved with deep lines and sinewy limbs protruding from old T-shirts. The look of watermen who'd spent their entire lives tugging on saltwater-laden ropes and baking in the sun.

He knew he should approach the table, try to strike up a conversation with the men, but he was discouraged. He had come to understand that perhaps the reason none of the articles about the inevitable disappearance of Frick Island included the point of view of any Frick Islanders was due not to gross negligence on the part of the reporters, but to an inability to get any of them to speak.

"Hey, weren't you just here? Couple weeks ago?"

Anders glanced up at the waiter. He was leaning back on the counter behind the bar, arms crossed, studying Anders.

"Yep," Anders said, eyeing him back. Was *this* the mysterious emailer? "I'm a reporter." He waited for a reaction, a knowing smile, a wink, a head tilt — anything that might let him know if this waiter was the person who had reached out to him. "Was covering the Cake Walk. Now I'm trying to do a story on climate change and its effects here on the island."

The guy grinned — that same Grinch-Who-Stole-Christmas smile Anders remembered, one that wasn't friendly as much as it signified finding joy at someone else's expense. "Good luck with *that.*"

"Yeah, it's not exactly been going so well. I can't get even one person to talk — well, I mean besides Mr. Gimby —"

The waiter nodded, wiping his hands on the dish towel tucked into his back pocket. "It's 'cause you're a Come Here."

Anders wasn't sure he had heard right. "A what?"

"A Come Here," he repeated. "On Frick Island, you're either a Come Here or a From Here. And you're definitely not a From Here."

"Oh," Anders said, his brow crinkling.

"Last guy that came was this developer from the mainland — had all these grand plans for the island, ideas to draw more tourists, revitalize the town. But he was unceremoniously shown the door when one of his first points of business was that the town start serving alcohol."

"Yeah, what's up with *that?*"

"It's always been a dry island." He shrugged, as if that explained it all. "Frick Islanders don't like change. Don't believe in it."

Anders nodded. That much was clear. "Including climate change."

"Including climate change."

"What'd you say your name was?"

"Jeffrey," he said, and before Anders could ask any more questions, he straightened up and plucked the rag from his back pocket and started wiping down the bar top between them. "You eating today or did you just stop in for a cold one? Soda, that is."

Anders's stomach growled, as if on cue. He checked his watch — still fifty minutes before the ferry left for the mainland. "I'll take the chicken basket again. And a Coke."

"Pepsi OK?"

"Oh. Yeah," Anders said. Being from Atlanta, he still wasn't used to Coke not being the primary soda brand.

Jeffrey disappeared into the back, and Anders sat hunched over the bar, letting his gaze drift along the fishing décor on the back wall — buoys and nets and paddles all hung so haphazardly it was hard to tell if it was actually ornamentation for the restaurant or storage. And then a loud bang caught Anders's attention, and he twisted his head toward the table of watermen.

"— it's out of hand! Not the boat, I don't care how long BobDan keeps it on planks for, but Piper! The entire thing." At the name "Piper," Anders's mind immediately flashed to the girl he embarrassed himself so fully in front of. "Look, Tom was like a

111

son to all of us after his daddy died, but it's not right, pretending he's alive like that. How long are we supposed to do it for? Piper needs to move on. The whole town does."

Anders's mind clicked into overdrive then, sorting out the sentences he had overheard; a few words, really, that kept replaying over and over.

Piper.

Tom.

Then memories began colliding in Anders's brain so fast, like keys fitting into locks, that he had trouble holding all of his thoughts in his head at once: Jess's newspaper article about the missing waterman, Tom Parrish. *Parrish.* That was the name that sounded so familiar when he read the article, not *Tom.* He remembered Jeffrey's words: *You're not the first to strike out with Piper Parrish.* He wondered if the two were siblings, and then remembered Jeffrey's other strange words: *She tell you she was married? . . . Depends on who you ask.*

That must have been what he had meant. If Piper and Tom were married, and they never found Tom's body, then it wasn't all that unusual for a wife to hold out hope that her husband was still alive — to want to believe that he was still out there some-

112

where, and not at the bottom of the ocean, or eaten by sharks, as Jess had so plainly put it.

He turned his attention back to the watermen, as another man chimed in: "That's not even the worst of it. You know what people are saying." He paused, and Anders subtly moved his body closer, hanging on to every word. When he spoke again, his voice was lower and Anders had to strain to hear. "That it wuddn't no accident, what happened to Tom."

Anders's entire world stopped then, as if someone had hit a pause button on a remote. The hair on his arms stood up.

You came all the way to Frick Island and missed the biggest story out here.

The narrowing of his world suddenly widened once again as he eagerly retrained his focus on the watermen, only to find that they were all staring directly at him, and not in a welcoming, kind way.

Face reddening for the second time in this restaurant, Anders quickly swiveled back forward in his stool and began reinspecting one of the many raised bumps on his arm, itching it intently with a stubby fingernail. After a beat the man began speaking again, but too low for Anders to hear.

The red plastic basket of chicken fingers

appeared in front of Anders on the bar top, and he looked up at Jeffrey. "Uh, thanks," he said.

"Need anything else?"

"Nope," Anders said, wanting Jeffrey to leave so he could continue eavesdropping. But as Jeffrey made his way back to the kitchen entrance, Anders heard the unmistakable squeak of chairs being pushed backward, the familiar rustling up of belongings. The men were leaving.

Anders stared at the deep-fried food, ignoring the déjà vu moment from just a few weeks earlier. *It wuddn't no accident.* If there were four more enticing words to a reporter, Anders wasn't sure what they might be. Were they saying Tom was *killed*? Were the police investigating it? Jess hadn't mentioned anything about that in her article.

"Hey," Jeffrey said, startling him out of his reverie.

"Yeah?"

"You know who you should talk to."

"Who?"

"Piper Parrish."

Anders just stared at him, wondering if he, too, had overheard the watermen. Or if he could somehow hear what Anders had been thinking.

"Remember the girl who was in here? The one you hit on —"

"I did not — I *was* not —" Anders stuttered indignantly.

"Yeah, OK. Whatever." Jeffrey grinned, with that same devilish edge to it. "Anyway, she's into all that stuff."

"What stuff?"

"Science. The earth. She'd probably help you."

"Huh," Anders said noncommittally. He had approached her once, to his spectacular regret. He wasn't eager to make the same mistake twice, especially now knowing that she was a woman deep in grief over her missing, likely dead husband. But . . . the fact that her missing, likely dead husband could possibly be her missing, likely dead, possibly *murdered* husband gave Anders a certain level of motivation to seek her out. If anyone would know about Tom's disappearance — and if there was anything nefarious about it — it would most likely be his wife.

Jeffrey motioned to Anders's uneaten chicken fingers. "You sure you don't need anything else?"

"Actually, I do," Anders said. "Is there anywhere else to stay out here besides that motel?"

CHAPTER 8

Pearl Olecki stood at her kitchen counter whisking the waffle batter in her smallest mixing bowl with more vigor than necessary. She hadn't slept more than two hours last night — or any night since the town gathering on Wednesday — tossing and turning in her heated irritation. A cell tower. *A cell tower!* How could anyone think a Lord-knows-how-tall metal contraption would be a good idea on their tiny island? Talk about an eyesore. Not to mention the radiation. Was everyone suddenly OK with getting cancer? If she wasn't a good Christian woman, she might have hoped that cancer would befall Steve Parrish for even bringing up the idea. Bad enough he brought that developer over here months ago who suggested they open a bar for the tourists — a bar! — and now this. Who needed a cell phone? Her landline had worked perfectly well for the past sixty years, thank you very much. And Internet? Well, anyone could just go down to the Blue Point market anytime they wanted to send an email (though what the point of that was, when one had pen, paper, and a post office, was beyond her). Mailing a letter never *killed* anybody. But cancer did. It sure enough did. She yawned, the action momentarily cutting into her thoughts, and she realized just how tired she was.

Fortunately, she only had three guests this Sunday morning — a couple from the mainland celebrating their twenty-sixth wedding anniversary, and the Mormon boy who dropped in unexpectedly late yesterday afternoon inquiring about a room. Thank goodness BobDan told Shirlene, who told Lady Judy, who called Pearl to warn her that he was in town. She also thought, in general, it was quite considerate of them to wear those short-sleeved white shirts, so they were immediately recognizable.

Proselytizers rarely made the trip out to Frick Island, mostly because, Pearl thought, ninety-nine percent of the island was already Christian, belonging to the Methodist church, even if they didn't all make it to the Sunday service as often as Pearl thought they should. In fact, Pearl couldn't remember ever meeting one, but she did open the door to a *World Book Encyclopedia* seller years ago, and that was three hours of her life and nine hundred dollars she would never get back. That was why she made Harold check the boy in and give him the short welcome spiel and tour of the house, just to be on the safe side. She didn't know how much he was selling those Books of Mormon for, but she knew she couldn't afford them.

The one thing she *did* know about Mormons was that they didn't drink coffee. She couldn't remember where she had read that — probably in one of those expensive encyclopedias. Either way, she was proud to show her sensitivity to his religion by not even offering it that morning when she was pouring for the anniversary couple.

Piper banged in the back door. "Sorry I'm late," she said, hurrying over to where her apron hung on the wall. "Tom likes to sleep in on Sundays, and I forgot to set my alarm."

"It's alright," Mrs. Olecki said, still whisking vigorously, and not batting an eye at the mention of Tom. Not anymore, anyway.

"Mrs. Olecki?"

"Yes, dear?"

"I think that batter is . . . mixed."

"Oh! Well, it sure is," she said, pulling the

whisk out and tapping it on the side of the bowl. The waffles certainly wouldn't be as fluffy as usual, but she hoped they didn't come out like bricks. "Could you warm up the vanilla maple syrup?" she said, looking over her shoulder only to realize Piper was already headfirst in the fridge, pulling out the fresh berries and then the syrup.

Pearl turned back to her batter, opening the waffle iron next to the bowl, the metal hot and ready. But just as she lifted the ladle to pour the first scoop, she heard it.

A scream.

And not just any scream. A high-pitched, toe-curling shriek that forced her hand to drop the ladle back into the bowl and her feet to sprint out into the dining room, where she half expected to find a young girl being hacked to death with an ax, blood everywhere — some kind of scene from those awful horror films Harold loved to watch every Halloween.

What she saw instead when she burst into the room, Piper at her heels, was the Mormon, his face white as his shirt, standing feet away from where he had been sitting at the table, his chair toppled over behind him. The two other guests sat at the table, eyes wide, toggling their gaze between the man and his empty plate. Well, not quite empty.

Mrs. Olecki bent at the waist and narrowed her eyes. And upon this closer inspection, she saw what looked like a small bug.

"What the devil?" Mr. Olecki said, drawing everyone's attention as he, too, appeared through the swinging door into the dining room and nearly collided with Piper.

"Everything's fine," Mrs. Olecki said, waving generally in Mr. Olecki's direction and closing the gap to the table in two long strides, quickly grabbing the nearest juice glass and flipping it on top of the critter to confine it. "We just had a little visitor at the table this morning."

"A visitor?"

Piper and Mr. Olecki both leaned closer for a better look. Trapped in the clear tumbler was an insect the size of a quarter, its gray wings freckled with black dots.

"Well, Pearl, that's just a little ol' moth," Mr. Olecki said. "What are you screamin' and carryin' on for?"

Mrs. Olecki cleared her throat, her eyes darting to the man, still standing.

As if on cue, the bug fluttered its wings, clearly trying to escape its enclosure, and the man flinched. And Mr. Olecki's eyebrows climbed closer to his receding hairline, as it dawned on him who had been doing the screaming. He shook his head and mumbled under his breath, "Coulda sworn that was a woman."

"It landed on my plate," the man said defensively. "I wasn't . . . It was . . . unexpected."

But Mrs. Olecki noticed that his pallor had quickly transitioned from ghost white to a few shades past the pink Double Knock Out roses she worked hard to keep alive on the bushes out front. And his gaze was no longer locked on the bug — it was locked on Piper.

Anders stood there, not believing the clash of his fortune and misfortune all at once. He had planned to spend the morning trying to find Piper, and here she was, right in front of him. But she was right in front of him because he had screeched — like a *woman,* apparently — at the sight of a tiny insect, and brought everyone within earshot running. And for the second time in the span of mere weeks, he stood red-faced in front of her.

Not that he necessarily cared how he looked in front of her. But still. He may have overreacted about the bug. And it was embarrassing to have so many witnesses.

Piper's eyes flitted to his, but if she recognized him, he couldn't tell.

"Well, no harm," Mrs. Olecki said gaily. "I'll just be taking this outside. Anyone need more —"

"No!" Piper said, and everyone joined Anders in looking at her. She frowned. "You can't release it."

"What?"

"It's a spotted lanternfly. I think. Caught one last week. The book said it's an invasive species — no natural predators. Not sure what one's doing out here, though." Piper squatted until she was eye level with the glass. "There are no crops here, silly bug. Did you get lost?"

Anders stared at her, eyes wide. He watched, trying not to flinch again, as Piper, in one swift motion, tipped the glass and plate over 180 degrees so that the bug remained trapped inside. "I'll take care of it," she said, and turned to go.

"Wait!" Anders shouted. He was afraid she wouldn't come back, and then what? But now he wasn't quite sure what to say, what with everyone's eyes on him. *Do you have reason to believe your husband was murdered?* It wasn't exactly something you shouted across a dining room, was it? He'd prefer to have a more private conversation.

Piper stood clutching the plate and the glass, waiting as he had requested, and he had to say *something.* He quickly scanned the table and spotted the empty mug, now grateful, instead of annoyed, that he had inadvertently been skipped this morning.

"Could I have some coffee, please?"

"What?" It was Mrs. Olecki, not Piper, who responded. And quite forcefully, as if Anders had asked for something outside the norm of polite social graces, like an erectile dysfunction pill.

Anders looked at her. "Uh . . . coffee? I'd love a cup if it's not too much trouble."

"Oh," she said, her forehead pleating in confusion. "It's just, I thought your . . . your . . . *people* . . . don't drink it."

"My people?"

"He's a Mormon," Mrs. Olecki explained to the room, as if Anders wasn't standing right there.

"I'm sorry — *what?*"

She brought her hand to her mouth. "Oh, dear. Is that not the proper way to say it?"

"I don't know the proper — I'm not a Mormon," Anders said, flustered. "I'm a reporter."

A collective gasp broke out around the room. Mrs. Olecki clutched her lemon-dotted apron.

"Are you undercover?" She peered at him with new eyes, and added in a near whisper:

"As a Mormon?"

"What? No!" Anders said, but he caught Mrs. Olecki glancing at his shirt, and that was when he remembered what he was wearing. And what his sister had said about it. He sighed. "I'm just here as a reporter. Well, a podcaster, really." He glanced at Piper when he said it, the thought occurring to him that perhaps she was the one who had reached out to him. If she did have her own suspicions about her husband's death, she'd likely want someone to look into it. But then, he reasoned, why wouldn't she just go to the police? Or come outright and say what she suspected? Regardless, Piper just looked pleasantly back at him. "I'm researching a story on global warming," Anders continued. "Its effect on the island."

The room fell silent. So silent, Anders could hear the bug's flittering wings as it tried to escape the glass. He suppressed a shiver.

And then Mrs. Olecki's mouth burst open with laughter. "Oh, honey," she said between guffaws. "I believe you might be a little late to the game. Do you know how many newspapers and magazines have written that exact story? *Newsweek,* the *Washington Post,* the *New York Times* — heck, I believe we were even in one of those food magazines, weren't we? Anyway, I think you've missed the . . . what do they call it, Harold dear?" She looked at her husband. "In newspaper terms."

"The scoop," Mr. Olecki provided.

"Yes! The *scoop*. I always liked the sound of that. Getting the scoop. Reminds me of ice cream. Now, that cell phone tower they're building out here — that might be something worth looking into."

"Yes, but," Anders started, his voice low, "all those articles were so one-sided; they didn't have the perspective of people who actually live here — of you guys. I don't know, I just thought maybe I could tell it differently."

But Mrs. Olecki was no longer listening. She had moved on, refilling the juice glasses of the couple and reaching in the cabinet of the hutch for a fresh one for Anders. In fact, the only person that seemed to have heard him, the only one even looking at him, was Piper.

"I'll get your coffee," Mrs. Olecki said, turning her attention to Anders once again. "Anyone need anything else? Waffles will be out shortly."

She breezed out of the room, Mr. Olecki following close behind. But Piper, still holding Anders's plate and the glass with the bug suspended between, stood there for a beat.

"You have a podcast?"

"Yeah," Anders said, searching her eyes to see if she already knew this. If she was trying to tell him something. But mostly all he saw was genuine interest, which made him shrug and feel the need to confess: "It's not exactly popular. Nobody really listens to it. Well, except my dad."

"Oh," she said. He cringed when he saw a flash of something that looked like pity in her eyes. "Well, if you're really interested in climate change, you should come to the Frick Island Wildlife Center. I work there on Saturdays."

Anders stared at her, partly stunned that he had so easily been able to get the outcome he'd wanted — without saying any actual words — and partly wondering if this confirmed it. That she was the tipster and she wanted to talk to him as much as he wanted to talk to her.

But before he could say anything, or even give her a meaningful glance to show he understood, Piper disappeared through the same door that had swallowed up the Oleckis.

Backpack slung over one shoulder, Anders stepped out the front door of the bed-and-breakfast, passed a couple of rosebushes, and walked onto the street, squinting at the bright sun reflecting off the bay water that pooled out from the bulkhead just steps in front of him and seemed to stretch out to the farthest edges of the earth, giving a new meaning to "waterfront property."

It was already brutally hot and it wasn't even 10:00 a.m., but he had loitered at the dining room table as long as he could, thinking Piper would reappear, eager to talk to him. He didn't believe she'd really make him wait until next Saturday. He was nursing his third cup of coffee when Mrs. Olecki reminded him that checkout was at 9:45 sharp. "I won't be late for church," she said, with the stern voice of a schoolmarm. Though she was round and soft in appearance, there was an edge to her. An edge that made Anders sure he never wanted to cross her in any way.

The ferry didn't leave on Sundays until noon, so Anders took a right onto the pockmarked road, figuring he would meander through town once more, hoping perhaps, if he stopped in all the storefronts again, he might just run into Piper somewhere, and if not, well —

Crrrreeeeeeak.

Anders turned his head toward the unmistakable sound of a screen door opening, which was coming from the end of a worn dirt-and-broken-oystershell path between the bed-and-breakfast and the house next to it. A set of stairs led up to the door of a small carriage house, and on the landing stood Piper, struggling under the weight of a large plastic basket overflowing with what appeared to be damp laundry.

She didn't even glance in his direction as Anders watched her make her way down the stairs, stunned once again by his luck. Until it struck him that in a town this small (could it even be called a town?), he supposed you were probably more likely than not to run into the person you were looking for. He paused, watching as a breeze lifted the tight coils of her hair off her neck, and just as he opened his mouth to shout hello —

"Yoo-hoo! Piper!" Mrs. Olecki's disembodied voice rang out from behind the bed-and-breakfast. "You and Tom coming to church this morning?"

Anders froze. *Tom?*

Tom was dead. Likely *murdered,* Anders hoped. At the very least, the man was missing.

"Shoot!" Piper said. "I lost track of time. We're coming." She hastily finished pinning a pair of frayed jean shorts onto the clothesline, then snatched the still-full laundry basket into her arms and ran up the steps as if it were suddenly light as a feather, without once glancing behind her. If she had, she would have spotted an open-mouthed Anders, feet glued to the ground in the middle of the street, trying to make sense of what was happening.

As Piper disappeared into her house, the banging of the carriage house door snapped Anders out of his fugue state. And the words the waterman said rang in his ears: *Pretending he's alive.* Suddenly other memories flooded Anders's brain.

Piper sitting at the table in the One-Eyed Crab talking to herself . . . the men at the docks the next morning waving hello to Piper *and* Tom . . . Piper saying "we" when it was just her standing there . . .

Pretending he's alive.

No. Anders shook his head. Surely he was misremembering. That would be crazy — crazier than the passionate poultry woman for sure. And yet. The hair on the back of his neck stood up, like a bloodhound picking up a scent.

He stared at the carriage house door, wondering who was going to emerge from it with Piper. He half thought he would lay eyes on a man who had been presumed dead, and the other half thought he wouldn't lay eyes on anyone at all, and he couldn't accurately say which prospect excited him more.

He quickly walked to the end of the neighboring house and then slipped into the pathway between it and the next one. He ducked behind a metal trash can, heart pounding at the thought of being spotted — how would he explain his strange loitering? But curiosity surged through him and he knew it was a risk he'd just have to take.

He waited, knees bent, back up against the splintered siding of the house, sweat dripping down the sides of his face. Minutes ticked by, and Anders started to get a cramp in his left calf. Just when he thought perhaps they had somehow taken a different route, he heard voices. He held his breath and peered at the road between the trash can and the edge of the house. Mrs. Olecki came into view first and then Mr. Olecki and then Piper, who had changed into a yellow sundress. He waited, but no one else was with them.

When they had passed out of view, Anders stood, the muscles of his legs slightly shaking. He walked around the trash can and back into the road, staring at the backs of the three people, now walking in a line even with each other. He searched his head for any other explanation, but none came.

Just then, a little boy shot off the porch of the house they were walking past like he was being ejected from a slingshot. He threw himself at Piper, wrapping his tiny arms around her legs.

"Bobby!" she giggled, bending at the waist to squeeze him back.

It occurred to Anders as he strained to listen to the voices that this was the first young child he'd seen on the island.

"You coming to church this morning, Bobby?" Mrs. Olecki's voice said.

"Yep! I just have to take this down to Lady Judy for my gran," the boy replied, holding up a brown paper sack in his left hand. He turned toward Piper but directed his attention to the air beside her. "Tom, can I sit with you and Piper?"

Anders's eyes nearly popped out of his skull. He gave his head a shake, wondering for an instant if *he* was the crazy one. But no. He was clearly looking at four people —

Mr. and Mrs. Olecki, Piper, and a little boy. A man named Tom was not among them. Because Tom — Piper's Tom — had been in a boat wreck and was most likely at the bottom of the ocean, never to be seen or heard from again.

"Of course. We'd love that, wouldn't we, Tom?" Piper said. "Run along now. We'll see you there."

Anders stood there, his heart galloping, as Piper and the Oleckis continued on their way toward the church. The boy, meanwhile, came running directly at him, full speed. "Hey!" Anders said, just as the boy was about to veer around him. He stopped. Wide-eyed, he regarded Anders, and Anders regarded him. The boy, though curious, did not seem wary of him in the slightest, even though he was obviously a stranger.

"Ooh, is that a camera?" the boy asked, pointing to Anders's chest.

"Yes," Anders said, considering the best way to formulate his question.

"Can I see it?"

"Uh, sure," Anders said. It was his personal camera, one he'd bought years ago and which was pretty much obsolete now, since the newspaper wanted him to use the new fancy Nikon that took far better pictures for print (heck, his *phone* took better pictures than this old thing). But when Anders didn't have the work one, he carried this one around out of habit — or maybe to strike a more professional posture. He removed the strap from around his neck and handed the camera to the boy, who had put his brown bag on the ground and eagerly started inspecting it.

"When you were talking to Piper just now . . ." Anders said, as the boy looked through the viewfinder and then methodically began punching every single button. "Was Tom . . . with her?"

The boy glanced up at him and then back at the camera. "Yeah."

Anders's head felt light and floaty. "What? I mean . . . did you . . . You could *see* him?" he sputtered.

The boy didn't respond immediately. He was clicking away, taking about twenty pictures in a row.

"Hey!" Anders said, and the boy gaped up at him.

"What?"

"You could *see* Tom?"

The boy cocked his head, as if he hadn't quite understood the question, and then his nose scrunched up and his mouth dropped open, his expression denoting that Anders might be just about the dumbest person he'd ever run across. "Of course not."

"But you . . . you *talked* to him, didn't you, just now?"

"Yeah," the boy repeated, nonplussed.

Hands on his hips, Anders stood staring, as his brain tried to sort out the confusion. "But he's not there!" Anders said.

"Right," the boy said, studying the camera once again.

Anders's eyes bugged at the infuriatingly circular path their conversation appeared to be taking. He grabbed the camera out of the boy's hands, shocking him with the abruptness of the action. Ashamed, Anders took a deep breath, in an attempt to keep himself from shouting at a child. In the middle of his exhale, he exploded anyway: "SO WHY DID YOU DO THAT?"

The boy, unruffled by Anders's ire, looked back at the camera. "Hey — can I have that?"

"Oh, for the love of . . . YES!" Anders felt sure he had never met a more infuriating boy in his entire life. "*If* you answer my question."

The boy's entire face lit up, and then he cocked his head, as if trying to remember the question Anders had asked. Then he shrugged. "Ma says just because *we* can't see him, doesn't mean Piper can't." And he snatched the camera out of Anders's hand, picked up the brown paper bag from the ground, and bounced off, leaving Anders standing there with his mouth gaping.

And Anders came to his second realization of the day: Maybe a woman thinking her dead husband was alive wasn't the strangest thing in the world.

Maybe the strangest thing in the world was a whole town pretending they could see him, too.

And a shiver ran down his spine as he came to his third realization of the day: Perhaps he *had* missed the biggest story on Frick Island. But he was pretty sure he had found it now.

CHAPTER 9

Six Months Before the Storm

Standing at the tin basin that served as a sink in her tiny carriage house kitchen, Piper attacked the hardened traces of chocolate icing left in the mixing bowl with a sudsy sponge, but her mind was on caddis flies.

She'd been keeping an informal count of them a few times every year, since her mother first taught her how to identify their larvae — the way they were constructed out of leaf matter, sand, and sticks, some of them free-floating on the currents in the marsh. If you didn't know what you were seeing, they just looked like any other organic debris in the water. The numbers always varied, went up and down, but the past few years they'd been steadily going down — and last week she hadn't seen any at all.

An unexpected cold hand gripped her waist beneath her shirt.

"Tom!" Piper shrieked, nearly dropping the

bowl she'd been rinsing under the torrent of water. "I thought you were sleeping." He did that some afternoons. Not often, but just on those days when the early wake-up time caught up with him, and he was bone weary from pulling in nets and cages from the ocean's bowels, beneath the tireless sun.

"Who can sleep with all the racket going on in here?" he said, his cold nose finding her neck beneath all her hair. It was late October, two days before Halloween, and fall had come raging through the island on a sharp cold breeze, chilling Piper to the bone. She shivered, and turned into her husband.

Husband. Would she ever tire of that word?

"Oh! I forgot. I found something today." She left Tom's embrace and, giggling, crossed the tiny room, stopping in front of the bookcase. "Gimby brought it in." Tom watched patiently, amused, as he already knew the "something" Piper found was going to be a record.

It was a collection she had started years ago, when they were walking through Gimby's antiques shop after school one day — neither one wanting to go home, to be away from the other for a second. They were browsing through dusty old albums, obscure ones with psychedelic covers that Gimby had picked up from yard sales on the mainland over the years. Problem was, people rarely got rid of anything good — so the collection was mostly music no one had ever heard of. Piper had stopped at an electric blue cover, a word catching her eye.

"Well, we have to buy this one," she'd said.

Tom had glanced at the band name — the Who — surprised Gimby had something recognizable, and then at the song title Piper was pointing at: "Tommy Can You Hear Me?"

It became the first of many in Piper's "Tom" record collection.

Now, in their den, she clapped her hands together, the excitement spreading her already large smile wider, her brown eyes even brighter. "Listen!"

A catchy banjo riff twanged into the air and a woman's southern drawl spoke over the top of it. "It's Dolly Parton," Piper whispered, still grinning. She held up a finger. "Wait for it."

Tom cocked an eyebrow at her but did as he was told. They listened as Dolly told her story, something about tent revivals, and then finally, the words Piper — and Tom — had been waiting for.

So preacher Tom wherever you may be —

"It's called 'Preacher Tom'! Have you ever heard of it?"

Tom shook his head no as Dolly started singing.

"This is . . ." Tom cocked his head, searching for the word to best encapsulate what he was hearing. "Awful."

"I know! Might be the worst one yet." Piper closed the gap between them and grabbed his hands, pulling him around in circles as she alternated jouncing her feet up and down as if she were in a square dance. Tom couldn't help but allow himself — as always — to get pulled into her orbit. He wrapped his arm around Piper's back and held it there sturdily and then started spinning her around the tiny room, making sharp turns every few steps to avoid the couch, the easy chair, the overturned crates that doubled as lamp stands and book stands and catch-all stands.

When the record started skipping toward the end of the song, Tom and Piper collapsed on the couch, causing the rusted springs within it to squeak and groan under their collective weight. Dizzy and out of breath, Tom turned toward his wife, staring at her profile — the freckles dotting the bridge of her nose, the errant corkscrew curls escaping from beneath her knotted silk kerchief, the way her nut-brown skin glowed, as if she had swallowed sunshine itself. He gently grabbed one of the loose tendrils, snaking a finger into it, around it, as though, if he tried hard enough, he could meld them together, and they'd be entwined just like that forever.

She's not magic, son. He heard his dad's voice, the thing he said to him all those years ago when he noticed Tom's gaze glued in Piper's direction, anytime she was anywhere in the vicinity. "Huh?" Tom had said, trying to drag his eyes away from her.

"She puts her pants on one leg at a time just like ever'body else. Do you good to 'member that."

And of course, the more he got to know Piper, and learned her all-too-human flaws — like how she dispensed toothpaste by pushing right in the center of the tube, or how she couldn't get rid of her favorite house slippers even though they smelled like rotten cheese, or how she was constantly running late, everywhere and for everything — the more he knew his dad was right. It was just that there were times, like now, when she looked as if she had eaten the sun for lunch, that he wondered if maybe his dad was just a little bit wrong, too.

Piper turned toward him, and maybe it was all that beaming light warming him from the inside out, or maybe it was just that they were young and newly wed, but his hand snaked around her neck and he reeled her in gently until their lips were a breath apart. "Preacher Tom," she whispered coquettishly. "This is quite the compromising position." And she giggled into his mouth when he kissed her.

Much later, when they were both out of breath again, and Piper got up to draw a hot bath, Tom plucked the book he was in the middle of off the overturned crates. He had only just found the sentence where he had left off when Piper came flying back into the den, wrapped only in a tattered terry-cloth towel.

"Tom! We're late! We're late! We have to go."

Tom eyed her from where he was lounging on the couch, then flitted his eyes to the football-size pewter crab on the wall, with a clock in the center of its shell: 6:56. Weariness overtook him. He had forgotten about the meeting at the church. Or rather, he had hoped Piper had forgotten about it.

"Come on! Why aren't you moving? Get dressed." She started picking up clothes that had been strewn on the floor and tugging her own on while tossing Tom's in his direction. His blue jeans hit him in the shoulder.

He clapped his book shut. "Do we really have to go?"

She stopped abruptly, like a spinning top paused with the tip of a finger. And when she looked at him, she could see it then, the thing she'd been trying to ignore for days. The dullness in his typically bright slate eyes. The grayish-purple half-moons hugging his lower lashes. The four days of stubble he had let grow on his typically fastidiously clean-shaven cheeks.

Every path has its puddle. That was what Mrs. Olecki always said. *No sense dwelling on them — you just gotta walk around them.*

And Piper felt that was her job — to show Tom the way around. Even when his puddles seemed so deep and so wide they threatened to take up the whole path as far as you could see. Especially then.

"Of course we have to go. That developer from the mainland is coming to speak, and we told Steve we'd be there." She flashed her bright smile at him, hoping it would cause a mirrored response. "And I made a cake."

Every time Frick Island gathered for a meeting — whether it was a Wednesday night potluck or the twice-yearly clothing swap or the monthly town hall (which was really just a gathering, as the island had no formal city council) in the meeting room of the church, a few people rotated the task of bringing a Frick Island cake. They rarely got eaten, most people having long grown sick of the overly sweet concoction, but it was tradition and there was nothing more important than tradition on Frick Island.

Tugging her sweater over her head, Piper

turned away from Tom, not wanting to linger any longer on his sullen face, and walked over to the kitchen area. She opened the half fridge.

"Son of a monkey!" she said, upon sight of the carefully chocolate-iced cylinder — which, at some point between being placed in the fridge three hours ago and now, had split right down the center, the inside yellow layers as visible as the stuffing in their threadbare couch.

Under Mrs. Olecki's tutelage, Piper had become proficient, if not good, at cooking all manner of breakfast staples, but baking was another skill altogether. And she had yet to create a Frick Island cake that she could actually take to a public event.

She plopped the ruined cake onto the counter with a thud and stared at Tom, who was upright and stuffing his scrawny legs one at a time into his jeans. He paused right before buttoning them up and studied the cake, then looked back at Piper. "Well, we obviously can't go now. They're gonna kick you off the island for showing up with that thing."

"Tooooom," she intoned.

"Piiiiper," he replied. But he was smiling now, and Piper's chest loosened a bit. She knew they would go to the meeting and hold hands and talk with their neighbors and everything would be fine.

Everything would be just fine.

Well, everything but the cake. There was no fixing that.

She slid it into the open trash can and went to find her boots.

Chapter 10

"Greta was just looking for you. Sounded important."

Anders glanced at Jess's face peering over the cubicle wall between them, and took in this week's do — her hair braided into a jet-black crown framing her forehead. He dropped his bag at the base of his desk and crumpled into his chair, massaging his face with his hands, trying to wake himself up.

"Jesus, get some coffee. You look like you're auditioning to be an extra in *The Walking Dead*," she said, before disappearing back down in her seat.

For a full week after he got home from Frick Island, he spent every waking minute trying to make sense of what he'd seen. He wrote down everything he remembered witnessing, filling four pages of his reporter notebook front and back with details and questions.

He peppered Jess about the missing waterman. Had Tom been married to a woman named Piper? *Yes.* Had she ever interviewed Piper after the accident? *No.* Was there any chance he had survived the accident (not that it would have explained anything; even if Tom was alive and on the island, he wasn't *invisible*)? *I guess. I told you, he's likely swimming with the fishes. But anything's possible.* Were the police actually ruling it an accident, or was there anything that suggested foul play? *An accident,* she said, but this was the one question that gave her pause, and she looked up at him with a crinkled brow. *Why?* "No reason," Anders said, not quite ready to go down that rabbit hole when there was so much more he needed to find out.

He scoured the far corners of the Internet for information — articles, studies, experts, *anything* that could help him understand. He Googled everything from "talking to the dead" to "seeing people who aren't there" and came up with a lot of weird information on séances and child psychology, but nothing that was helpful. At least, not until he typed in "seeing dead people." Hidden between all the *Sixth Sense* memes and Reddit threads about ghosts, Anders found something.

A study. A group of researchers in Italy

found that six out of ten grieving people have seen or heard their dead loved one. Sixty percent! They were called post-bereavement hallucinatory experiences, or PBHEs. And even though they were common, most people often didn't mention them, as they feared friends and family would think they were mentally ill.

Anders's first thought: Well, *yeah.* His second: Was *that* what was happening? Piper had recently lost her husband, that much he was certain of. Was she having some kind of prolonged PBHE? He shot off an email to the study author and got a response two days later.

Thanks for your inquiry. Please find my responses for your article on grief and spousal death as follows:

Yes, grief can manifest itself in many different ways, and yes, these "post-bereavement hallucinatory experiences," or PBHEs, are actually quite common for widows/ers, particularly in the days and weeks directly following the death. Typically they are momentary — not lasting for more than a few minutes, so to your next question: someone who was hypothetically constantly seeing their loved one and behaving as if they were still alive. Without being able to speak with the patient directly, it's hard to diagnose accurately, but the most likely explanation is a general psychotic break. Someone whose grief has gripped them so immensely they have disassociated with reality. Though I haven't dealt with that particular scenario, it brings to mind a news story I read a few years ago about a woman in Australia who lived with her husband's dead body in their home for weeks, until neighbors started to smell the decomposition. He had died of natural causes, but she simply couldn't let go. Perhaps you've come across that one in your research.

I hope this helps. Please let me know if you have any further questions.

Anders wrinkled his nose. At least Tom's body wasn't lying in wait, decaying in Piper's carriage house. He didn't think.

But he did think he finally had enough pieces to start pulling together an episode for his podcast. And he spent another week writing, recording, and editing it, until he had forty-nine minutes of a perfectly paced (if he did say so himself) story — beginning with the cryptic email he'd received from someone on Frick Island and slowly revealing his journey to understand climate change (peppering in a few of Mr. Gimby's wacky clips), which turned into a possible investigation into a missing waterman, which turned into the shocking realization that the wife of that missing waterman was experiencing a delusion on a grand scale — and that the entire island was going along with it.

Ira Glass himself couldn't have done it any better.

And last night at 3:20 a.m., he'd finally hit enter, uploading the episode to his website, posting it on Instagram and Twitter, and then falling into a deep, restful sleep. When he woke this morning with a start, sitting straight up, he knew without even glancing at the clock that he was wildly late for work. When he did look at the clock, he saw with a shock that he was nearly four hours late.

"Seriously, though, what's up with you?" Jess said, her head popping up again like a game of whack-a-mole. "Is this about all that Frick Island stuff again?"

"Kind of," Anders admitted, pulling his laptop out of his bag and powering it up.

Jess shook her head at him before disappearing once again. Last week, when Anders told her what he had seen, Jess was nonplussed. "I told you Frick Island was weird."

Now he waited as his computer screen came alive and then went through the motions of checking his emails, responding to any that needed responding to, checking the news headlines, and then pinging Greta to let her know he was in.

Then he clicked on his website to see if his father had listened to his podcast. It didn't load immediately — which was sometimes the case at work; the Internet was spotty no matter how much the higher-ups complained to the board, explaining that a slow Internet connection should probably not be an issue in a newsroom. Not knowing if it would be ten seconds or two minutes, Anders stood up to take Jess's suggestion of finding coffee. In the break room, as he was filling a foam cup to the brim with the hot liquid, Greta walked in.

"There you are."

"Yeah, sorry I was running late this morning. I overslept." He hadn't ever been late before, so he thought honesty was the best policy and hoped for leniency on his first offense.

Greta waved Anders's sentence away as if it didn't matter. "Listen, I need you to go out to Salisbury High School, like, fifteen minutes ago. It's on lockdown. A man knocked off a 7-Eleven with a hunting rifle and he's on the loose. Hector's covering a college visit today for that ninth-grade lacrosse phenom and he's all the way up in D.C."

"Why didn't you send Jess?" Anders asked, slugging down the hot coffee, not feeling it scald his throat.

"She's got to be at the courthouse at one for the record-pumpkin trial. It was the biggest story for us last year — she can't miss it."

Anders vaguely remembered Jess saying something about it. At last October's pumpkin festival, a local farmer had beat the record for largest gourd ever grown in the state — weighing in at more than 1,600 pounds. But another farmer claimed the vine had actually started on his land — that it was his pumpkin, even though it crawled over the fence and grew in the original farmer's garden. It ended in a knife fight, the vine-originating farmer stabbing the record-winning farmer, who spent months in the hospital on ventilation but fortunately survived.

"I'm on it," Anders said, getting a burst of adrenaline and confidence from this very Clark Kent–like experience, and he all but ran from the break room, yelling, "Text me the address!" over his shoulder to Greta. He

151

grabbed his laptop, closing it with his hand and shoving it in his bag in one quick motion, and was out the door.

The moon was high in the sky, the sun long gone, by the time Anders finally got back to his apartment that evening. The police didn't track down the suspect until 5:00 p.m. — he had been holing up in an empty shed more than six miles from the school — and the kids hadn't been allowed to leave until that happened. Anders had been on the ground, interviewing worried parents who — over time — morphed into angry parents who felt their kids were being held hostage inside the building while they were standing outside of it, when clearly any threat of the hunting-rifle robber was nowhere to be found. But protocol was protocol. When he got back to the newsroom, Greta informed him that not only would this be the lead story but that he would be penning three other related stories (about local gun laws, school safety, and community reaction), and that for the first time ever, every single byline on the front page would be his (his!), including the photos. He spent hours poring over each paragraph, sentence, caption, and word choice at least a hundred times, making sure the stories were perfect before turning them in.

When he let himself in, he barely glanced toward the kitchen to scan for cockroaches — he was too tired to do anything about it if he saw one — before slinking over to his mattress and collapsing onto it.

He kicked his shoes off and lay there for a minute, enjoying the rest. The silence. And then, as if his thought had jinxed it, the bass started thumping from upstairs. Anders groaned. He sat up and contemplated walking up to his neighbor's apartment to ask him to turn down the music, but it was too many steps. Instead he crawled over to where he'd dropped his laptop and pulled it out, along with his headphones, and then made his way back to the mattress, where he plugged the buds into his ears and the keyboard and sighed as an old *This American Life* episode filled his brain. He adjusted his stack of pillows behind him so they made a big cushion against the wall and then leaned into them, so he was sitting up, but comfortable.

Then he mindlessly checked his email, Twitter, the news, his eyes drooping heavily, thanks to his exhausting day and the music lulling him under. He slid the computer onto the mattress and nearly closed it before remembering his website, the podcast that he had uploaded the night before. He clicked on the URL, thinking he would glance at the stats before allowing himself to drift off for the night, but when he saw the numbers, he took a sharp breath and sat straight up.

There were 894.

He had 894 downloads. In one day. What in the world? He knew it had been good work; an intriguing premise, and he had told it well. But still, 894?

Heart thrumming in his chest, his gaze moved from the listens to the comments. He had six. Six! Wide awake now, he scrolled down. Leonard, of course, was the first.

LeonardC404: Riveting. Hope you don't mind, but I shared it with a few colleagues in the department. We've all got to know — what happens next? — Dad

Jsweets: An invisible husband? Haha! Dying for more — why are the people just going along with it?

StanforKeanu: This happened to my mom after my dad passed. She swore she could see him and talk to him. I didn't know it had a name, but yeah, I think it's more common than people know.

Dems4Life: Fifteen bucks it's a bunch of Repugnicans high on the meth they cook up in their crab shanties. You'd see people too if you were stoned all the time.
  Patriot1976: Libtard.

LDE4892898: I make $230,000 working from home. Want to learn how? Go to bit.x.z.url.com

Anders stared at the screen, a mix of pride and joy flooding his body (and only a touch of disappointment at the comment that was missing this time). His instincts had been right. People were responding to this story. What's more — they wanted to know what happened next! And Anders was going to give the people what they wanted. He could go over to the island on weekends — every weekend if he needed to. Until he could answer Jsweets's question, anyway, which was his question as well: Why *are* the people just going along with it?

His exhaustion quickly forgotten, Anders stayed up late into the night, revamping his website, archiving all his old podcast episodes, and leaving the two Frick Island episodes front and center beneath the title of his new serial, in a big-serif font on the home page: **WHAT THE FRICK?**

On Saturday morning, when BobDan spotted the familiar visage waiting on the dock at the Winder Cove Marina a hundred yards out, his heart stopped in his chest for a beat. Pearl had called Lady Judy, who told Shirlene at the market, who in turn told BobDan that the boy wasn't in fact a Mormon, as BobDan had incorrectly assumed, but a journalist. And BobDan — and the island as a whole — had even less use for one of those. The last thing they needed was some young Carl Bernstein wannabe snooping around, looking under rocks that were better left unturned.

He swallowed and pulled back on the throttle, letting the boat putter closer, and then killed the engine completely so he could drift the final yards up to the Winder docks. Instead of reaching for the boat line to help, the boy stood there engrossed in his phone — not that BobDan expected much else. Once he got the boat properly tied off and secured to the piling, BobDan stepped off onto the dock and reached his hands to the sky, stretching out the tight muscles hugging his spine, which seemed to grow tighter by the day. Then he reached in his back pocket for his pack of Winstons, shook out a cigarette, lit it, and inhaled deeply, before acknowledging the boy. "Well, if it isn't Bob Woodward himself."

The boy glanced up from whatever life-wasting app he'd been scrolling through. "Actually, my name's Anders."

BobDan rolled his eyes heavenward and let out a long exhale of smoke, his breath whistling lightly between his lips. His anxiety at a reporter coming to the island was lessened by the fact that at least this one wasn't very bright.

"I mean, I know who Bob Woodward is," Anders said quickly. "I just realized I've never properly introduced myself."

"You're doing one of those iPod things, huh?"

Anders cleared his throat. "A podcast. Yes, sir."

"On climate change?"

Anders nodded. Mumbled something.

"Speak up, boy. I can't hear you."

Anders shook his head. "It's not important."

"That's prolly true," BobDan muttered, and then louder: "Well, boat's not leaving for another twenty minutes."

"Yes, I just —"

"So why don't you make yourself useful." BobDan nodded at the day's cargo — a dozen cardboard Chiquita banana boxes holding the week's grocery orders for the island. Things they couldn't get at the general store, like kitty litter, fruit, any flavor of Utz potato chip besides plain. Apparently grocery delivery was the next big thing on the mainland — BobDan thought it was ironic that Frick Island had been doing it decades before anyone else.

He looked back up at Anders and noticed the boy hadn't moved.

"Well, go on."

"You want me to . . . load those up on the boat?"

"No, I want you to perform all five acts of *A Midsummer Night's Dream.*"

Anders blinked.

"Yes!" BobDan growled. "I'd like you to load those on the boat."

Anders blinked again. "Will you knock ten dollars off the ticket price?"

BobDan took a small step backward. He appraised the boy once more, seeing a glimmer of something he hadn't noticed on the boy before. He nodded. "Deal." And then he watched, amused, as the boy, scrawny as a toothpick with even fewer muscles, sweated and strained as he lifted the first

158

box — filled with Lady Judy's fifty-pound bag of birdseed. He groaned and grimaced under the weight, and nearly dropped it twice, but he didn't give up. And BobDan had to admit: If nothing else, the boy was persistent.

CHAPTER 11

Piper sat in Tom's easy chair in their small den, mumbling under her breath as she eyed the opposite wall and cataloged each and every insect housed in the fourteen shadow boxes that spanned it. It was a meditation of sorts, something she did when she was thinking or bored or just needed a reminder that the world could be constant at times. Familiar. It was also a memorization exercise to test her brain — to make sure she didn't forget.

She started with the beetle family: the acorn weevil, *Conotrachelus posticatus;* the banded net-wing beetle, *Calopteron discrepans;* the broad-necked root borer, *Prionus laticollis;* and so on, always pausing when she got to the northeastern beach tiger beetle. One of the quickest beetle species on earth (it actually ran so fast it went blind), it was the first bug Piper added to her collection when she moved to Frick

160

Island. But the insect was now considered endangered in Maryland, and though Piper knew the one that she trapped years ago was of little consequence to why they were now endangered, she still got a pang of guilt for taking it from its natural habitat.

She continued naming the insects one by one, even though she knew she should get up. She needed to shrug off her pajamas and pull on a T-shirt and shorts and go to the wildlife center, where Bill Gibbons would be expecting her, but motivation had been a hard thing to come by recently.

As she was trying to force energy into her legs, the trilling of the phone in the kitchen gave her the last burst she needed to finally stand. She reached the phone on the third ring and picked up.

"Hello?"

"Pipes!"

"Mom!" Piper was flooded with relief at hearing her mother's voice, mixed with a twinge of sadness. "Thank you for calling me back."

"Sorry it took so long. I've been out in the field all week."

"And how is the Gold Coast of Australia?" Piper asked, putting on the happiest voice she could muster. Her mom had moved there right after Piper graduated from high school — and Piper had only seen her once since, when she flew in for her and Tom's simple wedding ceremony a little more than a year ago.

"A mess. Flooded again." Only her mother could talk about devastating natural disasters with an edge of excitement in her voice.

Piper paused and narrowed her eyes at the pewter wall clock. "Wait — isn't it the middle of the night over there?"

"Early morning. Four a.m. Wanted to input this latest data before heading back out today."

Piper rolled her eyes. Her mother would work twenty-four hours a day if she could; and sometimes did.

"Tell me, what's going on with you? Three messages — must be important."

"Remember that stack of blueprints you had made — for the living shoreline and jetties project?"

"Of course."

"Where are they?"

"Why? Did the town change their minds? Is there funding?"

Piper hesitated, not quite sure how to explain why she needed them. "Not exactly."

"Piperrr . . ." Her mom drew out her name. "What are you up to?"

"Nothing."

162

"Don't 'nothing' me."

"Just — do you know where they are?"

"Hmmm . . . I think I gave them to Bill. If he didn't toss them, they're likely somewhere in that disaster of a storage room he calls an office."

"Oh, good. I'm headed there now."

"Please tell Bill I said hello. He's the only one on that island with any sense."

"The *only* one?"

"Tom is lovely, darling, but he did *choose* to be a waterman. He gets docked points for that — and for keeping you on that godforsaken place." At the mention of her husband, Piper's stomach went a little hollow. Her mother had never understood why Tom didn't want to get an education, make something more of himself, and consequently felt he was holding her daughter back as well. Not to mention, she thought deep-sea fishing was a dangerous career, which was why Piper hadn't told her mom about the storm months ago, not wanting to worry her even further. She felt a pang of guilt at keeping it from her, and a pang of something else, too, at the thought of that dreadful day. She swallowed and closed her eyes, picturing what Tom would likely be doing right now — standing on his boat, checking crab pots under the almost-noon sun, and she immediately felt a little better.

"I like this godforsaken place."

"I know you do. Which is why you don't have any sense either. I've gotta run, honey. Tell my favorite son-in-law I said hello."

"He's your only son-in-law."

"That's why he's my favorite. Oh, and Piper? Whatever you're up to, be careful. You know how people are out there."

Piper shivered.

"Love you, darling!"

"You, too," Piper said, but her words went unheard — her mother had already hung up.

Four long, desolate blocks off the main street, the Frick Island Wildlife Center was less a "center" and more a double-wide trailer that looked as if it had just fallen from the sky in a tornado, squashing a patch of seagrass instead of a wicked witch.

Anders stood outside near the cinder-block steps, sweating under the direct heat of the sun. If he had a life mantra, it would probably be the one his dad oft repeated, also known as the five Ps — Proper Planning Prevents Poor Performance. But for the first time in his life, Anders did not have a plan. Not a good one, anyway.

When working on a newspaper article or

podcast, he typically gathered all the information first, and then formed all his research into a story, with a beginning, middle, and end. But this story — well, he was still in the middle of it. He was recording as he went, the audience finding out along with him whatever he uncovered about this strange little island. And he hoped to uncover how and when this delusion started for Piper. But he couldn't exactly ask her directly. He had researched just enough about delusional disorders to know that if he contradicted what she believed to be true, she would just think *he* was crazy for saying that Tom was not alive.

And instinct told him — or maybe it was the way that waterman looked at him when he caught Anders eavesdropping in the One-Eyed Crab — that he couldn't come straight out and ask anyone else on the island about it either. At least not yet.

Fortunately, BobDan reminded him he had the perfect cover — he had told everyone he was doing a podcast on climate change. And he saw no reason to disabuse them of that notion just yet. He didn't like to lie — he was actually quite terrible at it — but he didn't really see a way around it for now. And anyway, it wasn't a complete lie in that he *did* talk about climate change in episode 2. Briefly.

He took a deep breath, wiped his sweaty palms on his khaki pants, climbed the three cinder-block steps, and pulled on the door, which squeaked on its hinges, the inevitable effect of salt air meeting metal. He stepped across the threshold, cool air enveloping him, drying the perspiration on his brow. This was a Frick Island first — air-conditioning. At least a powerful one.

As his eyes adjusted to the dimly lit space, the first thing he noticed was photographs, large and small, black-and-white and color, adorning nearly every free surface of wall, and then below them, the water damage. A clearly demarcated line rose about twelve inches from the floor, and considering the trailer was already about three feet off the ground, Anders stared at it, wondering at how large a flood would have to be to —

"Sandy."

Anders turned toward the voice, noticing for the first time a man standing at the far end of the room behind a desk. He squinted at the name tag affixed to the man's shirt: *Bill Gibbons.* "Huh?"

"Hurricane Sandy. That's what the water damage is from. Applied for government funds to get a new building — conservation center, the works. I got eight hundred dol-

166

lars." He pointed to the floor. "Enough for the carpet."

Anders looked down at the cheap but new-looking industrial carpet. He could feel the hard cement slab directly beneath it.

"You here for the tour?"

The tour? Anders glanced around the room, wondering what there possibly was to tour. All the photos had captions. Seemed pretty self-explanatory.

"Actually, I'm looking for Piper."

The man's eyes went hard. He studied Anders's face, a detective trying to determine motive. Or maybe turn Anders to stone. Either way, Anders squirmed under the scrutiny. Finally the man spoke. "She'll be along."

Anders waited, hoping Bill would add an estimated time to his sentence, but no such luck. "OK." He shoved his hands in his pockets and meandered over to the first large black-and-white photo on the wall: an image of a bird close up, the caption naming it a great blue heron. Anders skimmed the info about its habitat and history on the island, until the silence became overwhelming. He spoke without turning his head. "So are you related to BobDan, down at the docks? Noticed you have the same last name."

"Him and half the island," said an amused voice, but one that was decidedly not male. Anders swiveled his head only to lock eyes with Piper, who stood at the desk as if she had replaced Bill Gibbons with the flick of a magician's wrist and a puff of smoke. Before he could decipher where exactly she'd come from, recognition flashed in her eyes. "Oh. It's you." Her inflection didn't indicate pleasure at seeing him again. But it didn't indicate displeasure either.

"It's me," he agreed. His palms started sweating again, despite the cold air. He peered at her, as if studying an animal in its natural habitat. Now that he knew for sure that Piper had an . . . imaginary husband, for lack of a better phrase, his nerves were slowly overtaken by morbid curiosity. He felt the familiar buzz at that first deep dive into a new story; the anticipation of the things he might uncover, the answers to the five Ws and an H that he learned about in his first newspaper reporting class in college. And then a thought struck Anders — what if Piper thought her husband was in the room right now? His eyes darted around as if an apparition of Tom might appear.

"You OK?" She peered at him strangely.

"Huh? Yeah — yep." He rocked back on his heels, glancing around the room once more. Then he cleared his throat, trying to get back on track. "You told me I should come here . . . ?"

"I remember," she said. A coiled lock of hair fell in her line of sight, and she tucked it behind her ear. "I just thought it would be last week — and then you didn't show, so."

"Oh." Anders felt slightly shamed for breaking a promise he didn't remember making. "Hey, do you mind if I record our conversation?"

She narrowed her eyes. "For your podcast thing?"

"Yeah." He waited with bated breath for her response. If he could get her voice on the podcast, it would deepen the story so much more — and if she mentioned Tom? Anders got nearly light-headed with excitement.

"For your dad," she said, and he was surprised she had not only been listening to him that morning at breakfast but remembered what he had said.

"Him and a few other listeners," he corrected, which was more or less true. Nine hundred was a lot to Anders, but in the grand scheme of things, still not that many.

"I don't know," she said, hesitating. And Anders tried not to betray what he was feeling. If she said no, of course he'd be disappointed, but he'd respect her wishes. He could still get plenty of material for the podcast, but obviously Piper's story was what his listeners were most interested in.

"I guess no one out here would ever hear it," she said, though it wasn't directed at Anders as much as herself.

"I mean, they could," Anders said. "It's on the Internet. Anyone can find it if they want." It was something that occurred to him this week — that anyone on the island *could* listen to his podcast, and most people out here, given their propensity for privacy, probably wouldn't be thrilled with the content. But it was a risk Anders was willing to take. If people confronted him and wanted him to stop, well, he would cross that bridge when he got to it. For now, he was operating under the mantra that it was better to ask for forgiveness than permission. That seemed to be how podcasts worked — *Serial, S-Town.* The ethics of it were debated ad nauseam online, but they didn't follow the same tenets of newspaper journalism. In podcasts, story was king. And this was one hell of a story. Still, he wanted to be as honest with Piper as he could be, without scaring her off.

"Well, there's really only one computer

that actually gets Internet service on the island," Piper said. "It's at the market. And it's painfully slow."

"Really?" Anders said, although it made sense, Jess's words reverberating in his mind: *You're about to go back in time.* Well, that was one less thing for him to worry about.

Piper nodded. And then she shrugged. "Yeah. I guess it's fine to record."

While Anders nonchalantly dug his mini recorder out of his bag, trying to hide his excitement, and clicked it on, Piper bent down behind the desk, the entire upper half of her body disappearing from view.

Confused, Anders took a few steps forward, startling when she popped back up like a jack-in-the-box. "Here." She thrust a stack of papers toward him.

"What's this?"

"Research," she said. "About climate change."

Oh, right. He had nearly forgotten that was how this whole thing started — climate change. That was why she had told him to come to the wildlife center in the first place. She shook the stack, impatient. "Take it."

He did as he was told, scanning the paper on top. It was a photocopy of a scientific study published in the *Journal of Ecology* titled "Winter Mortality of the Blue Crab in Chesapeake Bay." "Where'd you get all this?"

"We have stacks of it in the office." She nodded to a door in the wall beside the desk, and Anders realized that must be where she'd come from and Bill disappeared to. "A lot of it's my mom's, actually."

"Your mom?"

Piper nodded. "She's an ecologist."

"Here? On the island?"

"She used to be. That's what brought us over here."

Anders's eyes went big. "You're a *Come Here*?"

She tilted her head, as if surprised Anders knew the phrase, and then nodded. "Yep. Since the sixth grade."

Anders took this in. She seemed so the embodiment of the island, he couldn't picture her living anywhere else. "What's your mom do now?" he asked, wondering if he had met her on the island and not realized it.

"Same thing. Just on the Gold Coast of Australia."

Anders stared, but Piper did not offer any further explanation.

"So you believe in climate change?"

"Of course."

"I was getting the impression that no one on this island did."

"From whom?"

"What?"

"From whom were you getting that impression?"

"Well, everyone," Anders said, then remembered his conversation at the One-Eyed Crab. "That guy at the restaurant said as much, what's his name — Jeffrey."

Piper's jaw went tight, and anger flashed in her eyes for the briefest second, so brief Anders wondered if he was imagining it. "Jeffrey's an idiot."

"Oh. Well, that Mr. Gimby at the antiques store. He definitely didn't believe in it."

Piper sighed. "Look, it's complicated. Most people here accept it's happening, just like they accept the sun comes up every morning. It's the *why* that's the trouble. They think it's cyclical — the climate changes, sure, but it's going to change back."

"Won't they be surprised when it doesn't," Anders said dryly.

"What did you say?" And there was no mistaking the anger that burned bright in Piper's eyes this time. "Is this some kind of joke to you?"

"What? No, no, I —"

173

"I should have known," she said, half to herself. And then fully to him: "You don't know anything about this island or the people here. You all just come here all smug and full of yourselves, wanting to gawk and laugh at how weird we are. Or ignorant. Or whatever it is you think about us. I thought — what you said at Mrs. Olecki's — I thought maybe you were different. That you actually realized there were *people* living on this island — people whose entire lives and livelihood are being affected, and that maybe you cared about that. I can see I was wrong."

Anders stood, openmouthed and flame cheeked, unsure of how the conversation went so bad so quickly, and searched for something to say to salvage it.

"Look," she said, in that way that let him know the conversation was over. "Did you want the tour? It starts in about five minutes."

"Oh, yes! That would be great." Maybe all was not lost. He'd get to spend more time with Piper and try to compensate for his cavalier observation. Maybe get back on better footing with her.

"Bill," Piper called, so loud it reverberated in Anders's ear. "He wants the tour!" She turned back to Anders and smiled sweetly.

"He'll be just a minute."

"Oh. Bill does the tour? I thought maybe that you —"

"Nope! I have things to do. Best of luck with your article." She disappeared through the side door, and as Anders stood clutching the thick stack of research papers Piper had given him and waiting for Bill to reappear, he decided that that couldn't have gone more poorly if he had tried.

The next morning, Anders woke up in the second-floor bedroom of the Oleckis' bed-and-breakfast. His feet hung off the end of the full bed, and sweat bonded the side of his face to the pillowcase, the warm breeze entering the screen of the open windows doing nothing to combat the heat. He blinked slowly, his head groggy with lack of sleep, his mouth gluey and dry. He had spent the majority of the night tossing and turning, the pure silence of the island deafening. There were no cars driving past outside, no sirens, no thumping music from an upstairs neighbor, no *people,* period. Nothing to hear but a few unidentified birdcalls (one particularly high-pitched and terrifying that jolted Anders straight up in bed, notwithstanding) and the sound of Piper's words replaying in his head.

I thought maybe you were different.

He felt bad, even as he wasn't sure exactly why. Maybe because everything Piper said hit a little too close to home. He did have preconceived notions about the island and its residents, and the first tenet of journalism — yes, even in podcasting — was to try to be as objective as possible. But if he was being honest, he *wasn't* objective — he thought she was crazy. He thought this whole island was crazy. And that wasn't fair. At the very least it was terrible journalism. The least he could do was try to be more open-minded.

But what was grating him was more than just being a possibly bad, selfish journalist. It was the look in Piper's eyes. The disappointment. Anders historically didn't care much about what other people thought of him, and he couldn't exactly say why it bothered him so much now.

All he knew was that Piper was disappointed in him. And Anders didn't want her to be.

By the time he woke up, his face pasted to the pillow, while most of his thoughts were still muddled, one thing was clear: Podcast or no podcast, he owed Piper an apology.

Downstairs, he sat at the dining table, staring at a plate of ham-and-cheese quiche, two pieces of maple-sugared bacon, and three orange slices. He shared the table with two amateur photographers who came to the island every summer to capture the scenery and wildlife with their lenses. Anders half listened as they casually spoke about their agenda for the day, but every time the door swung open from the kitchen, he craned his neck trying to catch a glimpse of Piper, to no avail.

"Is there something I can help you with?" Mrs. Olecki said finally, as she was clearing the dishes away. Her kind voice was belied by her stern eyes, her hand propped on her ample hip.

"Oh," Anders said, melting under her gaze. "I, uh, I was just looking for Piper."

"She's already left."

"So she's home, then?"

She narrowed her eyes. "Well, I don't rightly know. It's not really my business where she goes when she's done here." But the way she said it made it clear she thought it wasn't any of Anders's business.

"Right." He swallowed.

"Is there anything else I can get you?"

"No, thank you," he said, and excused himself from the table with haste.

Stepping out the front door of the bed-and-breakfast, Anders squinted against the morning sun reflecting off the calm water. He turned right on the one-lane road in front of the house and immediately turned right again between the bed-and-breakfast and the neighboring house onto the worn footpath that led to Piper's carriage house. Heart pounding, he climbed the steps and rapped on the screen door; he was partly relieved but even more anxious to hear footsteps from within.

"Hey," he said when Piper opened the door, leaving the screen between them. Barefoot, she wore a simple linen shift, and her hair was more wild than ever, if possible — curls shooting in every direction like a Fourth of July fireworks display.

"Hello," she said, her tone cold and formal.

He swallowed and gave a lame half wave. "Me again. Uh . . . Anders."

Piper just stared at him, her expression unreadable, her hand resting on the knob of the open door.

"Listen, I just wanted to say I'm sorry for . . . well, *everything* yesterday. I didn't mean to . . ." He cleared his throat. "What I'm trying to say . . . poorly, obviously . . . is that I was a jerk . . ." He paused. "Though, to be fair, I think *smug* was a little harsh."

She cocked an eyebrow.

He waved the thought away. "Doesn't matter. Point is . . . I'm sorry."

Piper remained silent. Anders searched for something else to say.

"Oh, and of course I want to say thank you. You know, for the research. You didn't have to do that, and it was really nice of you. So . . ."

Piper's eyes glazed over as Anders trailed off and he wasn't even sure if she was listening to him anymore. But then she tilted her head to the innards of her house. "What, hon?"

Anders cocked his head as well, straining to hear what she had heard, but the only audible sounds were a few birdcalls flapping in the air outside. The breeze. Nothing from the direction Piper was looking. Nothing from inside.

"Yeah, I'll be right there," she called, and turned back to Anders. "Sorry. It's my husband. He's color-blind and never can pick the right tie for church."

Anders stared at her for a beat. "Your husband," he said.

"Yep," Piper said.

"Your husband, Tom," Anders repeated slowly, for clarity.

"Yesss," Piper said, drawing out the word

and looking at Anders as if *he* were the one a few crayons short of a full box. "So you were saying?"

Flustered, Anders could hardly remember what he was saying. He knew this woman believed her husband, Tom, was here in the flesh; he had witnessed it with his own eyes! But the ease with which she spoke to . . . to . . . the *air* . . . was still unnerving. Or maybe she wasn't talking to the air. He remembered the email from the PBHE expert, about that woman who kept her husband's dead body in the house. He shivered. And then tentatively sniffed. Thankfully, he smelled only salt and the mild decaying scent of the marsh. At least he thought it was the marsh.

And then another thought elbowed its way in: Why hadn't he been *recording*? That would have been amazing for the podcast. He could have kicked himself for missing it.

"Anders?"

"Right. Sorry. Um . . . I was just saying . . ." He cleared his throat. "Thank you. You know, for the research."

"You're welcome," she said. "Is that all?"

"Well . . . yes," he said, still out of sorts. She gave a curt nod and moved to shut the door, and that was when he saw it again. That look in her eyes. The one that let him know she didn't *really* forgive him. Or think highly of him in any way. The look that cut him to the bone and made him feel — well, he didn't know what it made him feel. But it wasn't good.

"No, actually, that's not all," he said, putting his hand out, even though the screen door was between them and he couldn't do anything to stop her from shutting the other one. She stopped anyway and looked up at him. "Look, you were right. I don't know anything about this island. I came in with preconceived judgments about . . . well, everything. But I *am* different," he said, unable to hide the desperation in his voice. "At least, I think I am. I hope I am. I really do want to help."

And that was when it occurred to him that what he was saying was true. Maybe the focus of the story had changed since he first came to the island — and maybe he wasn't being completely forthright about that — but that didn't mean his motives were any less altruistic. How many people in America, around the *world,* struggled with grief, the death of a loved one? Sure, Piper's response was unique, but it was relatable just the same. In fact, Anders thought suddenly, everything happening on this island was relatable. Climate change, mental health issues, maybe even drug trafficking (he still wasn't sure about that part) — Frick Island was a microcosm for so many issues people faced all across the country.

Once the light bulb had clicked on, Anders could barely stem the exhilaration coursing through his veins. He could create a phenomenal podcast that was a metaphor for all of America's darkest struggles, forcing them into the light — who knew how many people it might drive to get the help they needed? Maybe it would even help Piper herself.

And everyone thought Superman was the hero.

"Is *that* all?"

"Well, yes," Anders said, but then immediately cursed himself. He'd obviously need to spend more time with her in order to get more material for this life-changing podcast. "Wait, no . . . I mean, I would love more help, you know, for the podcast."

"*More* help?" A hint of irritation crossed Piper's face, letting Anders know she thought she had done quite enough. "Like what?"

His mind raced. "I don't know. Could I interview you, maybe?" She was already shaking her head, but he kept talking anyway. "The climate change research is great, for background, but I really need to get someone that lives here on the record. Especially someone that" — he gestured at Piper — "understands what's at stake."

"No."

"No? But —" He'd really messed up. Yesterday she was giving him research and willing to be recorded. Today she wouldn't even open the screen door between them.

But Anders refused to give up, wracking his brain for another reason to be near her. "OK, well, can you tell me a little about the island? I'd like to understand it better, you know, what life is like here. Not tourist stuff, but . . . the real Frick Island."

Piper's eyebrows shot skyward. "You want the *real* Frick Island experience?"

Anders nodded.

The side of her mouth slowly curled up into a half grin. "Well, that I can do."

"You can?" He realized he had half expected her to slam the door in his face, for good. And that he probably deserved it.

"Yep. No problem. Meet me at the docks tomorrow morning, ten thirty."

Anders's shoulders relaxed, pleased that he'd been able to at least partly salvage the relationship with his subject. And it was quite ingenious on his part, if he was giving credit where credit was due — asking Piper to be his tour guide of the island, of sorts. She might not trust him to record their interactions again just yet, but at least he'd get to spend time with her. He grinned. "I'll be there."

CHAPTER 12

The sun burned bright and hot Monday morning as Piper walked to the docks for the second time that day. She had gotten up early to walk Tom to his boat and now she was meeting Anders, as promised. Even though it was Labor Day, tourism had been so slow that summer, Mr. Garrison hadn't blinked when she asked for the day off from working at the market. Though she wasn't sure why exactly she'd asked for the day off or why she had agreed to meet Anders.

Or why she'd opened her big mouth that morning a few weeks ago in the dining room at the bed-and-breakfast and told him she'd help him with his article — except there was something about him, an earnestness in his face. Or maybe that was just his freckles and unfortunate cowlick that gave him a look of vulnerability. And if there was one thing she understood, it was feeling vulnerable.

Or maybe it was just that she had a soft spot for Come Heres, considering she was once one herself. Though everyone treated her as nothing less than family now, she still remembered how it felt to be a knobby-kneed eleven-year-old, new to Frick Island. How people would smile, but not with their whole face. They would say "welcome" in a way that let you know you weren't. Not really. That you had to earn your place, though how, Piper had no idea. There wasn't an instruction manual. So Piper spent hours by herself, scouring the marshes and beaches for unusual insects to add to her collection. The silence and loneliness at first was novel, and then over time, so deep and painful, she thought she might not be able to breathe. She had her mom, of course, but more often than not, her mom was absorbed in her research, either physically working on it or mentally working on it, even when she was in the same room with Piper.

Or maybe it was that she was just too nice. That was what Tom was always accusing her of. If he only knew how hard it was to live up to the person he *thought* she was sometimes.

Regardless of why she had opened her mouth to help Anders, she instantly regretted it Saturday. How dare he be so flippant about what Piper knew would eventually be the *demise* of the island — the *home* — she had so come to love. Maybe it served her right — there was a reason why everyone on the island kept Come Heres at arm's length, and he had just validated that. And then, showing up on her doorstep like that yesterday morning? Even if it was to apologize, he was too nosy for her liking — and was quickly becoming a barnacle she couldn't scrape off.

When she reached the One-Eyed Crab and the docks came into view, she spotted Anders, his back to her as he studied Tom's skiff up on planks.

"In the market for a trawler?"

Startled, Anders turned, his clear brown eyes meeting Piper's.

"Even if I was, I probably couldn't afford even this one," he said.

"I don't know — I think Tom would sell it for a song at this point."

"Oh, it's Tom's?" he said.

"Yeah. It's got an issue with worms. See where they ate through the hull?" She pointed to the tiny holes, remembering how frustrated Tom was when he discovered those obnoxious pests. And then, of course, there was the matter of the time the boat had spent at the bottom of the ocean, rendering it completely unseaworthy, but Piper didn't like to think about that. "They're using his cousin Steve's trawler right now, until we get enough money to fix it."

"So, are you going to tell me what we're doing here?"

"Right now, we're waiting," she said, adjusting the strap of her pale pink tank top.

"For what?" Anders asked.

"You'll see."

He stood, staring at the horizon, and she used the opportunity to study him, from his skin, the same color of the blanched underbelly of a clamshell and lightly speckled across the bridge of his nose, to the tufts of hair sticking up like straw at the crown of his head, to his neatly creased khakis and the button-up shirt.

"Do you always dress like that?" The thought tumbled out of her mouth before she could catch it. She wasn't even sure she said it out loud until Anders looked down at his Dockers, at his short-sleeved work shirt, and then back at her.

"Like what?"

"I don't know —" She paused, nose scrunching as she searched for a tactful way to phrase it. "Like you're about to do

188

somebody's taxes?"

From the expression on his face, it was clear she had failed. She immediately felt a twinge of regret at what he surely interpreted as bald rudeness rather than simple curiosity. But then she remembered his own discourteous behavior in the wildlife center and clenched her jaw to keep from apologizing. There. Maybe they were even now. Movement caught her eye over Anders's right shoulder. "Ah! Here they are."

Anders turned to see a skiff puttering up to the docks, carrying two boys. Though Piper had known the Gibbons twins since they were rambunctious eight-year-olds, she saw them suddenly through Anders's eyes, and they surprisingly no longer looked like children. With matching crew cuts and sinewy, tan limbs, the boys looked hardscrabble — like they'd been in the Marines for five years, even though they weren't nearly old enough to enlist. When they reached the dock, one of them leapt onto it in a fluid motion, while the other cut the engine, but didn't take his hand off the wheel.

"Anders," Piper said. "Meet Kenny and Jojo."

"Hi." Anders nodded in their direction.

Kenny grunted, while Jojo grumbled

"hey" in return.

"They're going to take you progging."

"Bro-ging? What is that?"

"*Pro*gging," Piper corrected. "And you'll see."

Anders narrowed his eyes. "Why are they doing this?"

Piper shrugged. "Because I asked them to. And because you're going to give them forty dollars."

"Oh."

He stepped on board the boat, and when it bobbled under his weight, nearly pitching him into the water, Piper tried not to smile. "Might want to put your life jacket on," she called. Anders wasted no time picking up the bright orange vest from the fiberglass seat behind him, sliding his head through the neck hole, and securing the belt at his waist. By the time he looked up, Jojo was back in the boat, the engine was revving, and the boat was already pulling away from the dock, where Piper was still standing.

"Wait," he called. "You aren't coming?"

Piper just smiled and waved. "Have fun!" After a day out in the bogs with the Gibbons boys, she was fairly certain Anders — who didn't strike her as an overly outdoorsy type — wouldn't be in want of her help again, and she'd be shed of him for good.

190

■ ■ ■ ■

Four hours later, when the boat finally chugged back toward the marina, Anders was sweaty, sunburned, and wearing only one shoe. At some point in the middle of progging — which Anders quickly learned was really just mucking about in the mud to see what you could find (apparently old coins and "arraheads" were some of the treasures the boys had unearthed on previous expeditions) — the marsh sucked the other one right off his foot and swallowed it up. "Maybe someone will find it a hundrit years from now and put it in their collection!" one of the boys joyfully exclaimed, after Anders finally gave up digging in the sludge to find it.

When he first realized Piper wasn't going, he thought at least he could use the opportunity to interview Kenny and Jojo, but their conversation skills were limited to grunts — until they somehow got on the subject of hunting, and Anders learned more about tracking and killing muskrats than he ever hoped to know.

With a practiced grace, Jojo slid the boat between two others, the docks alive once again with skiffs and watermen, lugging nets

191

and traps out of their boats. "Today's Labor Day." Anders spoke his thought out loud, to no one in particular. "Don't they ever take a break?"

"Sure — every Sunday," Kenny said, and then stood in front of Anders, blocking his path off the boat, which Anders found disconcerting until he remembered Piper had promised he'd pay them. He reached into his back pocket for his wallet, which seemed to be the only thing on him not covered in filth, and plucked his last two twenties from it, handing them over, trying not to panic about how much cash he was steadily blowing on this podcast venture. Discreetly tucked beneath his napkin at breakfast that morning was the bill for two nights at the bed-and-breakfast. And while he had anticipated it, having spent the night there two weeks earlier, and while it was wildly reasonable — much cheaper than anything you could find on the mainland — there was no way Anders could continue to pay two-hundred-plus every weekend, on top of his rent.

Kenny snatched the bills and moved to the side, and Anders stepped off the boat onto the dock. Before he could even turn around to say thank you, the two boys were off once again, to God only knows where.

What were those weird names they were tossing about — Pitchfork Point? Dipstick Creek?

As Anders rubbed the back of his neck, sore to the touch both from the angle he'd had it bent all afternoon fruitlessly looking down and from the fire-hot sun that had surely left its mark, and stared at the retreating boat, he marveled once again that he was standing here, on this strange little island.

In the din of watermen shouting back and forth, a familiar voice drifted to his ears, drawing his attention to land. Sure enough, when he turned his head, he spotted Piper standing next to a bench, in animated conversation with BobDan.

He started walking toward them up the long dock, his stride slightly off-balance thanks to the missing shoe. And he noticed Piper glance his way, her eyes shining, her hand held up to her mouth but not quite covering a wide grin. He couldn't be sure, but it felt as though she were laughing. At him.

He stepped off the dock onto hard land, and when he finally reached the twosome, Piper dropped her hand. "Did you have a good afternoon?"

Anders bit off his instinctual reply — *Does*

it look *like I had a good afternoon?* — and plastered a manufactured smile on his face. "It was . . . something I had never experienced before. And it only cost me forty dollars" — he reached down to hike up his pants leg and show off his muddy-sock-clad foot — "and a shoe."

"A bargain, don't you think?" Piper said, her eyes twinkling. Anders peered at her, unable to shake the creeping suspicion he was in the middle of a game he hadn't signed up to play and didn't even know the rules for — and that Piper was winning.

Just then, BobDan put his hand on Anders's shoulder and squeezed. "Peter Jennings," BobDan said jovially. "Just the man I wanted to see. Think you could come help me in the office? I have a few boxes need moving."

Anders looked into the old man's eyes. Something felt off — BobDan had been nothing but gruff with him from the moment they first met, and suddenly he was being . . . friendly? And overly so. His hand dropped to Anders's elbow and he tugged — not gently. Were the boxes on fire?

"Wait!" Piper said, and Anders turned toward her. "Anders hasn't met Tom yet." She looked to the empty air to her right. "Tom, this is Anders, the journalist I was telling you about. Anders, my husband, Tom."

Anders froze, staring at Piper. It seemed ridiculous in hindsight that he hadn't planned for this eventuality. That he hadn't given any thought to how he would respond. Up until this point, this delusion of Piper's — and the islanders going along with it — was something that felt outside of him; something he was observing from afar. But now it was here, staring him in the face. Or not here, depending on how you looked at it. But something he was going to have to deal with, just the same. BobDan's grip tightened on his arm.

Anders's mind raced as he considered his options, and the story of the emperor with no clothes popped into his brain. When his father read him that fable as a child, Anders naturally saw himself in the role of the tale's hero — the little boy in the crowd who finally shouts out the truth. The emperor was naked! Everyone could see! It was frankly absurd everyone else went along with it. Of course *Anders* would never do that.

But now, here it was, happening in real life. And as the pressure mounted — BobDan's glare nearly burning a hole in his face, his bony fingers pressing harder into

Anders's elbow, Piper's brows drawing into deeper confusion as she waited for Anders to respond, and was it just his imagination, or had every waterman at the docks stopped what they were doing to watch this exchange? — Anders no longer had to speculate what he would or would not do.

"Hey, uh . . . Tom," Anders said to the same empty air Piper had looked at. "Nice to, er . . . meet you."

And just like that, the men at the docks seemed to spring back to life around him, BobDan's grip relaxed, and Piper smiled, her brows unknitting. "Oh, I've told Tom all about you. I'm sure he feels like he already knows you, don't you, babe?"

Tom, of course, did not respond.

"Anyway, we've got to go. Tom's mother is expecting us. Coming back next weekend, Anders?"

"Um, yeah. Yep. I will be here," Anders said, slowly enunciating each word, his brain still processing the encounter.

Piper walked off, and Anders watched her retreat, until she passed the One-Eyed Crab and was out of earshot. He turned to BobDan, who was looking at him with steely eyes. "Not a word, Dan Rather. Not one word."

"But —" Anders started. Surely that

encounter warranted some kind of explanation from the old man. Anders felt a spark of excitement — this was the perfect entrée to finally ask about Piper and Tom. He opened his mouth to ask if he could record their conversation, but BobDan cut him off before he could even get a word out.

"It's not any of your any mind what goes on around here. I want to be real clear on that. Looks like you've determined to be here for God knows how long, but I 'spect you to focus on your climate whatever and leave everything else the hell alone. Starting with her." He stuck his bony pointer finger out in the direction Piper had gone. "She's been through more than enough, ya hear?"

BobDan didn't wait for a response. Just turned on his heel and hoofed it toward the marina office. Anders stood there for a minute, gawking in BobDan's direction, something that felt a lot like shame creeping up on his face. He wanted to defend himself. He wanted to tell BobDan that he knew Piper had been through a lot — that he wanted to *help* her, which was more than it seemed like anyone else in this town was doing. But he was also lying about the actual story he was covering in his podcast and knew he didn't exactly have the moral high ground.

"Hey," Anders called after him, weakly. "I thought you said you needed help."

BobDan just growled and waved his arm in a shooing motion behind him, which Anders took to mean he did not want Anders to follow — nor did he need his help.

Having nowhere else to go, Anders sat down on the bench to wait for BobDan to come back out for the four o'clock ferry departure. As he waited, rolling the incident over in his mind, how easily he had spoken to a man that did not exist, how fiercely protective BobDan, and everyone else apparently, seemed to be of Piper, it occurred to him — not for the first time that day, he thought, peering at his one muddy-sock-clad, shoeless foot — that perhaps he was out of his depth.

"Caldwell!" The booming voice from across the room made Anders jump, though he should have been used to Hector Ochoa's baritone by now. The sports reporter sauntered over to Anders's cube, smacking on his ever-present wad of gum. He paused in midchew when he noticed Anders glaring at him, his finger pointing at the cell cradled between his ear and shoulder.

Anders turned his attention back to the voice mail that had just clicked on in his ear. "You've reached the therapy office of Janet Keene. Please leave a message at the tone. If you are having suicidal thoughts or this is an emergency, please dial 911." Janet Keene was a D.C.-area therapist specializing in delusional disorders. Anders hoped she'd be able not only to give him guidance on what he should do the next time he was face-to-face with "Tom," but also to offer some great expert insights to weave into his next podcast.

After leaving a vague message requesting an interview, Anders turned his attention to Hector, who was towering over his desk, his T-shirt taut over his ridiculously bulging biceps ("Grass-fed New Zealand whey protein, man," Hector had whispered to him once, as though he were offering him the secret to the universe, though Anders had never asked) and half tucked into the waist of his khaki shorts, which would look haphazard if the hem of his shirt weren't tucked in at the exact same spot (two inches to the right of his pants button) every single day.

"Dude, ever hear of sunscreen?" Hector asked, his lip turned up in disgust.

Ping!

Anders glanced down at his arms, where the skin had begun to scale and peel off in thin white crumbles. He sighed again. "What do you need, Hector?"

"The camera. Log says you checked it out yesterday. I got a game tonight."

Ping! Ping!

Anders dug in the shoulder bag beside his chair and produced the camera for Hector.

"Thanks, man."

Ping!

"You gonna get that?" Hector nodded toward Anders's computer screen. Anders glanced at the message box, even though he already knew it was his sister. He'd been so busy, he hadn't spoken to her since missing Labor Day weekend, and if her last text messages were any indication, she was pissed. He moved the mouse and clicked on the X to minimize the box.

"Porn chat room?" Hector gave him a knowing grin.

"No," Anders replied indignantly.

"Sure," Hector said, still grinning, then his squirrel attention span got distracted by the five-inch stack of papers on Anders's typically spotless and organized desk. "What's all that?"

"Research." Anders had decided if he was going to keep up this climate change story ruse, he should probably start digging into the studies Piper had given him, particularly in case she ever asked about them. But they were dense academic files and it took him most of the previous night to get through just two of them.

The one-word answer was enough to satisfy Hector's limited curiosity. He turned and sauntered back to his desk across the office, his leather flip-flops slapping the industrial carpet with each step, causing Anders to roll his eyes at Hector's ridiculous attire — this was a workplace, for Pete's sake.

But on the other hand — Anders paused and gave his head a shake. *God damn it,* he muttered to himself. He knew he was going to regret what he was about to say. "Hey, Hector, wait up."

Hector stopped and turned his head.

"Where do you get your . . ." Anders gestured his hand at his own shirt and pants. "You know . . ."

Hector cocked his eyebrows and grinned. Anders could see the gray gum squeezing out between his clenched teeth. "My effort-less ability to be cool?"

Anders closed his eyes. He regretted it already.

CHAPTER 13

Two Months Before the Storm

January on Frick Island, everyone agreed, was the worst month. Until February, anyway. And then February was definitely the worst. It was so cold, so wet, so miserable that only fifty-five or so of the ninety-ish people left on the island stayed for the entire winter, living in their battened-down houses like grizzly bears hibernating until spring. To make matters worse, this particular first week of February, a body-wracking cough was winding its way through the island, showing up like an unwanted houseguest and keeping everyone indoors, under blankets.

Piper had somehow been able to avoid it thus far, but looking at Tom's pallor where he sat at the kitchen table, intently repairing a scrape net, she thought he might not have been so lucky.

"Tom, you feeling OK?" She cringed immediately when she said it. It was the third time she had asked him that in as many hours. And she knew he wasn't. February was the hardest month for most watermen on the island. Tired of being cooped up and docile, they were ready to be back on the water. Not just because they were eager to start making money again but because, like German shepherds, they were most content when there was hard work to be done. For Tom, who mostly felt ambivalent about crabbing, fishing, and oystering, February was difficult for a different reason: It was the month he lost his father six years earlier.

Tom grunted, all his concentration on the mending task at hand, and Piper turned her gaze back to the menagerie of puzzle pieces in front of her, squinting at the swirls of purple for the one piece she currently needed. "Aha!" She spied it, up toward the corner of the table, plucked it up in her pincer grasp, and slotted it into the perfectly sized hole in the middle of the irises.

She glanced over at Tom again. He often teased her for her overenthusiasm in doing puzzles — her small shouts of victory or glee after completing the rectangular edge at the beginning or when discovering a particularly elusive piece. He at least jovially rolled his eyes or cocked a brow in her direction, a grin turning up one corner of his mouth. But today he just sat with his overly long needle, his brows furrowed, face solemn.

Piper frowned. Though he did often get this way around the anniversary of his father's death, her gut told her something else was eating at him. Something more. Maybe it was the visit with his mom two nights earlier, where it was impossible to ignore how much she was slurring her words over dinner (though they did ignore it) and how she nodded off in the middle of a bite of squash pie. And of course, there was the matter of the worms he had just discovered in his hull, leaving it looking like a tatted lace doily — and the fact that they didn't really have the money to fix it. Or maybe it was his shoulder — he had mentioned last night that it was acting up again. It hadn't really been right since he dislocated it last spring hauling in an overloaded net of snapper at a bad angle.

But at least he hadn't brought up that other thing. Not in weeks. After their last big fight about it, Piper hoped he'd put it to bed for good.

She stood up, as if to distance herself from the thought, and walked over to the two-burner stove to turn on the kettle. When the water was ready she poured two cups of tea and took one to Tom. "Here you go," she said, sliding it onto the table in front of him. He paused, holding on to the needle and net with one hand, and used his free one to gently squeeze Piper's elbow in gratitude.

"Oh my god," Piper exclaimed, when she felt the searing heat from Tom's palm. She touched the back of her fingers to his forehead. "Tom, you are burning up!"

As if on cue, Tom sneezed. "You need to be in bed," she said. He just shook his head, pulling a handkerchief out of his back pocket and dabbing at his nose. "I'm fine," he said. "I need to finish this and then I've got to get down to the docks to help BobDan pull the boat out of the water."

"No, absolutely not. I'll call Steve and he can help. You need to rest," she said in her best firm voice. "Come on. All of that can wait."

To her surprise, Tom set the net back in the basket he'd pulled it from, which was how Piper knew he really was feeling miserable. After she got him settled in their bed, tucking a quilt around his weary frame, she padded back out to the front room, retrieving her mug of tea and wrapping her hands around it to covet the heat, but the tea, in her absence, had gone lukewarm.

Piper stared out the window, at the clothesline strung between their house and the Oleckis', bereft without clean laundry hanging from it, and found herself wishing, for what seemed like the thousandth time that month, that spring would come faster.

CHAPTER 14

"The key is making each layer the exact same — not too thick, not too thin," Mrs. Olecki was saying as she poured the creamy yellow batter into the same five metal tins she'd been using since she was a little girl and her mother had taught her how to bake this cake. It wasn't really the key, of course — or not the only one, anyway. But Pearl couldn't give away the real secret to making Frick Island cakes or everyone would make their own and have one less reason to come over to the island. She didn't think of it as lying as much as it was just good business sense.

Of course, she wasn't sure if it made much of a difference anymore, seeing as how she used to give this class at her bed-and-breakfast every single Saturday afternoon of tourist season to six people (the maximum number that would fit in her kitchen), and now, tourism had dwindled so greatly, it was by request only — and this was only the second request she'd gotten that summer.

She'd once had ambitions — or fantasies, anyway — of being one of those cooking show hosts on television. She often watched reruns of Julia Child shows on PBS and sometimes, when she was sure she was alone, she narrated her recipes, as though she were on camera, talking to a rapt audience.

"Are you sure that thing can hear me?" she asked, eyeing the tiny rectangular recorder with a microphone the size of a golf ball that Anders had placed on the counter next to the metal tin full of flour.

"Oh, yeah," Anders assured her. "It's more powerful than you think."

Pearl had learned all about his little podcast, of course, long before he approached her after breakfast that morning saying Piper had recommended he take her cake-baking class, and could he possibly record the session? After he mentioned his podcast at breakfast that first morning, she had immediately called up Sue to ask her what a podcast was, who in turn asked Shirlene, who asked BobDan. The problem was *nobody* knew exactly what a podcast was. So Pearl called Lady Judy, and the two of them snuck over to the market under the cover of night — Pearl didn't want to be caught dead using the very technology she eschewed aloud every chance she had — thankful that Mr. Garrison never locked up in case someone needed to use the computer.

It took some time for the computer to boot up and then even longer for the dial-up to connect. Judy helmed the keyboard, as she had taken a typing class in high school when she thought she might leave the island and become a secretary.

"I think you have to use the Googler," Mrs. Olecki directed from behind.

"It's Google," Lady Judy said.

"That's what I said."

"What's the name of his pod thingy again?"

Pearl repeated what Harold had told her in a whisper. "Have you ever heard of anything so vulgar? To twist the name of our little island like that."

"I don't know." Lady Judy snorted. "I think it's frickin' funny."

Pearl lightly slapped her on the shoulder. "Honestly."

Between the loading time for the web page and buffering, it took them at least an hour to listen to six minutes of the first episode, but it was long enough to understand that

Anders Caldwell wasn't up to anything nefarious — he was just offering an outsider's look at their island. To a little over a thousand people.

Bless his heart. Her niece on the mainland had more followers on her Instantgram, or whatever it was called, than he did on his podcast, and she was fourteen.

Anyway, she called off the alarm, letting everyone know that Anders Caldwell was harmless. Of course, he was still a journalist and a Come Here, so he couldn't be fully trusted, but if he wanted to keep coming and spending his hard-earned money at her little bed-and-breakfast every weekend to, what? — do more podcasts on Frick Island and climate change, a story that had been done a million times or more? — she'd take it. And if he wanted to air her Frick Island cake lesson on his podcast to his very small audience, well, who was she to say no? Any publicity was good publicity.

But now, as the afternoon wore on, she got the feeling that the man she was teaching was interested in something other than learning how to bake the cake. She narrowed her eyes at Anders, the not-Mormon podcaster who had shown up for the third time at her bed-and-breakfast yesterday afternoon asking for a room, and waited patiently for the truth to out, as it always did if one waited long enough.

"Can I ask you something?" Anders said finally, when the first round of layers was in the oven baking.

She knew it. Here it was, the real reason he'd asked to take this class.

"Sure," she said, trying to keep the smugness out of her voice.

"So I was down at the docks last week and Piper introduced me to Tom." He was watching her carefully, and Pearl stilled.

"Tighter than ticks, those two are." She kept her voice steady.

Anders's eyebrows nearly flew off his face. "Yes, but —"

Pearl cut him off. "If you have any questions about the cake, I'm happy to entertain them. If you want to know more about that cell tower they're building out here and how it's going to give everyone cancer, I can talk at length about that as well." She paused to let that sink in. Surely that was a far better story than climate change, but Anders's expression didn't reflect interest. She sighed. "But the personal lives of other people? Well, I'm no two-bit gossip — and I'd certainly hope that you aren't either."

Anders looked appropriately chagrined. After a few moments of silence, the warm scent of baking sugar and butter filling the air between them, he spoke up. "Do you ever need any help around here?"

She furrowed a brow at the abrupt change in conversation. "Help?"

"Yeah, with, like . . . I don't know . . . cleaning the gutters or washing windows or yard work. Moving furniture? Things like that."

She stared at him, waiting for the rest.

"It's just . . . I'm probably going to be coming over here for a few more weeks at least, and I can't really afford it on my salary. And BobDan and I already struck a deal for the ferry — I'll be loading and unloading and doing a few other things around the marina for him, which is what gave me the idea . . ."

Ah. He wanted a discount. She eyed him carefully. Of course, she didn't fully trust him — was any reporter honest? — but there was something about him, an earnestness, at least, that she found appealing. Maybe it was the freckles. Or maybe it was the offer itself that was appealing. Harold was getting older, there was no denying that. Though he wouldn't dare admit it, she could tell getting out of bed was a chore, the aches and pains. And though he was as strong as an ox, as capable as every other

212

man on Frick Island, she didn't like when he had to get up on a ladder to fix a shingle. Heck, she worried about him on the ground, carrying suitcases in for guests. Of course Tom used to do some of those more challenging chores, but he wasn't around anymore, was he? Pearl let her eyes travel down from the boy's face to his scrawny arms, as thin as the toothpick she'd use to test the batter in a few minutes. He didn't look strong enough to lift the Frick Island cake they were baking, never mind a suitcase. But if he was willing to try . . .

A breeze greeted Anders as he walked out the front door of the bed-and-breakfast, and he paused on the top step to enjoy it. The weather was still warm this third week in September, but at least there were pockets of tolerability; reminders that fall was on the way. He popped in his earbuds and trotted down the three steps to the rosebush-lined walkway and out onto the road and breathed deeply.

Anders was in a good mood. Though the third episode of the podcast wasn't as great as the second one — not as many twists — it had still tipped him over 2,500 subscribers and climbing. He couldn't decide which part was best — Piper herself discussing other islanders' disbelief in climate change (irony at its best!) or his recorded conversation with the therapist, who had finally returned his call and offered solid advice on how to properly react to someone experiencing a delusion.

"It's as if the frontal lobe of their brain — the part of the brain responsible for critical thinking — is switched off," she had said. "So basically, if they believe they're the reincarnation of Elvis Presley, say, telling them they are not, in fact, Elvis Presley will result in them still believing they're Elvis Presley — but now also believing you're crazy for disagreeing. It can also be quite overwhelming for them to hear the truth, if they're not ready — and can cause quite a bit of stress and agitation, which can lead to further deterioration of their mental condition. All that said, if you go along with it — start calling them Elvis, for instance — you're just reaffirming their delusion."

Anders had paused in his note-taking and reread what he'd typed on the screen. *Don't disagree with the delusion, but also don't go along with it.* "Wait — so what *should* you do?"

"Safest bet is to change the subject. Gently. Don't acknowledge the delusion or allow them to dwell on it."

Regardless, he was definitely on a roll. And now, with Mrs. Olecki agreeing to give him thirty dollars off a room for every hour he helped out, the only obstacle in his way had vanished just like that, and he could afford to keep going.

Sure, she had shut down his line of questioning on Piper, but he had anticipated that — and the "tighter than ticks" quote was great. It being such a nice day, Anders decided to turn left out of Mrs. Olecki's and walk along the back end of the island, on a more desolate road where there were more empty plots of tall seagrass than there were houses. A door opened on one house, and a woman stepped out carrying a stack of packages and boxes so high, it half covered her face. "Lady Judy?" Anders said, stepping toward her in case the teetering tower toppled over.

She peered at him over it. "Anders."

"Can I help you with those?"

"If I needed help, reckon I would have asked for it."

"Oh — OK," he said. "Well, have a good day."

He carried on down the road, lost in thought about how he nearly apologized for offering help to someone and how backward that felt. And then he wondered what in the

215

world was in those packages. He hadn't realized how far he had walked until another figure up ahead caught his eye. He was almost to the wildlife center, and walking away from it was Piper, a football field ahead of him, carrying a very large duffel bag — big enough to carry a dead body if it was chopped up, Anders mused morbidly.

He would have been surprised to see her, had he not begun to understand that running into the same people over and over again wasn't a strange coincidence but more an expected consequence of being on a three-square-mile island with only ninety-some-odd other people. It was weird if you *didn't* see someone two or three times in one day. "Piper," he said when he got close enough for her to hear.

She stopped in her tracks and looked up, startled. "Oh, hi. I didn't see you there."

He closed the gap between them, and that was when he noticed her posture, tense and jittery, like a deer caught in a car's headlights trying to decide which way to dart back into the woods. If he had any notions she had forgiven him when he had gone to her house to apologize, they vanished the second she all but shoved him on the boat with those twin boys. And now, she clearly didn't even like the sight of him. Anders frowned, unsettled by how much her opinion of him mattered — why did it unsettle him so? And then another thought occurred to him, as he closed the gap between them — he had no idea if "Tom" was with her. He slowed his pace. Should he say hi to the air next to her or wait for her to say something? He wracked his brain — it was just after noon on a Saturday, and if Anders was to go by what he had learned of the watermen's schedule, "Tom" should be out working. He relaxed a bit at this thought, as Piper readjusted the strap of the bag on her shoulder, catching Anders's attention once again.

"Whatcha got there?" His earlier thought popped into his mind and then out of his mouth. "Dead body?"

He immediately regretted it as Piper's face twisted in disgust. "No," she said, the one word infused with her appall.

"Sorry, ah — I . . . It was a joke," Anders stuttered lamely.

Her face remained serious as she eyed him, her gaze drifting downward. Anders puffed his chest a bit, waiting for her to notice his new pair of shorts. They weren't Rag & Bone, because when he looked those up, he thought surely Hector had been joking. Who pays *one hundred and forty-three dollars* for any article of clothing, particularly shorts? Fortunately Old Navy had a pair that looked exactly the same for nine bucks. He threw in a pair of canvas shoes and a couple of T-shirts, and his new Frick Island wardrobe was complete.

"Oh!" she said, and Anders's grin grew. "Your fly's undone."

His eyes widened as his hand flew to his zipper and Piper quickly averted her gaze toward the hand-painted sign that said *Graver's Beach* with an arrow away from town. He struggled with the cheap zipper, which appeared unwilling to do its job. Finally, it came unstuck and he yanked it upward, hoping it would stay in place.

"Well, I guess I better . . ." Piper said, nodding her head in the direction Anders had just come from. "I've got to get this to Mr. Gimby." She took a step as if to go around him.

"Wait," Anders said, ignoring the warmth that had crept into his cheeks, embarrassed not only for his zipper but more that he was embarrassed yet again around her. He didn't want to end their conversation with that being the enduring memory. He cleared his throat. "When are you going to let me interview you?"

Piper didn't even blink. "I'm not."

"Oh," Anders said, his buoyant mood quickly deflating.

"But I'm happy to send you on another outing. You know, for the *real* Frick Island. That is what you wanted, right?"

Anders peered at her, trying to decipher if she was making fun of him. He wasn't sure if it said more about himself or her that he couldn't tell. "Right. Yes. What should I do next?"

Piper glanced behind her toward the wildlife center, as if her next words were written somewhere in the air between here and there and she was looking for them. She turned back to Anders. "Crabbing."

"Crabbing," Anders repeated.

"Yep."

He cocked his head, considering. "There's no chance that I can do that *not* in a boat, is there?"

She offered a half smile. "Nope!"

"Didn't think so." While he wasn't thrilled about another adventure at sea, he realized all might not be lost. "Am I going with Tom and Steve?" Tom's cousin and fishing partner would be a great source — and if he wouldn't talk, it certainly would make for a great anecdote for the podcast, that he'd spent the day on the sea with the invisible man in question.

"No. They take their workdays very seriously," she said.

"Oh."

"Jojo and Kenny would be happy to do it."

Anders raised an eyebrow. "For another forty dollars?"

"Eighty."

He sputtered, which turned into a full-on cough. He pounded his chest with his fist.

"You OK?"

"Yes. Yep." He cleared his throat. She adjusted the strap on her shoulder again.

"Can I help you with that? I can walk with you." It was a selfish last-ditch effort to spend time with her, but also a touch altruistic — the bag really did look heavy.

"Nope! I'm good. I really gotta —"

"OK, yeah. I'll see you around," he said lightly, masking the disappointment in his voice. Was there some kind of law on this island barring people from accepting help? He turned away from her, continuing on his path around the island, his buoyant mood from earlier nowhere to be found. When was he going to get to spend more than five minutes with Piper? How was he supposed to get to the bottom of what was happening around here without spending any significant time in the company of his subject, or anyone, for that matter, who would tell him *anything* about Tom or the storm or this crazy game of pretend the entire town was participating in? And while he was counting his disappointments, would he ever experience an encounter with Piper where he was *not* fully humiliated in some way? The pattern was becoming —

"Hey, Anders," Piper called out, her voice breaking into his reverie. "Nice shorts."

Anders paused, unable to keep a smile from pulling the sides of his mouth skyward. He wracked his brain, trying to come up with a witty retort, but nothing came to him. Anders had never been smooth by a long shot. But clever repartee? That was his wheelhouse, and he couldn't understand why his brain seemed to go disconcertingly blank every time he was around Piper. Finally, he turned to just offer a lame thank-you, but closed his mouth when he noticed Piper had already started walking off — in the opposite direction of town and Mr. Gimby.

And it was then he realized she never did say what she had in the bag.

WHAT THE FRICK?
EPISODE 6

Hokie4Life: Seriously? It was good at first, but don't think I'll keep listening. Nothing is happening. Meh.

Anders stared at the comment, letting the words cut him right open. Hokie4Life was right, unfortunately. The audience for episodes 4, 5, and 6 had been steadily climbing, but not at the rapid clip he had hoped. And there was the reason in black and white staring at him from his computer screen: *Nothing is happening.*

For the past three weekends, Anders had done everything Piper had sorted out for him: crabbing, bird-watching, kayaking. He had helped out at the marina — washing down skiffs, filling gas tanks, loading and unloading boats until his muscles were so tight and sore, when he crashed in his bed at night he thought he might never walk again. At the bed-and-breakfast, he did whatever Mrs. Olecki asked, lugging suitcases up and down the stairs, washing the sea-salt-gritted windowpanes, hauling heavy baskets of wet sheets to the backyard, pinning them up on the clothesline. Others on the island had apparently gotten word of his jovial willingness to work and started to ask him for favors, too. He mowed Lady Judy's small square of lawn and helped owner Sue clean out the deep freezer at the One-Eyed Crab; he even stacked and sorted big piles of wood for Bill Gibbons, the manager of the Frick Island Wildlife Center, who apparently dabbled in whittling on the side. Instead of money for that job, Bill gave him a carving lesson. At the end of four hours, Bill had a striking figure of a blue heron, cut from a thick branch of black walnut, while Anders had a piece of basswood that looked like it had been used for hatchet practice (which, he supposed, technically it had).

What he didn't have was any new information: on Piper and Tom, or climate change — or anything else for that matter. Anytime Anders brought up a subject on something other than the activity he was currently partaking in, the conversation shut down quicker than the gnats found his skin to feast on when he stepped outside.

And the podcast was stalling out, Anders could feel it. Flatlining, more like it, as Anders desperately searched for a pair of jumper cables to revive it.

He woke with a start in the dead of night Monday, the answer plain as day, and he couldn't believe he hadn't thought of it before now. The email! The one he got right after the Cake Walk. Maybe that wasn't a crazy person. Maybe it was the source he'd been looking for. The person who would go on record and explain everything he wanted to know about Piper and Tom. He tossed the blanket to the side and jumped off the mattress, making a beeline for his laptop in the dark, where he pulled up the email he had received weeks ago. After a few stops and starts, he typed out a reply on the glowing screen and hit send.

To: NoManIsAnIsland@aol.com
From:
  ACaldwell@TheDailyTelegraph.com
SUBJECT: Re: Your Cake Walk story

I think I found the story you're referring to, but I can't get anyone to talk. Would you be willing to meet?

Anders checked his email more often than usual that week, hoping to get a response before his Saturday morning ferry ride back over to the island.

But a reply never came.

CHAPTER 15

As soon as Piper stepped onto the front porch of Tom's mother's house, relief welled up in her like water filling a pot. Arlene was challenging to visit on her best days — and this day was certainly not that. She'd been in one of her talking moods and regaled Piper on everything from the argument she was currently in with Tom's grandfather Herbert (who'd been dead for twenty years) to the proper way to set a formal dining room table ("The edge of the butter knives must turn in toward the plates — you young people have no decorum") to the origins of the metal cell tower being built just outside of town ("It's the Russians! And everybody's just letting it happen!"). Piper loved her mother-in-law — she tried to visit at least every other day, and she and Tom took dinner over twice a week — but she was exhausting, at best. Arlene, who'd once been an energetic, with-it woman, had been on a downward slide ever since Tom's father had died six years earlier. But at least she hadn't been slurring today, which Piper hoped meant that Dr. Khari and Lady Judy had both taken her last conversations with them to heart.

Piper turned a corner, startled as a body collided with her knees. "Watch it, Bobby," she said, reaching down to set him upright.

"Sorry, Pipes!" he said, readying to take off again, with barely a glance at her.

"Hey, where are you headed in such a hurry?"

"Home. Ma says I have to finish my chores before I can play with this." He held out his pudgy hand, which clutched a plastic grocery bag, hard angles straining against its seams.

"What is it?"

"A camera!"

Piper cocked her head. Bobby's family was one of the poorest, if not *the* poorest, on the island. He went barefoot not because he hated wearing shoes, but because he likely didn't own a pair. "Where'd you get it?"

"Anders. I've taken more than a hundrit pictures! But they're stuck on here. He said he'll help me get 'em off."

"He did?"

"Yep. See ya!"

Feet rooted to the ground, she gaped after Bobby's fleeing form. Not many people surprised Piper. But in the weeks since first stepping foot on this island, Anders was proving to be nothing if not unexpected. She thought after that first adventure — the way he looked trudging back up the dock, sunburned, covered in muck, and missing a shoe (one shoe! — she had tried to paint the picture for Tom and Mrs. Olecki that evening but dissolved into giggles every time she attempted it) — that he'd leave this island for good and never look back. But she had to give him credit. He kept coming back for more. And there was something oddly charming, or at least admirable, about someone being so willing to make such a fool of himself at any cost.

And then there was the way he had begun pitching in — hauling old crab pots down to the incinerator for BobDan, mowing Lady Judy's lawn, and now this gift for Bobby — it was nothing short of . . . kind. But what she couldn't possibly understand was *why* he was doing all of this. For a silly old podcast? Yes, climate change was impor- tant, but Anders himself had said — and Mrs. Olecki confirmed — that he had a nearly nonexistent audience. What did he think he was going to accomplish that the

227

New York Times itself couldn't? Nobody on the mainland cared about what was going to happen to their island, that much Piper knew for sure. The question was: Why did Anders seem to care so much?

Movement in her peripheral vision caught her eye, and Piper looked up, surprised to see she'd already made it to Lady Judy's house while her mind was wandering — and further surprised to see Anders standing a few rungs from the top of a ladder at the side of her house, muttering under his breath as he clearly struggled to scrape the paint off the hundred-year-old window frames.

She stood staring up at him, as if his physical body might somehow offer clues to who he was and what he was doing here. A few wiry muscles she'd never noticed before flexed in his upper arms as he wielded the scrape, beneath skin that wasn't quite as pale as when he'd arrived, the contrast with his freckles less apparent. It seemed work on the island was agreeing with him, too. It wouldn't be long before he was as bronzed and sinewy as Tom.

As Piper appraised him, Anders paused in midscrape and leaned forward on the ladder, peering in the upper window of Lady Judy's house, eyes widening with each passing second. Piper froze — what was he, some kind of creeper? And then she realized exactly which room he was looking in, and a grin replaced her frown as she understood why he was so captivated.

"Whatcha doing?" she said loudly, and Anders startled, dropping the putty knife in his hand.

"Jesus. You scared me." He glanced back at her.

"Sorry." She bent over to pick up the knife and he carefully climbed down the ladder rung by rung until he was close enough to retrieve it from her grasp.

"Thanks," he said, and made to retrace his steps.

"Wait."

Anders paused.

"I ran into Bobby. That was real nice, giving him that camera."

Anders shrugged. "I didn't use it much."

She couldn't put her finger on it, but he seemed different today. There was a hard edge about him.

"You OK?"

He hesitated, as if weighing how to answer, and then jerked his head once. "No. I had a bad week."

Piper waited, wondering if a beloved pet had died, or he had a fight with a friend, or maybe even a breakup —

"My podcast isn't . . . going well."

"Your podcast," she repeated, blinking.

"I'm doing all of these things you're telling me to do, but I still feel like an outsider. Like everyone's keeping me at arm's length. No one will talk to me. Not about anything important, anyway."

"You *are* an outsider."

"I know I am, but . . ." He sighed again. "Never mind."

He climbed back up the steps as Piper chewed her lip. She had about a hundred questions but settled on one. "Hey. This podcast means *that* much to you?"

"Yeah," he said, his eyes as plaintive as his voice. "It does."

And she heard it then. The wanting. Up until that point, she may not have understood anything about Anders. Why he was really on this island. Or so hung up on a podcast, of all things. But *wanting.* Well, that was something she was familiar with — something she knew down to her bones. And in that instant she made a decision. She knew Tom would tell her she was being too nice, but she didn't care.

She nodded. "When you're done here, meet me at my house."

■ ■ ■ ■

Forty-five minutes later, Anders stood on the top landing of Piper's carriage house, wiping a sheen of sweat off his brow and inhaling through his nostrils in an attempt to slow his galloping heart. After Piper's unexpected invitation, Anders had scrubbed that window at lightning speed, nearly forgetting his curiosity about Lady Judy's strange room stuffed floor to ceiling with unopened boxes and packages on one side and a full wall of liquor and wine bottles on the other. Alcohol! On a dry island. He couldn't think about it now, because Piper was finally going to let him interview her. He could feel it. He could also feel a slight pinch of conscience for allowing her to continue laboring under the belief that he was solely focused on climate change. But as quickly as that cropped up, he swallowed it down, burying it as deep as it would go. This could be it — the big break his podcast needed. The thing that would reengage his listeners. And if not, well — he promised himself this would be it. He would quit. Leave Frick Island and Piper and their collective strangeness behind.

"Oh! I didn't expect you so soon," Piper

said when she opened the door. "Come in."

Anders stepped across the threshold, as if he'd just been invited into the Sistine Chapel. His eyes quickly adjusted to the dim light, and he darted his gaze around, committing to memory every detail in the dollhouse-like room — the tiny table with two ladder-back chairs, the round-edged minifridge and mustard-yellow half-size oven in the galley kitchen, the pewter crab wall clock — so he could properly paint the picture of Piper's house for his listeners. When his head panned to the wall on his right, he yelped, nearly jumping out of his skin.

Piper flicked her gaze to the literally hundreds of insects splayed and pinned under glass and hung on the wall, and then her eyes widened as if seeing them for the first time. "Oh. Guess I should have warned you about that. Forgot you don't like bugs."

Anders clutched his shirt, trying to slow his breath. When the initial shock finally passed, he cleared his throat. "No, it's not that. I was just alarmed to find that we have the exact same interior designer." He gestured to the bug displays, trying not to flinch. "She assured me my wall of dead insects was original and now I have to call and get my money back."

He grinned, so utterly pleased with himself that he had finally — *finally* — come up with a witty retort on the fly in front of Piper, but when he glanced at her, she was just staring at him, solemn. His face fell for a beat, until Piper opened her mouth in a burst of delighted, albeit belated, laughter.

Anders's pleasure at his cleverness returned twofold — or as pleased as he could feel in a room teeming with dead insects, anyway.

"Give me five minutes. I've got to go change."

Anders watched her disappear through the only other door in the room, which he presumed led to a bedroom and bathroom. Then he shoved his hands in his pockets and purposefully strode forward, suppressing a shudder and giving the vermin morgue a wide berth.

He skirted the sofa and stepped right up to the floor-to-ceiling bookcases, books stuffed in every which way like a game of disheveled Tetris, except for one shelf that held a record player and about fifty LPs. He casually flipped through them, not recognizing nearly any of the obscure bands, and then moved on to the books. He often thought bookshelves could tell you more about a person than the inside of their bathroom cabinet. This one was no different. There were the expected dry science titles — like *Field Guide to Chesapeake Bay Insects* and *Dragonflies: Behavior and Ecology* — and heavy classics mixed in with paperback mysteries and romances.

Then Anders spied a spine that gave him pause: *For Whom the Bell Tolls.* He plucked it from the shelf and eyed the cover, thumbed through the worn pages. It was an old edition, one that had clearly been read multiple times in its life. He flipped to the famous epigraph penned by John Donne, knowing what he'd find, as he'd had to memorize it in his tenth-grade English class.

No man is an island. The email handle of the mysterious missive he'd received weeks ago.

"That's one of Tom's favorites."

Anders jerked at the voice and looked up at Piper.

"I couldn't get through the first chapter, I don't think."

He blinked, and glanced back down at the book. *Tom's favorite.* Well, clearly *he* wasn't the anonymous emailer. Unless he'd found a way to type from beyond the grave.

He slid the book back in its rightful place.

"Come on, let's go."

"Where are we going?"

234

Piper side-eyed him. "I know you're a reporter, but you've really got to stop asking so many questions."

And that was how Anders ended up on a dead man's bicycle following Piper down the windy deserted path toward Graver's Beach.

The cracked paved road was flat, flanked on both sides by seagrass as tall as cornstalks. And though Anders knew the island was only 1.2 miles long, the road meandered for what seemed like miles, an unending maze, until finally — after twenty minutes of pedaling — the seagrass gave way to flush marshlands. Anders, sucking in deep lungfuls of air and sweating liberally, opened his mouth to ask how much farther, when Piper stopped, dismounting from her bike in one swift motion and setting the kickstand with her foot. Anders gratefully followed suit, although with much less grace.

He followed her along a footpath, around a bend, until they were dumped out on a rock-studded sandy expanse of land, dwarfed only by the never-ending breadth of sea lapping on its shore. Piper kicked off her shoes and led him to the middle of the beach, where she sat on a flat cloud-gray rock and patted the space beside her.

Anders hesitated before sinking beside her. He didn't know why they had to come all the way out here to do the interview, but Piper had told him not to ask questions and he thought it best to follow her directive, so as not to ruin his chances.

He waited for her to say something, but she just pleasantly stared at the water. So he took it as his cue to dig the recorder out of his pocket and set it discreetly between them, pressing the record button.

"I'm just gonna . . ." he said quietly, motioning to it.

She turned to look at him and then the recorder. She rolled her eyes before reaching for it and clicking the stop button.

"Wait! What are you —"

"I didn't invite you here for an interview."

"But I thought —"

Piper broke eye contact, jerking her head to Anders's feet, as if just noticing them. "Why do you have your shoes on?"

"I always wear my shoes."

"At the *beach*?"

"Well, I don't really go to the beach, if I can help it."

She stared at him incredulously, and then shook her head, muttering. Before he knew it, she had deftly reached down, grabbed his left shoe with both hands, and jerked it off his foot.

"Hey!" he protested, as she did the same with the other shoe, and he was left with his legs sticking straight out, his heels hanging inches from the gray loamy sand.

"Now put your feet down."

"No."

She cocked an eyebrow and Anders wondered if she'd been taking lessons in intimidation from Mrs. Olecki. Regardless, he would have protested again, except his thigh muscles had started quivering and he wasn't sure how much longer he could keep his legs hovering in the air. So he let them drop, making a disgusted face when the mushy, mud-like sand rose up to greet the sides of his feet, sliding between his toes.

"See? How does that feel?"

"Gritty. And slimy."

"I know," she said, sighing. "It's wonderful."

They sat in silence, Anders wondering what on earth Piper had brought him out here for if not for an interview, and how much longer he'd have to keep his feet in the sludge. When he finally opened his mouth to ask, Piper beat him to it.

"Better now?"

"What do you mean?"

"This is where I come whenever I'm

upset. Being out here . . ." She swept her arm at the craggy rocks, the sand, the water. "It helps."

They sat in silence for a few more beats and Anders stared out at the sea, watched as a seagull dove into the water in search of a fish but came up empty. He studied Piper from the corner of his eye, her face turned up toward the sun like a morning glory. Eyes closed. Peaceful. Content. Suddenly she opened one and caught Anders looking at her.

"You're still thinking about your podcast, aren't you?"

Guilty. Anders didn't respond, but apparently his expression was all she needed.

She closed her eye and sighed. "You can interview me, if you want."

"Really?"

"Yeah, why not?"

He had so many questions about her, her life, they swirled around in his head and he wasn't sure what to ask first. And wasn't sure he'd get the opportunity again. He pushed the on button on the recorder, and when it blinked red, he began.

"OK, you said you moved here in the sixth grade. What do you miss the most — about living on the mainland, I mean?"

"What do you mean?"

"I don't know — fast food, movie theaters, *driving.* Do you even know how to drive?"

"Not really. I tried on Bill's truck once but never could get the clutch part down, so I quit. And let's see . . . what do I miss?" She was silent for a few beats. "Oh! Girl Scout cookies."

"Girl Scout cookies."

"Samoas, specifically. A troop used to sell them outside the Food Lion in Winder and BobDan would pick up a few boxes for me, but they haven't been out there for years."

"So not technology or museums or concerts — wait, have you ever been to a concert?"

She shook her head again and Anders gaped at her. Not that he particularly loved concerts himself. He found them overly loud and hot and there were far too many people singing along with the words, when you hadn't paid to hear other people, had you? You paid to hear the person who originally sang the songs. But still, to never have actually had that experience in real life . . .

And then he remembered her record collection.

"Hey, tell me about your records."

"What do you mean?"

"They're just so . . . random. I've never

heard of most of the bands. I don't know —
I guess I took you for more of a Taylor Swift
kind of girl," Anders teased.

Piper's brow crinkled. "Who?"

Anders jolted, rounding on her. "You've
never heard of Taylor Swift?"

Unfortunately for him, when Kelsey was
in middle school she played "Shake It Off"
on rotation until the entire family was
begrudgingly humming it every waking
minute and ready to strangle Kelsey — and
Taylor, come to think of it. But even if
Kelsey hadn't been obsessed, Anders still
would have *heard* of her. She was ubiqui-
tous, like McDonald's or cold sores.

Piper's face remained frozen in confusion
for a beat and then melted into a lazy grin,
her dimples deepening. "Of course I have.
Just a little Frick Island humor."

She giggled as Anders groaned, tossing
his head back and half chuckling. When he
righted it and looked out at the water, he
felt something — a loosening — as if all his
muscles had been tightly holding on to a
tug-of-war rope and then just . . . let go.
The sand was still gritty and slimy. The rock
beneath his butt, hard and uncomfortable.
But the sun warming his skin, the repetitive
lapping of waves, the tang of the salt air filling his nostrils . . . Anders had to admit,

there was something soothing about it all. He sucked in a lungful of air and exhaled slowly, his breath joining the light breeze. He had a brief moment of understanding — of why people might like being on this strip of land. Not for good, of course. But visiting, perhaps, wasn't so bad.

He glanced back at Piper's profile. "What about your mom?"

"My mom?"

"Is she really in Australia?"

"Yeah."

"Do you miss her?" What he really wanted to know, but had no way of asking, was: Did her mom *know*? About what happened to Tom? About what was going on with Piper? How could she stay halfway across the world when her daughter so clearly needed her? Or needed *somebody*.

Piper turned and looked Anders squarely on. "I thought your podcast was about climate change."

He swallowed. "It is."

She raised one eyebrow.

"*And* the island. I'm trying to give listeners an idea of what life is like out here."

"What my life is like?"

Anders paused, a pit forming in his stomach. He cleared his throat to respond, but Piper beat him to it.

241

"I know what you're doing here," Piper said, her voice quiet.

Anders went cold, every single muscle in his body immediately constricting at once. "You do?" He tried to gauge the anger in her voice, but it was impossible. Had she heard the podcast? He had passed the cell tower construction — it wasn't even halfway done yet. But maybe she'd gone to the mainland, listened to it there? Was that why she had brought him out here — to scream at him in private?

"Yeah. You're not the first person to do it either."

"What?" Anders was genuinely confused now.

"All kinds of people have come to Frick Island over the years. Most of them stay a weekend, gawk at our quaint, outdated lifestyle, and never return. But every once in a while you get one that comes back. Or stays longer than he expects. Or never leaves at all."

Anders wasn't sure where she was going with this little speech, but he nearly choked on his words, he was so eager to assure her there was no risk of him *moving* here. Piper wasn't finished.

"They come from all walks of life — young and old, Ivy League educated, union workers — it doesn't matter. There's one thing they all have in common." Piper paused and Anders leaned forward despite himself. She turned and looked at Anders full-on. "They're running from something."

There was no malice in her expression, no judgment at all, really. Her face was bare, eyes sharp and shiny, and Anders found himself momentarily stunned by the visceral reaction he had to her full attention. There was something in the way she was looking at him. As though she could really *see* him.

"Running," he repeated.

She gave a small, barely perceptible nod, kindness and understanding pooling in her eyes, and Anders had the overwhelming desire to tell her things. Which surprised him, as Anders hadn't ever wanted to tell anyone anything in his life. Not anything important or meaningful, anyway. He preferred to keep his thoughts locked up tight in his brain, where they belonged.

Instead, he broke eye contact and chuckled. "You think I'm running," he repeated. "Did you even *see* me?" He gestured with his thumb back toward the path. "I got winded on a bike ride."

Piper half grinned and then abruptly stood, brushing off the back of her shorts. "I've gotta go. Tom should be getting in anytime now."

"Wait! I have more questions."

"I assume you'll be back next weekend, yes? You know where to find me." And with that, she turned on her heel and walked off. Anders searched his brain to find another reason to call her back, but came up empty. So he just watched her go, until she disappeared behind the dunes.

He turned his face up to the sun and closed his eyes, waiting for the pleasant feeling to overcome him once again; the loosening of limbs, the tranquility pooling in his belly. It was confounding because the same sun baked his skin, the same slurping of the waves filled his ears, the same hard granite pressed against the bones of his backside.

But the feeling never came.

Chapter 16

A cool breeze blew through the open window in Anders's room on the second floor of the bed-and-breakfast. The temperature, for once, was perfect. The bed, comfortable. Anders had even gotten used to the dead quiet of the nights, but he still couldn't sleep. He should have been on cloud nine for finally getting to interview Piper. It was nothing mind-blowing, of course, but it was a step in the right direction to make the next episode better. Problem was, Anders wasn't entirely sure he should make another episode. When he started, Piper had been a subject; an interesting character in an improbable story. But something changed on the beach, and instead of a character, a subject, he started seeing her for what she was — a person. An insect-loving person who was suffering from a bizarre delusional disorder and had terrible taste in Girl Scout cookies (everyone knew Do-si-dos were superior), but a person nonetheless. And being less than honest with her about the main focus of his reporting had grown from a pit in his stomach to a bowling ball. People were starting to lose interest anyway, he reasoned, and it wasn't as if he had some new bombshell to add to the story. Perhaps it was time to move on.

Except, Anders didn't want to move on. And therein lay the rub.

When the long hand of the clock ticked to 12:42, tired of tossing and turning, Anders slipped out of bed and stood at the dark window. The moon bathed the calm bay waters in a stroke of broken white light. And Anders had the sudden urge to be closer to it. To see it without the barrier of the window. He shoved his bare feet in his canvas slip-ons and opened the door to his room, stopping abruptly when the hinges let out a loud squeaky groan. He strained to hear any movement, and after deciding it was safe, he pulled on the door again, but this time moved at a glacial pace. When he finally eked open a large enough crack to pass through, he crept out into the carpeted hallway, then down the stairs.

It wasn't only that he didn't want to wake anyone. It felt clandestine — to be out and about this late. As if there were a curfew on the island and he was breaking it.

Once outside, he crossed the dark one-lane road that ran in front of the bed-and-breakfast and stepped onto the grass on the other side of it, walking up to the edge where the water kissed the land. As he stood there, in his plaid pajama pants and a worn T-shirt emblazoned with the logo of his college newspaper, staring at the glittering water and inhaling the briny air tempered with the scent of earthy grass, he tried to clear his mind but found it impossible.

A breeze came off the water, tugging at him, and Anders tore himself away from the view and followed it, thinking a walk might be just what he needed to help him sleep.

The bright moon and stars the only things lighting his path, Anders meandered up the one-lane road to the main street of town. If he thought Frick Island was desolate during the day, it was nothing compared to the dead of night. It was a strange feeling, to be so fully alone, every storefront, every house he passed dark and locked up tight.

Or was he? A movement up ahead in the dark caught his eye. He stilled, trying to focus. It was a figure, a person wearing dark clothing, but Anders couldn't make out much more than that. Out of curiosity — and without making a conscious decision to do so — Anders began walking in the same direction the person went, toward the marina. As he closed the gap, he squinted, trying to make out a face, but it was too dark, and the person's head was obscured beneath a ball cap. Anders paused when he reached the broken-down Chevy in front of the One-Eyed Crab, and thought about calling out, making his presence known, so if the person turned around, Anders wouldn't appear creepy in his lurking. But something about the way the man — at least he thought it was a man — was walking, furtively, with nervous glances to his right and left, kept Anders silent. And made the hair on his arms stand on end.

Anders stood still, watching as the figure quietly approached the boat on planks. Tom's boat. The man swiveled his head, looking around once more, causing Anders to quickly duck farther into the shadows of the restaurant.

What is he doing? Anders wondered, as the man stood at the boat, studying it. He walked slowly down its length, running his hand along the side, over the wormholes Piper had pointed out, as if he were assessing the damage. And that was when Anders noticed the object in the figure's hand. He squinted, the moonlight just enough to make out the shape of a hammer.

Oh. Maybe he was going to fix it up, as a kindness for Piper; a surprise, he thought, just as the guy cocked his arm back as far as it would go and drove it forward with force, slamming the hammer into the side of the boat with a dull thud.

Anders blinked. If this was part of fixing the boat, it was a process he was unfamiliar with. He almost stepped out to say something, to ask what exactly the person was doing, but something stopped him. Anders didn't like confronting people in general, much less men sneaking around under the cover of night holding hammers.

So he stayed put.

The man hit the boat once, twice, three more times, leaving the hull looking a sight worse than before, the wood cracked and splintered and even further beyond repair. Then he tossed the hammer onto the ground and, using the planks as steps, heaved himself up over the side of the vessel, disappearing into the cockpit.

Anders waited, dumbly, as though he were watching a television drama and had to find out what happened next. As he stared into the darkness, the stillness of the night was suddenly pierced with a deafening noise. A squawk of sorts, but it appeared to have no ending. Anders looked to the sky, thinking for a brief moment that he would come face-to-face with some kind of prehistoric bird, but the noise was farther away, behind him, somewhere on the island. Just as quickly as the noise started, it was over, and movement in the boat brought his attention back to the man, who had leapt from the craft as if it were on fire, and took off at a sprint.

Anders blinked to clear his vision, which had suddenly become blurred. And that was when he realized it wasn't his vision that was blurred — it was smoke floating up into the night air. The boat *was* actually on fire. And the man was running straight toward where Anders was hiding in the shadows, close enough that though Anders couldn't yet see his face, he could make out the color of the man's hat in the moonlight: green.

With his heart beating wildly, Anders's curiosity bumped up against his natural survival instincts — and the fear won out. Every muscle in Anders's body clenched and he closed his eyes, as a child might to render himself invisible. When he dared open them, the man was gone, out of sight. He exhaled, a short sigh of relief, until he remembered the fire. Turning back to it, it now looked as if the entire marina was

ablaze, the bright orange flames fully engulf-
ing the boat.

"Help," he said, but his voice came out
croaky and not nearly as loud as he anticipated. He cleared his throat and tried again.

"Help!" This time, the full force of his
breath propelled the word into the air, only
for it to be swallowed up by a siren, more
deafening than the loud birdcall.

A *siren*? Anders looked in the direction of
the high-pitched noise, expecting to see a
fire truck, though he had never seen anything resembling a fire station on the island.
Instead, his eyes landed on a gray pickup
truck, its headlights competing with the red
flashing bulb held tight to the roof by the
driver's hand. Anders couldn't make out
who it was, until the truck pulled up in front
of the flames, and he recognized one of the
burly watermen he'd seen at the One-Eyed
Crab and again at the docks. BobDan had
appeared, too, and Anders assumed he was
the one that called the . . . *firefighter* seemed
too strong a word.

They both hurried to the back of the
truck, where a large drum of water took up
the entire bed. The waterman grabbed a
hose and pointed it at the boat, while
BobDan turned a metal wheel, releasing the
water full blast onto the fire, and then put

his two hands on the hose as well, helping to hold it steady. Anders watched, waiting for the fire to die down, but if anything the flames seemed to grow higher.

Against all his better instincts, he unglued his feet from where they stood and ran toward the men. "Hey!" he yelled when he reached them, over the loud spray of the water, the crackle of the flames. "What can I do?"

BobDan glanced his way. "There's another hose over there." He jerked his head toward one of the docks crawling out to sea. "By the third piling."

Anders took off in that direction, but as soon as he turned away from the fire, it took a minute for his eyes to readjust to the darkness, and he didn't see the hose until he was almost on top of it. He turned the spigot as far as it would go and grabbed the nozzle of the hose, running back to the fire. Placing his thumb over the water spout to create a more powerful spray, he directed it at the boat, and though it wasn't much, combined with the force of the first hose, the fire finally started showing signs of backing down.

"Well," BobDan said fifteen minutes later, as the three men stood staring at what was left of the boat, essentially a pile of charred wet wood and smoke. Anders waited for BobDan to say more, before understanding that one word was likely his way — and the only way — of offering his thanks to anyone.

"I'll help you clean this up tomorrow," the waterman said, coiling up the hose on his elbow and shoulder.

"S'alright. I reckon I can handle it."

"Shouldn't we call someone?" Anders interjected, when he realized the men were in no hurry to do anything but pack up and call it a night.

BobDan eyed him. "Who?"

"I don't know, the police, maybe? Someone just committed arson."

BobDan didn't try very hard to conceal a half grin. "Knock yourself out, Barbara Walters. Nearest cop is about twelve miles thataway." He pointed a bony finger to the expanse of water beyond the dock.

Anders's eyebrows shot skyward. "So wait, what — you're not going to do *anything*? Don't you want to know who did it? I saw them — I mean, I didn't see much, but maybe . . ." He thought of the green hat and wondered if it was worth mentioning.

BobDan stared at him a beat. And then responded as if Anders hadn't even spoken. "It's late and I don't know about you fellas, but I'm gonna take these weary bones back

253

to bed."

Anders gaped. "You don't want to even *try* to find out who set your marina on fire?"

"Nope."

"But why not?"

"It doesn't matter. It's over now."

"But what if he does it again? Or something worse next time?"

"He won't."

And something told Anders BobDan already knew who had done it, just like he'd known it was going to rain when there wasn't a cloud in the sky. Or maybe, Anders thought suddenly, BobDan knew because he had *asked* someone to do it. Maybe he didn't know how else to get rid of the boat. And he was on the scene pretty quickly for being dead asleep.

But no — he thought of the furtive way the man skulked toward the boat like he didn't have permission to be there; like he didn't want to be caught. And another thought struck him, as hard as the blow of the hammer in the side of the boat — the waterman's ominous words he'd overheard at the restaurant a few weeks earlier, regarding Tom's death.

It wuddn't no accident.

If Tom's death *wasn't* an accident, fire would be an awfully convenient way to get rid of any evidence.

A chill ran up his spine, as he once again considered the very real possibility that he was in over his head.

And that his listeners were going to love it.

First thing Monday morning, Anders made a beeline for Jess's desk, only to find it unoccupied. He dropped his stuff at his desk and went to the break room, where he found her standing in front of the microwave, arms crossed, eyeing the lit innards of the machine, or more specifically, the pastry centered in the circling tray.

"Was there anything . . . weird about Tom's accident?"

Jess turned her head toward him. "Good morning to you, too."

"Sorry. Morning. So — do you remember anything weird?"

The microwave dinged and she removed the paper plate. She tapped the pastry with her finger. "Shit. Still frozen." After returning it to the tray, closing the door, and pushing buttons, she turned to Anders. "This is about the waterman thing again?"

"Yeah."

Jess blinked slowly and then yawned, in an overdramatic display of boredom at

Anders's prodding. "What do you mean 'weird'?"

"I don't know — did the police do a full investigation? Could someone have tampered with the boat?"

Her eyes brightened with recognition. "Wait," she said, scrunching her nose. "I do remember something about the boat."

Anders leaned forward, every nerve at full attention.

"When they recovered it, they said it had prior damage from some kind of wood pest or something. Maybe caused the boat to take on water faster?"

His shoulders dropped. Piper had mentioned the worms; he'd seen the holes.

"Nothing else?"

"Like what?" Jess said. "It was a storm. A bad one. Mother Nature has capsized bigger boats than Tom's and probably will again."

Anders gave voice to what had been niggling in the back of his mind since Saturday night. "Yeah, but Tom was an experienced boater. He grew up on the water. It just doesn't make sense. And why wasn't he wearing a life vest?"

"Watermen never wear life vests."

Anders thought of Kenny and Jojo. That much was true, at least.

"Why are you so hung up on this? Is it for that podcast thing you're doing? Sorry I haven't had a chance to listen to it."

"Yeah," Anders said, and ran a hand through his hair, smashing down the cowlick at his crown out of habit. "It's just that I overheard something. On the island. Something about Tom's death not being an accident."

"Really?"

"Yeah," Anders said. "And that's not all." He caught her up to speed about the boat, the fire. "Something just doesn't feel right about it. Any of it. I can't put my finger on it."

"You saw someone commit arson," she deadpanned. "I'd say that's probably what doesn't feel right."

"But why would they do it? Unless they were trying to cover up something?"

"I don't know. But I can tell you it was a cut-and-dry case. I've got the police report somewhere. I'll dig it up for you if you want."

"Thanks," Anders said, his cell buzzing in his pocket.

The microwave dinged. "Dang it! You made me overcook my strudel."

"Sorry," Anders said, glancing down at the screen. Kelsey. He was tempted to silence it, but he knew he couldn't get away with ignoring her texts and calls for much longer. Walking back toward his desk, he swiped his thumb across the screen.

"Well, you *are* alive. I'll call off the search party."

"Sorry, Kels, I've been busy."

"Too busy to *text*? My, Nowhere, Maryland, must have more breaking news stories than I expected."

"What do you need?"

"I don't need anything. I just thought you might like to know I got a part."

"In a *movie*?"

"Yes."

"Seriously?"

"Well, you don't have to act so surprised. Guess who's starring in it!"

"Who?"

"Guess!"

"There are literally thousands of actors and actresses. I'm not going to guess."

He could hear her frown over the phone and then: "Dwayne Johnson!"

Anders paused. "Who?"

"You know, The Rock!"

"The wrestling guy?"

"I mean, that's how he started, but he's kind of a huge deal as an actor now."

Anders thought that sounded familiar —

he could vaguely picture movie posters with The Rock at the forefront and large explosions in the background. "That's really great, Kels."

"Thanks. I mean, it's just one line, but I'll be in the credits! Girl in the Diner, Number Three. And, I'll be on the same set with *Dwayne Johnson.*" Anders could hear the pride in her voice. "Now, what have you been doing, besides avoiding us?"

"Working, I told you. I've been doing this podcast —"

"Oh, right! Dad said it's really good," Kelsey said.

Anders's eyes widened. "He did? He's listened to it?"

"Yes," she said, with a touch of surprise. "Haven't you seen his comments?"

"Oh, right. Of course."

"He's been telling literally everyone he runs into in the course of a day about it. Seriously — he made the gas station attendant yesterday promise he'd listen. Oh, and Celeste! I forgot to tell you we ran into her!"

"You did?" Anders paused, waiting for the requisite hollowing of his stomach or shadow of sadness to creep over him, as Kelsey droned on about spotting his ex across a crowded hibachi restaurant, but nothing happened. And it occurred to him — not unpleasantly — that he hadn't thought about her in weeks.

"Look, I really do need to go. I'm at work."

Anders hung up and stared at his phone for a beat, his mind back on his dad — not Leonard, of course, but his real dad, who still clearly had not listened to any of his podcasts. Who he hadn't even heard from in months. As he was swallowing his disappointment, Jess brushed by him, bringing him back to himself.

"Hey, Jess." He lifted his head so his voice carried over their cubicle divider. "Can you send me that police report when you get back to your desk?"

He had a podcast to record.

WHAT THE FRICK?
EPISODE 7

12,892 Subscribers
54 Comments

Hokie4Life: A murder! OK, I'm back in. [Image: Stephen Colbert eating popcorn]

CHAPTER 17

The Night Before the Storm

Piper stared at her husband as if he had sprouted a third eye. They were squared off against each other, the small kitchen table between them. She shook her head, trying to make sense of it all. "Tom, you can't do it! Not like this."

She had thought they'd put this crazy idea to bed months ago, so it was quite the surprise when he sprung it on her this evening, while she was studiously peering through her microscope lens at the venation in the wing of a dead dragonfly she had found on Graver's Beach that day, trying to determine its exact classification.

"Pipes, I have to, can't you see that? I can't live like this anymore. *We* can't live like this anymore. Do you know how many crabs I caught yesterday? Do you?"

Piper eyed him, her jaw set.

"Not even two bushels. And less than a

dozen peelers."

"Some days are like that. Some years, even," Piper said. "You've seen worse. And you'll see better. It's like BobDan says — crabbing ebbs and flows —"

"Like the tide. Yeah, yeah. He thinks everything ebbs and flows like the tide."

"Well, it does, really, Tom. That's life."

"No! That's not life, Piper. That's what I'm saying. That's an excuse to sit back and do *nothing* — to just let life *happen* to you — like everyone on this island has been doing for centuries."

Piper jerked her head back, narrowed her eyes. In a quiet voice, she said: "That's not fair."

Tom gripped the top bar of the ladder-back chair and leaned over, his knuckles turning white from the pressure. He looked up at Piper, his eyes rimmed red, his face more lived-in than most other twenty-four-year-olds'. "Look, don't you want something . . . I don't know. *More?*"

The truth was, Piper didn't. From the moment she first laid eyes on Tom, she knew he was all she ever wanted. Needed. That if she could just be with him, she'd never want for anything else in life.

"Tom, you're not *hearing* me. People aren't going to just let this happen."

"I know," he said. "That's why I have a plan."

"Yeah, some plan," she scoffed. "I know what it feels like to be a pariah, Tom. I'm not going to do it again."

"A *pariah*? Piper, there's not a more beloved person on this island than you. I mean, people practically bow to you on the street they love you so much."

"Not always. Remember? When I first moved here. It was awful."

"Piper."

"Tom."

They eyed each other, both barely breathing — and neither wanting to give in. Piper cracked first, reverting to her original point. "It's a terrible plan! I told you this two months ago and my feelings haven't changed. People will find out, Tom. And then what? When they find out —" She shivered. She couldn't even finish the sentence. "*Please* don't do this."

"I have to. It's time. And it's the only way."

Piper knew the look in Tom's eyes. It was the same look he got when he woke up in the middle of the night with a fully formed plan for a better scrape design and immediately began drawing it out, or when he turned to her a year earlier, lying on the bottom of his skiff, and said, "We should get married." She'd been with him for eight years, and in that time, she'd learned that when Tom got something in his mind, he moved forward like a speeding freight train that'd lost its brakes. Desperate, Piper grasped for something, anything that could stop him. "Think of your *mother,* Tom. Hasn't she been through enough?"

His blue-gray eyes went stormy. "Piper," he said, her name both a statement and a warning.

"What?" She leveled her gaze at him. "You haven't thought this through — you're not thinking about anyone but yourself."

"Are you kidding right now? You're *kidding.* Everything I do, Piper — everything! — is for my mother. For you. For everybody else in this freakin' town." He clenched his fists tight and raised them toward the ceiling, along with his gaze. Piper could see the veins in his arms, his neck, as he growled at the top of his lungs.

Tom glared at her once more, fire in his eyes, and then he abruptly straightened his spine to his full height and brushed past her, storming out the front door and letting the screen slam shut behind him.

Piper stood there for a minute, his words reverberating in her ears. She traced his steps to the door and stood at the screen, though Tom was long gone. And as much as she didn't want to admit it, she knew Tom was right. He did put everyone else first, starting with her, as if it were encoded in his DNA. There were good men and then there was Tom. He was good to the bone. And that was how she knew, as crazy as his plan might be, she was going to go along with it. She loved him and that was that.

She sighed once more and made to turn back into the house, when a slight movement caught her eye. Peering into the dusk, a form appeared — Mrs. Olecki standing on her back porch with a broom, looking up at Piper with one eyebrow cocked. And Piper wondered exactly how much she had overheard.

CHAPTER 18

On Saturday, Piper paced back and forth, traversing the length of her den in eight short steps, and then turning on her heel to cover the exact same area. Someone had set Tom's boat on fire last weekend. Well, not *someone*. She knew exactly who had done it. And though she had tried to ignore it all week and let it roll off her back, she had woken up that morning with a new rush of anger.

Logically, of course, she knew the boat had been beyond repair. And she had other things to worry about — like how her choices were starting to catch up with her. "Hope you're feeling better," Mrs. Olecki had said two nights ago over her shoulder while hanging laundry, as Piper tried to sneak past her up the stairs to her carriage house. She had lied to Mr. Garrison to get out of work, and should have known word would get around. It always did. "Uh, yeah.

I am," she had replied dumbly, unable to offer an explanation of where she had been.

She knew she needed to just keep her head down. Not rock the boat. But that was easier said than done — especially when people were going around destroying property that didn't belong to them.

And she couldn't pretend for another second that it didn't bother her. Piper knew she had a reputation in town for being perpetually happy, kind, unruffled. And if she was telling the truth, she rather liked the way people saw her. But more recently she was finding — disconcertingly so — that when she was sad or downright filled with rage (like right now), she was having more and more trouble holding it in. She was tired of pretending. And with that, she left her house, letting the screen door slam shut behind her, and stormed toward the docks.

"I'll just put these bags right here." Anders stood in the room adjacent to his own on the second floor of the bed-and-breakfast on Saturday afternoon, trying not to stare at the hat crowning the guest's gray curls, looking more like a dead peacock than a fashionable fascinator. "If you need anything, Mrs. Olecki will be happy to help. Oh, and there's fresh lemonade and chocolate chip cookies downstairs if you're hungry."

"Thank you, dear." The woman smiled, her yellowed dentures poking through her thin lips. "I think I'll take a short rest first."

Anders nodded, and with one last glance at the hat, he ambled down the stairs to help himself to one of the cookies Mrs. Olecki had just taken out of the oven. He'd only been on the island for an hour, but he couldn't shake the jittery feeling he'd had since stepping foot off the ferry and onto the dock. Was he sharing the same tiny strip of land with a cold-blooded killer? It didn't seem possible. For one thing, Jess was right, the police report had seemed pretty cut-and-dry — but still, something didn't add up. Who had set the boat on fire? And why? And what about the rumors in town that Tom's death wasn't an accident? Anders knew he had to be missing something, but he'd rolled the pieces around in his head all week and just couldn't seem to make anything fit.

"There you are." Pearl Olecki's voice cut into Anders's thoughts. "Only take two — the rest are for the guests."

Anders wiped crumbs off his chin with the back of his hand and started to remind her he *was* a guest, but realized he hadn't really felt like one in weeks.

"When you're done, can you help Harold move our china cabinet to the back shed? He's going to sand and restain it. This salt air wreaks havoc on the wood."

"Sure."

She nodded once and then opened the refrigerator and stuck the top half of her body in it. Anders heard the clanking of her moving jars around.

"Hey, can I ask you something?"

Pearl made a noise that sounded like assent.

"Do you ever worry about crime out here?"

While her chest remained perpendicular to the floor, Pearl peeked her head out just enough to look at Anders with eyebrows raised. *"Crime?"* She let out a hoot. "Heavens no." Back in the fridge she tutted, mostly to herself. "Crime. As if we've got drug dealers and street fighters running amok out here. *Crime.* Ha!"

Anders paused at her mention of drugs, remembering Mr. Gimby's senile ranting about a drug ring.

"So there's never been a crime out here? Not even once?" Anders found that hard to believe. Especially when the island had been home to more than five hundred people back in its heyday. There was no way five hundred people could be upstanding citizens at all times. It was Frick Island — not Pleasantville.

"Well, there was that one time," Pearl said, straightening up and shutting the refrigerator door with her hip, a bunch of celery and a head of lettuce clutched in either paw. "Lady Judy got her wallet stolen."

"Really? What happened?"

"She stomped all over this island, in a full-on fit, screeching to anyone who'd listen that whoever had taken her belongings had best be putting it back in its rightful place." The side of her mouth curled up. "And so Preacher Norm showed up on her front porch that evening, wallet in hand."

"A *preacher* had stolen it?"

"No. She'd left it in his house, when she'd stopped by to drop off her offering that she'd forgotten to take to church that morning."

Pearl chuckled and Anders joined in. He took the last bite of his second cookie and chewed, considering his next question thoughtfully. He knew Mrs. Olecki enough to know if he asked anything off-limits it would just shut her down. He decided go for it: "What about Tom's boat?"

He stared at her intently, expecting a reaction of some kind, but she remained unruffled as she ripped leaves of iceberg lettuce apart and dropped them in a bowl. "Oh, you heard about the fire, huh? Yeah, that was terrible."

"I didn't just hear about it. I was there. Helped them put it out."

At this she looked up. "You did? I didn't know that. It's a good thing, I guess. Unlike BobDan to be so careless with his cigarette butts, but accidents happen, I 'spose. Maybe if he didn't try to hide his habit from Shirlene — as if she doesn't know — he wouldn't have to dispose of the nasty things so quickly, but it's none of my nevermind."

Anders stared at her, not hearing her opinionated ramblings. His brain had shorted out, stuck on the first thing she said — BobDan had told everyone the fire was an accident.

BobDan had lied.

And Anders wanted to know why.

Clouds hung low in the sky, painting the town with a dreary brush — making every storefront and house appear even more dilapidated and depressed, if that was possible — and Anders shuddered in his cotton shirt, wishing he'd brought a jacket with him. It was the first weekend in October

and it reminded Anders a little of home —
how the blistering heat of summer seemed
to never end, until one day it was fall, just
like that. And then the cold of winter blew
in right on its heels. Autumn in the south
wasn't so much a season as a stopgap
between summer and winter.

After helping Harold move the china
cabinet (and feeling as though the muscles
of his lower back had ripped apart from
each other like Velcro in the process),
Anders had set out from the bed-and-
breakfast, his stomach rumbling. He had
half a mind to confront BobDan about the
fire, but knew that would get him precisely
nowhere. So he set his sights on the One-
Eyed Crab for a bite and maybe another
conversation with the waiter Jeffrey, who,
while not overfriendly, was the only person
who didn't seem to completely shut down
when Anders pressed him with questions.
He didn't outright answer anything, of
course, but his snide, sarcastic commentary
made Anders think he had a torrent of anger
running just under the surface and might
one day burst.

The door to the post office chimed as
Anders neared it, and Lady Judy stepped
out onto the street holding an armload of
packages so high, it nearly covered her face.

"Whoa. You need help with those?" Anders asked, reaching out for the top one.

"No!" Lady Judy barked, startling him back. "I've got it."

He held up his hands. "OK." He watched as she half hustled, half waddled up the street under the weight of her packages. He stared at her, perplexed. What was she receiving — more wine bottles? Or something else?

A drug-trafficking ring. Mr. Gimby's words floated back to him, unbidden. And then an image: Lady Judy as the kingpin of an island-wide heroin or meth ring — her large bosom straining against a Scarface-like suit, holding two tommy guns and cackling. Chuckling, Anders shook his head, dismissing the ridiculous idea at once.

Anders walked into the One-Eyed Crab, the screen door slamming behind him, announcing his presence. The place was empty save for two faces swiveling in his direction: Jeffrey, whose eyes looked like they could cut glass, and Piper, whose eyes looked like they could laser it all back together.

"Uh . . . hi," he said to the stony silence of the room.

"We're closed," Jeffrey said, cutting his eyes back to Piper.

"Closed?" Anders checked his watch

273

again. It was five minutes after three — an off time for a meal, to be sure, but he didn't remember the restaurant ever closing between lunch and dinner.

"Yep, tourist season is over. Which means locals only." Jeffrey still wasn't looking at him, but Anders got the distinct feeling that Jeffrey wasn't just talking about the restaurant anymore.

"Don't be a jerk," Piper said.

"Wait, is that why you weren't at the wildlife center last Saturday?" Anders asked.

"Yep. Season ends third week in September. A few tourists still trickle over, of course, but everything kind of shuts down after that."

"Oh."

Sue suddenly appeared in the doorway carrying a big stack of freshly laundered bar towels and brightened when she saw Anders. "Oh, hey there. You hungry?"

"Sorry, I didn't realize you were closed."

"It's fine." Sue waved him to come closer inside. "I'm happy to whip you up something. Least I could do for your help with the freezer."

"No, no. I can just go over to the market and find something."

"I'll come with you," Piper said, hopping off the stool. "I was done here anyway." She cut her eyes at Jeffrey one last time. Anders recognized the piercing look from his fumble in the wildlife center and felt overwhelming relief he wasn't the recipient this time.

Once they were a few yards away from the restaurant, Anders spoke first. "What was that about?"

"Nothing," she said, rubbing her arms through her sweatshirt.

"It didn't sound like nothing."

Piper shrugged. "Just Jeffrey being Jeffrey."

Anders knew, from the palpable anger he'd felt in the air, there was more to it than that.

"I take it you don't like him?" he pressed.

Piper sighed. "It's more . . . complicated than that." After a few beats of silence, Anders realized that was all she was going to say on the matter.

When they got to the market, the fluorescent lights were on, but the place was deserted. Anders stuck his hands in his pockets to wait for Mr. Garrison to return, but Piper walked right behind the counter.

"Are you allowed back there?"

"Of course. I work here."

"Really? I thought you worked at the bed-and-breakfast."

"Just in the mornings, helping Mrs. Olecki cook."

"So you have three jobs."

"I guess. But the wildlife center is volunteer, and I just help out at Mrs. Olecki's in exchange for rent. Kind of like you."

She slid open the refrigerator case door and pulled two crab cakes off the ice.

"Oh, I'll probably just have a turkey sandwich."

Piper peered at him over the counter. "The sandwiches are terrible here." Anders had ordered one before, cheap white bread stuffed with packaged deli meat and a square of plastic-wrapped cheese. Still, he thought "terrible" was an overstatement.

"I don't really eat seafood."

"Are you allergic?"

"No. I just don't like it."

"That can't be possible."

"To not like seafood? I think it's pretty com—"

She cut him off. "You haven't eaten the good stuff."

Realizing she wasn't going to take no for an answer, Anders remained silent as Piper moved to the flat metal grill next to the sink in the back. After lighting the fire with the turn knob and squirting oil onto the surface, she slapped both crab cakes on it with a satisfying sizzle.

When they were done, Piper flipped them both onto a paper plate and directed Anders to grab a couple bottled waters and follow her out to the covered porch, where two plastic chairs sat waiting. A light mist filled the air, minuscule raindrops not strong enough for gravity to pull to the ground, giving the whole island an otherworldly feel.

"Here," Piper said, offering him the plate after they sat down. She watched intently as he bit into the crab cake. Anders emitted a small grunt of surprise at the texture (somehow meaty and flaky) and the flavor (salty, buttery, with a hint of sweetness, but no fishy taste to be found). He swallowed. "It's good."

"Good?"

"Yeah," he said, confused at her clear disappointment in his response. "I like it."

"Are you always this enthusiastic about things you like?" she deadpanned.

"Yes."

She laughed. "Oh! I know what you should do for your next assignment."

Anders narrowed his eyes. "You mean I haven't done every single thing there is to do on Frick Island?"

"Not yet. You haven't picked crabs."

"Which is different from crabbing, I presume?"

"It is. You'd have to come Wednesday evening, though. That's when they do it."

Anders considered this. If he could convince BobDan to bring him over after he dropped off the afternoon passengers, instead of catching the noon ferry, he would only have to take a few hours off work.

"I could do that," he said, as a pinprick on his arm grabbed his attention. He cursed and swatted at the feasting mosquito. "These bugs!"

"Oh, don't kill her," Piper intoned. "She's just trying to make her babies."

Anders pulled a face. "On my *arm*?"

"No. She just needs your blood because she doesn't produce enough protein on her own to form her eggs. It's called anautogeny."

Anders wavered between being disgusted and impressed. "Well, tell her to use your blood, then." He scratched at his arm where a bump was already forming.

"You know, I've never understood why people love ladybugs and butterflies —"

Anders raised a finger, effectively cutting her off. "I don't like ladybugs or butterflies."

Piper blinked. "OK, I don't understand why *most* people love ladybugs and butterflies, but not mosquitoes or roaches. It makes no sense."

"It makes perfect sense. Mosquitoes are *parasites*. And roaches —" He shuddered again, not even sure where to begin with how disgusting they were. "Name one redeeming quality they have."

"I'll name five." She held out her pointer finger and began ticking points off. "They're survivors — they've been around for more than 280 million years. They can hold their breath for forty minutes. They play a major role in our ecosystem, converting just about everything they eat into nutrients that nourish growing plants. In China, they're breeding them to help combat their huge landfill problem." She paused, thinking. "Oh, *and* the Chinese believe cockroaches have medicinal benefits, so they eat them ground up in pills or fried."

Anders looked at the crab cake he was about to take another bite of, and lowered it back onto the plate. "Remind me never to go to Beijing."

Piper giggled. They sat in a comfortable silence, watching the mist turn into a dripping rain.

"Why are you here?" Anders asked suddenly.

She glanced at him, arching her eyebrows.

"Because you wanted lunch?"

"No, not *here* here. I mean the island. I know you said your mom brought you over. But she's gone. Why did you stay? Or I don't know — go to college?"

She sighed and turned her face back toward the rain. "You sound just like Tom."

"I do?"

"Yeah, after high school, he was adamant that I leave; go get a degree."

"And?"

"I don't know. This is my home. Everything I know and love. And *he* isn't ever going to leave. Why should I?" She shrugged, as if that explained everything. She adjusted in her seat and her knee accidentally nudged his. Anders felt the sudden warmth of her skin against his and then it was gone.

Well, he did *leave, actually,* Anders wanted to say. Instead he said: "Yeah, but you could always come back."

Piper cocked her head. "You don't really do small talk, do you?"

"What do you mean?"

"Most people chat about the weather. *What'd you do last night?* That sort of thing. But you — you always cut straight to the heart of things. *Why didn't you go to college? Do you miss your mom?*"

Anders paused. He'd never considered that before, but it was true. "I'm sorry. Occupational hazard, I guess."

"No, I like it. I never wonder what you're thinking."

"I wonder what you're thinking all the time," Anders said, and then snapped his jaw shut. Did he have to say *everything* that came into his mind?

Piper let the words hang in the air for a few seconds and then changed the subject. "Tell me about you. What's your family like? Why did you decide to be a journalist?"

For the next ten minutes Anders monopolized the conversation, telling her about Kelsey, his mom and dad — the condensed, easy-to-understand version that made his family sound as idyllic as a Norman Rockwell painting, even if that wasn't quite accurate. Then he explained about Superman and Clark Kent.

"Wait — you've known what you wanted to be since you were five?"

"Yep."

"And you never once wanted to be anything else."

Anders considered this. "I guess that's not entirely true. There was a full month in the fourth grade when I wanted to be a B-boy."

"A what?"

"You know, a break-dancer?"

"No." Piper's jaw went slack, her eyes round. *"You?"*

"Yeah. It was the first year *America's Got Talent* came on TV — you know that show?" Piper nodded. "They had this break-dance group that was amazing and I decided I was going to learn how. I watched a lot of YouTube videos and practiced in the mirror every night. I thought I was pretty good, too — until the talent show, when the entire audience erupted in laughter, quickly shattering my B-boy career dreams."

"Aw." Piper clutched her heart. "That's terrible."

"To be fair, I don't think they were trying to be cruel. I'm pretty sure they thought I was doing a sketch comedy routine."

Piper laughed and then sat up a little straighter in her chair. "Well, go on, then."

"What?"

"Show me some of your moves."

"Ah, no. Absolutely not."

"Please?"

"No. I literally haven't danced since. I've never even watched the video."

"Video. There's evidence?" Piper's entire face brightened at the prospect. "Oh, I *really* need to see that."

"Well, fortunately it's probably somewhere

in my parents' basement, never to see the light of day."

"I would pay *so much* money. I can't even picture you as a child, much less a *breakdancing* child. You seem like one of those people that was born as an adult."

Anders absorbed the observation. It wasn't far from the truth — he'd always felt different from his peers. Older in some way. But he was done talking about himself. They sat in comfortable silence for a few minutes, Piper with a small grin, at what Anders assumed must be the thought of him breakdancing, and he was glad to have amused her.

"You never finished telling me about your mom the other day."

"If I miss her?" Piper shrugged. "Of course. We email, though. She calls every now and then, but with the time difference and her work — well, we barely talked when we lived in the same house. She's the type of person who gets all consumed by her work. So even when she was here, she wasn't here all the time, if that makes sense."

Anders nodded and, his appetite having returned, picked up the crab cake to resume eating.

"Probably why I had an imaginary friend

as a kid."

Anders inhaled the bite of crab in his mouth and he pounded on his chest, eyes watering.

"You OK?" Piper looked at him with concern.

Anders grabbed the water bottle and unscrewed the top, taking a sip. "Yeah. Yep." He cleared his throat. *An imaginary friend!* "What was her name?"

"Bernadette Gertrude Pinkerton."

Anders sat back in his chair. "That's quite a distinguished name for an imaginary friend."

"She was quite distinguished." She grinned and Anders couldn't help grinning back — that is, until he remembered that his recorder was sitting in his back pocket, having missed the surprising snippet that would have been a perfect anecdote for the podcast.

But even more surprising — it was the first time since sitting down with Piper that he had remembered the podcast at all.

For the next two weeks, Anders redoubled his efforts, determined not to miss anything for his podcast. He started going over to the island on the Friday noon ferry, asking Jess to cover for him with Greta, just so he could spend a few extra hours with Piper at the market. There were rarely any customers — a local would pop in every now and then for a half gallon of milk or a paper sack of flour — so he spent the time asking her questions about the island and climate change and insects while helping her mop or take inventory or rearrange potato chip displays.

And then, side by side, they'd perform her closing duties and she'd leave at three to go meet Tom's boat. Anders wouldn't see her again until Saturday morning, when, after breakfast, she would take him to other hidden spots on the island — places Anders had passed but not given much thought to, like the abandoned schoolhouse that used to house upwards of forty kids during Frick Island's prime or the baseball field surrounded by a rusted, broken-down fence. Every two weeks Mr. Gimby religiously ran over the grass with his riding lawnmower, though Piper said it hadn't seen as much as a game of catch in more than a decade.

She shared other things, too — like how her mother had spent seven years studying the effects of global warming on the island. When she presented her findings along with a $9 million erosion-reduction proposal to the Army Corps of Engineers, they responded by offering half that amount to buy people out of their land and move off the island altogether, saying it was a waste of money to build barriers that sea-level rise would eventually overwhelm. And instead of being mad at the Army Corps, Frick Islanders were furious with her mother.

Piper talked about how the island was dying — and not just because of climate change, but because the residents were literally aging and dying off, without a new generation to take their place. Anders was right in assuming that Bobby, the kid he gave the camera to, was the only child on the island, besides a baby (belonging to Tom's cousin Steve) and the Gibbons twins, who were two years from being full-blown adults and were already looking at moving to the mainland once they graduated. They didn't want to be watermen and there were no other jobs on the island to be had.

Every Monday Anders would record another episode, and despite not having any new revelations — he still didn't know who set fire to Tom's boat or why BobDan lied about it or how Piper's delusion began — the podcast steadily grew in numbers.

He was up to more than thirty thousand listeners (thirty thousand!), and he began to wonder if they were drawn to it for the same reason he found himself drawn to spending more and more time on the island — to hear what else Piper had to say.

Turned out, crazy or not, she was a natural storyteller — animated and riveting — and Anders felt he could listen to her melodic, lilting voice read all 2.4 million words of the United States tax code and never want it to end.

And perhaps that was why, when Piper invited Anders to come over on a Wednesday to pick crabs in the island's cooperative building, even though it meant he'd have to take another day off work, Anders didn't hesitate before saying yes.

At least that was what he told himself, anyway.

It was for Piper's voice.

It was for his podcast.

It was *not* for how when she smiled, her dimples grew so deep it looked like Bill Gibbons had carved them himself with his whittling tool, or how when she got irritated, her nose burned pink and she cried out "son of a monkey!" or "holy barnacles!" or once — when she dropped an industrial-size mayonnaise jar while taking inventory at the store and it splattered all over the freshly mopped floor — "Frank Sinatra!" or how when she looked at him with her big, intelligent cow eyes, it somehow made his insides turn soft as bread dough.

It had absolutely nothing to do with any of that.

Chapter 19

Piper sat on the wooden bench at the marina, thumbing through the worn copy of *For Whom the Bell Tolls,* waiting for a boat carrying a man for the second time that day. This time it was the ferry and Anders Caldwell, instead of Steve's skiff and Tom.

Anders Caldwell. A few months ago she didn't think she'd even remember his name by now, much less be looking forward to seeing him. But she was. Aside from his debilitating neuroses — Who didn't like the beach? Or seafood? Or *butterflies,* for Pete's sake? — she liked how plainspoken he was. Or maybe she just liked how interested he appeared to be in what she had to say. Of course, it was his job to ask all those questions, but having a man truly listen when you spoke — well, she had lived long enough to know that was a rare thing indeed. It reminded her of the beginning with Tom, when he wanted to know every little thing about her, and they would talk breathlessly until the wee hours of the morning, as if the sun might not rise the next day. As if they might never see each other again.

Or maybe it had nothing to do with Anders specifically, and more that she just liked being around *somebody.*

She felt so lonely when Tom was gone. She was used to being a waterman's widow, of course — the nickname coined for the women during crabbing season who knows how many decades ago — but she'd never felt it more than she had this season. Fortunately crabbing season would be over in a few weeks — though she wasn't particularly looking forward to winter either, when everybody holed up in their homes, hiding from the cruel weather.

Or maybe he was just a nice distraction from everything else in her life that seemed to be going awry.

"Piper!" Anders's voice pulled her out of her reverie. She looked up at where he was waving from aboard the docking ferry and stood to greet him, an involuntary smile pulling her lips skyward.

"Hey," he said, after disembarking and reaching her. His cheeks were ruddy from the ride over, his now-familiar cowlick standing at attention. He hopped out of the boat effortlessly — a marked difference from mere weeks earlier, when she sent him off with the twins white-knuckling an orange life preserver — and shouted his thanks to BobDan, who had kindly agreed to bring him over on his return from the 4:00 p.m. run to the mainland instead of the noon, so Anders wouldn't have to miss a whole day of work.

Anders strode toward her and then slowed, his eyes darting from side to side. "Is Tom . . . coming?"

"Nope! This is a women-only activity." She turned to lead Anders away from the dock and he followed. "The men catch the crabs; the women pick them. It's all very 1950s."

"Oh," Anders said, and then abruptly stopped walking, eyes narrowed in concern. "You do know that I'm not a woman, yes?"

The Frick Island Crab-Picking Cooperative formed in the late eighties upon the FDA's shocking discovery that the watermen's wives on the island had — for decades — been steaming and de-shelling crabs in their own kitchens and selling plastic tubs of the unregulated meat to restaurants and grocers on the mainland. They immediately intervened and demanded rules! Gloves! Hairnets! Stainless steel sinks! And more regulations!

So a rectangular building was constructed and all the women started picking their husbands' hauls together and enjoyed the camaraderie so much, they wondered why they hadn't been doing that all along. They didn't wear the required hairnets and gloves, of course, unless an FDA rep came for an inspection, which only happened twice in the forty-plus years since.

"You start with the crab like so." Lady Judy clutched the crustacean in her left hand and a curved wooden-handled knife in her right. "First you peel off the back."

Piper looked on as Anders made sure his recorder was pointed squarely at Lady Judy and watched intently as she narrated her quick movements, deconstructing the crab and popping the white meat into a plastic tub on the table, the same way Piper had watched when she and Tom got serious and he suggested she might want to pick his haul like the other wives. Piper dissected exactly one crab, and though she enjoyed it from a scientific perspective, she had no desire to do it again and decided to leave picking to the experts at the co-op.

Currently those experts included Steve's wife, Jane; three other watermen's wives;

and Pearl Olecki and Shirlene, whose husbands were not watermen but whose fathers were, and they had spent their childhoods alongside their mothers picking crabs and saw no good reason to stop. The women were steadily mimicking Lady Jane's movements, taking crabs apart with a practiced speed that had once left Piper in the same slack-jawed awe Anders was now experiencing. They barely glanced at what they were doing, instead looking at each other as they chatted comfortably about various subjects — their children (who mostly lived off the island), then the disappointing upcoming Halloween season where only one child (Bobby) would be trick-or-treating, which turned into reminiscing about holidays past, when kids would run from house to house with a sock to collect change instead of a candy.

" 'Member that year BobDan came out the house with his mama's pantyhose? Determined to get the most money as anybody."

"He's always been resourceful." Shirlene beamed.

"He was tickled to death with hisself, too."

"Yeah, 'til his mama came shrieking out the front door, realizing what he'd done. It was her last good pair."

Chuckles peppered the air, as Piper watched Anders struggle with his first crustacean — he'd been at it for a full six minutes, enough time for Lady Judy to have dismantled four crabs. And the conversation turned to the construction of the cell tower.

"Should be done in three weeks' time, they said. Then we can all tune in to that podcast of yours, Anders. Like a listening party."

Piper felt Anders tense beside her and wondered if he was nervous picking his first crab under everyone's watchful eye, like she had been.

"Three weeks? That's what they said three weeks ago."

Pearl frowned. "It's the ugliest thing ever been on this island."

"I don't know — 'member ol' Dewey Winkins?"

The ladies howled. Piper caught Anders's eye and he grinned.

"He tried to get his cod in every cave he could find, didn't he?"

"Sure enough did."

Lady Judy looked up. "He never did try it with me."

The ladies howled even louder, as Anders dug his knife into a particularly tough part of the crab's shell. All of a sudden it gave, and the knife slipped directly into the ring finger on his left hand.

"Holy shit!" Anders shouted.

Piper gasped.

The room fell dead silent and every pair of eyes turned toward him. He looked up, stunned, likely from both the exquisite pain in his finger and the sudden quiet.

"Sorry," he said. "I cut my finger."

Piper jumped up and Pearl peered over the table at the red blood dripping down his hand. "Oh, dear. That's gonna need a stitch."

Anders swayed a little as Piper pressed the paper towels she'd retrieved into his hand to stem the flow. "Come on." She took his arm gently to help him stand. "I'll take you to the doctor."

They rushed out into the dark evening. "There's a clinic out here?" Anders asked, as they hurried down the street.

Piper hesitated. "Not really. He's more of a dentist."

"A *dentist*?"

"Well, retired now. We used to have a real physician, but he died a few years ago. Dr. Khari kind of took his place for all medical-related issues."

"Maybe I'll just wait until I get back to

the mainland." They both looked at the paper towel Anders was clutching; even in the dark, they could tell it was soaked through with blood.

"I don't think you can."

Dr. Sandeep Khari had just picked up his steaming chai tea when an urgent rapping at the door nearly made him drop his ceramic cup. He pressed the pause button on the remote, the Dowager Countess's mouth freezing in midbarb (he'd have to rewind that — he hated to miss the full effect of her quick-witted insults), and sat stock-still, mirroring the screen, hoping that perhaps whoever it was might go away.

When he first moved out to Frick Island after a long, exhausting career in the obnoxiously loud bustling city of D.C., he had hoped to live out his years in quiet solitude. He had no idea the impressive letters of a higher degree after his name would inexplicably earn him the business of any and all medical-related questions on the island — from malaise-ridden pets to reflux in babies to opinions on broken fingers and weird skin rashes — and that quiet solitude would be nearly impossible to come by.

The knocking echoed throughout the house again, more rapid this time and followed by a pleading "Dr. Khari?" Sandeep sighed heavily, put his cup down on the sideboard, and went to the door.

"Piper," he said, steeling himself for the same tongue-lashing she'd given him two months earlier, ordering him to stop procuring Valium for her mother-in-law. He had not. He took a deep breath. "I told you —"

"He needs stitches," she blurted out.

Anders stepped forward from the darkness behind Piper, startling Dr. Khari. He'd never met the boy, but he'd seen him before, once at the One-Eyed Crab and again at the market one afternoon. Yet, he knew his name was Anders and he was a reporter investigating climate change for a podcast, because you couldn't go five steps in this town without hearing all manner of other people's business whether you wanted any part of it or not.

To be clear, Dr. Khari did not.

The blood-soaked towel clutched in the boy's hand drew his attention and Sandeep raised his eyes to the sky, pleading with whatever gods would listen for the umpteenth time to send a doctor — a real, degreed medical doctor — to the island posthaste. And then, seeing as how his prayer hadn't been answered yet, and likely wouldn't be answered in the next five minutes, he ushered them both into the house and went to the bathroom to get his suture kit and lidocaine.

It wasn't until the two had been in his kitchen for nearly an hour, and he was halfway through the seven stitches the gash needed, that he noticed. (This wouldn't have surprised his wife, Adhira — God rest her soul — whose subtle and not-so-subtle hints of interest he didn't pick up on for *three* years when they met in dental school.) How Piper's forehead was creased in such concern over his condition, she resembled a shar-pei. Or how she let out a little gasp each time the needle pierced his skin, as if it were entering her own. Or how the boy kept glancing at her sideways (between his howls of pain — the numbing cream only did so much), as if he were afraid she'd disappear without his gaze pinning her to the room.

And Sandeep was a bit perplexed by the interaction, considering this was the same girl currently laboring under the delusion that her recently deceased husband was still alive. But at the moment she didn't look particularly concerned about him.

Oh, well. It was none of his business what went on in this town. After he finished the stitches, bandaged the boy's hand, and sent the couple out into the dark night, he settled back down into his microfiber recliner and picked up his now-lukewarm tea. After a less-than-satisfying sip, he pressed play on the remote, allowing the Dowager Countess to come alive and relishing the fact that he preferred his drama on television, where it belonged.

It was past ten thirty and dark as pitch by the time Piper and Anders silently made their way back to the bed-and-breakfast, like two soldiers just returning from war.

They turned down the lane between the houses, and at the foot of Piper's stairs leading up to the carriage house, Anders finally spoke.

"I'm, uh . . . sorry you had to see that."

Piper lifted her right shoulder and let it drop. "Blood doesn't really bother me."

"I was more talking about the crying? And the . . . squealing. I honestly didn't know my voice could go that high. Oh, and the cursing — I cursed, didn't I?" Anders had nearly blacked out from the pain of it all, and gratefully only had flashes of memory. He had the distinct feeling he'd be a lot more embarrassed if he remembered the whole of it.

"A lot." She nodded.

"Yes. Sorry about that." Anders's eye was drawn to Piper's right hand, where she was absentmindedly massaging her palm with her left thumb. "Oh, God, your hand!"

Anders reached for it, holding it gently in his uninjured hand. "I hurt you, squeezing it so tight?"

Piper wanted to respond — reassure him she was fine — but her breath had suddenly evacuated her lungs. The sensation of Anders's thumb slowly running over her knuckles, gently inspecting each one for damage, caused a jolt of electricity to run up her arm, making the tiny hairs stand on end. As if she hadn't been touched in months. As if she hadn't been touched ever. Piper took a small step backward, taking her hand with her.

"Glad you kept all your fingers," she squeaked, and then quickly turned and took the steps up to her carriage house two at a time.

"Good night," Anders called after her.

She pulled open the door and let it gently close behind her, shutting Anders and his words safely outside. Her eyes immediately scanned the couch for Tom's sleeping form, but he wasn't there. Panic gripped her lungs as she stood frozen with her back to the door. She thought of Anders. Of the warmth

of his hand encapsulating hers. And how —
God help her — part of her wished it still
was.

A noise jerked her head toward the bathroom. A clatter, as if something had fallen
onto the floor. "Tom? Is that you?" she
asked.

Tom, of course, didn't respond.

And as she made her way across the den
toward her bedroom door to check and see
if he was alright, she realized that was the
thing about loneliness. It made you suscep-
tible to doing a whole manner of things you
might not otherwise do.

Dr. Khari wasn't the only person to take
notice of the wildly unlikely, yet undeniable
growing attraction being Piper and Anders.

"Will you get away from that window,
woman?" Harold peered across the room at
Pearl from his comfortable position in their
full-size bed, where he was working on a
sudoku under the lamplight of the nightstand.

Pearl turned to him with that look in her
eyes he'd seen far too many times — the
look she got when she was minding everybody's business but her own.

"It looked like he was trying to hold her
hand!" She peeked out between the gap in

the curtain once more, glancing doubtfully down at the backyard where Anders now stood pitifully alone.

"Good for him," Harold murmured, returning his gaze to the stubborn lines of numbers, searching for the mistake he'd made causing the fourth line to have two threes.

"Do you think? I don't know. What about Tom?"

"I doubt he'll have much to say about it," he replied dryly, right before spotting and quickly erasing an erroneously placed seven.

"Harold! You know what I mean."

Harold brushed the rubber crumbs from the paper and looked up at Pearl once more. Her hands twisted around themselves so vigorously, Harold was surprised she hadn't rubbed her skin clean off.

"You worry too much. Let those children be. They'll figure it out."

But Pearl wasn't so sure. She wasn't sure of that at all.

CHAPTER 20

Two Months After the Storm

Piper woke up with a start on a Sunday in June, blinking at the empty pillow beside her, instead of Tom's familiar face. She lay still as a stone, listening for sounds in the small house, but heard nothing. Where had he gotten off to so early in the morning? They hadn't even had breakfast.

Warmth hung in the air like a preheating oven, even though she'd left a window open for the nighttime breeze. Summer had officially arrived, she thought — a little melancholy at how quickly the seasons seemed to change. Truth be told, she was also feeling melancholy to find herself alone, but she quickly brushed it off. She'd been alone most of her life before Tom came along, especially when it was just her and her mom — and she'd been just fine. What was one morning?

She slipped out of bed and padded to the kitchen to turn on the kettle for tea. While she waited for the water to boil, she ambled around the small room, stopping at her prized display of insects. She stared at the shadow box filled with dragonflies and put her fingers gently on the glass in front of the pygmy snake-tail, her rarest find, with its neon-green body and delicate, tissue-paper-thin wings. She stared at it for a pleasurable beat and then moved along, crossing the room to the floor-to-ceiling bookshelves. Running her hand along the spines of some of Tom's favorite books, she imagined his own fingers gripping the same spots. Then she casually flipped through the records, the rush of memories each one contained playing like a mash-up of movie clips in her mind, warming her belly. She tugged out her favorite one, by the Who, but just as she was about to slip the disc from its sleeve, the phone rang.

Now who could be calling her so early on a Sunday morning? Her first thought was Tom's mother, who had taken to calling more often in the past few weeks. As she crossed the room, the ringing appeared to grow louder, more demanding — convincing her it was, in fact, Tom's mother. She plucked the receiver off its base.

"Arlene?" she said.

But as soon as she heard the voice on the other end, she realized it wasn't Tom's mother.

It wasn't Tom's mother at all.

"Oh," she breathed. She put her hand on her heart, as if checking to make sure it was still there. Still beating. For the first time since the storm, her eyes pricked with tears. "Oh, Tom."

The teakettle whistled, an insistent shrieking, but Piper could barely hear it for the roaring in her ears.

CHAPTER 21

Thursday morning, if the trilling of Anders's 5:00 a.m. alarm hadn't woken him, the throbbing of his bandaged finger would have. He groaned and rolled to his side, slamming his good hand onto the clock to silence the ringing, and then sat up. He was exhausted, but he had to catch the buy boat back over to the mainland so he'd have time to shower and change at his apartment before work.

But by the time he got to the docks, BobDan informed him the boat had left a full hour earlier (Anders couldn't comprehend why anybody on the island even owned clocks, at this point, since they clearly never chose to go by them), and he'd have to wait for the mail boat. He didn't get into the Winder docks until eight, which gave him no choice but to drive straight to the office without stopping by his apartment like he had planned.

306

And his backup plan to immediately get coffee was thwarted when he spotted Greta, standing cross-armed and stern at his desk. "My office. Now."

Anders dropped his bag and, heartbeat speeding up, followed his boss to her office, where she shut the door behind him. Probably not a good sign.

Once they were both seated in chairs across from each other, Greta's desk between them, she opened her mouth to speak, but then sniffed the air, wrinkling her nose.

"What is that?"

Anders sniffed the air, too, the distinct scent of not-so-fresh briny crab juice filling his nostrils.

"Er . . . I don't smell anything," he lied.

Greta's eyes narrowed. "Where were you yesterday?" Before Anders could respond, she waved her hand. "It doesn't matter. What matters is you weren't in the office. And you weren't out on assignment, though that's what Jess tried to convince me of. I haven't said anything the past few Fridays you've cut out early — and yes, I noticed. But a Wednesday? Anders, I can't have that."

"I'm sorry," Anders started, his bandaged finger throbbing in earnest.

"It's not just about the days either. Yes,

you're getting your work turned in, but you're making careless mistakes. I had to field a phone call this morning from Earl on the school board — you misspelled his last name."

She thrust the paper across the desk, her finger pointing at a line in his latest article, and Anders's eyes grew big as walnuts. Anders had used a mnemonic device to remember Earl's last name, Fuquall, by thinking "Fuckall." And now everyone who read the paper knew the way he remembered it as well.

"I don't know what's going on with you, Anders, but consider this your warning. No more leaving early. No more distractions. I know we're a small paper, but we're a small paper that's using a considerable amount of our small budget to pay you to be here. And not *fuckall* of it up."

Anders raised a brow, impressed with her quip, but something told him she didn't expect a laugh in return. "I understand," he said.

"Oh, and Anders?" Greta said, shuffling papers on her desk as he stood to leave. "Take a shower. You smell like you crawled inside a tuna fish can to die."

Back at his desk, Jess peeked over their cubicle divider. "Sorry," she said. "I tried to cover for you."

"It's not your fault."

Jess squinted at him. "Isn't that what you were wearing yesterday?"

In his periphery, Anders saw Hector's head pop up from his desk like a meerkat. His booming voice carried. "Caldwell got lucky?"

Jess raised her eyebrows. "Did you?" she whispered.

"No, I —"

Hector appeared beside him, slapping him on the back so forcefully Anders's chest almost crashed into his desk. "Let's hear deets," he said, before immediately clapping his elbow across his face. "Dear God, man."

"I know, I know." Anders pinched the bridge of his nose. "It's crabs."

Jess let out an involuntary gasp, while Hector took a small step backward, shaking his head. "You gotta wrap it up, dude. That's rule number one."

"No, not . . . I'm talking about *real* crabs. Crustaceans. I was helping —" Anders sighed. "Never mind. It doesn't matter."

Hector slowly backed away and Jess shot him a concerned look before disappearing behind the cubicle. Anders sank into his chair and massaged his temples. He had plenty of headache-inducing problems, starting with the powerful throbbing in his tightly bandaged ring finger, the whole-body exhaustion from rising so early, and the most recent conversation in which he nearly lost his job and only source of income.

But the thing Anders couldn't stop thinking about was the cell phone tower currently nearing completion on Frick Island. He had forgotten all about it until yesterday evening, when the women brought it up at the crab picking.

Three weeks.

Three weeks until anyone and everyone there who so desired could listen to his podcast. Of course technically he knew they *could* have been listening to it all along, using the albeit "painfully slow" Internet connection at the market, but it was clear no one had much interest or had bothered — and even more clear that Anders had become a little too comfortable with that fact. Now it was as if a countdown had been set — he could almost hear the ticking of the clock until the bomb detonated — because he felt certain he wouldn't be welcome back on the island once everyone found out what he was really doing.

And he had so many questions! He still didn't know why everyone was going along with Piper's delusion. Or who set fire to

Tom's boat. And was there really a drug ring on the island? Why did Lady Judy receive so many packages? And who on earth was the anonymous emailer, NoManIsAnIsland?

But something else was bothering him, and it had nothing to do with the story arc of the podcast and whether he could bring it to a satisfactory conclusion. His hands started sweating as he realized that over the past few months he'd been living under a delusion of his own: that the Frick Islanders were never going to hear the podcast he was making. Or if and when they did, he'd be long gone and on to something else. He never anticipated he'd still be there when the cell tower was finished. Or that he'd want to still be there, even after it was done. Or that he'd care so much what the islanders would think when they found out.

And by islanders he meant *islander,* of course.

And by islander, he meant Piper.

Piper.

His stomach dropped when he thought of her listening to it — and not just because she would learn that Anders had been lying to her. But his mind kept drifting to something that therapist had told him in her interview. *It can also be quite overwhelming for them to hear the truth, if they're not ready*

311

— and can cause quite a bit of stress and agitation, which can lead to further deterioration of their mental condition.

Not only might it make Piper hate Anders forever, but it could actually make her delusion *worse*. And Anders couldn't decide which consequence troubled him more.

He pulled out his laptop and opened it on his desk, clicking through to his podcast website, as if it might give him the answers he was looking for. Staring at the screen, he thought of only one: He could delete it altogether. The latest episode had 42,932 subscribers — and though it would be difficult to just erase all his hard work from the last few months, he doubted the listeners would mind too much. There were plenty of other podcasts for them to move on to. And if it meant helping Piper . . .

He froze, replaying that sentence in his head, and wondered why he hadn't thought of it before. He could *help* Piper. He *had* to help Piper. He had been on that island for months and it was clear that no one else was going to do it. There had to be a way to get her to come to terms with her reality, to help her to understand that Tom was no longer alive. It would be hard, of course, but she couldn't go on like this forever — she'd have to face it sometime. And he could be there for her when she did. To comfort her and support her through it.

And *then* once she was facing reality, he could tell her about the podcast and how many other people it could help. And maybe, just maybe, she'd understand.

Or maybe not.

But it was the best chance he had.

Reinvigorated, he sat up and tugged out his cell phone to call the therapist. If he was going to help Piper, he needed to know how. And quickly.

He only had three weeks to do it.

"I don't think I can do this anymore," Piper whispered into the clutched phone Friday morning, her heart thudding in her chest.

"What? What do you mean? We're so close," said the man on the other end of the line.

"I know, but when people find out . . ." She couldn't even finish the thought. She'd been up half the night, thinking about it. Worrying over how mad people were going to be. She remembered the way her mom was treated, after sending her proposal to the Army Corps — the way the townspeople gave her the cold shoulder, glared at her on the street, made her feel as unwelcome as Piper had felt when they first moved there.

The islanders didn't take kindly to betrayal. And what she was doing? It was definitely a betrayal. She couldn't even fathom how she had agreed to it. There were reasons, she knew. Good reasons. But she couldn't remember any of them just now.

"Listen . . . don't make any rash decisions," he said. "Meet me tomorrow. The usual spot. I'll pick you up. Let's talk it out."

"OK," Piper said after a long silence. "I'll be there."

On the ferry Saturday morning, Anders both dreaded and eagerly anticipated what he thought would likely be one of his last weekends on the island. Janet Keene hadn't been overly helpful in her advice on how to treat someone with delusional disorder. "It's really hard to generalize a treatment plan, as it needs to be tailored to the specific needs of the patient. These conditions are very difficult to treat, and may need a mix of antipsychotic medications as well as supportive therapy." Lacking access to antipsychotics, Anders pressed her on the details of supportive therapy. "After building a rapport — which can take weeks, even months — I'd ask questions that gently start challenging the nature of their belief. For instance, using the Elvis example again, I might ask what it was like singing 'Blue Suede Shoes' for the first time or if they remember where they were when they sang it. When they have trouble answering specifics, it can help them start to question their problematic belief."

So that was Anders's plan — to gently ask questions that Piper might have a hard time answering. He wasn't quite sure what that looked like, but he hoped it would come to him.

By the time he finally got to Mrs. Olecki's Saturday morning (he had wanted to go over on Friday and have as much time as possible with Piper, but after Greta's threat of firing, he knew he had to wait), he was a speedball of nervous energy. He rushed in the front door of the bed-and-breakfast, only to find it completely empty. No guests. No Mrs. Olecki. No Harold. He ran through to the back porch and up the stairs to Piper's carriage house. He rapped briskly on the door.

No answer.

He was about to knock again, when a voice from below called his name.

Anders looked to find Harold's head poking out of the shed door. "Something on fire?"

"No, sorry," Anders said. "Was just looking for Piper."

"I noticed."

"It's just that she's always here around this time. We usually . . . hang out."

"I noticed that, too."

Anders paused then, trying to understand the underlying meaning of Harold's words — or if there was an underlying meaning. He ran his palm over his cowlick. Finally, he said, "Well, do you know where she is?"

"Nope. Haven't seen her all morning, come to think of it."

"Oh."

Anders slowly took the steps back down, thinking of where in town he might begin his search for Piper.

"Hey, do you mind giving me a hand?" Harold said.

Anders hesitated, glancing at his escape route up the alley between the houses where he could be on his way to find Piper. Then he looked at Harold, who had been nothing but kind to him, and he dropped his head a bit. "Of course. What do you need?"

Anders spent the entire afternoon prying the rusted-to-the-frames screens from the bed-and-breakfast's windows and replacing them with the storm glass stored in the shed. At every window while he worked, he kept his gaze outward, glancing at the street, the backyard, the alley, hoping Piper would suddenly appear.

"You know, I'm starting to get a little of-fended," Harold said, as they were carrying a stack of screens back to the shed behind the house. "All these months you've been here, and you haven't asked me once what *I* think about climate change."

"Oh," Anders said, a bit dazed. Why *hadn't* he asked Harold for an interview? "Well, I assumed, you know . . . Pearl —" He stut-tered, unsure what excuse to give.

"I'm just ribbing you," Harold said. "Everyone knows that's not what you're here for."

Anders's head jerked up. "They do?" he asked, his heart suddenly pounding in his ears.

"Anyone with two eyes and half a brain" — he paused, cocking an eyebrow — "who's seen the way you look at Piper."

"Oh." Anders's face relaxed. Harold didn't know, after all. But then he looked up at Harold again and squinted. "Wait — what do you mean?"

"Hoo, boy," Harold said, chuckling, and then mumbled something that sounded a lot like: *You're worse off than I thought.*

When they were done with the windows, Anders shot out of the house and walked

the entire length of town three times looking for Piper, to no avail. He even nabbed
Tom's bike from behind the bed-and-
breakfast and rode all the way out to Graver's Beach. She wasn't there either. On the
way back home, he pedaled slowly, as if
she'd step out from behind the seagrass lin-
ing the roads at any second.

She didn't appear.

Not at three, when she should have been
walking Tom back from the docks.

Not at dinner, when Pearl invited him to
help himself to the pot of chili on the stove.

Not after dinner, when she dished out
bowls of apple crisp and turned on PBS,
while Harold sat at the kitchen table dealing himself a game of solitaire.

As the sun dropped from the sky and they
sat watching an antiques expert appraise an
opulently jeweled egg for a hopeful blue-
haired woman, Anders kept one ear out for
any sign of life outside: footsteps, doors
opening, anything that would indicate Piper
coming home. While he was listening, he
noticed something — a full silence in the
house, save for the slow card-flipping by
Harold.

"No guests this weekend?"

Pearl looked over at him. "No. I don't accept reservations from October until April."

Anders's brow crinkled. There hadn't been guests for three weeks' time and he was just now noticing? He must have been more consumed with his podcast than he thought. With the podcast and Piper.

Piper. His knee involuntarily jiggled and Anders felt like he was going to come out of his skin if he didn't say something. "Is anyone else worried about Piper?"

"Worried?" Pearl tilted her head. "How so?"

"She's gone! I searched the whole island. She's nowhere to be found."

Pearl shrugged. "Well, I'm sure you didn't explore the *whole* island. She's probably off in one of the marshes or something. She's always liked to explore."

"In the dark?"

"Sure," Pearl said, as if walking through swampy creeks in the pitch black was as normal as getting a tub of popcorn at the movies. Pearl shifted in her seat and, after a few moments, glanced up at Anders again. They each sat in matching Victorian armchairs, a side table separating them. Pearl leaned slightly over the table, and in a low voice said: "Listen, Anders. About Piper —"

"Pearl." Harold's voice shot out from the kitchen. A warning.

Pearl pursed her lips and straightened her

spine, turning her full attention back to the show, where, alas, the egg was not one of the sixty-nine fabricated in Imperial Russia after all, due to its lackluster hot pink. "Fabergé layered his colors," explained the expert, "giving them a richness that's difficult to mimic."

Anders stared at Pearl's profile. What had she been going to say?

"Do you know where she is?" Anders whispered.

Pearl shook her head but kept her eyes on the screen. And she didn't open her mouth again until the show ended and she and Harold headed upstairs together to go to bed, and with a meaningful expression that Anders couldn't read to save his life, said: "Good night. Sleep well."

CHAPTER 22

Anders blinked into the darkness and glanced over at the alarm clock on his nightstand. It was analog, not digital, so he squinted to try to make out the hands in the shadows — eleven thirty? And then tried to determine what had wakened him. A noise? He had a fuzzy memory of a light plinking sound, but listened carefully and heard nothing now. He closed his eyes to return to sleep when suddenly something hit the window with such force, his eyes popped open at the report and he sat directly up in bed. He stared at the glass, taking in the three-inch spiderweb fissure, then slid out of bed in the dark room and carefully walked over to it, hackles raised, every muscle on alert — but for what he wasn't sure. He stayed on the periphery of the window frame, on the very off chance it was some kind of attack. Perhaps a world war had broken out, and they were attacking Frick Island first. How would he know? It wasn't like his cell got any alerts out here.

He poked his head forward and peered out. Not seeing any fighter jets, he scrolled his eyes downward, until his gaze landed on Piper, lit up by the glow of the back porch light, her shoulders hunched around her ears, her hands clutching her cheeks in a look of dismay. Chalking up the weird buzz in his stomach to relief that he was not in the midst of a battle for mankind, he raised the window carefully, waiting for the shattered glass to fall out of the pane at any second. Fortunately, it held.

"Oops," she whispered, when he stuck his head out into the night air.

"What are you doing?"

"Shhh. Not so loud."

"You want *me* to be quiet?" he whisper-shouted. "You just shattered a window."

She scrunched her nose. "It always works in the movies. How was I supposed to know the storm windows were in?" Her bottom lip protruded in a slight pout.

A grin threatened to pull Anders's mouth skyward, but he forced it to remain passive, remembering his exasperating search for her. "Where were you all day?"

"Come here. I want to show you something."

He narrowed his eyes, irritated she didn't answer his question. Not only had he been waiting around for her all day, but now — in the middle of the night — she just expected him to jump when she said so. And he was even more irritated that he knew he was going to.

"It's really late."

"Are you a senior citizen?" she said, still whispering like they were children playing a game of telephone. "It's not even midnight."

"Fine. Give me five minutes."

"Hurry," she urged.

He was downstairs in two.

Three differences stood out in Anders's second ride to Graver's Beach in the span of seven hours: (1) He wasn't alone. (2) Moonlight, instead of the sun, lit the path in front of him. (3) Despite the cold night air, his thighs burned like fire with the exertion of trying to keep up with Piper.

"Why are we going so fast?" he huffed, the wind tearing through his sweatshirt as if it were made of tissue paper.

"I don't want to miss it."

"Miss what?"

"You'll see."

Anders suppressed a growl, growing progressively vexed at Piper's secrecy — and his willingness to go along with it.

After they dropped their bikes, Piper tossed Anders a flashlight and they took off, picking their way through the rocks on the beach, crabs skittering sideways out of their bright rays of light, until they finally reached a sandy stretch. Piper abruptly stopped and put her hand out.

"Turn off your flashlight. It'll confuse them."

"*Them?* Oh, God," Anders breathed. Knowing her, it was a colony of cockroaches or a cluster of . . . maggots. Or something else equally horrifying.

After their eyes adjusted to the darkness lit up only by the moon, Piper scanned the sand. "There!" she said. "Come on."

Anders tentatively followed at her heels and stopped beside her, mimicking her movement — bent at the waist and peering down into a large patch of sand that looked like it had been messed about by an enthusiastic child with a shovel.

"Shoot. They're gone," she said. "We missed it."

"What did we miss?" Anders whispered.

Piper straightened her spine. "It was a sea turtle nest. We haven't had one out here for two years. And then I found this one a few weeks ago. I wasn't sure, though; it's really late. They usually lay their eggs in May and hatch late summer. So I don't know if the warmer water messed them up or this mom got lost or what. I've been keeping an eye on it, and when I saw the movement earlier tonight, I knew."

Anders stared at her as it dawned on him that she was at Graver's Beach earlier this evening — had he just missed her? How had he not seen her? He opened his mouth to say something, just as movement in the sand caught his eye. "Wait — what's that?"

He squinted as Piper leaned back over and they both watched with bated breath, the grains of sand tumbling to the side, as if pouring out of a broken hourglass. Suddenly, something darker than the sand protruded from the surface. A tiny turtle nose, and then, on either side, tiny turtle flippers.

Piper let out an appropriately tiny squeal. Once it was free of the sand, the turtle struggled to orient itself. When it finally did, it started pushing forward on the sand with its flippers.

"Oh, no, it's listing left. Go straight," she urged, as if the turtle understood English. "It's got to make it to the ocean to survive."

"Should we pick it up?"

"No! We can't touch it or it won't imprint.

Give it space."

Anders had no idea what imprinting was, but he stepped back. The turtle's path skewed more left. "Wait!" Piper said. "I have an idea. Go stand at the ocean and turn on your flashlight!"

Anders did, and whether it was the beam of his light, or Piper's continual gentle prodding and encouragement, the turtle finally found its way down the beach to the water, until it was swept away in a gentle wave.

"Oh my gosh!" Piper said, throwing herself at Anders. Startled, he wrapped his arms around her tiny body, which he could feel vibrating with pure delight, and then he was further startled when he realized he didn't want to let go. She stepped out of his embrace, her face completely flushed with pleasure. "That was amazing!"

Anders would have responded in the affirmative — that it *was* absolutely amazing — but he found he could scarcely breathe, he was so mesmerized by the sight. Not of the turtle making it to the ocean, but Piper's pure joy. Adrenaline pulsed through his veins and his brain scrambled.

"It was," he finally said, finding his voice. "It was amazing."

"Right?" she said, her face so bright, the moon paled in comparison.

And then a thought hit Anders as hard as if Piper had picked up a rock and leveled it at his head. Piper left the turtle nest when she saw them hatching and came all the way back to town . . . for him. "Why did you come get me?" he asked. "Why didn't you bring Tom?"

She frowned, and Anders instantly hated himself for asking. "He was asleep," she said, but Anders could have sworn that her eyes shifted before she spoke. And he thought this might be it: an entrée to gently press her and make her face the fact that Tom wasn't actually in her house. Asleep or otherwise.

"I was asleep, too," he said carefully, while staring intently at her face. And this time he wasn't imagining it — she squirmed uncomfortably, as if her brain was overloaded.

He knew he should change the subject, that if he pushed too hard, it could agitate her unnecessarily and undo the small progress he hoped he was making. But he was like a dog with a bone and didn't want to let it drop. He opened his mouth to ask another question, but she beat him to it. "Let's go make sure there aren't any other turtles left."

Her face had found its light once again,

and Anders found he didn't have the heart to dim it.

Anders and Piper rode side by side back to town at a much more leisurely pace and in a comfortable silence, giving Anders the opportunity to replay the events of the evening, or event, really, as he couldn't stop thinking of Piper hugging him — and the way her body felt pressed against his.

"How's the podcast going?"

Anders slowly turned his head to her. "What?"

He noticed she gripped one handlebar on her beach cruiser loosely, letting her other arm hang casually by her side. She blinked at him, repeating her question. "How's it going? You've been recording so much, but you haven't said how it's doing."

He opened his mouth. And then closed it. The guilt pulsed through his veins and he wanted to tell her the truth. So badly. How he had messed up. Made the podcast about her, without thinking about the repercussions, about how it would make her feel. But he couldn't. Not yet. "It's going well, actually. The last few episodes have been especially good, I think because of you. You're kind of a natural."

"Really?" she said, her mouth turning up

in a half grin. They pedaled in silence a few more feet. And then: "Are you ever going to tell me why it's so important to you?"

Anders crinkled his brow. "What do you mean? I've told you. Because I was born with a single-minded drive to be the most successful journalist of all time. Remember — Clark Kent, *Spotlight,* the whole bit? And now, I've added Sarah Koenig and Julie Snyder to that list — they're the podcasters who created the first *Serial.* It's this whole murder mystery thing . . ." He trailed off when he realized she was staring at him with a cocked eyebrow. "What?"

"Tell me the truth," she said.

And if she had used any other word, Anders might have just brushed it off, changed the subject, but it was as if she could read his mind — could see how badly he wanted to tell her just that. And the least he could do was tell her the truth about this. He squeezed his handlebars tighter and then loosened his grip and sighed.

"It's for my dad."

"Right, you told me that. How your dad is the only one who listens to it."

"No, I know, but . . . it's actually my step-dad, Leonard, who listens to it. It's my real dad that I *want* to listen to it. They were never married — him and my mom. And we don't see him much."

"Where does he live?"

"Chicago. He's a CEO for a logistics firm. I don't even really know what that is, except he strolls around in custom-tailored suits and says things like" — Anders lowers his voice to a deep baritone — " 'Success is walking from failure to failure with no loss of enthusiasm.' "

"Ah," Piper said, as if that explained it all. Maybe it did.

"Anyway." He squeezed the handlebars once more. "Leonard came on the scene when I was around six. Kelsey took to him immediately, even started calling him Dad when it became clear he was sticking around, but I was . . . more difficult. We already *had* a dad — even if we didn't see him very often — and I thought he would be as appalled, *offended,* as I was that Kelsey was calling Leonard that. But when I told him, you know what he said?" Anders half chuckled at the painful memory. " 'That's probably for the best. You could just call me Rob.' "

"Ouch."

Anders nods. "He's kind of a walking stereotype, my dad. And I guess I am, too, because no matter how shitty he is, I still want to . . . impress him or something. For as long as I can remember, all I've ever wanted was to become really successful at something in order to . . . to . . ."

"To earn his affection," Piper supplied gently at the same time that Anders spat out: "To completely rub his face in it." He paused, letting some of his knee-jerk, decades-old anger dissipate. "And yeah, probably to prove I'm lovable or something. I'm sure that's what a therapist would say."

After a few beats, Piper said, "I get that. My dad was married when I was born. Not to my mom."

"Oof."

"Speaking of clichés, she was a graduate research assistant and he was her professor at a university in Kentucky. That's where we lived before here." And Anders found once again, he couldn't picture Piper anywhere but Frick Island.

They both maneuvered their bikes to the right, rounding a corner and then slowing as the bed-and-breakfast came into view.

Piper lowered her voice to a near whisper. "His wife wasn't . . . thrilled, needless to say. But she came around, and I got to spend time at their house some. But I always felt like the fifth wheel. An outsider. Then we moved here. Now he sends cards for birthdays and Christmas, when he remembers."

"Wow. I think you might have me beat," he said, quieting his voice, too. They slowed their bikes, and then both dismounted, walking them the rest of the way to the bike rack at the front of the house.

"In the deadbeat-dad department?" Piper whispered back. "Let's call it a tie."

After racking the bikes as quietly as they could, they both stood with their backs to the house looking out at the water, as if neither one was ready to go inside. "You know," Anders said, "it's amazing we're not both strippers."

Piper's eyes rounded at Anders and then laughter burst out of her. She quickly clamped her hand over her mouth to trap the noise, but it didn't hide her wide smile. Anders grinned back at her, and then found — just like on the beach — he couldn't look away. He was transfixed, glued to her face as though he were seeing it all over again for the first time. Piper dropped her hand and let her mouth relax into an easy smile as Anders's gaze traveled down the slight slope of her broad, sturdy nose, and then to her lips, which even in the moonlight shone shell pink and ripe as a summer peach. He swallowed, trying to ignore the palpable heartbeat in his chest, the adrenaline pulsing through his veins, the all-consuming sudden urge he had to close the gap between them. He lifted his eyes back to hers, searching. She was no longer smiling, but she wasn't unhappy; it was more like she was considering. Waiting. As caught off guard as he was by the moment. And, in retrospect, that was what caused Anders to do a very un-Anders-like thing: He took a chance — though it wasn't driven by choice as much as an inner compulsion. Heart pounding, he slowly tilted his head forward.

"Relationships are complicated," Piper said suddenly, tearing her eyes away from his, turning her head toward the ocean. The spell broken, Anders froze. "Tom has a complicated relationship with his dad, too. Had, anyway. His dad passed a few years ago. When he was eighteen. Did I tell you that? I can't remember."

Tom.

Right.

He straightened his spine and cleared his throat. "Oh. I don't think I knew that. That's awful, I'm sorry."

Piper kept talking at a clip about Tom's dad — how Tom cared about what he thought more than anyone in the world, that was why he became a waterman — but Anders was only halfway listening. The other half was busy berating himself for being so stupid. Piper was married! Or at least, she *thought* she was married. And he . . . ugh. Heat crawled up his neck, as he replayed the moment. He was suddenly glad for the cover of darkness. That Piper couldn't see his embarrassment. Or his disappointment.

Or the dawning realization that perhaps there was another reason he wanted Piper to accept the fact that Tom was no longer here.

CHAPTER 23

It was just after 2:00 a.m. when Pearl, perched in the Victorian chair in her fleece robe and slippers, watched Anders creep past her in the dark living room and tentatively place his foot on the bottom stair.

"You need to be careful there," she said.

Anders gasped sharply and clutched his chest, his eyes wild and groping in the direction her voice came from. "Oh my god, Mrs. Olecki. You scared me."

She kept her piercing gaze on his and pursed her lips. "I don't think Piper's ready for . . . whatever's going on between the two of you."

Anders chuckled nervously and then lied: "What do you mean? We're just . . . friends." Pearl could tell he was lying because he was a terrible liar.

"Mm-hmm."

Anders sighed and Pearl saw the distress cross his face like a cloud. "What else could we be? She thinks she's still married."

Pearl paused and then clucked her tongue. "Yes, well, that girl's always had a very vivid imagination."

Anders rounded on her. "*Imagination?* Is that all you think this is?"

"Keep your voice down," Pearl admonished him.

He lowered his voice and pressed on. "You really don't think it's more serious than that? Is that why no one is helping her?"

Pearl set her lips in a tight line. She was no two-bit gossip and she'd already said too much.

Anders took a step forward, the desperation written all over his face. "Mrs. Olecki, please. You have to tell me. Why is everybody going along with it?"

Pearl sighed. Clearly the boy was smitten, just as she feared. And she supposed he'd spent enough time out here — and with Piper — that he did deserve to have his questions answered. But how could she explain? Especially when she didn't fully understand it herself. "Come sit," she said, resigned. Anders looked at her a beat and then crossed the room, taking the chair next to hers in a mirror image of how they had sat hours before. And Pearl thought back to that morning months ago, a few weeks after

Tom went missing, when Piper waltzed into the kitchen, as if nothing had happened, declaring that Tom no longer snored, and then waltzed out with eggs for his breakfast.

Frick Island, it was often said, didn't have a newspaper because by the time one came out, all the news would already be old on account of how quickly word spread by phone, reaching nearly every one of the ninety-four residents of the island in a matter of hours (or minutes, for really good gossip). Which was why Piper hadn't yet made it to the front door of her carriage house that day before Mrs. Olecki had recovered enough to grab the handset to the rotary phone on her wall and turn the dial seven times in correlation with Lady Judy's number. When Judy picked up, Mrs. Olecki skipped her usual pleasantries. "Was Tom Parrish revived from the dead and nobody thought to tell me?"

"If he was, nobody thought to tell his mother, God bless her soul. I just got back from checking on her — I don't think the poor thing has moved from that recliner for forty-eight hours. Anyway, what are you on about?"

Pearl briefly told Lady Judy about her odd morning with Piper, and when she was done, Judy tutted. "Well, that is quite strange. I suppose we ought to call the doctor."

"Yes, I thought so, too."

Dr. Khari — who was more of a dentist than medical doctor, Pearl admitted — after listening on a three-way call where Mrs. Olecki related the encounter with Piper, took a deep breath. "I'd say it appears the girl is in denial, a quite common stage of the grieving process."

"What should we do?" the women prodded.

Dr. Khari, possessing zero knowledge of psychoanalysis, didn't rightly know, so he did what he always did when confronted with questions on the island that he wasn't necessarily equipped to answer: He said whatever first came to his mind, and did so with great gusto and confidence. "If that's what's bringing her comfort right now, I don't see any reason not to go along with it. She'll come around when she's ready."

And the women, feeling a bit maternal, as they always did in their protection of Piper, ever since that poor girl's mom left to go halfway across the world to study dirt of all things, took his advice to heart and made it their mission to inform every last resident of Frick Island that while Piper had finally left her house, she believed her husband was not only alive but still living in her house, and that not one person was to contradict that belief, under strict doctor's orders, in the best interest of her grieving process.

At first, that was all it was. People loved Piper and didn't want to cause her any more distress than necessary, so when they saw her at the Blue Point market or walking to the docks, they just avoided the topic of Tom's death. When Piper started walking "Tom" out to the docks in the morning and back again in the afternoon at her usual time to meet Tom's boat, most of the watermen just looked the other way, giving the grieving woman her space. It was unclear who the first person was who waved to him, calling out, "Good haul today, Tom?" across the marina. Some claimed it was Old Man Waverly, while others pointed the finger at Bobby, a child who always held Tom in great esteem when he was alive. Regardless, it broke something open in the town, and most people found that they enjoyed waving at Tom, talking to him. Maybe Piper was onto something, they thought. And before anyone really knew what was happening, even though they couldn't see him, it was like Tom Parrish had never left.

A few weeks later, when Mrs. Olecki was out pulling cloth napkins from the clothesline in the backyard and she saw Piper coming up the drive, animatedly talking to the air at her side, eyes bright and smile wide, Pearl found herself smiling despite herself. "Evening, Piper. Tom," she said, nodding twice, even though she could see only one person standing in front of her.

"Hi, Mrs. Olecki," Piper said. "See you in the morning." And then she giggled as if a phantom ghost had tickled her side. Maybe one had.

Anders stared at her. "That's it?" he said, dumbfounded. "The entire town decided to pretend Tom was still alive on the advice of a *dentist*?"

"Well . . . yes," Pearl agreed.

"But that's insane!"

"Is it? It seems to me you've been going along with it just like the rest of us. Does that make you insane?"

"Well, I didn't exactly have a choice, did I? If I was the only one who said something, it would —"

"It would what?" she pressed him.

Anders paused, considering. He thought about what the therapist had said; how agitated Piper had gotten on the beach when he pressed her on Tom. "I don't know . . . it would hurt her."

Pearl raised her eyebrows knowingly and made a high "hm" sound with her throat. "It's amazing what people will do for the ones they love."

Love? Anders's eyes nearly popped out of his skull. He opened his mouth to protest, but Pearl suddenly looked past his shoulder out the front window.

"Oh, goodnightinthemorning," she said under her breath, and then took off for the front door. Unsure what was happening, Anders stood up and followed her, as Pearl opened the front door and stepped out into the night.

"Arlene," she hissed. "Stop right there."

Over Pearl's shoulder, Anders spotted an old woman in a long nightgown, hair shining white in the moonlight. She stopped as directed, turned, and spotted Pearl, then shouted, "No!" and began shuffling her slippered feet faster away from them.

Pearl exhaled a great sigh and walked down the steps and out into the street. She easily caught up to the woman and put her arm around her, talking in a hushed voice, when suddenly the woman's face twisted up in anguish and she let out an earpiercing shriek so loud, Anders had to cover his ears. It took him a second to realize two things: He'd heard that shriek before. But this time, the shriek sounded a lot like the name "Tom." A light flew on upstairs, and Harold came plodding down in his nightshirt, wearily brushing past Anders on the stoop and heading out toward the two women.

"I've got her, Pearl," he said gently, once the shrieking had subsided. He slid his arm around the woman's frail shoulders. "Come on, Arlene. Let's get you home."

He escorted her slowly back up the street and Pearl returned to the porch and Anders, who was standing there with his mouth open big enough to fit the baby sea turtle he'd seen on the beach.

"Who was that?" he asked.

"That's Arlene. Tom's mother."

"His *mother*?" Anders's eyebrows shot up even higher, if that was possible. The woman, with her streaked white hair and frail frame, looked old enough to be his grandmother.

"She had Tom . . . later in life. She was forty-eight, forty-nine maybe? She and Tom Senior had accepted long before that having children wasn't in the cards for them, and then surprise!" Pearl smiled at the memory. "That was a happy day. Anyway, you should have seen her ten years ago — so energetic, full of life. But after her husband died, and then her son, well — the years have not been kind."

"I've heard that sound before," Anders said. "At night. I always thought it was some kind of wild bird."

"Yep," Pearl said, wiping her house shoes off on the porch mat and crossing the threshold back into the house. "She likes to wander at night. Hates when someone finds her and we make her go back home. We'd let her be if it wasn't for that time we found her waist-deep in the water, like she was trying to drown herself." She said it as easily as if she'd come upon the woman eating an ice cream cone.

"She tried to kill herself?"

"I don't think so. That was probably just the dementia. That's Dr. Khari's best guess."

"The dentist."

"Mm-hm. Piper and Tom tried to take her to a doctor on the mainland once. That didn't . . . go well. Anyway, Dr. Khari keeps her in Valium, which is the only thing that seems to help calm her, though Piper and Tom were never thrilled with that. Said it made her sleepy and slur her words." Her brow crinkled. "I don't think that's the Valium, though."

"What is it?"

Pearl looked at him then, as if she just realized he was standing there and she was not, in fact, talking to an empty room. "Well, that's none of your business, is it? I'm no two-bit gossip." With one last stern look and a huff for good measure, she bid him good night for the second time that evening.

But Anders did not go to bed. When Harold got home from walking Arlene back to hers — giving her one of her pills with a glass of water to wash it down, staying on until he made sure she was good and asleep — he found Anders sitting at the dining room table, staring at the floral chains of roses on the wallpaper. Harold paused and thought about speaking, but then remembered the anguish of being a young man in love. And wanting nothing to do with that, he gratefully took his creaky back and knees upstairs to bed.

Anders was still sitting at the table when Pearl came down a few hours later to start the coffee. "Well, you're up early," she said brightly, as if the entire previous evening had not been one of the most eventful of Anders's life. Though he'd had plenty to mull over — how the next episode of the podcast would nearly write itself, what with Pearl's explanation of why the town was going along with Piper's delusion — Anders hadn't spent the past three hours contemplating any of those things.

All he could think about was Piper. The way she threw herself at him with such joy on the beach. How sorely he wanted to press his lips to hers under the moonlight. How extraordinarily unqualified he was to help her in any meaningful way. And — what was occupying most of his thoughts — how deeply hurt she would be by his podcast, one way or another.

There was no getting around it, and it made Anders sick to his stomach that he could be the cause of pain to her in any way.

By the time Harold came down and took the seat across from Anders, taking out his deck of cards and dealing another game of solitaire, as if he were just picking up from the evening before, and Pearl circled the table pouring them both glasses of freshly squeezed orange juice, Anders had made a decision.

The second he got home, he would delete the podcast.

At the ferry, BobDan greeted him with a solemn nod. "Anderson Cooper."

Anders nodded in return, barely noticing the rib, and loped over to the fiberglass bench, where he spent the entire boat ride back to the mainland convincing himself he was making the right choice. It would be fine to delete the podcast. Sure, it was the first story in years that had captivated any kind of audience, but at least he had an audience now. Nearly fifty thousand of them, to be exact. And surely some of them would stick around for a new story. If he could find one.

That was how things worked. People moved on to the next bright and shiny. Some of them might be irritated that they weren't going to get any kind of satisfying conclusion, but then they'd forget about it. And he could keep his friendship with Piper, maybe even convince her to get real therapy. Though if he deleted the podcast, he didn't really have an excuse to keep returning to the island, and that made his stomach sink even further than Tom's poor boat.

"Your pants are singing." BobDan said, jolting Anders out of his self-pitying reverie. He looked up and found they were already within sight of the Winder marina, and sure enough, his pants were buzzing and chiming with all the missed texts and emails and notifications he had received while over on Frick Island. Usually it was two or three, max — maybe a message from Greta about an upcoming story or Kelsey with an inconsequential text or a link from Jess with yet another rescue dog that needed a forever home. But today, his phone kept buzzing, as if it were on the fritz. Frowning, he stuffed his hand in his pocket, withdrew his cell, and glanced at the screen to determine who had been trying to contact him.

But it wasn't the paper. Or Kelsey. Or his coworker. Anders stared at the phone, unable to comprehend what he was seeing. And then, like a fuzzy television screen that all of a sudden comes into focus, Anders understood.

Holy Frank Sinatra.

CHAPTER 24

WHAT THE FRICK?
EPISODE 10

1,752,034 Subscribers
2,643 Comments

Anders blinked at the number on the screen in front of him.

On the boat, once he realized all the messages were alerts from his Instagram — literally thousands of new likes, follows, and comments — he had clicked through to his podcast website and thought surely there was some mistake. A glitch of some kind. And now, staring at it on a bona fide computer screen in his apartment for the last ten minutes, he still thought it must be a glitch. He slowly shook his head, trying to make sense of it all. How could his audience possibly have grown — he couldn't even do the math, but *exponentially* for sure

— in two days?

His cell phone buzzed for what felt like the thousandth time in the past two hours, but when he glanced at the screen, he saw it was an actual call. His sister. His motions were slow, robotic from the shock he was wading through, and it took him longer than usual to answer.

"There you are!" Kelsey said, her voice high-pitched and animated. "I've been trying to get ahold of you for days! Did you see?"

"See what?" he asked, his mouth dry, his eyes still locked on his computer screen.

"The post! He tagged you in it!"

Anders's brain felt foggy, a step behind. "What? Wh-Who?"

"Dwayne! Didn't you get my message? It was *so* embarrassing. I forgot my lunch at home last week and Dad drove it over for me — and *brought it onto the set.* In front of *everyone* like I was in the fourth grade or something. And Dwayne just happened to be standing there, chatting with one of the grips — he's so down-to-earth, it's crazy. Anyway, Dad just walks up and introduces himself! Like it was no big deal! And then, because Dwayne's so polite and cool, they got to chatting, and because Dad couldn't help himself — I swear he has, like, Proud

Father Tourette's or something — he told him all about your podcast. I really thought we were both going to get kicked off set. Or that I would die of humiliation."

Anders sat up straighter, his mind reeling. "Kelsey. What are you saying? Dad told who about my podcast?"

"Dwayne," Kelsey said, drawing out the word as if English were not Anders's first language. "Johnson?"

"The *Rock*?"

Kelsey let out a growl of exasperation. "Yes! And Dad showed him the link, and Dwayne actually listened to the first episode while he waited for his call time and loved it so much, he posted it to his Instagram and now you have all these followers! Isn't it *amazing*?" She giggled happily. "Oh, and did you see? People have made T-shirts! Dad and I both bought one."

T-shirts. Anders tried to repeat the word but found he had no breath in his lungs. He looked at his hands, as if they weren't attached to his body, and saw that they were trembling. "I gotta go," he said. Or he thought he said it, but no words actually came out, before he hung up the phone and then sat there, in the folding chair in the middle of his cheap apartment, in a catatonic state for hours, wondering what in the world he had done.

There were not just T-shirts, Anders learned the next day as he sat at his desk, still numb from the previous day's events and weeding through search engine link after link. There were baseball caps and Koozies and car window decals and, on Etsy, a cross-stitch pillow, all with the now-iconic name of his podcast in big bold print (or in the case of the pillow, a frilly script font): WHAT THE FRICK?

And don't get him started on the blogs — hundreds of them — filled with reviews and synopses and think pieces. Dear God — the think pieces! They were everywhere. On *Medium, The Cut, Slate,* analyzing how Anders's podcast — *his* work — was *important to the cultural dialogue of mental illness* or was *completely exploitative of and detrimental to people with mental illness* or had *nothing to do with mental illness and everything to do with the way American culture is unable to speak in any real way about grief and death.*

Anders's in-box overflowed with messages and emails, not just from listeners asking for — nay, *demanding* — another episode, but from journalists and bloggers from all over wanting to interview the man behind the overnight (literally) podcast sensation.

His mind swirled as he sifted through it all, trying to understand how people could not only listen to the entire podcast in such a matter of days, but then also pen critiques of it — and create merchandise!

"Anders?"

He turned and aimed his blurry eyes up, into Greta's concerned ones. "I just got off the phone with corporate. They want to know if you're *the* Anders Caldwell behind some podcast? Said it was about Frick Island."

And that was when Anders froze. Not because he was worried about corporate or his job but because Greta had said "phone." It had naively not occurred to him until that second — even with the sudden rabid popularity of *What the Frick?* — that there would be any consequence for him on Frick Island. It still felt so insulated to him, so off the grid, with no cell service and hardly any reliable Internet to speak of.

But phones they had.

The world shifted, as he imagined someone calling Piper that instant. Or Pearl. Or BobDan. His body swayed and he bent over at the waist.

"Anders?" Greta's voice filled with alarm.

"I'm gonna be sick."

"Oh." She took two large steps back. "Why don't you, uh . . . head home? We can talk about this later."

Anders didn't even look at her as he bolted for the door.

If BobDan was surprised to see Anders sprinting toward his ferry at the Winder marina just as he was pushing off from the dock at 12:01 p.m., he didn't show it. He eyed Anders calmly and said one word: "Jump."

And Anders did, nearly overshooting the boat altogether and landing in the Chesapeake Bay. Fortunately, the railing on the far side of the boat caught him in the thighs and BobDan managed to grab an arm, pulling Anders back into the boat, where he tumbled onto the floor with a thud.

"Welcome aboard, Walter Cronkite," BobDan said, and then ambled to the front of the boat and settled into the captain's chair.

Once docked on the island, Anders leapt from the boat and ran directly to the Blue Point market. He had no idea what he was going to say to Piper; all he knew was that if he had any kind of chance of protecting her, he had to get to her before anyone else. He vaulted up the few rickety wooden stairs of the tiny store and burst through the front door, red-faced, clammy with sweat, and breathing hard.

The market was empty, save for an older gentleman in a white apron and glasses, whom Anders had seen around the island but not officially met. "Mr. Garrison?" he said.

"Yes?" The man peered at him over his thin wire frames.

"Is Piper working today?"

He frowned. "No. Called in sick today. Don't think she ever fully got over whatever it was she had a few weeks ago."

Anders paused at that, as he couldn't remember Piper ever being sick. He glanced around the tiny store. "Do you sell soup here?"

With a foam cup of microwavable chicken noodle in hand, Anders walked to the bed-and-breakfast, staring at his shoes, unsure what he was going to encounter. As he turned the corner, he saw Mrs. Olecki kneeling at the edge of the yard with a garden trowel in one gloved hand and a flower bulb in the other. He slowed his pace, wondering how to explain his sudden reappearance on the island. He'd have to tell

Pearl sooner or later, and everyone else out here. But he was determined to tell Piper first. If he could get her to understand, then maybe . . .

"Well, speak of the devil!" Pearl said brightly.

Anders stopped in his tracks. "Huh?"

"The phone has been ringing off the hook this morning!"

Anders tried to swallow. His heartbeat revved. "It has?"

"Seems like that little podcast of yours has people interested in visiting our island. Who'd have thought?"

Anders pushed out a laugh. "Oh, ha ha! Wow. Who *would* have thought?"

"Well, I've told them tourist season is over, of course. But we're already completely booked up for the first two weeks of May."

"That's . . . great."

She narrowed her eyes, as if just realizing the day. "What are you doing back so soon? Didn't you just leave yesterday?"

"Yeah. I, uh . . . heard Piper was sick and thought I'd bring her some soup." He lamely lifted the cup up a few inches.

"You came all the way back over here to bring . . . soup?"

"Yep."

"Ohh-kay," she said, as if the actions of young people were beyond her comprehension and she wasn't going to worry herself trying. "Well, can you go through the kitchen and take the trash out on your way? It's near overflowing and Harold won't be back 'til later on this afternoon."

"Sure," Anders said. He walked past Pearl and up the steps to the porch.

Just as Anders put his hand on the front doorknob, Pearl spoke again. "Hey, Jeffrey." Anders turned his head in time to see the One-Eyed Crab waiter ambling down the side alley between the houses. Walking toward Piper's. Wearing a green baseball hat.

Anders blinked, pausing at that detail.

What on earth was Jeffrey coming over for? It was clear they weren't exactly friends. Unless . . . Oh, God. He had heard about the podcast and was coming to tell her before Anders could.

Anders stepped across the threshold and ran to the back of the house, lifting the storm window facing the back porch as quietly as he could. The roof overhang obstructed his view of Piper's porch, but he could see Jeffrey's boots walking up her steps.

Thunk-thunk-thunk.

Jeffrey rapped on the door in time with

Anders's racing heartbeat. And then the silence stretched out so long, Anders thought — he hoped — Piper must be asleep.

Finally, he heard the door creak open. "What are you doing here?" Piper whispered harshly. She did not sound happy to see him. Jeffrey mumbled something in return and Anders strained to hear, his heartbeat now pounding in his ears.

"Jeffrey, you're drunk. Go home."

Drunk?

"Please. Don't send me away. I don't want to be alone." Anders heard it then. The slurring.

"Jeffrey, you have to stop coming here. It's too much."

"I can't," Jeffrey said, his voice breaking. "Don't you understand?"

Piper's voice went even softer and Anders could only make out every few words: ". . . have to get over it . . . it was never meant to be . . ."

Jeffrey was full-on crying now. Sobbing, more like, and Anders, though relieved, was wildly confused.

"Piper? Everything OK up there?"

"Yes, Mrs. Olecki," she called back. And then, her voice a little louder: "I have to tell Tom, Jeffrey."

"No!" Jeffrey wailed. "Piper, stop. Please stop."

Anders quietly closed the window, uncomfortable eavesdropping on such raw pain. He stood there for a moment, trying to make sense of it all.

His first thought, the obvious: Jeffrey was in love with Piper.

His second thought: *Who wouldn't be?* Objectively speaking, of course. And then he recalled Jeffrey's words that first night at the One-Eyed Crab. *You're not the first to strike out with Piper Parrish.*

Or the last, apparently, Anders thought wryly. But something didn't make sense. Piper had said he had to *stop coming here,* which meant this wasn't the first time he'd done this. Why would Jeffrey continue to lay himself bare, especially given that Piper was a married woman? Well, technically Piper was a widow, but still. She *thought* she was married. Anders's head was beginning to hurt.

He saw Jeffrey's boots come back into view as they clomped their way down the stairs and out of sight. He listened as Piper's door creaked closed and decided now was not the best timing to visit her and offer his confession.

And then he remembered the trash. He

walked into the kitchen and hefted the plastic bag out of the bin. After tying the top into a knot, he walked it into the backyard, where the metal bins rested alongside the shed.

"Anders?"

He froze and then turned his head slowly to find Piper sitting on the top step of her porch, her eyes bloodshot and swollen. He hated to see women cry — his mom, his sister, Celeste once. It made him feel ungainly and awkward, as if he suddenly had three extra limbs and didn't know how to wield them correctly. He hated to see men cry, too, for that matter. That was why he never watched *Good Will Hunting* a second time. Or *Cast Away*. But there was something about Piper crying that made him feel worse than awkward. It made him hurt down to his bones.

"Oh," he said weakly. "I thought you were —"

"What are you doing here?"

He glanced at the bag in his hand. "Taking out the trash?" he ventured, and then, completing the final steps to the bins, he finished his chore and walked back toward the bottom steps. "Are you OK?" It was a stupid question, like pointing to the sun and asking if it was the moon, but it was the best he could come up with.

"Yeah," she said, wiping under her eyes and inhaling a big lungful of air. He fought the urge to ask her what in the world Jeffrey's drunk visit was all about. And then fought the greater urge to vault up the steps and hope that she'd throw herself in his willing arms again. It didn't help that he knew what he needed to tell her was going to upset her all over again. He stood rooted to the bottom step, feeling helpless, and shoved his hands in his pockets, trying to think of a way to soothe her. Fortunately, something popped in his blank mind.

"You know what I do when I'm upset?"

"What?"

"I pedal a bike eight hundred miles to the other side of the island until I think my legs are going to fall off and then I sit on an extraordinarily uncomfortable rock and watch sad lonely birds hunt for their supper."

A sound a bit like a hiccup escaped Piper's mouth. "You do, huh?" she said, a touch of shine reentering her eyes. "Do you stick your feet in the sand?"

"God, no. I'm not a sadist."

She offered a full-on smile and Anders felt his stomach untwist a bit. Suddenly, something moved in Piper's lap and he noticed a ball of fur stick its head up and look at him. He stared back at it and cocked his head, recognizing it as the black-and-white-patched cat he had seen before at Mr. Gimby's. But he'd never noticed it at Piper's house before.

"Is that yours?"

Piper glanced down at the animal as if she was also surprised to see it. "Oh. Yeah. I mean, he's not really mine. He kind of comes and goes as he pleases."

"Oh. So do you want to go? To the beach? I'm not doing anything right now."

She hesitated. "No. I'm not feeling well. I'm just gonna rest for a while." She stood and the cat landed on all fours on the porch and started circling Piper's legs.

"OK," Anders said. And then both Piper and the cat disappeared into her house.

Pearl was waiting for him, hands on her hips, when he walked in the back door. "Don't you know anything?" she hissed.

"What?" he asked, startled to see her.

"When a girl is crying, you give her a handkerchief."

"I don't have a handkerchief."

Pearl rolled her eyes up to the ceiling, made a loud huffing noise, threw her hands up in the air, and turned to go.

"Wait!" Anders said.

Mrs. Olecki paused and cocked an eyebrow at him.

"What's the deal with Jeffrey and Piper?"

"What do you mean?"

"Is he . . . I don't know . . . in *love* with her?"

Mrs. Olecki stared at him then, long and hard, until the straight line of her lips slowly turned up and what started as a small chuckle eventually grew into short hoots and long howls of laughter. Her entire body shook with it. "In love with *Piper,*" she muttered. And then she fixed Anders with one last look. "You're not the sharpest knife in the drawer, are you?" With that, she turned and left the kitchen for good, still chuckling as she went, leaving Anders alone, his forehead wrinkled in confusion, contemplating all his many failures as a man.

It wasn't until the front door slammed closed behind her that he remembered the soup.

An hour later, Anders was sitting at the dining room table playing solitaire with Harold's deck of cards, plotting what he was going to say to Piper when he got a chance to talk to her. Half of him tried to convince the other half that he didn't need to say anything. Being out here, he felt it again —

the isolation, the feeling that the real world, his real life, was miles away. Maybe no one on the island would ever find out — maybe they'd just get a nice bump in tourism and everyone would be so thrilled they wouldn't dig any deeper into why. But he knew that was wishful thinking.

So, around the fifth game, he moved on to hoping Piper slept all day, and all evening, and then maybe by tomorrow he'd have figured out how to tell her.

As he lost his eighth game of solitaire, he heard the unmistakable long creak of Piper's front door open. He got up and walked to the window, watching her canvas-shoe-clad feet come into view and tiptoe down the stairs. Was it his imagination, or was she trying to be quiet? He stepped to the side so she wouldn't see him ogling her through the window. And he watched as she came into full view, furtively glancing from side to side while hurrying to her bike. Then, instead of walking it out down the alley to the main road, she threw her leg over the frame, hopped onto the seat, and took off to the right of the shed, through to the neighbor's backyard, and then she was gone.

Anders stayed put at the window, considering her actions: Maybe she was feeling better and wanted fresh air. Perhaps she wanted to go out to Graver's Beach, after all. But if that was the case, what was the point of being so sneaky about it? And then, like a light bulb clicking on, Anders remembered all the times the past few weeks when Piper was less than forthcoming regarding her whereabouts and how she'd apparently been sick a few weeks ago and today — but aside from her swollen sad eyes, she'd appeared perfectly healthy.

And though it probably didn't take a journalist or someone with keen observation skills, Anders had a deep gut instinct that Piper was hiding something — and he was determined to find out what it was.

He ran out of the house, grabbed Tom's bike, and took off after Piper, pedaling as hard as he could through the neighbor's backyard. Fortunately, the grass had been tamped down by Piper's tires, creating a clear track, which he pursued until it ended at the road. Betting on instinct, he turned left. Sure enough, when he got close to the Graver's Beach sign, he saw her figure atop the bike up ahead, her curls blowing behind her in the breeze. He kept his distance, without losing sight of her, and made sure he stayed far enough behind that if she turned around she wouldn't spot him.

By the time he reached Graver's Beach,

Piper was nowhere to be seen; the only evidence she had come that way was her bike lying sideways on the edge of the road. He dumped his beside it and snuck down the sandy path to the beach, expecting to find her sitting on a rock basking in the late October sun. But she was not.

Anders walked the entire length of the beach twice before accepting the fact that Piper had somehow vanished.

So he sat on a rock in the late October sun and waited for her to reappear.

And four hours later, just when Anders was ready to give up, she did.

Anders stood up as he watched a boat approach the shore and then slow to idle. He shielded his eyes from the glare of the sun and recognized Piper, as she hopped over the side and started wading in the knee-deep water. And then his gaze drifted to the man helming the boat. And his heart full-on stopped. His jaw dropped to his chest.

And he stared at the man that — from a distance — looked exactly like Piper's dead husband, Tom.

CHAPTER 25

Piper held her skirt bunched around her upper thighs with one hand and her shoes in the other, as she waded from the boat to the shore, and kept her eye on the figure standing on dry land waiting for her, trying to decide what exactly she was going to say to Anders when she reached him. She had seen him following her, of course. She just hadn't thought he'd actually wait around this entire time for her to return. Turned out she'd underestimated him a lot these past few months. And she knew she needed to tell him the truth. She had wanted to so many times — and she almost had, too, right there on the beach when he asked why she had come back for him but not Tom. What was it about being surrounded by darkness that made it easier to lay your soul bare?

But then — how on earth to explain? If he didn't already think she was crazy, he certainly would now. And Piper wasn't sure why she cared so much about what Anders thought of her, but she did. She sighed, as her feet sunk into the wet muck of sand, and then she was free of the tide lapping around her ankles altogether and was standing in front of Anders.

Sweet, freckle-faced, logical Anders.

"Hi," she said nervously, wishing she could just rewind time and tell him the truth from the get-go.

Anders didn't smile in return. He looked shell-shocked. "Who was that? On the boat with you?"

Piper looked behind her to the retreating vessel and then turned back to Anders, feeling a little sick to her stomach. "I can explain."

"Was it Tom?"

Her eyes flew wide. "Tom? No. Of course not." She squinted, picturing the man in her mind's eye, and then realized how Anders could think that, with their similar build and sun-kissed buzz cuts. "It's all really . . . complicated." She looked around. "We should probably sit." She walked to the nearest rock to lower herself onto it, then waited for Anders to follow suit. When he did, she wasn't quite sure how or where to start, but thought the beginning was best.

She looked at Anders, took a deep breath, and said: "So . . . you remember that cat?"

Piper, of course, knew the cat was not her dead husband, Tom. Well, *now* she knew. But when she woke up sick with grief two weeks after Tom's disappearance and a cat she'd never even seen before was curled on Tom's pillow staring intently at her with those briny blue-gray eyes, well, she could be forgiven for having the thought. She wouldn't be the first or the last distraught widow to imagine such a thing — a bird that comes daily to your windowsill, a butterfly, an owl staring into your soul. It would have crossed most people's minds, because the truth was, no matter what you believed, everyone wanted a sign, didn't they? That your loved one was still here in some way. Still with you.

And so Piper did. Believe that the cat was Tom — for a few days at least. Long enough to mention something to Pearl that morning in the kitchen of the bed-and-breakfast, which, in retrospect, was what started the whole mess. When she got back home, it wasn't just the lack of snoring that forced Piper to accept that this cat was not in fact harboring Tom's late soul. After the cat inhaled the plate of eggs, Piper tried to caress his soft cheek, and the cat promptly scratched her hand and jumped out the open window above the sink. Tom would never have been so rude.

Still, she was sad when the cat left and she was once again alone. So she started leaving the window open and a bowl of milk on the counter to entice him back. And three days later, he returned. He took to sleeping on Tom's pillow, and it comforted Piper to have another living creature in her space that she could talk to when the loneliness and silence in her house became overwhelming.

She named him Tom. Not because she thought he *was* Tom. Not anymore, anyway. But because he was a tomcat and she knew it would have made Tom (her husband, not the cat) laugh. And when Tom (the cat, not her husband) was in her house, she was a little less lonely, which was how Tom always made her feel, so maybe she did name him a little bit for Tom. But she thought maybe she could be forgiven for that, too.

"Anyway, that's all it was," she continued, ducking her head, unable to meet Anders's eyes. "A blip. I was grieving and I had a tiny little break with reality that lasted all of about two days. How was I to know Pearl would take it so far?"

Anders stared at her, his jaw so slack, it looked unhinged.

"I know I should have said something, stopped it. But in my defense, I didn't even realize what was happening until a few days later at the docks. I'd been walking there in the morning and the afternoon, because I thought it might make me feel better to do something that felt routine — and be around people, rather than wallow in my house, which is what I had been doing. Imagine my surprise one day when someone shouted out to Tom! Asked if he had a good haul or something. And then before I knew it, everyone was waving to Tom, and I had no choice but to smile and pretend that he was right there with me."

"No choice! They were doing it for *you*. You could have said something."

"I know," Piper said, filling with both relief to have said it all out loud and shame at how long she'd let the pretense go on. "But everybody seemed so happy. I didn't want to take that away from them. And . . . if I'm telling the truth, I guess selfishly, I didn't want it to end. It was so nice, hearing his name all the time. People smiling at me instead of pitying me."

Anders's mouth moved open and closed, searching for words. He finally clamped onto some. "Let me get this straight. This entire time — these past however many months — you've been *pretending* to have had a psychological break?"

Piper flinched at how awful it sounded out loud and she could barely muster the strength to push the word out of her mouth with a puff of air. "Yes?"

"Oh. My. God." A large purple vein was noticeably pulsing in Anders's neck and he looked so angry Piper felt the need to defend herself.

"It's not like it's been easy!"

"Then why did you do it?"

This was the question Piper dreaded; the one she didn't have an answer for. Or a good answer, anyway. How to explain that it was easier in a way? Because if she stopped pretending, then she'd have to face the truth: that Tom was really, truly gone. But before she could begin, Anders rounded on her again.

"So wait . . . that time you said Tom was asking you what tie to wear when I was on your porch — you were *messing* with me?"

"It's not like that," she said. "And to be fair, he *was* colorblind. That part was true."

"And the marina!" The vein grew larger and more purplish. "I said hi to him! And you knew —"

371

"Right. I did feel bad about that."

Anders was silent for a few beats, absorbing it all, and Piper wasn't sure what to say without making everything even worse. "So why don't you just tell them the truth? It's not too late. Or you can just pretend that you're . . . better or whatever."

"I don't know. Every time I think I'm going to, I just can't."

"But you *have* to."

"Why?"

"Because it's not real!"

Piper got quiet and looked out to the water. Seconds turned into minutes as she tried to put words to how she felt. Finally she said: "It is to me."

"What?" Anders's forehead crinkled in genuine confusion. "But you just said —"

Piper put a hand up. "I mean, not the way everyone is pretending — the way *I've* been pretending. But . . . sometimes I swear I can feel him beside me, his breath in my hair. Or I can hear his laughter. I talk to him, too. All the time. When I tell him things, I know exactly how he'd respond" — she felt her voice begin to crack and brought her hands up to her chest to try to quell the rising emotion — "and when I close my eyes, I can hear him say it."

Anders nodded, solemn. "Those are called

PBHEs."

"What?"

"Post-bereavement hallucinatory experiences. It's the scientific term for . . . never mind." He shook his head. "It doesn't matter."

They sat in silence for a few beats and then Piper spoke up again: "Have you ever read *The Phantom Tollbooth*?"

"No."

"It was one of Tom's favorite books as a kid. I never really got the appeal, but there's this one line that says: 'If something is there, you can only see it with your eyes open, but if it isn't there, you can see it just as well with your eyes closed. That's why imaginary things are often easier to see than real ones.' "

She felt Anders's eyes on her, and then he, too, turned to look out over the water, and they sat like that, side by side, in silence, watching the sun drop closer to the horizon.

Finally, Anders broke the silence. "So who was that guy on the boat?"

Piper took a deep breath and exhaled. "Jacob. He's a real estate developer."

Anders continued to look at her, his eyebrows raised, waiting.

"Back in October he came to the island

373

with all these ideas to boost tourism and use the money to rebuild our infrastructure. He wasn't the first — we've had so many people come over the years to peddle their ideas to 'save' us. They all want to build high-end resorts or waterparks or, one time, a casino."

"Wait, wait, wait." Anders held up his hands to slow Piper and try to process what she was saying. "Why would somebody want to build anything on an island that is purportedly sinking? Doesn't sound like a very sound business decision."

She paused. "I thought you understood."

"Understood what?"

"The island can be saved."

"What?"

"Or at least protected. That was the conclusion of my mom's study — we can't stop climate change, but we can build jetties from bargeloads of sand and get taller, stronger bulkheads and create ripraps, which are basically rock walls that can shield the island on its most vulnerable sides from storm surges and wind to help prevent erosion."

"But I thought the Army Corps said it was a waste of money."

"Well, *they* think it is, because to them we're just ninety crazy people that could solve all of our problems by moving to the mainland. They don't think we're worth saving. But all developers see is a big dollar sign. This island *could* be here for eighty or a hundred more years — that's plenty of time to get a return on their investment and then some."

"And that's what this guy — Jacob — wants to do?"

She nodded. "Yeah, but he's different than the other investors. Or at least Tom thought he was. That he would work with us and let us have a say in the changes that were made. And that Jacob's motives were more altruistic than selfish. I told him he was crazy — at that meeting everyone made it clear that they didn't trust him — and I thought that was the end of it. But then I found out Tom had secretly kept meeting with him. We fought about it." She paused, not trusting her voice, but also compelled to finally say it out loud. "The night before he died."

She took a deep breath and continued. "I thought it was a social death wish, going behind everyone's back to work with this stranger. I was terrified everyone would be furious when they found out. I accused him of . . . only caring about himself." Piper inwardly cringed, thinking of the last words she'd said to her husband. "And then he . . .

died. He was gone, just like that." She waited a few beats for her voice to steady once again. "I forgot all about the developer, until one day, out of the blue, he called. He hadn't heard what had happened to Tom, even though it was all over the paper. And when he asked for him . . . well, it brought the entire night screaming back to me, and I decided right then and there that I would pick up where Tom left off. If it meant that much to him, it was the least I could do. And maybe, somehow, that would be enough."

"Enough for what?" Anders asked.

She hesitated and then: "For him to forgive me." She was silent for a beat. "But I don't think I can go through with it."

"What? Why?"

"People are going to be furious. I've gone through every single idea Jacob has, decided which ones I could convince people to accept and which ones would be a flat-out no — like serving alcohol at the One-Eyed Crab. But the truth is, I don't think it matters. They're not going to trust him and they're going to be furious with me for going behind their backs and nothing is going to change — except the only place I love, the people that are my *family,* will never forgive me."

Anders looked at her. "I get that I'm new here, but even I can see that everyone loves you. Of course they'll forgive you."

Piper pressed her lips together and just shook her head, her eyes filling with tears.

In a quieter voice, Anders said: "And I didn't know Tom at all, but I don't have to know him to tell you he already did."

"Why do you think that?" Piper asked, her voice small. The tears in her eyes escaped down her cheeks, as she remembered that last morning when she was still angry at Tom and refused to get up to walk him to the docks. What if she had? She'd thought it a million times. Would it have changed anything that day? Logically, she knew it probably wouldn't have, but what she wouldn't give to have had those last few moments with him.

"Well, you've single-handedly humiliated me on a number of occasions and I've forgiven you."

"You have?" She reached up to dry her face with the back of her hand.

Anders nodded. "Piper Parrish, you are eminently forgivable."

Anders wasn't prone to pacing, but if a passerby were to look in his window on the second floor of the bed-and-breakfast later that evening, they would have found he struck a comparable resemblance to Baloo, the Andean bear at the Salisbury Zoo that nervously patrolled the length of his enclosure nonstop.

Piper did not have a delusional disorder after all. And though that should have given Anders some form of relief or gladness, he couldn't help but wonder if it was somehow crazier to go along with a delusion you knew wasn't real.

But that wasn't why he was pacing. He thought the movement might work up his nerve to finally confess about the focus of his podcast. It should be easy — *easier,* anyway. The main obstacle was out of the way. Piper knew Tom wasn't alive, so the revelation wouldn't come as a shock to her or be damaging to her psyche in any way.

It would just be damaging to Anders's relationship with her.

And that was what made his stomach twist in knots every time he thought about confessing.

That and how beautiful Piper looked on the beach that afternoon, bunching her skirt around her tanned thighs. The warmth of the sad smile she offered, just for him, when he said she was eminently forgivable. Hell, even her swollen eyes and red nose were somehow alluring.

He shook his head sharply, and then, finally accepting that wearing a path in the wooden floor wasn't going to change his circumstances, Anders girded his loins and stormed out of the room, down the stairs, out the back door, and up the stairs to Piper's front door.

He rapped on it with his knuckles and took a step back, resting his hands on his hips, rolling the words he had practiced over and over in his mind along with a mantra: *Just tell the truth, just tell the truth, just tell the truth.* But then, she opened the door, and when he saw her standing there with her red nose and wild lion's mane, words left him completely and he stood mute, his mouth gaping.

"Anders?" Piper said, cocking her head, her big beautiful eyes searching his face. He came back to himself, remembering the sentences he had rehearsed, and opened his mouth.

"I have to tell you something," he said.

"What is it?" She waited patiently.

Just tell the truth, just tell the truth, just tell the truth.

He opened his mouth. "I think I'm in love with you."

He snapped his jaw shut abruptly and

couldn't decide who was more shocked — Piper or himself. They were not the words he had practiced.

But it was the truth.

Piper blinked. She'd read enough romance novels to know that as declarations went, this was not the most quixotic. It wasn't even top ten, really. But still, the profession caused a flutter in her stomach, as light as a dragonfly's wings, and her heart skipped a beat. Maybe it was his intensely earnest eyes that made her feel like suddenly she was the only person in the entire world, or his sardonic smile, which she had begun to seek out when they were together, or maybe it was because for the past six months, she had experienced a depth of loneliness that was so cavernous, she felt as though, at times, she were swimming in an interminable black hole.

Regardless of the reason, she reached out for a handful of his shirt and pulled him across the threshold, until the length of his body was pressed against hers. Then she tugged him down, and when his face was close enough, she kissed him. Anders — freckle-faced, gangly *Anders*! — needed no more of an invitation. In one swift motion, a hand wove itself into her hair, gently cupping the back of her scalp, while the other encircled her waist, steering her backward until she was pressed up against the wall. The sharp edge of a wooden frame jabbed her between the shoulder blades and she came back to herself for a moment. "My bugs!" Piper yelled against Anders's lips. Anders stopped and pulled his head back from her so his wide eyes could meet hers. "Well, that's definitely something I've never heard a woman scream out before."

Breathing heavily, the rise and fall of her chest matching his, Piper stared at him, taking in his swollen lips, ruddy cheeks, and mussed hair, and then she cracked, her mouth splitting open, laughter erupting from her gut. Smiling, Anders leaned in, as if he could eat the joy right off her face, and pressed his lips to the side of her mouth. Steering her away from the wall and toward the couch, he planted kisses all the way up to her jawbone, until his breath filled her ear with the roar of the ocean, both overwhelming and familiar.

Piper closed her eyes and let herself be swept away.

Later, as they were both drifting off in a tangle of Piper's bedsheets, Anders propped himself up on his elbow. "Piper."

"Mm?" she said, without opening her eyes.

"Tell me something."

"Mm," she intoned, this time an affirmative statement.

"What on earth is Lady Judy getting all those packages for?"

Piper opened one eye. "They're supplies."

"Supplies? What for?"

Piper yawned. "She makes candles. Out of old glass bottles. Sells them on Etsy. Makes a good amount of money, I hear."

Anders started chuckling, all the pieces finally fitting together. "Do you know I saw all those bottles in that room in her house and actually thought she was selling alcohol on the island?"

Piper closed her eye again. "Yeah. She does that, too."

"What?" Anders's brow crinkled. This island never ceased to amaze him.

"Anders?" Piper said, rolling over on her side away from Anders and taking his arm with her, tucking it around her stomach.

"Yeah?"

"Your pillow talk needs some work."

He grinned, settled his head on the pillow, pulled her warm body closer, and waited for sleep to come.

CHAPTER 26

The first thing Anders saw Tuesday morning when he woke up, a sleepy grin plastered on his face, was the cat, curled on Piper's pillow, its briny-gray eyes staring stonily at him. He rolled away from its judgmental gaze and looked from the open door of the bathroom to the open door of the bedroom. "Piper?"

The air remained silent.

He sat up, rubbing the sleep out of his eyes, the sheets pooling at his waist, and tried again: "Piper."

Nothing. He slipped from the bed and pulled his boxers on, and then, to ward himself against the chill in the air, pulled a blanket off the bed and wrapped himself in it. It took roughly ten seconds of walking the length of the carriage house to determine with certainty that Piper wasn't in it.

He was alone. Well, him and the cat.

He glanced at the pewter crab wall clock:

8:32 a.m. He sat at the kitchen table, wondering where Piper had gone. Maybe to work? He glanced at the wall of bugs and tried to suppress a smile at the memory of the night before, to no avail.

It had certainly not been the plan. But Anders was starting to see the appeal of spontaneity.

He knew he still needed to tell her about the podcast, but something had occurred to him as he watched Piper sleep peacefully before he, too, succumbed to exhaustion — Piper had been working so hard to come up with a strategy to increase tourism, thereby increasing the town's funds to invest in the infrastructure. Well, according to Pearl, his podcast was doing just that — drumming up interest in Frick Island — and didn't she say the bed-and-breakfast was already booked for the first two weeks of tourist season next year? Maybe even more than that by now.

He had the hope that not only would Piper *not* be angry at the (very slight, really) mischaracterization of his subject matter — she would be thrilled! He popped up from his chair and walked back to the bedroom, picking up each article of his strewn clothing on the way. He would find her and tell her, and then — if he was lucky — they would tumble back to her carriage house in mutual giddiness and celebrate their amazing turn of fortune properly. Preferably more than once.

The bell on the door of the Blue Point General Store chimed as Anders stepped inside. Piper stood behind the counter pushing a mop around, and the second he spotted her, his smile grew so large, it threatened to take over his face. Any other observer might have seen the sweat at her brow, the few haphazardly loose coils of hair grazing her neck, her blemished white apron, the worn but sturdy canvas shoes, and let their gaze move right along, but Anders stood struck by her splendor. In his eyes, she was nothing short of perfect.

With a small bounce in his step, he walked toward her, and Piper looked up from her mopping.

"Hi," he said, beaming at her.

"Hi," she replied, but didn't return his smile, causing his to dim exponentially.

"You OK?"

"Mm-hm."

He paused, trying to comprehend the sudden change in last-night Piper and this-morning Piper. "Where'd you go this morning?"

"Work," she said, her face remaining expressionless.

Anders mentally hit his head with his palm, realizing the obviousness of his question, though it wasn't really what he'd been asking. He wanted to know why she'd left without waking him or saying goodbye. "I know, I meant —"

"After I walked Tom to the docks, of course."

Anders went cold, his smile now a distant memory. "What?"

Movement caught Anders's eye and he glanced at the back door to the office, where Mr. Garrison was entering. "Piper, can you run inventory on the spices after you —" He saw Anders. "Oh, hi there. I see you found our girl."

Our girl.

Anders didn't know anything for sure in that moment, except that Piper was certainly not "his girl." He had a feeling she wasn't Mr. Garrison's girl either. She wasn't anyone's girl — except maybe Tom's. And he realized how very foolish he was to think that one night would change that. Anders looked from Mr. Garrison to Piper. "Yeah," he said. "I did. Sorry to bother you at work, Piper." Face aflame, he turned and walked out as quickly as he could. Halfway down the street, he heard his name and turned. "Wait!" Piper was rushing toward him and his heart swelled a bit. Maybe he'd jumped to conclusions; surely Piper was going to tell everyone the truth about Tom — she just hadn't had the chance.

She caught up to him and he stood silent, waiting for her to catch her breath.

"I'm sorry," she said.

He exhaled. Thank God. This was an . . . unusual situation. He just needed to be patient and sensitive. "It's OK. I didn't expect you to, you know — for everything to change immediately." He had, actually, but he could be flexible. "I'm glad you came out here, though. There's something I need to talk —"

"It was a mistake," she said, cutting him off. Her face was steely, hard.

The breath left Anders's lungs in a puff. "What?"

"Last night." She shook her head, and he noticed water rimming her eyes. "I love Tom. I shouldn't have —"

Anders shook his head. "I know. Of course you do. But, Piper . . . you don't have anything to feel guilty for." He paused and lowered his voice, to make it softer, gentler. "Tom's not here."

"How do you know?" she shot back. Then

she closed her eyes and crossed her arms over her chest, hugging herself. A tear dripped from her lashes, falling to the ground. "Maybe he is."

Anders stood still for a beat, and then reached his arms out to encircle her, pull her to him. He could be here for her. Help her through this. He'd do whatever she needed; wait as long as it took.

"Don't," she said, shrugging him off.

"Piper, you don't have to go through this alone. I'm here. Let me help you."

When she looked at him, her brown eyes turned black with sudden anger. "I don't want you here! Can't you get that through your thick skull?" She was near shouting now and Anders took a step back as if to somehow dodge the venom. But there was no escaping it. "Please leave," she said, and if he thought he heard her voice waver a bit, she corrected that notion when she said, steady as an arrow directed at his heart: "And don't come back." Piper turned on her heel and left Anders standing there, feeling exactly like one of those crabs after a picker was done with it — as if everything that was good inside him had been turned out and there was nothing left but a worthless cracked shell.

■ ■ ■ ■

The docks were desolate, as empty as Anders felt, and he sat hangdog on a bench waiting for BobDan to finish whatever he was doing in his office, so he could leave the island. For good, this time.

"Women, huh?"

Anders looked up, squinting against the sun's bright rays — which did nothing to warm the chilly late-fall air — and right into Jeffrey's mocking face.

"Told you to steer clear of her."

Anders dropped his head, not in the mood to speak with anyone, least of all Jeffrey. Maybe if he ignored him, he'd leave. But then he considered Jeffrey's words, and a rage that had been brewing in his gut boiled over.

"You know what? You didn't tell me to steer clear of her, actually. You told me I should seek her out — that she'd be the perfect person to help me with my podcast, if I recall. It's almost as if you take some sick pleasure in orchestrating people's embarrassment. Or pain. Is that it?" He paused, his jaw twitching. "All the while, you're madly in love with her. That's pretty sick, if you ask me."

Jeffrey scoffed, his blazing eyes matching Anders's. "For an observant guy, you really do miss *everything,* don't you?"

Anders stared at him, wondering what he had missed, and then something clicked in his mind. He'd heard that phrase before. Or seen it, anyway.

"*You're* the emailer. NoManIsAnIsland."

Jeffrey narrowed his eyes. "What are you talking about?"

Anders mirrored Jeffrey's expression. "You didn't send me an email? A few months ago?"

"No."

"Oh," Anders said. He'd been so sure for a split second. "So wait — what are *you* talking about? What have I missed? You're saying you're *not* in love with Piper?"

"No," he said, with a sad chuckle. "I'm not in love with Piper."

"But I overheard you, at Piper's. You were so upset and she said . . ." What had she said? *It was never meant to be.* But then he remembered Mrs. Olecki's reaction as well, when he had asked if Jeffrey was in love with Piper, and he wondered what he was missing. As he searched the corners of his brain, Anders stared at Jeffrey and really *looked* at him. And it was then that he saw the raw pain in his eyes, the same pain he'd seen mere moments ago . . . in Piper's. And that was when it hit him.

"Oh my god. You're in love with Tom."

Jeffrey didn't respond. He just chewed his lip and studied the toe of his boot, as he dug it into the wooden plank he was standing on.

"Did Tom know?"

Jeffrey tilted his head to the sky as if the answer were somewhere floating in the clouds, and then, exhaling slowly, sat at the opposite end of the bench. "I never came out and told him, if that's what you're asking. I'm not a glutton for punishment."

Anders leaned back, absorbing this new information. He could feel the change in Jeffrey's demeanor, the fight having left him, the relief at his admission. Jeffrey took his silence as an invitation to keep talking. "We were best friends, me and Tom. Since we were no bigger than ankle biters. Growing up, I was different than the other kids on the island — there were more of us back then — I just didn't know how. But the other kids, they saw it and poked fun at me. The red hair didn't help." He grinned wryly and pointed at his scalp. "Tom always stood up for me, told me it didn't matter what anyone else thought. We ran all over this island like we owned it, dreaming up big

391

plans for the future. Stuff like he was gonna write for *National Geographic* and I was gonna take the pictures. Never mind I didn't even own a camera." He half chuckled and then stared off, like he was lost in the memory for a minute. "We were like those double Popsicles — you ever eat those as a kid? Always stuck together."

Anders realized where this was going. "And then Piper moved here."

"And then Piper moved here," he repeated. "It was fine at first. I knew Tom had it bad for her, but I didn't mind. Was even happy for him when they started going together. But then Tom's dad died — and it rocked him. It would rock anybody, but Tom, I think he got one of those predispositions or whatever you call it for sadness. It was deep. And dark. Even a blind man could see he needed help, but he wouldn't listen to me. I tried to talk to Piper, but she'd just brush it off. *It'll pass, it'll pass,* she'd say. It did, of course, but then it'd sneak up on him again. It never left him alone for good. Or for long."

Anders crinkled his brow. "That doesn't sound like Piper," he said, repeating a phrase he'd heard Pearl say once: "She'd help a crab cross the street if she came up on one."

"Yeah." Jeffrey nodded. "She might do that. But she also bleeds sunshine and rainbows — and when something's ugly, she'd rather pretend it wasn't." He raised his eyebrows at Anders. "She's the Great Pretender, in case you haven't noticed."

Anders's jaw went slack. "Wait. You knew?"

"That she's faking it? 'Course."

His eyes grew bigger. "Did everyone?"

"No, I don't think so. I begged her to make it stop. I couldn't stand hearing his name a thousand times a day. Seeing his mangled boat up on those planks."

"So why didn't you just tell?"

Jeffrey hesitated. Chewed his lip some more. "I do care about her, despite how it sounds. I knew she was hurting, too. I didn't want to hurt her any further. I tried . . . other things, though."

And then Anders remembered the green hat and he knew. "You burned the boat."

Jeffrey didn't respond right away. "I didn't plan to. I . . . wasn't in my right mind."

Anders remembered how bewildered he was by the hammer, and the fact of the person wielding it being drunk made a lot more sense.

"So much for this being a dry island," Anders deadpanned.

"Do as we say, not as we do," Jeffrey quipped. Then he rubbed his palms over his jean-clad thighs and stood. "I should get going. See you next weekend?"

Anders bristled, Piper's words ringing in his ears. "I don't think you will, actually."

Jeffrey just nodded and then walked off. A few paces in, he stopped. "You know what I saw on that boat right before I set it on fire?"

"What?"

He paused, looking at Anders purposefully. "A life jacket."

Anders furrowed his brow, trying to understand what Jeffrey was implying, what he'd said about Tom's depression. And then he remembered the words of the waterman from the restaurant: *It wuddn't no accident.* And finally, he understood. "Maybe he didn't have time to grab it."

"Maybe," Jeffrey said slowly. "Or maybe he just didn't want to."

Anders watched as Jeffrey loped off and then gave his head a shake. What in the hell was wrong with the people in this town? There were more buried secrets on this island than on a sunken treasure ship, and Anders was tired of uncovering them.

For the rest of the week, Anders continued to try to lie to himself that he was glad to be done with Frick Island, by trying very hard not to think about the place. Or Piper. Which meant that he constantly thought about the island. And Piper. And while he was thinking about the island and Piper, he robotically performed the motions of his life. He went to work, wrote his articles, and ate tasteless microwaved dinners at his folding table before going to bed on his sad floor mattress, alone and miserable. He largely ignored the podcast, and all the emails and messages he was still receiving, except to apologize to Greta for not giving her a heads-up about it.

When he woke up on Saturday, the day stretching ahead of him empty and unscheduled for the first time in months, he lied to himself again, telling himself this was a good thing, that Frick Island had taken over his life. And now he could do more important things. Like . . . (and this was where his mind went blank for a few minutes). Oh! He could get a dog. Or start working out! Maybe he'd ask Hector what gym he went to. But the thought of having to sit through another diatribe on the merits of protein powders again deterred him from that path instantly. He rolled over on his mattress and clicked the television on, trying not to think of Piper, which was really all he could think about. He missed her. And the idea of never seeing her again squeezed his heart so tight, he thought he might literally be having a heart attack. Panicked, he sat up and scrolled through his phone until he found a list of symptoms on WebMD and then spent the next hour hyperfocused on his left arm and chin, trying to decide if it was tingling or if he was short of breath because he thought he might be having a heart attack or because he was actually having a heart attack.

Fortunately, his phone rang, giving him a short reprieve from his spiraling.

"Hey, Kelsey," he said in a slightly irritated voice, not having fully forgiven her for his podcast exploding, even though at one point that was all he ever wanted, and it wasn't technically her fault.

She didn't respond, and at first he thought they had a bad connection. He pulled the phone away from his ear to check the bars. When he saw they were full, he put the phone back to his ear.

"Kels?"

He heard a squeak and then a ragged sob. "You have to come," she said, in a voice so distorted it was almost unrecognizable. "It's Dad."

And from the fear and pain and love pulsing through the line, Anders didn't have to ask which one. And his chest constricted all over again.

CHAPTER 27

The Hartsfield-Jackson airport in Atlanta was not only one of the busiest airports in the world but also had the distinct honor of having the longest span from the last terminal (E) to the first (A) — a little over two miles. An underground train quickly transported passengers between them, but naturally, the night Anders flew in, his plane docked at terminal E — and the train was out of commission. So Anders ran two miles carrying a duffel bag in one hand and his phone in the other, waiting for an update from Kelsey on their stepdad, who was currently in surgery after suffering a stroke.

He took a Lyft to Northside Hospital, and as soon as the car pulled into the parking lot, Anders bolted and didn't stop running until he found his mom and sister in the waiting room of the ER.

After embracing both of them, he sat down, still slightly out of breath. "Is there an update?"

His mom shook her head, her face wan.

"What happened exactly?" Kelsey had been so distraught, he couldn't understand half of what she had been saying on the phone.

"I don't know," his mom said, her eyes watery. "One minute he was eating a turkey sandwich and telling me about the new idea he had to keep squirrels out of the bird feeder. Then his words started running together like he'd had three scotches in a row, when he hadn't had a drop to drink! Next thing I know he was slumped over in the chair and his sandwich was on the floor. It was terrifying."

Anders couldn't even imagine how scary that must have been.

"Then the paramedics showed up and we followed the ambulance here. We just ran out of the house. I don't even have my purse."

"I called 911 when I heard Mom scream," Kelsey interjected.

"They took him back for a CT scan, said it was an ischemic, whatever that means, and then wheeled him into the OR to unblock the blood vessel or something or other. Kelsey's been researching it on her phone."

"Did they say how long he'll be in surgery?"

"About two hours, so not much longer."

"OK." Anders nodded, even though all of this information did not give him the only piece they were all looking for — whether his stepdad was going to be alright. "Do you want me to go get your purse?"

"Would you? And maybe Dad's flannel pajamas, too. He's going to hate that flimsy gown."

"Of course," Anders said, grateful to be of use and have a task to focus his mind. "Text me if you think of anything else."

The house was dark when Anders walked in the front door. And quiet. Too quiet.

He flipped light switches as he moved from room to room and then he padded up the stairs and poked his head in his old bedroom. His mom had always threatened to turn it into her craft room or a home gym the second he left for school, but it looked exactly the same. His eyes roamed the walls from the framed world map over his bed to the four movie posters tacked up in a row (*All the President's Men, Superman, The Paper, Spotlight*) to the Chicago White Sox flag his dad had sent him one year, even though Anders didn't even like baseball.

He moved on to his mom and stepdad's room at the end of the hall. He spotted her purse on the dresser and Leonard's flannel pajamas in the fourth drawer down, exactly where she'd said they'd be. On his drive home, his mom had texted that perhaps he should bring a change of regular clothes as well, so he picked out a pair of jeans and Leonard's favorite sweatshirt, which announced will golf for beer, along with a couple pairs of boxers and socks. He laid everything on the bed and walked into the closet, looking for a bag to put everything in. Not spotting one on any of the shelves, he remembered that his mom kept suitcases in the attic.

Down came the foldout wooden stairs in the middle of the hall, and up Anders went, tugging on the string at the top, illuminating the bright light bulb. He spotted the cluster of suitcases immediately and picked a small roller-bag carry-on wedged between the plastic tub of Christmas ornaments on the left and a stack of two cardboard boxes on the right. The top box caught his eye, because it had his name in bold letters on top. He nearly turned away from it, assuming it was maybe old clothing that his mom hadn't donated yet, but curiosity got the better of him and he paused, opening the top flap. And then he realized what it was — his mom's collection of his childhood belongings. There was Elmer, his stuffed elephant that he refused to part with until at least third grade, maybe even longer. Scribbled artwork, stacks of handwritten stories, report cards, photos. He briefly rifled through it all, not remembering half of it, until he got to the middle of the box and a stack of VHS tapes, the top one with the words, in Leonard's handwriting: *Anders's 4th Grade Talent Show.*

He paused, half cringing and half laughing at the memory — not of the actual talent show but of telling Piper about it and her delighted reaction. He felt a pang in his chest. And then he pulled the tape out of the pile and closed the box.

After packing up his stepdad's belongings, he walked downstairs to the den with the video, slid it into the VHS player on the built-in bookshelves, and turned on the TV. It took him a few minutes of fast-forwarding, but then there he was, a gangly nine-year-old in a backward baseball cap, standing stone-still and alone in the middle of the stage in his elementary school cafeteria. And then the first electronic strains of the Beastie Boys' "Intergalactic" filled the air, followed by his mom's voice. "Is the red button on, Leonard?" "Yep, we're rolling," his stepdad replied. "Shh! He's starting!" his mom said, and likely nudged him, causing the camera to jerk before Leonard righted it, zooming in on Anders. Anders watched as his younger self moved his limbs, jerking and spinning and throwing himself to the ground with all the rhythm and awkwardness of a giraffe on roller skates. The laughter began about twenty seconds in, starting with surprised snickers until it built on itself, rippling through the crowd like a tidal wave. Anders squirmed for the boy onstage as if he were watching someone else, someone who had all the enthusiasm in the world, and none of the talent. He watched as the laughter reached young Anders's ears. He saw the light go out of his eyes, the smile leave his face, and he suddenly remembered that moment so vividly. How had he forgotten the humiliation? But then, above the roar of laughter from the crowd, he heard something else — something he certainly hadn't heard all those many years ago. It was his stepdad's voice, loud and booming: "Woo-hoo! You've got this, Anders! Good job, son."

Back at the hospital, Anders's mom was sipping hot tea from the cafeteria and waiting some more. Leonard had made it out of surgery but hadn't come to yet. The doctor let his mom see him briefly, and then said someone would let them know when he woke up. The three of them sat in silence, lost in their own thoughts, until at some point Anders nodded off.

He woke up to his sister shaking his arm, drool hanging from his mouth, a painful crick in his neck. "Huh," he said, looking up, trying to make sense of his whereabouts. He wiped his lips with the back of his arm and remembered.

"Come on. He's awake," Kelsey said.

They walked single file down the hall, his mom in the lead like a mother duckling with her chicks. Anders's stomach tightened with each step, unsure what they were going to find. Kelsey had briefed them on the possible side effects of stroke: being paralyzed, confused — and what Anders thought would be the worst — unable to speak.

But his worst fear was quickly squelched as they got closer to the room and heard Leonard's booming voice drift out into the hall. "You'd think at least one of them would have ducked."

It was his infamous "three men walked into a bar" joke that both Kelsey and Anders had heard so many times growing up, they often said the punch line with him. His mom took off as soon as she heard his voice, with Kelsey and Anders at her heels, and they rushed into the room and found him, head wrapped in bandages, laughing more at his own joke than the nurse taking his blood pressure.

"Well, there they are!" he said, spotting the three of them in the doorway. "Alisha, this is my family. My wife, Carol, my daughter, Kelsey, and my son, Anders."

Anders's mom hurried over to Leonard's side.

"Kelsey's about to be a world-renowned actress and Anders is a famous podcaster. Have you heard of *What the Frick?* Everyone's talking about it. Even The Rock."

"Really?" Alisha said kindly, as she slipped the blood pressure cuff off his dad's arm. "I haven't heard of that."

"Take a listen. Great stuff."

"How are you feeling?" Carol asked, her voice filled with concern. She looked him over up and down like she used to with Anders when he was a kid and fell off his bike.

"I'm just fine! 'Course I'm OK! You think a little stroke is gonna take me out?" He paused. "Can't move the left side of my body, though."

"Oh my god. Are you serious?" Kelsey said.

"Yeah. I mean, I did have a stroke. Doctor says it's nothing a little physical therapy can't sort out."

"How did it happen? Could it happen again? What are they doing to prevent it?" Anders went straight into reporting mode. Gather as many facts as possible so you know exactly what you're working with.

Leonard shrugged, though only his right shoulder actually moved. "Just one of those things, doc said. Said they'd run some tests."

"They better," Anders said, crossing his arms. *One of those things* was absolutely not an acceptable diagnosis when somebody's life lay in the balance.

For the next three days, Anders took turns with his mom and sister visiting the hospital until Leonard could regain enough strength to go home. Anders mostly spent the time online researching everything he could about ischemic strokes and then grilling the doctors and nurses whenever it was his turn to be at the hospital.

"Anders," Leonard said one day, after the doctor had nearly tripped over his feet getting out of the room as quickly as possible

406

when Anders walked in. "Can you do me a favor?"

"What?" Anders asked. He was moving a vase of puffy chrysanthemums from Leonard's bedside table to across the room, as Leonard kept sneezing and thought it might be the flowers. Anders's phone buzzed in his pocket, and he set the vase down, then tugged it out of his pocket. After glancing at the screen, he tossed it on the bedside table, in the empty space the vase had left.

"You gotta tone it down a little bit."

Anders stared at his stepdad, and nearly laughed at the irony of someone who was gregarious and over-the-top in every aspect of his life asking *him* to tone it down. His phone buzzed again, and Anders ignored it.

"Are you kidding? We need answers! This is absurd. Your risk of having a second stroke doubles for up to five years after the first one — and they can't even tell us why you had the first one. How are you supposed to prevent it?"

Leonard looked Anders squarely in the eyes and said calmly, "Maybe I'm not supposed to prevent it."

Anders's head jerked forward on his neck like a chicken. "What? What is *that* supposed to mean? You're OK with just dying next time?" His phone came alive again, and

Anders wasn't sure if it was his imagination or if it was buzzing more loudly, more insistently, this time. Leonard glanced at it, too, and then back at Anders.

"Well, no, I'm not *OK* with dying. I'd prefer not to, if I can help it. But some things in life are out of our control. Most things, actually."

"That's absolutely ridiculous," Anders said, as his phone went off for a fourth time.

"Are you going to get that? Sounds important."

"No," Anders said.

"Who is it?"

"Nobody."

Leonard raised an eyebrow at him.

"It's *Good Morning America.*"

Leonard laughed, but quickly stopped when Anders's face didn't change. "Are you serious?"

"Yeah. They want to do a segment on *What the Frick?*"

"Anders! That's amazing! Why aren't you answering the phone?"

Anders sighed. And then he sat down heavily into the chair beside his stepdad's bed and slowly began to unravel the entire story, starting with his dishonesty from the outset, through to Piper's confession and her secret meetings with the developer, and ending with Piper never wanting to see him again.

"Well," Leonard said when he was done. "You sure made a mess of things."

"I know. And I don't know how to fix it."

"What's your gut tell you?"

"That I need to explain everything to Piper — whether I do *Good Morning America* or not. Though I think I should — and not just for me, but because I really think it could help. The publicity from a platform that big could be a boon to tourism there, bringing sorely needed money into the island, which is exactly what she's trying to accomplish."

"True," Leonard said thoughtfully. "But maybe that's not the way she's trying to accomplish it."

"What do you mean?"

"Just that, from your podcast anyway, it sounds like the people on the island are very private — and maybe they wouldn't view that amount of attention or exposure in the same way."

Anders absorbed this, and then, realizing Leonard was right, felt even worse that he had done exactly that with his podcast. Leonard reached over and patted Anders's hand.

"Chin up. You're a good kid. You'll do the

right thing."

Anders's hackles raised — as if Leonard had scratched his fingernails down a chalkboard. Anders *wasn't* a good kid. He wasn't good to the people on Frick Island and he hadn't been good to Leonard, certainly — growing up he'd been difficult and temperamental and ungrateful. He'd shouted horrible things at him. Anders cringed remembering the unoriginal juvenile insults he'd lobbed Leonard's way: that he wasn't his *real* dad, that just because his mom loved him didn't mean he had to, and worse, that he hated him, he hated his stupid laugh and his stupid jokes and his goofy smile. And Leonard took it, in his roll-off-the-back, life-is-ducky, I'd-prefer-not-to-die-but-whatever-happens-happens! kind of way.

"Why do you do that?" he said, irritated.

"Do what?"

Anders thought of the video — of Leonard's raucous cheering — and he thought of the ridiculous comments he left on every single one of his podcasts. And he thought how he didn't deserve any of it — especially not for the break-dancing, anyway. "Why do you believe in me, when I've given you absolutely no reason to?"

Leonard cocked his head, his eyes dancing with amusement, as if he knew the

410

secret to the universe and Anders was just too thick to see it. "For the same reason the people on Frick Island believed Piper."

Anders raised his eyebrows. "Because you're insane?"

Leonard chuckled. "Yes, that's it. Because I'm insane." He looked pointedly at Anders. "And because I love you. So very much."

Anders stared at his stepdad for a beat, until his nose started to tingle and his vision blurred. And then he decided perhaps he was allergic to the chrysanthemums, too.

CHAPTER 28

Anders's stomach twisted in a hundred knots as he rode the ferry back to the island. He had spent three days at home, mulling over his choices, until finally he called the producer back at *Good Morning America* and asked her to give him one more day to decide. He had considered calling Piper, but he didn't have her phone number, and even if he could find it, he decided this was likely a conversation he should have face-to-face — if she would even see him. He was going to tell her everything — lay it all out on the line and then leave it up to her. If she wanted to do the talk show, if she thought it would help, he would do it. If not, simple as that, he'd say no.

As the boat pulled closer to the dock, Anders saw a huddle of people — mostly watermen — standing around, and as they got even closer, he could see their faces were long, drawn, and he knew in his already twisting gut that something was wrong. When they reached the pilings and Anders stepped off the boat to tie it off, BobDan's wife, Shirlene, noticed them and peeled off from the group. Wringing her hands, a worry line carved deep into her forehead, she approached the boat and glanced from Anders to BobDan.

"What is it?" BobDan asked, and the gravity of his voice further cemented Anders's concern.

"I tried to get ahold of you, but you left the radio."

"Tell me."

"They found his body."

"Who?"

"Tom."

BobDan sucked in a sharp breath.

Shirlene explained how a large industrial fishing boat from Boston hauled it in on their trawling net a few days earlier. Took some time to get to the right authorities and then run the proper identification tests.

"Does Piper know?" Anders interrupted her.

Shirlene nodded. "She was here when the call came through. Took off before I could do anything. Pearl went to check on her, but she wouldn't open the door."

Shirlene kept talking, but Anders didn't

413

stick around to hear any more. He ran. Past the huddled watermen, past the bench. Down the deserted main street, past the general store and the church. And though his heart was pounding in his ears and his lungs were screaming at the cold air being forced into them, he kept running all the way to the bed-and-breakfast. He sprinted down the alley to Piper's carriage house, took the steps two at a time, and didn't even bother knocking. He threw open the front door and burst in, nearly tripping on Piper, who lay crumpled like a pile of discarded clothing on the floor, her entire body convulsing with sobs, as if she'd taken one step into the house and then hadn't had the strength to go any farther.

Anders immediately scooped his arms beneath her and she collapsed against him, limp with grief. He carried her to the couch, where he just held her while she blindly cried into his chest. He wasn't even sure if she knew it was him — or if she'd be angry when she realized it, considering the last time they saw each other she had told him in no uncertain terms to leave. He only knew that he couldn't, he *wouldn't,* leave her alone like this.

Finally, the fresh waves of crying seemed to slow, with longer lulls in between, and she lifted her head to look at him. His breathing shallowed, bracing himself for her ire. "I know it's stupid," she said, her voice small and hoarse. "But I think I was holding out hope this whole time. I thought maybe he could somehow . . ." She hiccuped. "Still be alive."

Anders smoothed her hair. "That's not stupid."

She pressed her cheek back against his chest and began crying anew, albeit calmer this time, and Anders let her, methodically stroking her curls. It was peaceful, sitting here, and Anders imagined he could stay exactly in this position for days, if not weeks, and not find himself wanting for anything.

And then the door burst open once again, startling him. He looked over to see Mrs. Olecki filling the door frame, holding a metal whisk in one hand — which may not have been so strange, if the expression on her face didn't look so angrily purposeful, as though she were intent on using it for something other than to mix cake batter.

"How *dare* you," she said, coming straight for Anders. Piper sat up, confused. Pearl kept her blazing eyes glued on Anders and didn't stop moving until her whisk was inches from Anders's face.

Anders pressed himself into the back of the couch as far as he could, his palms facing forward in a *don't shoot* motion. He eyed the whisk. *Don't swat.*

"Mrs. Olecki?" Piper said, bewildered, but Pearl didn't even glance her way.

"*Good Morning America* called!" she said, and Anders sat stunned for a beat that they hadn't waited like he'd asked them to. And then flooded with relief. *That* was what this was all about? Granted, it wasn't the ideal way to introduce the information to Piper, but he was coming to tell her anyway, and now he could explain. "It's about you, Piper," Pearl spat out, as if the words tasted bad in her mouth. "His little podcast has *nothing* to do with global warming — and everything to do with you and Tom."

Piper turned her head slowly until she was looking fully at Anders, her eyes wide, cheeks still wet with tears. "Is that true?"

"Yes, but —"

The parallel lines in Piper's forehead deepened, her brow furrowed. "You lied to me? You've *been* lying to me this entire time?"

"Well, technically yes, but —"

"And *Good Morning America* . . ." He could nearly see the wheels in her head turning, as she made sense of it all. "I thought you said you only had, like, four listeners."

"Well, it's increased slightly — I told you it was doing better."

"How much better is better?"

Anders mumbled the number quietly.

"I can't hear you."

"A little more than one million."

"ONE MILLION PEOPLE!"

"Give or take."

"You've been blabbing all the details of my personal life to *one million people* without telling me, without my *permission,* so that, what . . . you could be some famous podcaster?"

When she put it like that, Anders's confidence faltered and shame started to flood his veins. His mind raced, trying to figure out how to explain so that it sounded less horrible, but he couldn't — because that was exactly what he'd done. Piper straightened her spine, her entire body going as stiff as it had been limp just minutes before. She pointed to the door. "Get. Out."

"Piper, please," he said, the positive aspects of this horrible thing he'd done slowly coming back to him. "I was coming here to tell you. This could actually be a good thing —"

"GET OUT OF MY HOUSE!" Piper

screamed so loud, the silence afterward hung in the air like a presence. Her eyes were on fire, her entire body vibrating with anger.

And Anders had no choice but to leave, Mrs. Olecki following a step behind him, with her whisk poised and at the ready.

"I knew it! I knew that boy was up to no good," Pearl fumed later that evening to Harold, over their dinner of cod stew and corn bread. She'd been repeating some variation of that sentence, sometimes muttering it, sometimes shouting it to the air, all afternoon. "What a slimy, good-for-nothing, dishonest . . . *journalist.* And to think we let him stay under our roof! Fed him, even. We housed the enemy, that's what we did, Harold." Harold wasn't sure that was an accurate assessment, but he knew better than to contradict his wife when she was on a tirade.

Instead he took a thoughtful bite of his corn bread, swallowed, and then said: "Business sure does seem to be picking up. Maybe next summer we'll finally be able to put a new roof on the house, huh?"

Pearl narrowed her eyes at him. "I know exactly what you're doing. You think just because some little bit of good came out of his lying, backstabbing betrayal, I should just forgive and forget. Well, I will not do it. The way he lied to us all right to our faces and hurt Piper! As if that girl hasn't been through enough. I should just cancel all those reservations! That's what I should do. It's blood money! That's what it is."

But Harold knew she wouldn't do that either. His wife might be overly opinionated and particularly fond of Piper and prone to dramatic angry outbursts — but she was also quite a shrewd businesswoman.

He dug into his stew and blew on a steaming spoonful, as Pearl carried on in her dismantling of Anders and his character, and was glad for the boy's sake that he was only on the receiving end of her invective in theory and not in person.

Back at his apartment Anders stood — stunned — at what a turn of events the day had taken. Tom's body had been found! And while Piper was trying to process her grief over that, Pearl had to butt her nose in and complicate matters — adding to Piper's overwhelming heartache for no good reason. But eventually the shock melted into shame and self-pity, as he knew he had no one but himself to blame. There were so many times he could have explained himself to Piper —

prevented her from finding out in the way she just did — and he had chosen not to. He let fear of her reaction stand in the way, only to all but guarantee the terrible reaction this afternoon with his continued dishonesty. He jammed the pad of his pointer finger onto the numbers on his phone screen, dialing the producer at *Good Morning America* and leaving a message that he would not be appearing on the show after all. Then he hung up and stood in the center of the room, staring at his podcast equipment.

Glaring at it, really, as if the equipment itself had gotten him into this mess. The urge to swipe it all off the metal table in one swift motion and watch it fall to the floor in a satisfying crash overtook him. But then he remembered how much the microphone alone cost, and he settled for angrily — but gently — packing it all away, piece by piece. As he worked, his anger at himself (and the equipment) slowly morphed into frustration at all the work he'd put into it, all the time he'd spent creating this story that so many people had responded to — and now he couldn't even finish it. He'd blown it with Piper, everyone on the island hated him, and he didn't even have a full podcast to show for his efforts. As he coiled the final USB cord around his elbow, he paused, the thought slowly dawning on him that he could, technically, finish it. Piper had made it clear that she never wanted to see him on the island again. It wasn't like he had to face anyone over there anymore. And he had so much he wanted to say, so much to get off his chest. Maybe it would be good for him, too, cathartic even, to finish what he'd started. Put it to bed. And then move on from Frick Island for good.

Slowly, he pulled out each piece of equipment, plugging them in one by one. And then he sat down on the uncomfortable metal folding chair, adjusted his microphone, pressed record, and began to speak.

CHAPTER 29

January on Frick Island, everyone agreed, was the worst month. But for Piper, this year, November had it beat.

It used to be her favorite — crabbing season was officially over, the bed-and-breakfast was closed to guests, and she had Tom all to herself. They sometimes went days without seeing another soul on the island — hunkered down in their tiny carriage house, cuddled under blankets, drinking tea and doing puzzles or lying on each other in various configurations (sometimes her feet were in his lap, or his head was on her belly, or his arm was draped casually across her shoulders, but always touching), reading books, lost in their own worlds, but still together.

Now all she had was a cat.

She had to give Tom (the cat, not her husband) credit, though. Instead of leaving first thing in the morning as had become his routine, he now stuck around most days (likely because it was frigid outside and he preferred the warmth of the carriage house, and not out of any duty or loyalty to Piper). He didn't say a word when the first letter from Anders came in the mail, and he watched with one whiskery eyebrow raised as Piper — instead of throwing it out or promptly sending it back — chucked it onto the kitchen table unopened. He also kindly didn't seem to mind Piper's hours-long crying jags, or the times Piper used his fur as a mop of sorts for her mucus- and tear-streaked face, or the incessant playing of the Who's "Tommy Can You Hear Me?" over and over and over again on her record player.

Piper had never realized how prescient the words of that song were. One time, when the depths of her grief felt so overwhelming, so unmanageable, she shouted them into the void of her carriage house: TOMMY CAN YOU HEAR ME? CAN YOU FEEL ME NEAR YOU?

And then, realizing how ridiculous she likely looked and sounded, she began laughing. Hysterical peals of laughter that made her stomach muscles start to cramp up and tears run down her face, and that of course eventually turned into hysterical sobbing because Piper no longer had control over anything, including her own emotions. Alarmed, the cat slipped out the window Piper still left cracked over the kitchen sink, and then Piper was really, truly alone. She thought she had grieved Tom, in the months when she was pretending he was alive, alone and silently in their bed at night. But apparently she hadn't even scratched the surface.

And now, her face swollen, her throat raw, it felt like grief was a never-ending corn maze with plenty of surprising turns but no actual solution. Exhausted, she curled up into the chair that Tom used to read in, hoping to feel him somehow. Where was he? She knew, of course, where his body was now — in the graveyard behind the church where they'd exchanged vows and thin gold bands. But where was *he* — the essence of him? Was it in these books he used to hold or the pillow he laid his head on night after night or in the coffee mug in the sink filled with mold because she still couldn't bring herself to wash it out? She sat in the chair, waiting to feel him, his breath in her hair, his laughter in her ear. But all she felt was the cold draft from the cracked window over the kitchen sink and all she heard was the crackle of a log disintegrating in the woodstove.

And she knew that Tom — her Tom, the greatest love of her short, pointless life — was gone. And she would never, ever see him again.

At the end of November, a knock on the door roused her from an afternoon nap. Lady Judy had taken to leaving food on Piper's stoop once again, but rarely knocked anymore, as she knew Piper wouldn't answer the door. Piper planned to ignore it, but the knocking kept up at intervals, only becoming more insistent, until finally she heard the door creak open of its own accord. And then she heard a familiar voice. "Piper?"

She sat straight up, wondering if she was hallucinating. "Mom?"

She threw the covers off and ran to the den, stopping at her bedroom door to take in the woman she hadn't seen in more than a year — since the day she married Tom.

"Oh, my baby," her mom breathed, her face crinkled in concern. "Why didn't you tell me?"

Piper slowly shook her head. She knew she didn't have to explain right then. That saying it out loud, especially to her mom, would have made it all too real. "How did you —"

"Pearl called. Lord knows how she found

my cell number. I booked a flight immediately. But, God, Pipes, *months*! And I had no idea. And the funeral?"

A sob lodged in Piper's throat. She covered her mouth, as her mom spread her thin arms out like a bird about to take flight. "Come here." And Piper did, collapsing into her mother's embrace.

Her mom stayed through the holidays, which were sad and awful, but a little less sad and awful than they might have otherwise been because at least Piper was no longer alone.

Anders continued to send letters, and sometimes a package, and Piper added them, unopened, to the stack on the kitchen table that was coming dangerously close to teetering over and spilling onto the floor.

She dodged phone calls from Jacob, the developer, deleting his messages, one after the other, until he finally stopped calling. What was the point of trying to fix up the island? What was the point of *anything*? Tom wasn't here to see it.

At the end of January, four months past its first scheduled date of completion, the workers finally finished the cell tower. Tom's cousin Steve invited everyone to a ribbon-cutting ceremony and Piper decided to go, if for no other reason than to give herself an excuse to shower and get dressed. As Steve talked about the importance of the island having decent Internet and cell phone service — being connected to the greater world — Mrs. Olecki stood scowling and Steve's baby, who was now toddling around on her chubby legs, charmed everyone in town, even grumpy Mr. Gimby. Bobby took pictures of the whole thing with his camera and said he was going to get them developed and make a newspaper just like Anders. At the mention of his name, Mrs. Olecki scowled even harder, and everyone studiously avoided Piper's eyes, and she found herself wishing she hadn't come after all.

February dragged on, as February tended to do, and Piper found herself growing increasingly restless. She spent several sleepless nights tossing and turning, until finally early one morning before the sun came up, she came to a decision. She slipped out of bed, bundled up in her coat and mittens and boots, and, under the cover of darkness, snuck over to the Blue Point General Store, let herself in, and booted up the computer — which now got high-speed Internet thanks to the new cell tower. When the search engine screen popped up, she hesitated, wondering if she was doing the right thing. She could turn off the computer and go right back to her carriage house and pretend she wasn't curious at all.

Instead, she stayed put and typed the words: "What the Frick?"

She slipped in her earbuds, clicked on the first link of the results, and then, before she could stop herself, clicked on the first episode. Anders's voice instantly filled her ears and she sat up, drinking it in. The image of his face formed in her mind and she grinned, thinking of his funny smile, his ridiculous cowlick. She allowed herself thirty seconds of missing him, and then remembered what he'd done, how he'd lied to her, manipulated her, all for a stupid podcast. How millions of people around the country now knew her name and private details about her life — and also likely thought she was certifiably insane.

Anger ripped through her, but she continued listening anyway. And then she came back early the next morning. And the morning after that. And the morning after that. Until she finally reached the last episode.

This is Anders Caldwell. And you're listening to *What the Frick?*

The now-familiar musical intro that sounded like a quirky duet between a banjo and piano filled Piper's ears and then Anders's voice returned.

Watermen on Frick Island get up before the sun. They don't wear sunscreen. Or life jackets. They don't check the weather on cell phone apps or chart their course with GPS. They don't have to — they know the waters, the tides, by heart.

It's backbreaking, toiling work. Decades of pollution and overfishing and the change in water temperatures in the Chesapeake Bay have made recent years difficult. Some days they only get a few crabs for their efforts. And even less money. So the question is: Why do they continue to do it?

Motivation can be a challenging thing to pinpoint. It's often the most difficult question to tackle in reporting — the who, what, when, where, and how, those are typically the easy bits. But the *why?* That's what drives a good story. It's the question at the root of my reporting.

And criminal investigations, too, come to think of it.

Why do people do the things they do?

Why do those watermen get up day after day and put in so much effort, for so little reward?

429

Is it out of habit? Tradition? Sheer force of will? Insanity?

"Insanity" is an interesting word. We throw it around liberally. When food tastes amazing, it's insane. In that usage what we're literally saying is: It's "crazy good." That album or those kicks or that penthouse condo is insane. But then there's the flip side of the word, when "insane" is not meant as a compliment. When something is crazy, in a bad way. There are a hundred synonyms, none of them any kinder: deranged, batty, mad, psychotic, cracked, nuts, unhinged, mental . . .

When I first learned that Piper Parrish thought her dead husband was alive, I thought she was insane.

Was I using the word "insane" because I thought she was literally crazy? Well, yes. But it's more than that. We use it to describe someone whose beliefs or actions we can't comprehend. Someone whose behavior is so far out of the realm of our life experience that it can't be normal.

And as a journalist, when something is outside of my realm of experience, I try to understand it. I study it. I gather facts.

These are the facts. Tom Parrish woke up one morning, after a fight with his wife, and went out on a boat to try to catch crabs in the middle of a storm. Some people think when his boat started to sink, he could have grabbed the life jacket he had on board and saved his own life. Some people think he may have chosen not to. But I don't know what Tom was thinking in his last minutes on that boat. Nobody knows.

What I do know is, for months I couldn't understand why Tom was on that boat. He didn't have to be a waterman. He was a voracious reader. He enjoyed writing. He dreamt of adventures with boyhood friends on faraway lands. He could have done so much more with his life. Why did he stay there? Why does anybody on Frick Island stay there, when the land is disappearing so fast, it might not even be there eighty years from now. Or ten. Or five. Or one, if a hurricane hits it at the right force and speed.

But then, sometime in the past week, I wondered: Why do any of us do anything?

Living, in itself, is a risk, with only one guaranteed outcome. And we get up each day, and we make our toast and kiss our spouses or kids or parents or cats or dogs and go to work or school and come home to yet another pile of laundry. We do all of these things with no guarantee that we'll even make it through the day. See the sun come up the next morning.

Somebody could make the argument that it's pointless. Somebody might say that it's insane.

And maybe it is.

But maybe it's something else, too: hopeful.

Every human being — every single one of us — wakes up each morning hoping, *believing,* that today is not our day. Not our time. That the storm is not yet here. That our island will not be wiped out. That we will see the sunrise the next morning. That life is worth living.

Otherwise, we wouldn't bother getting out of bed.

I spent months on an island trying to understand why the actions of the people on it were so incomprehensible, only to find that they were nothing out of the ordinary, after all.

If it's insane that Piper loved her husband, Tom, so much, she pretended he was still alive, right beside her, because the alternative was too much to bear, and if it's insane that the entire town went along with it, because they loved her so much, well then . . .

May we all be loved and love each other so insanely.

May we all be so human.

"Piper?"

She jerked her head, suddenly coming back to herself, remembering that she was in the plastic molded chair in the corner of the general store. Mr. Garrison peered at her, taking in her mussed hair, her pajamas, with a look of concern. "You OK?"

Piper slipped out her earbuds and stared at the computer screen, and then, through her ridiculous stream of never-ending tears, she managed one word: "Yes."

CHAPTER 30

"Sure you won't come to trivia tonight?" Jess asked as she walked by Anders's desk. "We could use you. Hector and I overlap on sports knowledge, and his only other area of expertise is — and I quote — 'the Kama Sutra.' "

She pulled a face, and Anders forced a grin. "Nah. I've got to . . ." He couldn't even remember what lie he had conjured up earlier when he said he couldn't go. That was the level of pathetic he had reached.

"Eat ice cream out of the carton and cry yourself to sleep?" Jess supplied.

"Is it that obvious?"

"Your sad puppy-dog eyes these past few months are worse than actual sad puppy-dog eyes," she said, before patting him on the shoulder and telling him the name of the bar in case he changed his mind.

Anders had been trying to move on, he really had. The final podcast had soared, reaching more than 1.9 million listeners, and though four months ago that would have been Anders's wildest dream come true, he couldn't even enjoy it. Now, instead of wanting his dad, Rob, to listen to it, the only person he wanted to hear it was Piper.

He had sent her at least twelve letters — the first few pouring his heart out, explaining how and why he had messed up so badly; the last few he whittled down to the essence of what he wanted her to know: "I'm sorry." She had yet to respond.

When he wasn't penning letters, he kept his head down, did the assignments given to him at work, and, at night, sifted through all the emails and messages that still flowed into his in-box, though the current had slowed down some. Some of them — his favorite ones — were heartfelt, from people who enjoyed the podcast or wanted to know how they could help Frick Island and other cities most threatened by climate change, or who felt they understood a friend or family member a little better after listening to it. There were not-so-nice ones, too, of course, criticizing Anders or the people on Frick Island, spewing a level of profanity and hate that always took Anders aback in how angry people must be to e-shout vitriol like that to a stranger. He even had a few job offers —

radio stations, a newspaper in Texas that wanted him to start up a podcast department, an agent who thought the podcast could be turned into a book. Anders was flattered, but he also felt stuck, as if he couldn't move on, couldn't capitalize on this newfound fame, because he had garnered it by hurting others, and therefore didn't deserve it.

Only two messages really surprised him. The first was an email from his dad in Chicago. He sat up when he saw it and eagerly clicked on it (though he was irritated with himself for being so eager).

Anders —
Looked at the link you sent me. Nearly 2 million subscribers? Tell me you're capitalizing on this properly. Advertisers would murder their family dog for that audience. You need, at the very least, a sales director and a lawyer. You should be getting a cut of all proceeds from any related merchandise. Call me, I've got some recs.

— Rob

Upon reading it, he wasn't surprised after all.

The second message was a voice mail.

From a developer named Jacob. Who wanted to meet.

Up close Jacob didn't look like Tom at all, Anders realized, as he sat across from him in a booth at Rise Up Coffee. Or at least, the pictures he'd seen of Tom. They did have the same shorn blond hair, but that was where the similarities ended. Where Tom's face was relaxed and open, Jacob's was pinched and closed, his nose crooked, as though it had been broken at some point and never healed correctly.

Since sitting down, Jacob had explained that his phone calls to Piper were going unreturned and, being that she was his only point person on the island, their plans for the island were indefinitely on hold.

"OK, so what do you want from me?"

"I came across that podcast you did — and I was hoping you could talk to her for me."

"Wish I could help you. Piper's not talking to me either."

Jacob pounded his fist on the table. "Dang it."

Anders peered at him. "Why are you so invested in this? You could just move on to another project."

"I know," he said. "It's just — I've always

had a fascination with the island. My grand-parents took me over to visit when I was a kid. Back then, a lot more people lived on it and it was kind of this bustling community, but its own separate place. I was enamored with it. When I started to see the articles about its imminent demise, I couldn't imagine it not existing — what would happen to the people living on it?"

"You're telling me you're doing this out of the goodness of your heart?"

"Well, not exactly. I mean, it's a passion project, yes. But I'm a capitalist, to be sure, and there's money to be made here. It's just that, unlike other developers, I do think the strength of that island is its uniqueness. I don't want to change it by building a casino or making it an exclusive resort for wealthy people. I want to improve on what's already there."

Anders could see why Tom liked him. Jacob did seem honest — as honest as a real estate developer could be.

"Tell me about these ideas. Piper didn't go into the details."

Jacob sat up and Anders could see the excitement flash in his eyes. "First and foremost, they need a public ferry. BobDan does a great job, but his boat is small, so there are only so many tourists that can go over on a given day and there is only one time people can go. A public ferry could offer a cheaper fare, a more reliable schedule, and more frequent runs."

Anders thought of all the times he'd been stranded on the island or wanting to go over or leave only to be at the whim of BobDan, and he agreed that was exactly what they needed.

Jacob went on to explain his plan to repair and upgrade the docks and marina, repave the roads, and rebuild the bulkheads, taller and sturdier to protect against the rising tides. "Once we get some of that basic infrastructure in place, then we can focus on the businesses open to the tourists, to make sure they're being utilized to generate the most revenue possible."

"I still don't understand," Anders said.

"What?"

"This all makes so much sense. Why is it so hard to convince them to do this?"

"Trust," Jacob said, echoing the same explanation Piper had given. "If I invest my money, then they're afraid they'll lose control over their community. I can't blame them, really. Corporations and developers don't have a great track record for keeping communities' best interests at heart."

Anders stared at him, a thought suddenly

taking shape in his brain. He knew exactly what he could do to make things up to Frick Island. To Piper. "Maybe they don't need your money."

It took only four days for the salesman Anders's dad had recommended to make his first deal for a banner ad on his *What the Frick?* website. Anders couldn't believe his eyes when he saw the amount of money on the contract, but it wasn't nearly as big as the second and third.

Two weeks later, Anders sent a check to Piper with a letter saying that it was for the island, for them to decide how to invest it, with a promise of more to come.

A few days passed and Anders didn't hear anything from Piper. He looked at his bank account every day to see if it had been cashed, but the money was always still there. He'd started to wonder if maybe the check got lost in the mail or if she'd chucked it in the trash, which was where he'd started to think all of the letters and packages he'd sent her over the past few months had ended up.

Finally, a full week after he'd sent the check, Anders trudged from his car to his apartment door, head down to keep the bitter cold off his face. When he reached his apartment door, he was surprised to see someone already standing there.

"Piper?"

Heart thumping in his ears, Anders felt a mix of relief and joy and wariness all at once. She wasn't smiling. But she wasn't not smiling either, and Anders took another step forward.

"You are truly unbelievable," she said, her face remaining unreadable.

He nearly smiled at the compliment, until he saw the glint in her eyes of unmistakable anger. And then he saw the check clutched in her clenched fist.

"The arrogance!" she shouted.

"What?"

"You have such a savior complex! You are not Superman! Or Clark Kent, or whoever it is you think you are. This isn't a *movie,* Anders," she growled. "Why can't you just leave us alone?"

"I'm trying to help!" he said.

"No, you're not. You're trying to buy my forgiveness," she spat out. "And it's not for sale."

"No, that's not . . . Piper, you have to understand. I don't want your forgiveness."

She cocked a sharp eyebrow, jerking her head back.

"No, that came out wrong. Of course I

441

do. I'm so sorry, you have no idea. And I'm sorry that that's what you thought this money was for," Anders said, desperate for her to understand. But then he realized that he felt something else, too — something that felt a lot like anger. "You know what? I'm not sorry, actually! It's ridiculous that anyone could be mad at someone for trying to help — to make your lives better. And it's even more ridiculous how you all think you don't need anyone. People *want* to help. Sometimes you just have to let them in."

Piper growled one last time and then threw the check in Anders's direction. He watched it flutter to the ground and then watched her turn on her heel and storm off, leaving Anders standing at his door. She turned the corner to the parking lot and he wondered if there was a cab waiting on her. If she was just going to take off and he'd never see her again. Defeated and simmering with anger, Anders bent down to pick up the check, before realizing that he'd rather be in the company of an angry Piper than no Piper at all. He ran up the walkway and turned, following her path, and then stopped short before he nearly ran into her, as she was stomping her way back to him.

"And another thing," she said, sticking her index finger straight out from her hand, nearly poking Anders in the chest. Her nose flushed red with anger. "Tom did *not* kill himself. I don't know who told you that. But it's bullshit. He would never leave me on purpose. Never."

Anders wasn't sure what surprised him more — the fact that she'd cursed or that she had obviously listened to his podcast. He wanted to reach out and grab her hand, entwine it with his, pull her to him, but instead, he stuck his hands in his pockets.

"I know," he said.

"What?" Her finger remained between them, angrily pointing.

"I agree that no one would ever want to leave you."

"Oh." Her face softened and she curled her finger back into her fist and dropped her hand. "He said he'd never leave me. He swore it." Her face crumpled and the tears came swiftly.

This time Anders followed his instinct to reach out for her. She fell into him and he just held her and let her cry, wetting the front of his down-filled coat with her sadness, and relief flowed through his veins at having her in his arms once again. Finally, when she started to calm down, she mumbled something, her face smushed against him, muting the words.

"What?"

"I'm still mad at you."

"I know," he repeated.

She extricated herself from Anders's arms and the sudden emptiness left him bereft.

"The whole town is mad at you. Furious, really."

"Everyone?"

Piper hedged. "BobDan. And Mrs. Olecki. Mostly Mrs. Olecki."

Anders thought of her intimidating glares. "Well, she's enough."

Piper stared at the ground, kicking invisible pebbles. "People have been coming over to the island, you know. A lot of people, even though tourist season doesn't start for another two months and nothing is open, including the bed-and-breakfast. They want to see the places you were talking about. The people."

"I know it's not the way you wanted, but this is a good thing. You guys can capitalize on it."

Piper offered a half grin. "Mrs. Olecki already is. She's charging people five dollars to get a picture with her. For ten dollars they get a frame."

"See? And with this money, you could do so much more. Maybe get the ferry Jacob was talking about? Open a gift shop."

"It's not just up to me."

"What do you mean?"

"If you really want to give our town this money, you need to come ask them if they want it."

Anders stared at her and swallowed. He'd never imagined giving away money would be quite so difficult.

BobDan crossed his arms and shifted his weight in the squeaky metal folding chair set up in the meeting room at the bottom of the church. Then he set his best glare on Anders, who was standing off to the side, waiting for Harold to call the meeting to order. He knew that boy was trouble from the moment he laid eyes on him. A *reporter*. He shook his head. Troublemaker more like it. And how! Even he couldn't imagine the boy would have stooped so low. If Pearl hadn't called Lady Judy, who told Shirlene, who told him all about Anders's lies, he never would have believed it.

And he never would have brought the boy over on the boat this evening if it hadn't been for Piper. She asked him, and against every bit of good sense in his brain, he begrudgingly agreed. He never had been able to say no to that girl. But he didn't have to be happy about it. And he certainly didn't have to talk to the boy. Or forgive him.

A scowl on his face, BobDan glanced around the room at the people lowering their heads together, murmuring back and forth, not a smile to be found. The mood hadn't been this somber at a town meeting since they found Tom's body. Nobody had even brought any cakes! Which was how he knew he wasn't the only one who didn't give a care what Anders had to say. The place was packed, though. Every single person in town had shown up for the same reason people slow down to look at a car accident. No one wanted to miss the gore, or worse, hear about it secondhand.

Harold finally knocked the gavel against the wooden podium. "This town hall meeting on Wednesday, March the third, is hereby called to begin. We only have one order of business on the table —"

"Two!"

"What?" Harold looked up at Lady Judy. "Oh, right. Lady Judy would like me to inform you that she has a new candle scent for the spring."

"It's called cucumber lemon mint. I brought a sample for all those who want to smell it." She held up a glass wine bottle that had been cut off at the midpoint and filled with wax. "I brought a sample of what used to be in it, too." She grinned and nodded to the travel coffee mug in her left hand.

"You and your drugs!" Mr. Gimby shouted. "Ruining this island."

"OK," Harold said quickly, before the longtime feud between Lady Judy and Mr. Gimby could escalate further. "And now I'll turn the floor over to Anders, who's come to . . . well, I'll let him tell you what he's come here for."

With that, Anders walked over to the podium, looking like a fish on the hook, his eyes wide and frightened. If BobDan hadn't been so angry, he might have even felt bad for the boy.

Anders swallowed, his Adam's apple bobbing up and then down. "I want to start off by apologizing. I know I misled a lot of you about what I was doing out here for all those months, and I didn't mean to."

"You lied!" someone shouted. It sounded a lot like Mrs. Olecki, but Anders couldn't spot her in the crowd.

"I did. And I shouldn't have. I ended up hurting the people I care about most." His gaze locked on Piper, and then scanned the rest of the room. BobDan intensified his scowl, so Anders couldn't miss it. "And that's why I'm here tonight, not just to

447

apologize but because I care about the island and what happens to it." He paused and took a breath. "Recently I met with the real estate developer — Jacob — who came out here some time ago."

Everyone started screaming at once.

"We won't have outsiders telling us what to do!"

"This is a dry island!"

And most surprisingly: "Traitor!" Even BobDan thought that insult was a bit over the top.

"Just listen to him!" Piper shouted over the din. "Please. If not for me, then for Tom."

At the invocation of her dead husband's name, the room quieted a bit.

"Tom?" someone shouted from the back row.

"Yes, Tom," Piper said, quieter now. "He agreed with Jacob. He thought he was different; that he had good ideas for our island. In fact . . ." She hesitated. "He'd been secretly meeting with him before he died. And then I started to as well."

The crowd gasped.

"Look," Anders said. "I understand that you guys don't want to have some stranger coming in and telling you what to do. I get it — I do think Jacob has good intentions, but I understand. The thing is, you have to do *something.* If you don't, this island is going to be gone, and your way of life with it, and that's just the truth." He paused, waiting for another outburst, for people to object, but there was only some low grumbling. And it was then he realized that even if people didn't agree on the cause, they did know their island was in danger. "I don't want that to happen," he continued. "This podcast, it's making a lot of money now. And it's yours. All of it. I want to give it to you. It's the least I can do for what I did. And you all can vote how you want to spend it."

The roar swelled again.

"Why should we trust you?"

"Why don't you leave us alone?"

"Nobody asked you to come out here!"

Anders looked in the direction of where that last voice came from and something occurred to him in that moment. "You know what?" he said, raising his voice to be heard above the crowd. "That's actually not true. Somebody *did* invite me out here."

"Who?" BobDan asked, the first word he'd uttered during the meeting. He didn't believe a word Anders said and he wasn't about to let him peddle lies up there.

"I don't . . . know," Anders faltered. "It

was an email. From somebody called NoManIsAnIsland."

"What?" Piper breathed. And though the word was barely audible, her sharp head snap grabbed the attention of the crowd — that and the fact that her bronzed skin had turned ghostly pale. Silence enveloped the room once again as everyone looked from Piper to Anders. "That's Tom's email address."

The crowd gasped again.

"Tom?" Anders's brow crinkled. "But it was after . . . I don't think it could have been . . ."

"Goodnightinthemorning." A loud exasperated sigh came from the back of the room, along with a squeak of metal chair as someone stood. "It was me."

Every head turned to look at Pearl Olecki standing with her hip stuck out and her head cocked, a look of irritation on her face. "I emailed you."

"From Tom's account?" Piper asked, confused.

"Well, I didn't know it was Tom's email, did I? I don't know how those darned things work. It was open on the screen when I booted it up. I thought it must be a community account or something."

"But that was months after he . . ." Anders

said. "Why was his email account still open?"

The crowd fell quiet, as if waiting to find out that Tom had really been alive after all.

"I used to go to the store some nights," Piper finally offered quietly. "When I couldn't sleep, and I'd already been through all the notes and pictures he'd left behind. I liked reading his words." She shrugged. "I must have forgotten to log out."

Anders paused for a beat, wishing he could swallow Piper's pain and make it his own, if only so she wouldn't have to feel it. Then he turned his attention back to Mrs. Olecki's admission, trying to wade through his confusion. "Wait a minute." His eyes narrowed at her. "So you *wanted* me to come do a story on Piper and Tom? But —"

"No!" Pearl's eyes shot heavenward and she lightly growled, as if she couldn't believe anyone could be so obtuse. "I wanted you to write about that good-for-nothing cell tower they're building out here. It's too close to everyone, and we're all gonna get cancer, but no one seems to give a care! Any self-respecting reporter would have looked into it, but you couldn't take your eyes off Piper long enough to do your job."

"Pearl," Tom's cousin Steve said with a steady, patient voice, only slightly tinged with anger. "I've told you a hundred times that cell towers do not increase the risk of cancer. I even showed you the research from the American Cancer Society about the non-ionizing radiation, remember?"

"And that's supposed to make me feel safe?" Pearl shot back. "Your fancy name for radiation? Radiation is radiation."

"But you thought I was Mormon!" Anders said. "You didn't even know who I was."

"Well, I didn't know what you looked like when I emailed you."

Harold stood up. "OK, I think we've gotten a little off course here."

Pearl glared at her infernally patient, sensible husband. He swallowed. "Look. If Piper thinks this developer has some good ideas, then I think we owe it to her — and Tom — to listen to what they've got to say. The truth is, people are coming here whether we like it or not, thanks to Anders's podcast." He nodded toward Anders and caught his eye, but Anders found no malice in his expression. The crowd began murmuring again and Harold held up his hand. "Now, we could turn them all away. Shut down the island. Cut off our nose to spite our face. Or we could come up with a plan. Together."

■ ■ ■ ■

Three hours later, after a lot more squabbling and shouting, the town had voted 64 to 27 to accept Anders's money and voted on a five-member committee to spearhead what to do with the funds, with the caveat that selling alcohol at the restaurant and/or general store was still strictly off the table. When the meeting was adjourned, people got up and started congregating in groups of three or four, then slowly filing out. Nobody approached Anders, and in all his time on Frick Island, he had never so strongly felt like the odd man out. Like the Come Here that he was.

Still, as he snuck out a side door into the dark night, he was unable to keep the grin off his face. Maybe he wouldn't ever be fully forgiven — maybe he didn't deserve it — but at least he was able to carve some good out of his colossal mistake.

"Hey, where do you think you're going?"

Anders paused, and turned to see Piper standing behind him on the road. Then he considered her question and frowned, a pit forming in his stomach. "I don't actually know," he said. He didn't think BobDan was going to give him a ride back over to the mainland this late, nor did he expect Mrs. Olecki to offer up a room. "I think I'm stranded."

"Serves you right."

He dipped his head. "It probably does."

They stood facing each other in silence, Anders regretting once again how sorely he'd messed everything up. And then he saw the tears well up in her eyes, and he felt even worse.

"I think Tom would have been really happy with tonight," she said when she spoke again, her voice cracking but not breaking.

Anders nodded.

"I really miss him."

"I know," he said.

She bit her lip and looked up. "But what's even worse is that I missed you, too."

Anders didn't think that was worse at all. He thought it was the best thing he'd heard in a very long time.

Piper's eyes overflowed and Anders dug in his pocket for the handkerchief he'd remembered to stuff in there just for this purpose. He handed it to her, and his chest puffed up a bit, wishing Mrs. Olecki could see him now.

"I forgot to thank you for the Girl Scout cookies," she said, dabbing at her eye with the cloth.

He raised his eyebrows. He had begun to assume that she hadn't opened the packages he'd sent.

"And the Taylor Swift record."

"You're welcome," he said.

She sniffed again. "And the video."

"Did you watch it? I didn't know if you had a VCR."

"Jeffrey has one. We watched it together." She dabbed the handkerchief at her eyes, her nose. "You are a spectacularly bad dancer."

"I know."

"You would have been a terrible stripper."

He grinned. "Yes."

She sighed and slipped her arm through the crook of Anders's elbow. "Come on. I guess you can stay at my house tonight. Since you're stranded."

"Really?"

"On the couch," she said, eyeing him purposefully.

"Next to the *bugs*?"

She smiled and Anders's entire heart filled. He stared at her beaming face, wishing with everything in him that he could kiss the smile right off of it. But he knew for now he'd just have to imagine it. Something he learned could be almost as good as

the real thing.
   Almost.

CHAPTER 31

Nearly Six Months Later
August

Pearl Olecki stood in her lemon-dotted apron, mixing the yellow batter with her rubber spatula and holding the bowl slightly away from her so her rapt audience of fifty people or so on the green space in front of the church could see the proper consistency. She spoke into the tiny microphone clipped onto her apron strap.

"You don't want to overmix it. That'll take the air right out of it and then your layers won't rise properly." That wasn't true, of course. With Frick Island cake you didn't want the layers to rise too much, because then they wouldn't stack right. But she wasn't about to give away all her secrets.

She glanced over at Lady Judy, who was under the white tent next to hers, hawking her new line of Frick Island Bay Breeze candles, along with the only officially licensed *What the Frick?* merchandise: T-shirts, hats, key chains, tote bags, baby bibs, and coffee mugs.

Pearl looked back at the crowd gathered round her, including the Barretts, a new family that had just moved to the island, buying the abandoned house next to Lady Judy, along with four others. The wife had been a general contractor on the mainland and spent her days renovating the homes, with the intent to sell them when she was done, and the husband was a stay-at-home dad to their three young boys. Kids! Bobby took to them instantly and had been running them ragged all over the island since the day they moved in. And they weren't the only new residents. A young man had also renovated a storefront on the main road, turning the top floor into his apartment and the bottom into his own private practice. A bona fide doctor. And good-looking, to boot! At least Jeffrey seemed to think so. Pearl smiled, remembering how close they sat together at the One-Eyed Crab last Friday night during Jeffrey's shift break — they might as well have only had one chair. Anyway, she wasn't sure of the doctor's specialty, but she hoped he at least knew a little about cancer, seeing as how everyone was now going to be afflicted with it thanks to that godawful cell tower. She glared at the metal contraption just beyond the church, and then gave her head a good shake. Never mind that for today.

"Now, we'll put these pans in the oven." She slid them on the shelf beneath the table she was working on. "And with the magic of Frick Island, they bake in an instant." She snapped her fingers and then pulled the layers she had baked earlier from the same shelf and set them on top of the table, grinning. Take that, Julia Child.

As she began the icing part of her demonstration, Pearl, who wasn't overly prone to nostalgia, found she was suffering from a touch of it anyway. This Cake Walk was as big as the ones from twenty years earlier or more. If not bigger.

Not that it surprised her, of course.

It just reminded her of what BobDan always said: Everything ebbs and flows like the tide.

And she supposed he was right.

Piper zipped up her suitcase and set it on the floor, where Anders hefted it up by the handle. "Is that everything?"

Beyond Piper's open window, they could hear the low rumble of tourists BobDan had brought over by the boatload on his new seventy-five-seat ferry — and beyond that, the near-constant hammering and drilling and electric sawing that didn't seem like it had stopped since the Frick Island Renewal Committee had completed their visionary plan four months earlier. Piper hated to leave the day of the Cake Walk, but freshman orientation at Cornell was in two days and she wanted to settle into her dorm and find her way around the campus before everyone got there.

"I think that's the last one," she said, and followed Anders out into the den. The cat slipped around her legs, purring, and then moved on to Anders. He lifted the cat in his other arm and nuzzled him.

Piper took a deep breath. She'd known this day was coming since she got her acceptance from the university's entomology department in May, but suddenly she felt completely unmoored by it.

"Can you give me a minute?" she said.

Anders looked at her and offered an understanding grin. "We'll be outside."

Piper watched him go and then turned to look around her carriage house one last time. She'd be back, of course. On breaks from school, summers, but she knew Mrs. Olecki would most likely be renting it out to guests now that tourism had picked up

460

again. And it felt like the last time this house would be fully hers.

She studied the room, letting all her memories flood in, competing for space in her brain. Dancing with Tom around the tiny space, trying to avoid crashing into the furniture, sitting side by side in comfortable silence while she pieced together puzzles and he mended nets or read. She even remembered all the fights — the glorious screaming matches fueled by passion and anger and love.

And then she tried to take a mental picture, so she could always remember it just this way: the pewter crab wall clock they'd picked out together at the antiques shop, the threadbare easy chair in the corner, the book lying facedown on the upturned crate — all of it still, silent. As if each inanimate object were holding its breath, still waiting patiently for Tom to return.

And then, just like that, he did.

She let out a little gasp when she spotted him, there in the worn seat, his blond hair shorn tight against his tan skull, his briny-gray eyes smiling at her in the way they always did — slightly amused, full of adoration. She stared back at him, her eyes suddenly pricking with tears, her heart swelling with relief, joy, and love.

Always love.

She cocked her head and waited, willing him to say something, *anything.* But he didn't. So she just smiled back, drinking him in one last time until, finally, she blinked. And then — just like that — he was gone.

She stood, staring at the empty chair, allowing herself to slip into her grief for a minute like a familiar winter coat.

And then she straightened her spine and walked out the front door into the wide world that was waiting for her. Well, Anders and the cat, anyway.

Hands shoved in his pockets, his unfortunate cowlick sticking straight up in the air, Anders looked up at her. "You ready?"

Piper considered the question. She thought of all the things she was leaving behind, all the things she was going to miss: Tom (her husband, not the cat) and Pearl and the general store and Arlene and her perfect little carriage house and Tom (the cat, not her husband) and Anders. They promised to see each other often, of course, despite the three hundred and fifty-two miles between them. (Or less, if Anders took one of the many job offers in New York that had come his way. He was taking his time making a decision, though, and Piper couldn't help but think — though he'd never admit it — that Anders had an affinity for Frick Island. And didn't want to stray too far from it.)

Still, Piper felt a little misty-eyed and a lot terrified because she had no idea what lay ahead of her; what her life was going to look like. But she felt something else, too, for the first time in a long time.

Hope.

She picked up her suitcase with one hand and the other she tucked through the crook of Anders's arm.

"I am."

AUTHOR'S NOTE

My grandparents Hugh and Marion Oakley were adventurers. They loved nothing more than exploring the world and seeing how other people lived — except for maybe sharing and instilling the love of travel in myself and my siblings. They whisked us away to many far-flung foreign cities, but one of the most memorable trips was the time we boarded a ferry on the coast of Maryland and ended up on an island smack in the middle of the Chesapeake Bay. I'll never forget how I felt when I first laid eyes on Smith Island, and understood that the people who lived there, though they were Americans, experienced a very different existence from mine. Even back then, when I didn't know I was an author in the making, the wheels in my teenage brain were turning, and I knew the island would be the perfect setting for a story.

Fast-forward some twenty-plus years, and

when the idea for a novel about a widow who still thinks her husband is alive and the entire town goes along with it popped into my head, I knew exactly where it would take place: my own version of Smith Island. While Frick Island was clearly inspired by Smith Island and there are many similarities (you can only reach the island by ferry, a famous Smith Island layer cake exists — and it is delicious! — and climate change threatens the very existence of the island), I feel obligated to point out that there are also a number of incongruences. The layout of the town and businesses in it were all created to suit the needs of my story, as well as all the characters — they are figments of my imagination and do not resemble anyone who actually lives on the island.

However, I would not have been able to write this book had the citizens on Smith Island not welcomed my mother and me with open arms when we went to visit for research purposes. If you ever get the chance to go, make sure you stay at the lovely bed-and-breakfast Susan's on Smith Island and eat a slice of her famous Smith Island cake (though I'm sure it's hotly debated by Marylanders, I think hers the best). Her husband, Otis, runs the ferry, and they can both tell you stories much more interesting than mine of what life was like growing up on the island. Jim Adkins, who lives Smith Island–adjacent, was a grand tour guide and answerer of all my many questions about the topography of the area, details of the ferry, and minutiae of life on the island.

My research also included the fascinating book *An Island Out of Time,* by Tom Horton, which I highly recommend if you want a nonfictional account of what it's like to move your family from a typical American life to a remote island in the middle of the Chesapeake. Also, the plan to save Frick Island, as detailed in Anders's conversation with Jacob, is based loosely on the Smith Island Vision Plan, a list of strategies created by the community in 2015. Fortunately, they are way ahead of the residents of my Frick Island and have been proactive in trying to preserve their island and way of life for future generations. It is my sincerest wish that they succeed.

ACKNOWLEDGMENTS

As always, first and foremost, I am in deep gratitude to my readers — from those who have been along on this ride with me since my very first book to the newcomers and to everyone in between. Thank you from the bottom of my heart.

And thank you to the following people:

My agent, Stephanie Rostan, who came waltzing into my career mid-dance and never missed a step. I'm so grateful for your expertise and enthusiasm.

My wonderfully sharp and brilliant editor, Kerry Donovan, and the indefatigable powerhouse of Team Berkley, including Claire Zion, Craig Burke, Diana Franco, Fareeda Bullert, Tara O'Connor, Sarah Blumenstock, and Mary Geren. Thank you for all of your hard work shepherding my books into the world and getting them into the hands of readers.

My first agent, Emma Sweeney, who

found my debut manuscript in her slush pile and expertly crafted a career for me in this industry. Thank you. May you enjoy your well-deserved retirement!

My publicist, Kathleen Carter, for your passionate and tireless work promoting this book.

My foreign publishers, who have helped my books find devoted readers all over the world. Thank you for exceeding my wildest author dreams.

The people of Smith Island, especially Susan Evans and Otis Tyler for their warm hospitality, and Jim Adkins in Crisfield, Maryland, for sharing his wonderful stories and thorough history of the island.

Pat Campbell for walking me through the particulars of entomology. Any mistakes pertaining to the study of it are mine alone.

My aunt Wendy and aunt Jeanne and their families for giving me a home away from home in Salisbury, Maryland, while researching.

My talented friend Lindsay Champanis for the gorgeous map of Frick Island at the front of this book.

My beta readers, who I'm also lucky to call the very best of friends: Caley Bowman, Brooke Hight, Megan Lobe, Kelly Marages, Laurie Rowland, Jaime Sarrio, and Shannon Tilley.

My fellow writers who have become a much-needed and beloved community in this wild roller coaster of an industry, including Nicole Blades, Karma Brown, Emily Giffin, Kimmery Martin, Aimee Molloy, Kirsten Palladino, Amy Reichert, Taylor Jenkins Reid, and Karen White.

Megan Oakley, Jason Oakley, Kathy and Bill Oakley, Jack and Penny Wyman, and the rest of my Tull, Wyman, and Oakley families for a lifetime of boundless love and support. Special thanks to my mom for being the best tour roadie a gal can have and for never forgetting the crossword puzzles.

Henry, Sorella, Olivia, and Everett, my four children, who inexplicably love me despite my many failings as a parent. Never forget: I love you most.

My husband, Fred, who makes everything possible. I'm so glad I hit on you in that bar.

Finally, thank you to my grandparents Marion and Hugh Oakley, who were intrepid explorers, as well as my biggest cheerleaders on this earth. While I have no idea what adventure they're on now, I know that wherever they are, they're together — which always seemed to be the most important bit, anyway.

■ ■ ■ ■

READERS GUIDE:
THE INVISIBLE
HUSBAND OF
FRICK ISLAND

COLLEEN OAKLEY

■ ■ ■ ■

QUESTIONS FOR DISCUSSION

1. Frick Island is certainly an unusual place. Why do you think the author chose to set the book on this island? Have you ever been to a remote island like Frick? What was it like?

2. At the end of chapter 1, Tom returns home — or at least seems to: "He was going to come home. Of that one thing, Piper was sure. And then one morning, just like that, he did." What did you think when you read that last line? Did you think he had actually returned or something else?

3. When we first meet Anders, he appears to be single-mindedly driven by his career and success, as many young twentysomethings can be. What does success mean to him at the start of the story? Do you think his viewpoint changes over the course of the book?

4. At one point, Pearl muses that the differ-

ent ways people grieve are "as varied as the waves that lapped up on Graver's Beach at the far end of the island." Do you think that's true? Has grief ever surprised you in the way it's manifested itself in your life?

5. The author uses flashbacks every few chapters to offer a glimpse into Piper and Tom's relationship. Do you feel like you got to know them as a couple? What do you think of their relationship?

6. Within the community of Frick Island, there are lots of distinctive personalities: BobDan, Pearl and Harold Olecki, Lady Judy, Mr. Gimby, Dr. Khari, Jeffrey. How are they similar and different? Did Anders's feelings toward them change over time as he got to know them? Did yours?

7. Anders returns to Frick Island hoping to do a story on climate change and its effects on the island. How does climate change — and whether people believe in it or not — fit into the bigger themes of the novel?

8. In his research on Piper's "condition," Anders learns about post-bereavement hallucinatory experiences, or PBHEs. Have you ever heard or seen a loved one after they passed?

9. In Chapter 11, Anders realizes that

between "climate change, mental health issues, maybe even drug trafficking . . . Frick Island was a microcosm for so many issues people faced all across the country." Do you think that's true? Why or why not?

10. When Anders first "encounters" Tom face-to-face at the marina, he has to decide whether he will go along with the charade and speak to a man who doesn't exist. What do you think would have happened if he had chosen not to greet Tom? What would you have done?

11. At one point, Anders asks Piper what she misses about living on the mainland. What do you think you would miss? What would you enjoy about living somewhere like Frick Island?

12. When Anders realizes that the nearing completion of the cell tower will allow the islanders to hear his podcast easily at any time, he panics. Do you think he was deceptive about the content of his podcast on purpose? How could he have handled it differently?

13. When Pearl finally tells Anders how and when the town decided to go along with Piper's delusion, she says: "It's amazing what people will do for the ones they love." Have you experienced any examples in your own life that exemplify this idea?

14. Why do you think it takes Anders so long to realize he's in love with Piper?

15. This book explores the theme of faith, how it can sometimes be hard to understand why another person believes something so different from your own beliefs. In Anders's final podcast, what does he conclude about those differences? How have his thoughts on faith and belief changed over the course of the novel?

ABOUT THE AUTHOR

Colleen Oakley is the *USA Today* bestselling author of *You Were There Too, Close Enough to Touch,* and *Before I Go.* Her books have been named best books by *People, Us Weekly, Library Journal,* and *Real Simple,* and have been long-listed for the Southern Book Prize. She lives in Atlanta, Georgia, with her family.

CONNECT ONLINE
ColleenOakley.com
Facebook: WriterColleenOakley
Twitter: OakleyColleen
Instagram: WriterColleenOakley

The employees of Thorndike Press hope you have enjoyed this Large Print book. All our Thorndike, Wheeler, and Kennebec Large Print titles are designed for easy reading, and all our books are made to last. Other Thorndike Press Large Print books are available at your library, through selected bookstores, or directly from us.

For information about titles, please call:
(800) 223-1244

or visit our website at:
gale.com/thorndike

To share your comments, please write:
Publisher
Thorndike Press
10 Water St., Suite 310
Waterville, ME 04901

CPSIA information can be obtained
at www.ICGtesting.com
Printed in the USA
BVHW082124300821
615664BV00001B/5